# ELIZABETH

This novel covers the first 30 years of the reign of the great queen, Elizabeth I of England. At her accession the country was impoverished, weakened, and torn by religious strife; thirty years later she was one of the greatest rulers in the world, and her small kingdom was the equal of the European powers who had hoped to destroy it.

The legendary character of the queen has overshadowed the nature of the woman, but in this book the painted, glittering, poker-faced figure of the portraits comes to life in all her strength and her weakness, her magnificence and her pettiness. Elizabeth's great passion was power, but she was also, to her sorrow, capable of more human passions, such as her love for the worthless Earl of Leicester. Her feelings also complicated the long and bitter struggle with her cousin Mary, Queen of Scots, for the throne of England.

Evelyn Anthony has skilfully and vividly described the passions and emotions of the great queen, her favourites, her vanities, her political intrigues; and has set them against a colourful, exciting historical background to give us a compelling story, and a rare insight into one of the most intriguing figures of English history.

# *Elizabeth*

## EVELYN ANTHONY

HUTCHINSON OF LONDON

Hutchinson & Co (Publishers) Ltd
3 Fitzroy Square, London W 1 P 6 J D

London Melbourne Sydney Auckland
Wellington Johannesburg and agencies
throughout the world

First published in Britain by Museum Press Ltd 1960
Published by Hutchinson 1976
Reprinted 1978

Printed in Great Britain by litho by The Anchor Press Ltd
and bound by Wm Brendon & Son Ltd
both of Tiptree, Essex

ISBN 0 09 125950 9

## Author's Foreword

ELIZABETH TUDOR was the greatest of all the sovereigns of England and in writing the story of the first thirty years of her reign, I have tried to be as accurate as possible. Many of the conversations and all the extracts from letters are authentic; I have compressed the Northern rebellion and the Ridolfi Plot and changed the details of its disclosure by Dudley for the sake of cohesion, and given a shortened account of the long marriage negotiations with Alençon. No one knows the true facts of who killed Amy Dudley; I have advanced a theory of my own, based on a study of the slight evidence still in existence, but it is only a theory and cannot be supported by proof. However, it is generally accepted that Robert Dudley was responsible for her death. This is the first riddle in the story of Elizabeth Tudor; the second, and the more impenetrable, is the extent of her sexual relations with men. Whatever the psychological injuries she suffered through her appalling childhood and her initiation with her own stepfather, I believe that she remained unmarried because for her "the passion for power was truly greater than the lusts of the flesh". Ruthless, cynical, brilliantly clever, she remains one of the most fascinating women in the history of the world. I have tried to present her, and her Royal cousin and antagonist, the unhappy Mary, Queen of Scots, as fairly and as faithfully as I could.

EVELYN ANTHONY

London, 1960

# Chapter 1

I t was November, the saddest of all the English winter months, when the last yellow leaves had been stripped from the trees by a vicious wind, and the ground was soft with rain. The year 1558 had only two more months to run, and it had been a year of tragedy and unrest, symbolic of the rule of the Queen of England who was lying ill in her Palace in London.

Mary Tudor had reigned for six years, and the majority of her subjects hoped that the illness she was suffering would be the last. The country was desperately poor, riven with religious strife, engaged in a war with France which had brought nothing but humiliation and defeat, and the Queen herself was a sick fanatic, wasting of dropsy and heartbreak.

Thirty miles outside London, in the County of Hertfordshire, Queen Mary's half-sister Elizabeth stood by the window of her room at Hatfield House, looking out over the drenched park and the skeleton trees. She had known that view for the most part of her life; as a child she had played in the same room and ridden through the grounds on her first pony. Hatfield was her only home. Elizabeth had very few attachments, but she loved the old red-brick house with its associations of her childhood. She spent long hours alone, preferring solitude and her own thoughts to the companionship of the women who attended her and spied on her for Queen Mary. She was not as tall as she appeared; her very slim figure and erect carriage gave the illusion of height, her pale features were striking rather than conventionally beautiful, with a high-bridged nose and heavy-lidded eyes. They were strange eyes, large and brilliant and as black as pitch, inherited from her mother, Anne Boleyn, who had been so infamously beautiful; but she had the fair skin and blazing red hair of her Tudor father, the enormous, tyrannical Henry VIII. The wintry daylight was fading into dusk and it was too dark to sew or read; the house was very quiet and Elizabeth stood staring out at the rain.

So much of the past belonged to Hatfield, so many of her earliest memories, confused and dim, belonged to the old

7

house where she had come to live, when she was heiress to the throne of England—a tiny child of two years old, with a retinue of servants and pages and ladies-in-waiting. There were visits from a strange, dark woman who smelled very strongly of scent, whom she knew to be her mother, and a memory of a huge, fair man, so heavy that the floor shook under him as he walked, lifting her up to the window. By the time she could climb the window-seat herself all her ladies and pages had been sent away and she was suddenly addressed as Lady Elizabeth. The spoilt, bewildered child had beaten her fists against the glass, demanding to know where everyone had gone, and why the few remaining members of her household did not curtsy and called her by her Christian name. No one had been able to explain to her that she was no longer a princess, that her mother was divorced and she had been made a bastard by her father's order.

There were no more visits from her mother, and when her governess Lady Bryan told her gently that Anne Boleyn was dead, Elizabeth had only stared at her, not understanding. Death was a word which meant nothing to a child. She was fretful and insecure and the more questions she asked the less she understood the answers, but years later, when she could look out of that window without climbing up, a servant girl had whispered to her how her mother the Queen had died, and Elizabeth screamed and ran to her washing bowl and vomited. For a long time she woke shrieking after nightmares where she saw her father standing with a bloody axe uplifted in his hands.

She could remember her half-sister Mary, who was an old maid of twenty-two, coming to her once in the middle of the night, and lighting the candle and sitting by the bed until she fell asleep. Mary did not like her, but she did strange things which puzzled the child; she made her presents at Christmas and New Year, and she assured her that their father was a good and kindly man, deserving of his children's love, in spite of what Elizabeth and she knew he had done.

And when their father finally died, Mary went to Mass every morning and prayed for the repose of the soul of someone who must surely be in hell, if he possessed a soul at all. She never understood Mary.

Mary had fallen in love with Philip of Spain and she had married him against the wishes of her people. But as a woman

8

with a husband, as a Queen with undisputed power, she had never known as much about human passions and political opportunities as her sister. Love had come early to Elizabeth in the guise of the boisterous, handsome man who had married her stepmother Katherine Parr, after the old King's death. She had lived in their house and at thirteen her immature body had been subjected to the cunning assaults of the Lord Admiral, and her immature feelings had been roused into a dangerous passion, dangerous and fatal, because the intrigue had brought the Admiral to the scaffold and put the girl he had used for his ambitions in peril of her life.

He had not seduced her completely; he was widowed when she was fifteen and his design was marriage; so Elizabeth was still a virgin, but mentally he had despoiled her innocence, and his violent death and her own danger nearly crippled her emotionally. She had grown up within days; she had lied to her accusers with terrible precocity, stifled her feelings and repressed her tears when the man she loved had died. And through her own cunning, she had escaped the traps set for her. At fifteen she had learnt the perfidy of men and the cruelty of relations; her own brother Edward was King, and Edward would have signed the warrant for her execution as lightly as he had signed the Admiral's, who was his blood relation and his friend. Elizabeth had saved herself, but the shock to her system was so violent that for four years she was prostrate with ill-health.

When she recovered properly she was nineteen and she desperately wanted to live, and to live in the one way which would bring her fulfilment. She wanted to survive her sister Mary and succeed to her throne.

And she had known then what simple, stupid Mary Tudor only learnt at the cost of her happiness and her people's loyalty; there was no place for love in the heart of a Prince.

" Madam ! "

Elizabeth turned round slowly. Her lady-in-waiting, Frances Holland, stood in the doorway. She held a candle and it lit her excited face, the flame wavering in a strong draught.

" What is it? I was just about to ring for you; the fire is low and I need lights."

" Madam, Sir William Cecil is downstairs in the Great Hall. He is asking for you urgently."

9

"Cecil?"

Elizabeth's thin brows raised. William Cecil was Mary Tudor's Secretary but he had always been her very good friend. Through the vicissitudes of the last six years, when the affectionate older sister had been transformed into a jealous sovereign who saw Elizabeth as a rival for the throne, Cecil had managed to advise her secretly on several occasions.

"Shall I send him up, Madam?"

"Not till I can offer him more than a pauper's welcome in a place without heating or light! Ask him to wait, and have this fire mended and candles brought and something hot to drink. And hurry!"

Twenty minutes later Cecil found her sitting in a high-back chair sewing tranquilly by a blazing log fire. She looked up at him and her pale, chiselled face was quite expressionless.

"This is an agreeable surprise, Sir William. Forgive the delay in admitting you, but I am not accustomed to visitors. I have ordered a hot cordial. It's a dismal journey from London in this weather and you must be chilled to the bone."

"Your Grace is very kind."

He was a slight man with prematurely grey hair and a stoop, the legacy of a life spent at a writing-desk. He looked older than his thirty-eight years; his voice was quiet, almost toneless; there was nothing about him to suggest that he was one of the few men clever enough to stay in office under the Protestant rule of Edward VI and the turbulent Catholic revival of Mary. Elizabeth glanced at the door. It was shut, but she knew that her sister had spies in her household.

"I understand that you come with the Queen's knowledge, sir: you must assure me of that before we proceed any further."

"Madam, the Queen is in no condition to know anything. I am here to tell you that she is dying."

"Dying? What are you saying?"

"She has named you her successor. I have ridden from her sick bed to tell you. It is only a matter of days, perhaps hours, before you will be Queen of England, Madam. And may God grant you a happier reign than the one which is closing now."

"You are so reckless, Cecil," Elizabeth said slowly. "I feel she is dead already. . . ."

"Not yet." Cecil's pale eyes gleamed for a moment, and she

saw the hatred shining in them. " But soon, and not soon enough for all of us."

" Sit down, sir. And temper your spleen. Remember that she is your Queen and my sister."

" She is not my Queen," he answered. " I served her because I wished to live, instead of burning like my friends. And she so far forgot her sisterhood to you, Madam, that she came near to killing you."

Elizabeth smiled; it was a cynical smile and it gave her pointed face a wicked look.

" She had good reason to get rid of me. Had I been in her place and heard my name on every rebel's lips, I fear I might have done more and threatened less. Come, pour some cordial for both of us and tell me everything."

As she listened to Cecil describing Mary's illness, and the onset of the coma which preceded death, Elizabeth wondered why he had always been her champion. What did he hope from her accession to make him work for it even when the possibility was most remote? If she was really going to trust him, and she wanted to, that question must be answered.

" Tell me," she said suddenly, " what is the Court doing? "

" Preparing to come here as soon as they can mount up," he answered.

" The Queen is dead, or dying, rather.—Long live the Queen! Poor Mary. Please God I'll never see the rats deserting me, even before I sink! "

" She is not loved," Cecil said quietly. " And all men are not rats because they seek the sun that rises in preference to the one that sets."

" What must I do to be loved, Cecil? What am I to you and all those you tell me are hurrying out here to show themselves? And what have I been to you for all these years when you helped me and paid lip service to my sister? "

" You were my only hope for England," Cecil said. " I saw in you the only sovereign who could save England as surely as you saved yourself. And save the Protestant religion. We've had enough of a Papist Queen who was half Spanish and married a man like Philip of Spain against her people's wishes."

" You have no pity have you, Cecil? What will you do if you find me harsher than my sister—will you follow where I lead or will you pretend that you are loyal and cast about for someone else . . . ? "

Cecil shook his head.

"I couldn't even if I would. There is no one else but Mary Stuart your cousin, and she is a Catholic. Yours is the only road that does not lead to Rome."

"By God," she said dryly, "I never thought to hear you make a joke! And I believe I've found an honest man! Give me your hand, my friend, and swear that you will serve me faithfully. Swear that you'll tell me the truth no matter whether it's pleasing to me or not, that your advice will never be swayed by fear. Swear that of all the men in my kingdom and my Council, I can trust at least one, and that one William Cecil."

He knelt to her, awkwardly, for he was not a man gifted with grace of manner, and lifted her hand to his lips. For a moment their eyes met, and though she stared at him as if she could see into his brain and read his thoughts, he did not waver.

"I swear."

"So be it," Elizabeth said. "You are my man, Cecil. I am a jealous mistress; I will never let you go back upon that oath and live. From this day we will work together, you and I."

That promise and that partnership were to endure for nearly forty years.

In London, where the Queen lay dying at Whitehall Palace, the confusion of the Court had communicated itself to the common people, and the London mobs gathered in crowds along the river bank and routes out of London, and cheered the increasing flood of place-seekers who were hurrying out to pay homage to the future Queen. It was safe to give expression to their hatred for Mary the Papist and for Philip, her detested Spanish Consort; so violent was the public reaction that all Spanish nationals were warned to keep off the streets and barricade their houses against attack, and the Catholic friends and servants of Queen Mary huddled around her deathbed and whispered about what was to become of them. Everyone knew that the new Queen would favour the Protestants; no one knew whether that favour would extend to retaliatory persecution of the Catholics.

There were many who were both English and Catholic who hated Spanish influence and deplored the dying Queen's fanatical pursuit of heresy; to them the new reign promised release from Spain, and a cessation of the war with France which the infatuated Mary had undertaken to please her husband. If she had not loved Philip so blindly, she might have been mourned by her people—even those close to her admitted this.

Mary was the victim of her own fanaticism and of the ruthless exploitation of her husband, Philip, who knew how to bend a doting woman to his own ends. She had begun her reign with mercy, pardoning her cousin who had been proclaimed Queen and surrendered to Mary's army after a reign of nine miserable days.

The Duke of Northumberland—John Dudley—had been executed, because he had led the rebellion, but Mary spared the rest of his family. However, the surviving Dudleys were imprisoned in the Tower when a second rebellion broke out six months after the first. Stung by the ingratitude of those she had pardoned, Mary punished the rebels with a ferocity worthy of the old King Henry. Jane Grey and her husband Guildford Dudley were beheaded and hundreds were hanged, and Robert Dudley, who was only twenty and passionately fond of living, expected to die with them.

He was an extremely handsome man, favouring his father the Duke who had been a fine athlete. He was very dark, with a swarthy skin and brilliant black eyes and an insatiable desire for importance and power. He had married an heiress at seventeen, and tired of her within a year, and as soon as his kin were settled in their graves, he boldly addressed himself to Queen Mary and begged for his release. He wrote cunningly, pleading his youth and ignorance and the influence of his father, and he managed to touch Mary; she was naturally soft-hearted and, remembering her own girlhood, blighted by imprisonment and loneliness, she ordered Dudley's release. When he chanced everything by presenting himself at Court and explained that, as the son of a traitor, he was penniless, the Queen gave him a position and restored some of his family's lands.

Dudley was not grateful to her: he was too healthy and ruthless to feel anything but contempt for the tired old maid who had been influenced by all the lies he told her. He took her favours, made himself agreeable and, when she finally showed signs of mortal illness, he sold some of his land and secretly sent the proceeds to Elizabeth at Hatfield. The old Queen was obviously dying of dropsy; her hysterical belief that she was pregnant no longer deceived anybody. Robert Dudley had known the young princess Elizabeth as a child and seen her once or twice before the scandal of the Lord Admiral removed her from public life. They had been close friends when they were children, and he had heard that she was always pressed for money. She would be the next Queen of England, and he hoped she would remember his gift and be grateful.

Now, immediately after the news of Mary's death, he was riding hard down the road to Hatfield on a November morning. He had kept horses ready for days, and hung round Whitehall Palace without sleep, waiting to hear of the Queen's end. He wanted to reach the new Queen while she was excited and exalted by her accession, and more likely to be generous. He had a valid claim on her friendship, if only he could make it before all the positions were filled and she had nothing left to give away. Mary had died at six in the morning, and everyone was racing towards Elizabeth on horseback and in carriages.

He kicked his horses into a gallop; there was only another mile or two before he reached Hatfield. Dudley began to hum as he rode. He felt excited and full of optimism. He had escaped the consequences of his father's treason; his tiresome little wife Amy was away in Norfolk; he was exactly the same age as the woman for whom life was expanding in such a glorious manner, and there was no reason in the world why his fortune should not be linked with hers. At one period in their lives, they had been prisoners in the Tower at the same time during the late reign. If he had the chance, he could remind her of that.

He turned up the drive towards Hatfield House and reined in at the gates. The old red-brick house was like a bee-hive; he could hear the noise coming out of the windows, and the courtyard was full of horses and servants. He pushed his way through the open door to the Great Hall, and found himself hemmed in by a large crowd. Elizabeth was sitting on a chair on the dais where the principal table usually stood, and he could see William Cecil and the Lords Sussex and Arundel and the Duke of Bedford standing round her. He began to struggle, using his elbows and his fists, and at last he had reached the front rank of those waiting to be presented. Then he saw her clearly, sitting very calmly and very straight-backed, wearing a dress of deep black velvet and a pearl and diamond pendant, with her hair blazing round her head. He was surprised to see how handsome she had become. In spite of her dignity, her eyes were sparkling, and she was obviously so happy that she could not repress a constant smile. For one more moment Dudley hesitated. Then he stepped forward to the foot of the dais and fell on his knees in front of her.

"Lord Robert Dudley, Madam! My life and my possessions are at your service."

He looked into her face and saw that she had recognized him.

"Welcome, Lord Robert. Have you come to collect your debt?"

This was not Mary, roaring with temper one minute and shedding sentimental tears the next. This was a composed and self-confident young woman and she was looking at him with an expression of mocking amusement. But Dudley's skin was as thick as his father's; he did not redden or hesitate.

"The Queen is in no man's debt," he answered quickly. "May God grant you health and long life, and may you grant me the chance of being of service to you."

Elizabeth smiled.

"We are old friends, my Lord. You did not forget me and I shall show my gratitude; remain at Hatfield, and I will find some place for you."

He kissed her hand, noticing how delicate and long her fingers were, and stepped back into the crowd, waiting until she rose and went upstairs with the Secretary and peers. She walked slowly and gracefully, pausing to smile and speak to people who had not yet been presented to her, and Dudley watched her with admiration. She was clever and she was a good actress, she knew how to please without losing her dignity; it was a rare gift and her sister Mary had never possessed it.

There was a loud spontaneous cheer and a cry of "God save the Queen" as she stopped at the head of the stairs and waved. Then she disappeared into her own apartments with the members of the Council. Dudley went to find food and drink and returned to the Great Hall to wait. Late that evening, when he was beginning to think she had forgotten him, a page summoned him to a private audience with the Queen.

On November 28th a glittering procession moved slowly through the narrow, crooked streets of the city of London. It had begun at the Cripplegate, where the new Queen left her gold and crimson chariot and, dressed in a riding habit of purple velvet, mounted a magnificent white horse. The animal had been specially chosen for its colour and breeding; it was saddled in scarlet and there were jewels and beaten gold worth hundreds of pounds sparkling in the bridle reins. The Queen's new Master of the Horse led it forward, and bowed. He was dressed in red and silver and there were rubies in his sword-hilt and his doublet. It was a vulgar, dazzling costume, and only Robert Dudley could have carried it. Only Dudley would have squandered so much money on the accoutrements of the horse, and persuaded Elizabeth to leave the clumsy chariot at the Cripplegate and ride into London, arguing that she was too good a horsewoman to be hidden in a litter. Her Councillors objected, resenting the innovation, and resenting Dudley who was being officious with advice and interference after the Queen had given him his appointment.

She had indeed been generous; his office brought him a handsome income, and kept him in constant attendance upon her. And the Queen publicly thanked him for the idea, over-ruled all objections and left the arrangements for her transport into the Capital in Dudley's hands.

He gave her his hand as she mounted, and for a moment she smiled at him. Then she gave a sign and the procession began to move forward.

The Lord Mayor of London, ruler of the City of London, which was not only the powerful centre of English commerce but an independent kingdom within the kingdom, rode at the head with the Garter King-at-Arms, chief of the Royal Heralds, who carried the gleaming golden sceptre, followed by the Gentlemen Pensioners of the Crown in their dress of red damask, carrying the gilded axes, and behind them the heralds. Elizabeth's contingent, the breasts and backs of their red and silver tunics emblazoned with her cypher E.R. in gold thread.

The Earl of Pembroke walked on foot, holding the Queen's ceremonial sword, its scabbard thickly encrusted with pearls. There was a gap between him and the Queen, slowly walking her horse. Dudley watched her from behind, noting the slim back, so straight that the spine might have been made of steel. He had only seen her gay and relaxed during the last few days at Hatfield; she had relegated him to her leisure hours as an amusing companion, and though Dudley joined her informal supper parties and played cards at her table in the evenings, he still knew nothing of the woman who stayed shut up with her Council for hours at a time. He had already concluded that she had two faces, and that the one she showed to him and to his kind—the unofficial jesters who flattered and amused her—was very different from the countenance that Cecil saw behind closed doors. He watched her closely, noticing how she turned in her saddle to wave to the crowds who pressed in on the procession. And what crowds there were—he had never seen the City streets so packed with people and so profusely decorated. Tapestries and hangings and brightly-coloured bunting hung from every window and were strung across the narrow space between the leaning houses. The gutters, usually choked with kitchen waste and the foulest refuse, had been flushed clean, but even so the smell was overpowering and Dudley smiled as he saw Elizabeth sniff occasionally at the pomander which hung from her waist.

Bands of musicians played on every corner, their music muffled by the cheers which seemed to increase in volume. The procession halted frequently while the Queen accepted flowers and gifts and listened to long addresses of welcome; several times she paused to speak to the ordinary citizens who crowded round her horse's head. The noise of cannon grew louder as they went deeper into the City, and when they rounded the sweep of Mark Lane, Elizabeth raised her hand and the procession halted. The grey walls and turrets of the Tower rose ahead of her, standing like a jewel of stone in the centre of the deep, still moat. The drawbridge was down, and she could see the Governor of the Tower, standing with the yeomen warders in their crimson tunics and breastplates, making a glow of colour under the shadow of the massive spiked portcullis. Never had the Tower seemed more majestic or more remote; it was strange that a place of dread and torment should be so beautiful—for though it was a Palace as well as a prison, she thought of it as a prison and she always would.

Memories pressed in on her, isolating her for a few seconds from the splendid cavalcade, the glittering uniforms, the dignitaries, the cheers and trumpet fanfares. If she heard anything it was the steady boom of gunfire as the Tower cannon fired a Royal salute. And yet only six years before she had come to that same place, arriving by water, and under another portcullis, while the rain lashed down and the whole teeming City was silent, its citizens at Church. She had come in by the

Traitor's Gate, the prisoner of her sister Mary, suspected of a plot against her life, and neither she nor the men who escorted her, men like Sussex and Arundel who now rode behind her in the procession, no, not one of them had thought she would leave the Tower alive.

The moment lengthened, its significance began to shadow those who witnessed her triumph, and when she turned she saw her own memories reflected in their faces. Her voice was clear; it had a deep tone which carried; her words went beyond the ears of Dudley and Pembroke and Sussex:

"Some have fallen from being Princes of this land to being prisoners in this place; I am raised from being prisoner in this place to being a Prince of this land. That dejection was a work of God's justice—my advancement is a work of his mercy. I swear by it that I shall be merciful to all men as He was merciful to me."

As the last members of the procession moved under the Tower gatehouse, and the Queen passed out of sight, the crowds broke up, reforming into groups round the musicians; they began to dance and sing, and fought round the street conduits which were running ale instead of water. All through the night the London crowds celebrated round bonfires blazing in the streets, and someone found a man who kept a dancing bear and dragged the poor beast out to perform. It was a drunken, rowdy celebration, and here and there fights broke out when a known adherent of the dead Queen Mary was identified. The splendid hangings were quickly drawn in, out of reach of grabbing hands, scavengers attacked the tableaux, smashing them to pieces and making off with bits of cloth and garlands. By the dawn of the following day the City looked like a battlefield, its drunken or injured casualties lying in the streets, but the lawlessness was an excellent measure of the popularity of the new Queen. Her words on entering the Tower were repeated and embellished; those who had called out to her and actually received an answer, lived on their anecdotes for days. The people of London were as sentimental as they were rough; the idea of a sovereign who appeared to care for them fired their loyalty. It was a fine contrast to her sister Mary, who used to ride among them without a smile or a gesture of awareness that they existed.

Hearing the reports Cecil was well satisfied. He had cast his lot for good or evil with Elizabeth. As he had told her, there was no alternative claimant to the throne but the Catholic Mary Stuart, fortunately living in France as wife to the heir to the French throne; but even so, Cecil was too cautious to be entirely sanguine.

However, he was safer than he might have expected. Elizabeth had a genius for touching hearts, which he thought to be strange, for he had discovered that her personality was secretive and cold on close acquaintance. She puzzled him, and he disliked that, for he preferred to document his fellow humans; but there was no pigeon-hole in which she fitted. She spent her evenings playing cards or dancing, decked in Mary's jewels, but she sat with her Council for hours at a stretch and never complained that she was tired or tried to defer the most tedious business till the following day. She gave the impression of spontaneity, when he knew from working with her that she weighed every word before she said it. She expressed herself with beautiful simplicity, as she did as she rode to the Tower, but she could speak and write in riddles when she wished to confuse an issue. He knew she was clever, more clever than he had ever supposed; he imagined she was susceptible to flattery—yet he doubted if she were deceived by it. He supposed many things about Elizabeth whom he had elected to serve and follow for life, but he was sure of very little.

The morning after her entry in London, one of the Queen's pages came to Cecil's apartment in the main building of the Tower, with a message to attend upon her.

He was admitted to her Privy Chamber, a small, primitive room with a narrow window which admitted inadequate light. Elizabeth was seated at a table writing, with two candles burning beside her. She wore a loose gown of blue velvet, her hair confined in a net of gold thread sewn with pearls. She had a habit of receiving him and other members of her Court in her dressing robe. He privately thought it unbecoming in an unmarried woman to be so lax, but he dare not tell her so. He was discovering every day that there were more and more things he dared not do or say to Elizabeth.

"Master Cecil—good morning to you—if you can see whether it's morning or midnight in this pest hole! It's so dark here that my ancestors must have been cats if they could read and write in such a gloom."

"Your Grace finds it a strain on your eyes?" Cecil knew that she had short sight and suffered from headaches. Certainly the lighting was poor.

"I find the Tower itself a strain. It's cold as the devil and damp as hell. I can't wait to leave it and go to Whitehall. It's only fit for prisoners. Take that stool, Cecil. I've been seeing into some costs and I want your opinion.—If this place is bleak, it's only matched by my Treasury. I find I come to a bankrupt throne.—Look at these figures."

She continued while he read. "Trade is poor; my sister's war with France has swallowed every spare penny, *and* taken the men who should be busy at their trades. The coinage is so debased that our credit is a laughing stock abroad. These are the opinions of Sir Thomas Gresham; I heartily agree with them."

"What does he propose we should do, Madam?" Gresham had a genius for money; Elizabeth's financial adviser was as well chosen as her Master of the Horse. It was typical of her that she had so much in common with two men who had nothing in common with each other.

"Call in the debased currency and restore the old value. Curb spending and expand trade. In the meantime, he undertakes to go to Flanders and borrow for us. He'll tell his own tale to get the money, and he's confident that he can succeed."

"I shall draft the Bill to go before Parliament. As you know I'm not an expert in finance, Madam, and I'm content to follow Gresham."

"If you're not one now, Cecil," she said, turning a page in front of her, "then you must learn. Money is the lifeblood of a Government. Without it, you cannot bribe, you cannot wage war, you cannot stand any man's equal. As soon as the Coronation is over, all the Crown's expenses must be cut."

"May I suggest, Madam, that you begin before your Coronation, and limit the sum to be spent on the late Queen's funeral?"

It was more than he could bear to hear her threatening economy and ordering him to learn finance like any counting clerk, while she proposed to lavish money on the interment of Mary Tudor.

"£40,000 is excessive, even for a sovereign," he added.

Elizabeth looked at him, and laid down her pen.

"Would you have me bury my sister like a pauper? Excessive or not, that is the sum I shall spend on her. Spare me any more quibbling; I'm sick of hearing you and the others sniffling over halfpennies."

"But when you are prepared to stint yourself, why throw your money away on this—this burial? Madam, for God's sake, at least allow me to understand you—why must Queen Mary go to a more sumptuous grave than any other sovereign of England?"

"Because," Elizabeth spoke very slowly and distinctly, "because, my friend, she forbore to send me to mine. I will not sit here squabbling about the cost of her coffin. She was my father's daughter and Queen of this realm when she lived; she is no less in death."

Mary had spared her life, that was the reason she gave Cecil for a funeral which was going to cost nearly as much as her own Coronation. But there was more to it than that. There were memories of early years at Hatfield, and the sister who was kind and soothed her nightmares. The little cap, sewn with pearls, and the dress made from a length of blue brocade —she had them still, reminders of Mary's generosity, when she emptied her meagre purse to buy the child Elizabeth a costly present. No, Cecil couldn't be expected to understand that; she hardly understood it herself. She only knew that now she could make a present to Mary and bury her with all the pomp and splendour of the Roman Catholic Church she had loved, and Cecil and the rest of them could go to the devil.

The Secretary had no idea what was passing through her mind; she appeared perfectly composed, frowning over some item in front of her, the argument over Mary's funeral apparently forgotten. But he did know that he had lost again in the contest of wills.

"You're very silent, Cecil," Elizabeth said suddenly. "Come, I have some human feelings—don't condemn me for it."

"God forbid," he coughed and changed the subject. He was embarrassed and not quite as proof against a woman's charm as he supposed.

"The Duke de Feria has been to see me, Madam. He's asking for another audience with you. He wants assurances of your continued friendship for his master King Philip."

"Don't worry, he shall have them. Better still, Philip shall hear of them in person. Last night I drafted a letter to send to my dear brother-in-law. Here, read it."

It was a long letter, written in her exquisite Italian copper-plate hand. He had seen other letters equally long in which she had managed to confuse her meaning to the point where it was impossible to make any sense of the contents at all. But this was a masterpiece of clarity.

She began by telling Philip of her accession, reminding him of how much was due to his intervention on her behalf with the late Queen. Not once, but many times, she wrote, Philip had protected her from the false accusations of her enemies. Cecil read the last paragraph aloud:

"'My only motive in writing this to your Majesty is to let you see that I do not forget your great kindness to me. . . . I shall be able to show my gratitude to your Majesty by doing all that it prompts me for your service and in your interests. . . .'"

He put down the letter and looked at her. She smiled at him across the table, the same wry, twisted smile which made Dudley vaguely uncomfortable.

"Words," Elizabeth said, "just words; they cost nothing and they mean less. I dare not let him know his influence here died with my sister. When he does realize it, I will be strong enough to suggest that if he was fool enough to believe my letter he deserves to eat it—all ten pages!"

"If you do owe him all that you say here, no wonder he expects the alliance to continue."

"I owe him nothing. How long would I have kept my head if Mary had borne a child? He knew she would die early and I would inherit. And now, my friend, he has to support me whether he wants to or not!"

"Even when he knows that you are a Protestant, Madam? I saw his religious fervour, blackening the English skies with smoke from burning honest men and women; why should he support you when he knows you are the opposite of everything he stands for?"

Elizabeth stood up and began to walk up and down, her long gown trailing the floor, one hand opening and shutting in a gesture which always betrayed either nerves or excitement in her.

"Religious fervour is just another name for policy where that man is concerned. His god is Philip—he worships at his own shrine and says his prayers to himself! Don't make the mistake of judging him by the burning of a few cranks and Puritans! That was my sister's error, not his!"

"Madam, do you describe Bishop Latimer, Archbishop Cranmer as cranks?"

It was Cecil's recurring weakness, this obsession with the Protestant martyrs of the previous reign, whose number he had not elected to join when he had the chance. At that moment it jarred on Elizabeth and she swung round on him; for a second her temper blazed.

"Don't drag me into your religious bear pit! Latimer, Ridley, Cranmer, and the rest! What the devil does it matter what I call them? They burnt Catholics, that precious trio of saintly clerics, and then a Catholic burnt them! That's the long and short of it as far as I'm concerned. Know this, Cecil, once for all time. I'm no bigot—I care nothing for how men worship or whether they worship at all. It's a matter for their conscience, and the only time I'll take a hand in it is if my throne is threatened. I'm a Protestant because that's what the people want me to be, and because according to Catholics I'm a bastard with no claim at all! Now do you understand me, and will you let me finish about Spain, which really matters, and not interrupt about things that aren't worth a finger's snap?"

He flushed at the rebuke but said nothing; there was nothing he could say. He waited, tense and silent, until the angry light died out of her eyes and she began to pace up and down again.

"Philip married my sister for one reason only. To prevent her marrying a Frenchman and thereby uniting the power of France and England. *You* said," she went on, suddenly pointing at him, "that there was only one alternative to me as Queen, and that's my cousin Mary Stuart. A Catholic—yes, Cecil, I can see it forming on your lips. But half French by blood, and married to the future King of France. If God or Fate or my enemies dispose of me, then Mary, Queen of Scotland as she now is, and Queen of France as she'll become, is the only true claimant to my throne. I tell you one thing, your head will roll off your neck quick enough if that day dawns!"

She laughed and mocked suddenly at him. "So have a good care for me, as you would for yourself—now *I* digress, Cecil, forgive me—a union between England, France and Scotland, all under one woman, would mean the end of Philip's power in Europe. He'd lose his hold on the Netherlands overnight, for

France has long been eyeing them. He'd face a combination of such strength that all Spain's might wouldn't be able to resist the armies which would stream over his frontiers. And that's why I can tell you that he is on my side, because he *has* to be, for his own interests. I shall send this letter—it can do no harm, and visible sign of his friendship may make France pause a little. We are in a triangle, Cecil, and thank God I think we are the base, which is the side that keeps the balance."

She had only been Queen of England for twelve days, but her grasp of the strength and weakness of her own situation would have done credit to a seasoned statesman. It was so remarkable that Cecil forgave her the jibe about his execution at the hands of a successor. But there was one point she had overlooked or, rather, deliberately left out.

"If, as you say, Philip married your sister to stop her marrying a Frenchman, whom will he permit you to marry, Madam?"

"He has many relatives," Elizabeth said coolly. "He may even propose himself—I shall consider them all in turn."

"But you won't choose one of them?" She saw the surprise and alarm in his face, usually so grave and impassive, and she laughed.

"Oh, Cecil, Cecil, how little you know me to ask that question! Do you suppose that I would give myself to that Spanish codfish, and die of neglect as my sister did—do you think I should be fool enough to marry one of his cousins, and provoke France into declaring war on me in favour of Mary Stuart? But I'll tell you this, I have a value in the marriage market, and I shall make the best of it; Spanish suitors, French suitors, Catholics, Protestants, let them all come, and I'll give them an Englishman here and there to balance the odds."

"But when you *do* choose," he persisted, "and you must, Madam—for your own safety and the safety of the realm you must follow."

"Not if I marry an Englishman," Elizabeth countered swiftly. "That might be the answer for the future. I have no stomach for foreigners."

"And what Englishman could possibly aspire to you?" Cecil's voice was deceptively quiet. From the moment of her accession he and Arundel and Sussex and the other lords had been concerned about the question of Elizabeth's marriage. They had been so busy considering the implications of an alliance with any of the Royal houses abroad that the possibility of an English candidate had never occurred to any of them. But the man who married Elizabeth would be the first man in the kingdom; he would automatically take the title of King, and the lives of Cecil and his friends and co-Councillors would depend upon that man as much as they did at the moment on Elizabeth herself. An Englishman! Cecil's heart jumped like a stag at the idea that the Queen had already seen someone, or had long intended marriage with a secret lover. In the name of God he could think of only one man who received any sign of favour from her in the last twelve days. Dudley, Robert Dudley! That cunning, self-seeking upstart!

"Have you a man in mind, Madam?"

"Content yourself, my friend. I have no secrets from you. I have seen no one who moves me towards marriage. I doubt if such a man exists. We have talked about 'when' I marry—it would be closer to truth to say 'if'."

The audience was over; Cecil kissed her hand and hurried back to his apartments where an enormous amount of work was waiting for him. When he finished that, he arranged for a watch to be set on Robert Dudley and the times and places and duration of his meetings with the Queen to be reported to him every day.

Philip of Spain's ambassador to England was a remarkably astute diplomat. Don José María Jesús de Córdoba, Duke de Feria and hidalgo of Spain, was one of the handsomest and most ambitious of men, who had entered England in the entourage of Mary Tudor's husband. He combined all the courage and courtesy of his nation with a pleasing wit and an observant mind, unlike most of Philip's courtiers who were universally loathed for their stiffness and their unfriendliness. He had fallen in love with the prettiest of the Court ladies, Jane Dormer, and married her. He thus had a link with England which won him the post of ambassador, and he continued in it after Elizabeth's accession.

He had been granted a long audience with the new Queen, in which she spoke of Philip in the warmest terms, and held out promises of undying friendship with Spain. As he wrote to his Master afterwards, she was at such pains to be agreeable to him that her affability increased his suspicion of her motives. This was a remarkably shrewd assessment; he had come under the full force of her charm and her verbal gifts and remained unconvinced of her sincerity. Elizabeth did not dupe him, as she was apparently duping Philip himself. Feria was alarmed when his King's despatches mentioned an affectionate letter from her, full of gratitude for his kindness in the past; he wrote off and begged Philip not to attach too much importance to anything she wrote or said, as he was convinced that she was lying. Everything would depend upon her choice of husband just as everything depended upon the first laws promulgated after her Coronation.

At one point it seemed unlikely that she would be crowned. The Catholic Bishops, scenting a Protestant revival, refused to officiate. Then, no one knew by what means, either by bribery or threats or in the hope of effecting a compromise, the Bishop of Carlisle agreed to crown her. The clergy had made the first protest against Elizabeth, and it had failed. On January 15th she was crowned Queen at Westminster Abbey, with enough pomp and magnificence for a Pope's Coronation and ten days later she opened her first Parliament. At last Feria's warnings were justified. He had watched the ceremony that day, and he sat in his room in the Spanish Embassy, writing a bitter, detailed account of the Queen's perfidy to King Philip. The Abbot and monks of Westminster had met her in procession, carrying candles. Elizabeth had stopped her carriage and ordered them to get out of her way; she had no need of torches, she said at the top of her voice, she could see well enough. . . .

The incident outside Parliament was only a foretaste of what was to happen within.

King Philip's affectionate sister-in-law, the self-styled friend of Catholic Spain, had proclaimed herself Supreme Governor of the Church of England, a euphemism which deceived only those determined to escape the truth: for it was the same heretical claim as her father's title in the Act of Supremacy which had cost so many noble lives. She had destroyed her sister's work for a Catholic restoration by establishing an official form of worship which combined all the worst tenets of Protestantism and, at the same time, she had been cunning enough to delete the more offensive passages in the standard Prayer book which referred to the Pope.

The Bishops who had attempted to stop her Coronation, were now paying for their defiance in prison. It was a further instance of the heretical tendencies of her people, that, instead of rising

26

in defence of their priests, the commonalty approved the outrage.

In Feria's opinion, the new Queen had no religion in her soul; her assault on the Catholic religion was committed in cold blood, dictated by expediency and without any saving grace of personal conviction behind it. She made a public show of repudiating the monks and their tapers while using candles in her private Chapel, he had seen them there himself.

He begged King Philip to beware of her; he also reminded him that she was surrounded by men of the worst character and religious beliefs, heretics all of them, or else so besotted with riches garnered from the Dissolution of the Monasteries that they were prepared to forfeit their souls' salvation to avoid a restoration of Church lands.

It was also rumoured, so he spitefully wrote to Philip, that Queen Elizabeth's morals were inherited from her mother. When she was not plotting the destruction of God's Church, she was spending every spare moment in the company of one of her courtiers, Lord Robert Dudley, the Master of her Horse. Her preference for him had grown so marked, and her familiarities so blatant, during the weeks since her accession, that he was almost certainly her lover.

# Chapter 2

THE Queen was at Windsor during the early spring of 1559, and the old grey Castle was transformed with colour and activity; it became the home of her Court, the meeting place of the most talented, rich and powerful men in the kingdom. The roads carried an endless stream of couriers from the ports and the City, for the business of Government followed the sovereign from place to place, like the Lords of the Council.

It was a gay Court as well as an active one. Like the woman who ruled it, it was characterized by vigour and despatch. There was always something happening, someone arriving. It was a life in which each member of her household played a part, from Cecil and her Councillors who found themselves keeping pace with a mistress who never tired of work, to the humble cooks and pantry boys who provided food for over five hundred people twice a day. Elizabeth rose early, attended a service which was neither the Mass nor the plain form of worship favoured by her more Protestant nobles, breakfasted in public, gave audiences, dealt with her vast correspondence, and then usually went hunting before the light failed.

She had always been an enthusiastic horsewoman; now, with the best mounts in the country at her disposal, she was able to indulge her passion for hunting. She was a magnificent shot; the hart which fell with an arrow through its breast was usually the Queen's victim. When she did not hunt she hawked, and there were days when she took a small company of a dozen enthusiasts with her and galloped through the Park at Windsor until the horses were tired out. She was known to be restless; she spent most of her time on her feet or on horseback; when the evenings came or the weather precluded outdoor exercise, Elizabeth danced or organized an impromptu masque with her ladies and gentlemen. She had an appetite for work which was fully equalled by her capacity for enjoying herself. The wits, the poets, the best dancers and musicians were sure of a place in her circle of intimates, and the women who attended her, the Countesses of Warwick, Lindsay, Essex, the Ladies Sidney and Dacre, were as cultured and talented as she was herself. She hated bores and fanatics and a rigid mind annoyed her. A lively tongue, a quick wit, and a handsome appearance were requisites without which no one could hope to attract her attention, and Robert Dudley possessed these qualities in abundance.

Her initial preference for him was innocent enough. She enjoyed his company and found him a pleasant contrast to the sober men with whom she spent the serious part of her life. He was young and full of enthusiasm, and he could talk about their childhood, resurrecting the few happy memories that she had ever known. He never irritated her, or crossed her will; he agreed with her opinions without appearing to flatter, they shared the same irreverent sense of humour and the same tastes. He danced so well that he was a suitable partner when she wished to display her own talent, and he played efficiently enough to accompany her in duets on the virginals. It was all so casual and so natural that she failed to realize its essential artificiality. She was in a unique position; she could command amusement, homage, companionship from whoever she wished and no one could refuse her. It was not till spring of that year, when tongues had been wagging for weeks with scandals about her and Dudley, that she found that she could no longer refuse Robert.

They had come back from hunting. It had been a brilliant afternoon, cold enough to make the rough riding an invigorating pleasure, and she had come out into the Long Gallery after changing her hunting dress for a costume of warm red velvet. The colour suited her; her usually pale cheeks were flushed, her black eyes sparkled. The first person who came up to her, having hurried over his own change of clothing, was Robert Dudley; he was always the first to greet her, whatever she was doing or however long he had to wait. The Gallery was crowded; her ladies were sitting in the window-seats, or clustered round the two fires which burnt at either end of the long passageway. Their voices rose in a pleasant hum which ceased as she appeared in the doorway from her Privy Chamber.

Smiling, Elizabeth gave her hand to Dudley.

"Take me to the window, Robert; I've no mind to be surrounded by a crowd."

"Nor have I," he said quickly. "It's a rare pleasure to have you to myself, Madam, even for a few minutes."

Elizabeth laughed.

"You're always with me—don't you ever tire of the same company?" She sat in the wide window-seat, spreading the vivid red skirts around her, the light of the setting sun turning her hair to copper.

Dudley knelt on the floor at her feet; he was looking into her face when he answered and there was an expression in his eyes which she had never seen before. They were always laughing, darting with energy, seeing a dozen things at once; now it was as if a mask had dropped, and the man's soul gazed at her, urgent, desperate, determined upon something.

"I could never tire of you if I lived to be a hundred, Madam. Sometimes I don't know which is the greater torture to me—seeing you every day and longing for you without hope, or trying to find the courage to leave you for ever."

She stiffened and the colour slowly left her face.

"What do you mean, leave me for ever?—What are you saying?" Elizabeth repeated. "You cannot leave me unless I permit it!"

"How can I stay?"

"Will you for Jesu's sake stop talking riddles and come out with what you mean!" The flash of temper warned him but it exhilarated him too. He knew the signs of a quarrel between lovers; he had seen that expression on other women's faces when he spoke of leaving. . . .

"I cannot stay here," Dudley said quietly, ". . . because I love you."

Suddenly she turned away from him; only her hands betrayed her. They were clenched till her rings cut into the flesh.

"All loyal subjects love the Queen." Her voice was strained. "You are talking nonsense."

"I love the woman," Dudley answered. "Say that you forgive me and will let me go."

Slowly Elizabeth faced him.

"I love the woman."

He would not let her escape; he had destroyed her attempt at subterfuge, the opening she had offered him which would have allowed them to remain as they were.

"You have a wife, my Lord, have you forgotten her?"

"Completely. From the moment I saw you at Hatfield she ceased to exist."

It was as if they crossed swords, fencing with words and

emotions as skilfully as two enemies in mortal combat. He was making a desperate bid for the unattainable, risking his future, his fortunes, possibly his life, and she knew that he understood not only the value of the prize but the penalty for failure if he had misjudged.

" Then if you have forgotten her, what point is there in going back to her? "

Her heart was beating so quickly that one hand touched her breast as if to calm it; but her mind, swift as the hawks she loved, dared him to parry that thrust, if he could. . . .

" There is no point in going anywhere or doing anything, unless I can have my heart's desire," Dudley answered without hesitating. " And since that is forbidden me, then I can only bring dishonour by staying at Court. I can't hide my feelings, Madam. Don't ask me to try, it's beyond Nature. And don't ask me to stay here, watching you day and night, touching your hand, as I did a few moments ago, and knowing that I would give my life to take you in my arms."

" Not only your life, but mine too. I am no King—only a woman, and a Queen cannot take a lover."

His back was between her and the Gallery; he caught one of her hands and found it deadly cold. Suddenly he pressed her palm against his mouth.

" Take me," he whispered. " Nothing will befall you. . . . I know what you fear. Take me, just for one hour. . . ."

" So another man said," Elizabeth wrenched her hand away, fighting a serpentine quiver of response that frightened her so much she could have hit him. " He lost his head and I came near to joining him. Get off your knees, you fool."

She stood up then, and immediately the laughter and talk in the Gallery ceased as everyone sprang to their feet.

" You are dismissed, my Lord."

She walked past him into the centre of the room and beckoned to Lady Warwick to join her. Then she turned and looked at him over her shoulder.

" Until this evening. I lost to you at backgammon last night, and I want my revenge."

Lady Warwick held out the silk embroidered slipper, and eased it over the Queen's foot. Covertly she watched her mistress. She had been watching her for several weeks now, performing her duties in the Royal bedchamber with such

31

diligence that Elizabeth suddenly demanded whether she expected to find someone under the bed. Lady Warwick blushed; she was quite sure that if Dudley were anywhere to be found, it would be inside the curtains, not underneath them. And everyone said he was, though nobody knew when or how it was arranged. But she had not watched Elizabeth for that; she was spying in order to test the truth of a far more serious rumour and one which could not be hidden even by someone as adept as the Queen. If she was pregnant, Lady Warwick would find *that* out. Elizabeth was certainly nervous enough, and so irritable that she had slapped poor Dacre for dropping a scent bottle. But she was thinner than usual, and not sick, nor given to whims about food. No, there was no child, Lady Warwick could swear to that. A sudden angry kick sent the slipper flying into a corner.

"Not that one," Elizabeth snapped. "They pinch; find me another pair, and stop daydreaming, woman. There's a deputation waiting for me."

"Is it about your marriage again, Madam?" Lady Dacre, rather unnerved by the violence and speed with which the Queen delivered a blow, asked her question from a safe distance. She was locking up the Queen's jewel box. Elizabeth had chosen a massive chain of emeralds and pearls with a matching brooch as big as a child's fist. The stones winked and blazed against her black and gold dress. A collar of stiffened lace framed her head.

"It is. They come to urge me to marry the Archduke Charles. How will you like another Spaniard for a Consort? Better than I should, I daresay!"

"It's a shame to worry your Grace, so," Lady Dacre twittered on, unaware of the angry gaze directed at her back. "Why should you be pestered to take a husband till you wish for one? The Lord knows, I wish I were a maiden!"

Elizabeth suddenly burst out laughing. Poor Dacre! Her sympathy was quite genuine. She saw marriage in the light of her own unhappy union with a middle-aged boor who bullied her unmercifully when she was not at Court under the Queen's protection.

"You'd be wise to keep that wish from your Lord husband," she said. "Come here."

Lady Dacre approached her uneasily and knelt. To her own surprise Elizabeth pinched her cheek.

"You are a wise old matron of nineteen and I'm but an old maid of twenty-six," she said. "If you advise against marriage, I shall take your word. You've given me a weapon to use against my persecutors.—Come, ladies, give me my fan and my gloves. I must go forth and defend my virgin state." And she gave the inquisitive and suspicious Lady Warwick a look that took her breath as effectively as any blow.

The Archduke Charles was Spain's candidate; a second candidate, if one considered Philip's tepid offer to marry Elizabeth himself. Though she had expected it, the proposal had filled her with repulsion and rage. The idea that she would welcome the man who had married Mary and hurried her to her grave with a broken heart, had first made Elizabeth laugh and then spit with anger at the impertinence. She must not expect him to spend much time with her, the ungallant proposer added, even if he should leave her pregnant. She had shown the letter to Robert, and he had read with his arm around her, one hand absently caressing her waist in the gesture she loved. She was gratified to see how angry it made him; it gave her the opportunity to sooth his temper and assure him that he had nothing to fear from Philip, or from anyone else. . . . Not for as long as she could withstand her Council and her Parliament. Now Spain was proposing the Archduke, and so alarmed were her advisers, both by her unmarried state and by her apparent liaison with Robert Dudley, that even Cecil was prepared to stomach a Consort who was a Roman Catholic.

They had resurrected every bogey, real and imaginary, which they thought could frighten her into making a decision. The only effective one was her cousin Mary Stuart, whose husband, the French King, had died after a reign lasting only a few months. Mary had now no longer anything to keep her in France, she was waiting to return to her native Scotland, where her presence as Queen and her claim to the English throne would deprive Elizabeth and her advisers of many hours' sleep at night. Fortunately the Protestant nobility of Scotland had chosen that moment to revolt, and large sums of English money were spirited across the Border to assist them and prevent the arrival of the Queen of Scots. Elizabeth denied all knowledge of the money, and promised severe punishment for any of her subjects who assisted the rebels. But the money and the encouragement continued. Elizabeth had at first rejected

33

Cecil's proposal to enter the conflict openly by sending troops when the Scottish rebels appeared to be losing, but the Secretary threatened to resign unless she agreed. The threat had its effect: an English army marched into Scotland, and by July of that year they entered Edinburgh. A treaty was signed between Queen Mary's nobles and the rebel Lords, but the terms were dictated by England, who could at least frame a political and religious settlement in that unruly country which would hamper and dispirit the eighteen-year-old Queen of Scots when she finally arrived there.

Spain's anger at her intervention had been so intense at the time that Elizabeth had hurriedly encouraged the Archduke's suit. But now that she had won her war and got her way in Scotland, there was no need to continue the pretence. The deputation, made up of the Spanish ambassador—an amiable but foolish Bishop who had replaced Feria—and members of her own Council, could safely be dismissed.

When she told them she preferred maidenhood, she watched the anger and the disappointment on some faces, the disbelief and cynicism on others. She had made a fool of the ambassador and his candidate, and deceived her own advisers. Most of them supposed the reason to be political, and these were right; others imagined the cause was Robert Dudley, with whom she was said to be in love.

They were lovers in all senses but the true one. She had allowed him growing intimacies on the understanding that he did not attempt the last of all.

The danger of pregnancy was too obvious to need stressing; Elizabeth refused to contemplate such a risk, but with Dudley at least she was too honest to pretend that her nominal chastity was due to moral scruples. If she could take a lover, she would take him. Those words, wrung from her in a moment of passionate abandonment, fed Dudley's innermost ambition and made the rules governing their strange relationship not only bearable but proper.

Elizabeth refused to become his mistress, and he no longer urged her, because he had conceived the fantastic ambition of making her his wife. He had watched the progress of the Archduke Charles' courtship, terrified that Policy and the promptings of her Council would encourage her to place herself beyond his reach. But the longer the negotiations dragged on, the more ambassadors and politicians did the Archduke's wooing for him, the more confident Dudley felt that no man would win Elizabeth in cold blood.

He showed that he was jealous in order to be re-assured; jeering at the paper courtship, as he called it. And he waited patiently for the obvious solution to their problem to present itself to her. If and when she saw the point of marrying as her subjects demanded, and choosing a husband to her own taste, he would need every friend at Court he could enlist. It was all planned in his quick, unscrupulous mind. He would divorce Amy, whom he hardly ever saw, since he forbade her to come to London, and Amy would agree as she agreed to everything he said. And he, Robert Dudley, would be Consort, perhaps even King of England. Even his father, who had been un-crowned King in Edward's reign, had never conceived an ambition as daring as this one.

If Dudley's intentions were kept secret from Elizabeth, they were obvious enough to her advisers. Cecil's worst fears were being realized, and all the antipathy of the old nobility towards the elevation of an upstart concentrated in a clique against Dudley, headed by the Earl of Sussex. He was a middle-aged man of great courage and discernment; he had befriended Elizabeth when she was Mary's prisoner, and she was known to respect his opinion. She was also so averse to criticism that the other members of the Council, Cecil included, gladly elected Sussex as their spokesman.

She was in her Privy Chamber, playing the virginals with her ladies, when the Earl asked permission to see her privately.

She was in a good temper, soothed by the melody and her own musical skill, and by the memory of the exasperation on the face of the Spanish ambassador when she told him she could not consider the Archduke as a husband because of his religion and her own reluctance to get married.

" My Lord Sussex, Madam."

She continued playing, well aware that the Earl liked music and that she presented a lovely, graceful picture, seated at the instrument in the light of the setting sun. After a moment she looked up and smiled and beckoned to him.

" Welcome, my Lord. You find me idling, I fear. Music is my greatest relaxation. Have you come to divert me for a change or to harry me with business? "

" Neither, Madam. I come to you, as I always will, as a loving servant and councillor. May I see you alone? " At a sign from the Queen, her ladies rose, curtsied, and left the room. Elizabeth left the virginal board and took her favourite position in the window. As a special sign of her favour, she patted the ledge beside her.

"Sit down, my Lord. What do you want from me?"

Sussex faced her without flinching. He had known her for many years; he admired her courage, her natural dignity and intelligence, but his view of her was still coloured by his experience of the nineteen-year-old Princess he had once escorted to the Tower, who wept and seemed so pitifully frail and feminine in her distress. Even the sharp contest of wills in the Council chamber where Elizabeth over-rode some of the toughest men in England had not taught him that she was not now the wilting girl he had befriended long ago.

"I've been charged by the other Councillors to give you a warning, Madam."

He was too gruff and forthright to notice the narrowed eyes, suddenly fixed on him like points of steel.

"If they chose you to be spokesman, they must have known I should dislike it, whatever it is. Don't be too ready to be other men's tongues, my Lord. What is this warning that they dare not give themselves?"

"It concerns Lord Robert Dudley."

"Yes? What of Lord Dudley?"

Her voice usually rose when she was angry; she asked the question lightly and again Sussex was misled.

"He's bringing scandal on your good name. He is a married man and we have reason to believe that he intends to put away his wife and attempt something which would involve your Majesty in ruin."

"And what," she asked softly, "do you mean by my ruin, Sussex?"

"He hopes to marry you himself, may God forgive him!"

"Marry me. . . ." The thin brows arched with surprise. "What makes you think any such thing—and by Jesus, my Lord, in what way would I be ruined by a man's honourable intentions?"

"They are not honourable!" Sussex burst out. "He seeks you from ambition to be King of England! And I tell you, as I shall tell him, that he won't live to carry out his plan. He's taken advantage of you, Madam, and for that alone I can never forgive him. Only a base-born dog, the son of a base-born

36

traitor like his father, would dare dangle after an innocent woman and try to advance himself at her expense!—I come to warn you of it, before it is too late. I come to ask that you dismiss him from Court."

She swung round on him then, and he was startled at the fury in her face. The deadly, murderous anger of her father blazed up in front of him, and though he had never known fear, Sussex recoiled.

"You come to ask!—in that language? Take care, my Lord, take care. You talk of my ruin because you suspect that Robert Dudley hopes to marry me. You sit there and you dare to say he seeks me from ambition, as if I were so unwomanly it was impossible that he should love me for myself! Oh, by God, you say I'm an innocent woman, and all you mean is that you take me for a fool! Now you're united, all you squabbling grandfathers, because you suspect a young man may succeed where these paper Princelings fail! And you dare to threaten him and indirectly threaten me. Believe me when I tell you this. If anything befalls Robert, I'll send a dozen of you to the Tower."

"That's in your power, Madam." Sussex stood up, his heavy face crimson. "But there was a time when you yourself went there under my keeping, and I showed you more favour than you show me now, when I seek to help you once again."

She looked at him, and again it was King Henry, on whose friendship no one could rely once he was crossed.

"You presume too much on the gratitude of Princes.—You already owe your life and your position in my Government to what you did for me. My debt to you is paid. Remember that. You've delivered your message, now go and be my spokesman. Tell my Council that when I marry and if I marry an Englishman might well be to my taste. And thank them; until now I had not thought of Robert Dudley. From this time I shall seriously consider him."

# Chapter 3

July was the hottest month for nearly ten years; the country baked under a cloudless sky and a brassy sun. The water supplies fell dangerously low in some areas. There was a drought which killed off crops and cattle, and the plague broke out with ugly virulence in London. The wealthy had left their big houses on the City outskirts and taken refuge on their country estates and the Court moved from Whitehall Palace to Hampton Court.

There were so many reminders of her mother and father at Hampton that some people had expected Elizabeth to avoid it. The beautiful red-brick Palace was haunted by memories of Henry, and Anne Boleyn, who had come there as his Queen; she had slept and eaten and made music in the rooms Elizabeth used every day, walked through the same formal gardens by the river bed, and watched jousts from the tournament tower, where her daughter now sat in Royal state.

As Elizabeth sat sewing in the shade with her ladies, she could see the graceful cornice where workmen had carved Anne's initials with the King's, bound by a lovers' knot in stone. The same motif, ordered by the infatuated Henry, had once decorated porticos and ceilings in the Palace. But they were gone, erased to make room for the initials of her successor, Jane Seymour. And further down the garden walk there was a little artificial hillock, called the Mount, where Henry had stood on a clear May day, listening for the Tower cannon to announce Anne's execution. Once only, Elizabeth went there and gazed up the shining stretch of the river. In spite of the heat, her two attendants saw her shiver. She went back to the Palace without speaking, and she never climbed the Mount again.

She spent most of the evenings in the Long Gallery, where the windows opened out, admitting the cooler air from the river, and the sound of music and voices drifted out into the deepening twilight.

The middle day of the month had been so stifling that the

Queen had stayed in her room, drinking cordial and fanning herself while a hot, tired Lady Warwick read to her aloud. When it was cooler she dined informally, and frugally, in spite of the variety of dishes which were always set in front of her, and then to her attendants' relief, decided to go into the Long Gallery and join her Court for the evening.

She was not an easy mistress; even gentle Lady Dacre admitted that, and she had already forgiven that box on the ear. She was too tense and restless; always uncertain tempered if she was denied exercise, she prowled up and down her apartments, demanding to be read to or played to or entertained with conversation, and though some of her ladies were several years her senior, they felt constrained and on edge. Elizabeth was bored by women, and she showed it. After a time their chattering irritated her; and she often turned on them with a curt order to be quiet. They had a spiteful explanation for their failure to amuse her or get close to her; in fact Elizabeth's refusal to make intimates of any of her women provoked them most of all. She was short tempered and impatient because she wanted the Lord Dudley with her day as well as night, the wagging tongues declared. Her unfortunate attendants had to pay for her observance of propriety, and God knew what she did observe was scant enough. . . . Like most explanations of human behaviour, it was partially true. She missed Robert when she had to be separated from him; she missed him because she was not in Council or out hunting or doing anything that interested her, and like both her parents she could not suffer tedium with any show of patience.

She missed Robert that day, when it was too hot to go out or venture into the crowded Gallery until the evening. But after dinner she dressed in a long, light gown of white silk, the bodice and sleeves shining with milky pearls, her hair hanging down to her shoulders and drawn back from her face with a narrow crescent, spiked with diamonds.

She walked out into the Gallery, preceded by her gentlemen ushers crying: "Make way for the Queen's Majesty! Make way for the Queen!"

She knew without looking that Robert Dudley was pushing his way forward towards her. Always pushing, always determined to stand where the limelight fell, she thought, but she made the observation indulgently, amused by the characteristic she knew so well. He was ambitious and thrusting, but those

39

traits were part of him; they gave him that keen, hunter's eye, the agile body, radiating energy; he possessed a ravening hunger for life and all that life could offer, and the prize which dazzled all men's eyes was herself. Only Robert, the grandson of a grasping lawyer without a drop of truly noble blood in his veins, would have dared try and take that prize before all the princely competitors in Europe.

"Madam—at last! This has been not only the hottest day but the longest, because of your absence!"

She gave him her hand to kiss, and mischievously dug her nails into his fingers because he held it to his mouth too long. But she was smiling, and her dark eyes sparkled; the boredom and irritation which had frayed her temper all day had vanished without trace. He was the only man except the Admiral who had ever brought this feeling of excitement, of expectation, when they met, as if she were seeing him for the first time and always with new eyes. There was a crowd round her, murmuring compliments—there were half a dozen men, stifling in their best silks and velvets, all trying to claim her attention, but it was Dudley who fell into step with her and brought her to a seat by the open window.

"By God, Robert, I feel as if I'd been baked in one of my own ovens! There's enough sweat running down your neck to melt your ruff!"

"As always you look like a goddess and talk like a stable-boy," Dudley grinned. "But then you always did, my adored Lady; when we were children I remember being beaten till I couldn't sit for a week because of some oaths you'd come out with, which my father supposed I had taught you!"

"More likely you learnt them from me," Elizabeth laughed. "You're always saying what a hoyden I was—don't you know that my tutor described me as the best-lettered Princess in Europe?"

"Oh, you can swear in ancient Greek better than most men can talk plain English," he retorted. "It's part of your charm, Madam, that no one knows what to expect of you. Have you boxed poor Kate Dacre's ears today?"

"Poor Kate Dacre is devoted to me now, so it must have done her good. I can think of a few others who may benefit in the same way if they're not careful."

"Not me, I hope?"

"No." Elizabeth leaned back and fanned herself lazily.

40

"No, not you, my Robert. Only a fool of a woman would hit you and think you too much the gentleman to strike her back. If I ever gave you a blow, which God forbid, it would have to be a mortal one."

He laughed and took the fan away from her, and began to wave it.

"Let me cool you, Madam, and allay that blow while I can."

"Cool me now, only to heat me later," she said softly, watching him. "I know you, my Lord Dudley. Be careful; everyone is watching us."

"I know, and they're busy damning me to hell because they're not in my place."

"How reckless are you? " she asked suddenly. "Do you know that Sussex came to me as the Council's spokesman and asked for your dismissal from Court? "

The rhythm of the fan was interrupted for a second; when it resumed the pace was faster.

"On what grounds, Madam? "

"On the grounds that you were bringing me into dishonour, Robert. He didn't pick and choose his words, I can assure you."

"I warned you what would happen if I stayed with you," he answered. " You should have let me go when I asked, before your Councillors force me out."

"No one," Elizabeth said sharply, "will send you packing except me. I told my Lord Sussex to mind his tongue and his manners; but there was something else he said—the real reason why he came, I think. He said you were planning to put away Amy. Is that true? "

"Yes," Dudley answered without hesitation. "I intend going to Norfolk next week if you will give me permission."

"And when you are a bachelor, what will you do then? "

He laid the fan in her lap, and glanced round at the crowded Gallery.

"If we were alone I could tell you," he said. "But not here, with every pair of eyes searching our faces. Will you walk in the garden with me, Madam—I have so much I want to say to you. . . ."

"I can take Dacre with us," she said, "and tell her to wait when we are out of sight of the Palace."

She made a sign and her gentleman usher preceded her, carrying the rod of his office, and the call went down the

41

Gallery again, "Make way for the Queen's Majesty! Make way!"

Elizabeth walked through the lines of men and women who curtsied and bowed as she passed; she paused for a word with one or two, and smiled at the rest. She stopped before Sussex, who was still smarting from their encounter over Dudley, and suddenly held out her hand to him.

"My Lord Dudley takes me to the garden for some air," she said. "I require the strong arm of a Sussex to guide me down the stairs. Come, my Lord."

It was a signal honour, and ignoring his enemy's presence on the other side of her, Sussex kissed her hand before placing it on his arm and led her to the end of the Gallery, past the sentries at the entrance, and slowly down the wide oak staircase into the Great Hall.

"I have seen too little of you," Elizabeth remarked. "You are not to skulk out of my sight because we had a disagreement, my Lord. I am too fond of you to be abandoned."

Sussex crimsoned with mixed pleasure and embarrassment. He could never understand how a woman who had lacerated with her tongue a few days, or even hours before, could heal the wound with a few words and put her victim sweetly in the wrong.

"I thought you wouldn't wish to see me," he said awkwardly. "I thought your Majesty was still angry with me."

"There's no real anger between friends," she said. "And we are friends, my Lord, from many years."

At the entrance to the garden she stopped, and turned to him.

"Thank you for that strong arm." Elizabeth smiled slowly at him, and he thought with emotion that he had never seen a lovelier expression on the face of any woman. It was so full of sympathy and affection, as if he were the only man in England that she really trusted. . . .

"It is always at your service, Madam. From now until death withers it!"

"I know that, and I thank God for the knowledge." Then followed by Lady Dacre, she passed out into the summer dusk with Dudley by her side.

They left Lady Dacre sitting on a little stone seat behind a yew hedge in what had once been Cardinal Wolsey's herb garden; she watched the pale figure of the Queen in her white

42

dress shadowed by Dudley in his gleaming doublet, until they turned a corner by the fountain, and disappeared from sight. Lady Dacre sighed, and crossed her small feet, anticipating a long wait. She disliked Lord Dudley; he was too dark and fierce looking, and his eyes flicked over her with something rather like contempt. She was a gentle creature, and though she was afraid of her, she genuinely loved her mistress and defended her reputation among the scandal-mongering ladies-in-waiting with a vigour that surprised them. The Queen embodied all those characteristics of courage and presence that she knew to be lacking in herself. Perhaps a woman as strong and self-confident as the Queen was not afraid of men like ordinary mortals. Perhaps she could use them as they normally used women, without ever surrendering her freedom or completely losing her heart. Kate Dacre stared through the soft summer gloom till her eyes ached; they must have wandered far because she could not hear their voices. Well, whatever they did, Jane Warwick and Lady Bedford would hear nothing about it from *her*.

They had come to the stretch of lawn beside the river bank, and in the shelter of a cherry tree, Dudley tried to take Elizabeth in his arms. To his surprise she pushed him back; she was much stronger than she looked.

"We came to talk," she reminded him.

"We spend our lives in talking," Dudley said impatiently. "We spend our time like puppets on a stage, living our lives before an audience. God knows it's seldom enough we are alone like this—— Come to me, give me a few moments of joy, I beg of you!"

She shook her head and moved swiftly away to the edge of the river parapet so that he had to follow her.

"What will you do if Amy agrees to be divorced?" she said. "Tell me, Robert."

He stood beside her, leaning against the rough stone, and gently put one arm around her shoulders.

"I'll set out to win the only woman in the world I want," he answered. "And you know very well who that is."

"Would you aspire to marry me, Robert?" She looked at him, her face very pale in the dim light, her eyes as black as the river which ran past their feet.

"I would, and I'll never rest until I do."

"I am not to be taken by intrigue or force of arms," her

43

voice was a whisper. "Do not mistake me for a venture, Robert, and think in terms of power. Who gains me will never gain my throne. I have to tell you that."

"There is no need," Dudley told her quietly. "I told you before, I love the woman, not the Queen."

She turned suddenly, and this time she came into his arms, one hand holding his cheek, gazing into the face bent over hers as if to read the same sincerity in the eyes as she heard in his voice.

"Do you really love me, Robert? Just for myself, and not for what I can give you?"

"More than my life," he whispered, and in that moment when success seemed within reach, he had an odd suspicion that he meant what he said.

"If I were free, and I will be, I promise you, would you marry me?"

"I don't know." She was staring past him, out over the shining Thames, beyond into the increasing darkness. "I don't know, Robert. I am afraid to marry. We stand here, you and I, talking of love, and have you ever thought who may have stood in this same spot and kissed and whispered, just as we are doing now?"

"No," Dudley shook his head. He had no idea what she meant.

"My mother and father."

The next moment she had stepped back from him, and there was something about her that stopped him from touching her.

"He was supposed to love her," she said harshly. "He turned England upside down to marry her and then he cut her head off before I was three years old. That is what marrying for love has meant to me. God knows, perhaps that's what marriage means itself, I can't be sure. I am sure about everything, Robert, everything in life that I want or must do, except this one thing that all men believe to be so easy for a woman. You ask me to marry you and I can't answer."

"Yes, you can," Dudley urged. "Banish your ghosts, Madam—banish your fears with them! Pity your mother if you wish, but for Christ's sake don't take her as an example."

"I don't pity my mother," Elizabeth interrupted; she was staring across the river, her face as hard and pale as stone in

44

the light of the moon which had just risen. " She died a whore's death and that's all I know about her. I should never have spoken of this, even to you. And I never will again. I forbid you to speak of it either."

" As you desire," he answered quickly. " Let the dead rest; and let us talk of the living. Do you believe I love you? "

" Yes." Elizabeth looked at him, and smiled almost wistfully. " I believe you love me as much as you know how to love, my Robert."

" And knowing that, you cannot answer me, or give me any hope? "

" How can I promise anything, when you already have a wife? "

" But I am going to divorce Amy," Dudley protested. " You know that, my beloved."

" When you are free," Elizabeth said, " it will be time to ask and the time for me to decide. And now you must take me back, Robert. We've been away too long already."

It was nearly dawn and she had woken after three hours of restless sleep. Elizabeth pulled back one corner of the bed curtains; she could hear the snores of her ladies in the ante-chamber, and the rising birdsong outside her open windows. It was a sound she loved, the gentle twittering that grew into an excited welcome for the rising sun. A peaceful sound, happy and unaware that the day brought the human enemy out to hunt and took the hood off the deadly falcon's head.

She never used falcons; the falcon was her mother's favourite bird, a white falcon was her mother's crest. " She died a whore's death." Those were her words to Robert when they were at Hampton a week ago, and she could not dismiss them from her mind. She had never mentioned Anne Boleyn to anyone before, not since the day she learnt the truth about her death and her alleged offences. She never wished to speak about her or think about her; there was no profit in the past once its initial lessons had been learnt. Learn by the mistakes of others and then forget who made them. Learn not to trust a man's love.

For all women were weak, and if she once surrendered her independence, she could never hope to get it back. Robert would try to dominate her—when she imagined that domination her feelings came close to hatred instead of love. She did not want to marry him, but she didn't want to lose him either,

45

and she lay at Windsor, after yet another wretched night, cursing him and herself and wondering when he would return from seeing his wife, Amy Dudley. She was a foolish, unsophisticated girl who had never said anything but yes to her husband. *She* could not hinder Robert; he would force her to agree and he would come back to Court and the whole struggle must be fought again. Elizabeth leant back against her pillows. Her head ached; it always did when she was worried. She loved him in many ways, perhaps more than she would admit. He could give her the warmth, the laughter, the closeness which was essential to true happiness. Indeed he gave it already, as much as their irregular relationship allowed. And he would give her children, heirs to stabilize her throne.

"No woman is truly happy until she has borne children."

She could hear Cecil saying that in his dry voice, urging her to marry the Spanish Archduke, or one of the Protestant German Princes who were suing for her hand. It amused her to hear him; she could never think of Cecil begetting anything with his dull wife except a Latin treatise. . . . He had not understood her mockery; he thought her unfeminine, because he was devoted to his family while she had as little faith in children as she had in men. Sons and daughters would only grow up to envy each other and wish her dead so that they could inherit. She did not want Robert for children. She wanted Robert for her own sake, for her own happiness. But she did not want Robert as joint sovereign of England, and she knew in her heart that he would not be content with less. She did not want any human creature to partake in the power which was hers alone; the man who mounted a throne beside her would cease to be a husband and become a rival. That was another thing she knew Cecil did not understand when he preached of the joys of wifely functions, in relation to some man she had not seen and might not even like. He wasn't pleading Robert's case—no one pleaded that except Robert himself. . . . Cecil did not understand that there were human beings in whom the passion for power was far stronger than the lusts of the flesh and that she was one of them.

The sun was up, flooding into her bedroom. She reached out for her silver handbell and shook it. It must be half-past five, and she had a mass of paperwork to attend to and a Council meeting after the morning service. Suddenly her head was clear and her heart light; she felt refreshed and eager at the prospect.

46

The problem of marriage and Robert Dudley had ceased to exist.

Cumnor Hall had once been the property of the abbots of Abingdon, and the house and parklands had passed to the Crown when Henry VIII seized the monastic estates. It was not a large house, and showed little trace of its religious origins by the time Robert's treasurer Anthony Forster leased it for his own use. Shortly afterwards Robert had suggested that his wife, Lady Dudley, should make her home there until a permanent residence was chosen for her. It was typical of Amy that she agreed to be boarded out with friends and associates while her husband stayed in London, or wherever the Court happened to be. She had once suggested that he might bring her to the Court and present her to the Queen, but he had told her it was inconvenient because he had so many duties. That was a long time ago, and she had not asked again. As the time passed, rumours of his advancement reached the quiet backwater where Amy lived, and there were occasional visits from Robert, who was always splendidly dressed and mounted and accompanied by a train of servants. The visits were not only infrequent but very short; they were only undertaken because of some business which could not be transacted by letter, for Amy had inherited several estates from her father, and Robert administered these and collected their revenues.

She had not seen him for six months when she received the letter advising her of his arrival. The few days before he came were spent in preparations; the best bedroom was aired and cleaned, sheets put on the double bed, food stocked into the larders, and Lady Dudley's modest wardrobe was inspected for her best dresses to wear in his honour. It was a pitiful attempt which deceived nobody, not even Amy. She had been ill with an abscess on her breast; this had mercifully broken, but she was pale and thin and burst into tears over her reflection when she saw it in the mirror. When they married, nearly ten years ago, she had been pretty, very pretty in a plump way, with soft fair hair and large eyes; the world had been a kind place, full of promise, and her husband had been desperately in love with her. During the endless evenings when she sat alone, and the longer nights when she sat up in bed, sewing because she could not sleep, Amy remembered their marriage and the first months of happiness which had suddenly declined, almost without warning, into the farce of their present life together. For nearly a year Robert had been in love with her, amused, protective and gay, and then, almost without transition, he was satiated and bored.

When she cried, it made him restless and drove him out hunting, or up to London, where his father, the Duke of Northumberland, was so powerful, and where he could amuse himself with women if he chose. Amy, who was not as simple as she seemed, knew very well that he did choose, and the jealousy which tormented her for the next nine years corroded her looks and downed her spirits.

He had left her to court Queen Mary's favour, and stayed on to establish himself with the new Queen, Elizabeth. And for over a year, Amy had been hearing rumours that Robert was the new Queen's lover. She had never taxed him with it; she had never dared. She only smiled nervously and chattered, and fidgeted, and made timorous overtures of affection which he pretended not to notice. She had no place in his life but the nominal position as his wife, and she only saw him when he wanted something, but at least she saw him, and for that she had begun to live, expecting nothing more.

She was waiting for him in the hall, wearing a dress of dark blue velvet which was six months behind the fashion, a collar of stiffened lawn framing her face, which was pinched and strained, and anxiously smiling. He saw her companion Mrs. Odingsell, standing in the background, the two Forsters, and another woman, Mrs. Owen, who had left her husband and attached herself to Lady Dudley. Robert kissed her cheek, greeted the others and in reply to Amy's question he explained brusquely that he was only staying for one night, and then went up to his room to wash and change his riding clothes.

They dined well that night; the conversation was rather forced, until Mrs. Odingsell asked questions about the Court. While Robert talked, his wife sat quietly, picking at the food on her plate, glancing up from time to time to see the animation in his face as he discussed the personalities whose names were famous, describing a Ball or a brilliant masque, his eyes glittering whenever the name of the Queen was mentioned.

"Is she as beautiful as they say, my Lord?"

Robert smiled at that old harpy, Odingsell, sitting there with her mouth open like a seal, hungry for verbal scraps.

"Not beautiful, no. But more fascinating than any woman

48

alive, I should say. Handsome, handsome as the devil, the best horsewoman, the best dancer—why, the best at everything, that's all I can tell you."

There was a moment of awkward silence, broken by Mrs. Owen.

"Why, you've eaten nothing, my Lady! Try some of the chicken pasty—it's really excellent."

"No thank you," Amy smiled up at the plain, anxious face of the only real friend she had in the house. She was grateful to Beth Owen, who had repaid her shelter by countless acts of kindliness. "No, I'm not very hungry."

"We're well buried here, my Lord," Mrs. Owen said aggressively. "But even we heard rumours that the Queen is about to marry a foreign Prince. Is that true?"

"You are indeed buried, if that is the latest you know." Robert's eyes considered his questioner with hostility. When he settled with Amy he'd make sure Madam Owen found another benefactress. . . .

"The Queen is besieged by suitors, and has rejected them all. And now, Madam," he bowed to Amy, rising from the table.

"I know the company will excuse us. I have travelled far and I have many things to discuss with you, and not much time. We will see you tomorrow, ladies, and you, my good Forster. We must have a word about finance before I leave. Come to me in the gallery before noon."

They went into the long, panelled room which had once been the Abbot's private chamber; the August light had faded, and a big iron candle branch burnt on either side of the fireplace. As she took her place in the chair opposite to him, Dudley noticed her dress trailing in a pool of half melted wax. She had always been a bad housekeeper, useless with servants, who either cheated and defied her or doted on her for the wrong reasons, extravagant over trifles, and maddeningly forgetful. The smooth running of Cumnor was due to Forster and his wife. They were a clever, efficient couple. He could trust Forster with anything.

She did not open the conversation. He had shown temper with Beth Owen, and she knew he was still irritated. While she sat there, Dudley watched her for a moment. She was always so nervous, he thought contemptuously. She moistened her lips and kept looking quickly at him and then away, and twisting her chain of pearls round and round her fingers. It would have been so much easier if she showed a little spirit. He actually deluded himself for a minute that he might have still cared for her had she been of tougher temper, shown anger or defiance, taken a lover—done anything but wait for him like a sick dog, which would rather be kicked than ignored. He had already decided to ask for the divorce quite simply and gently and avoid a scene if he could, and therefore his first words were a surprise to her.

"You don't look well, Amy."

"No—Oh, I've been ill for some time, Robert, but I'm quite cured now. I won't tell you about it, and I didn't write because I know how sickness distresses you. But it's left me a little pale, I think."

"You should have a change," he said. "You could arrange to go to the North; the air there is very good."

"I'm quite happy here. If I went to the North, I should never see you."

He leant forward suddenly, both hands on his knees.

"Amy, I must talk to you. I must talk to you from the heart. We can't go on in this fashion any longer. You can't sit here, wasting your days waiting for a husband who has too many calls on him to *be* a husband. We married in great haste, when we were both too young to know what marriage meant. Let us dissolve it now, while we are friends and wish each other well. I want my freedom, Amy, and I want you to have yours. Another man will make up to you for all that I've lacked."

He was surprised because he had been so certain that of all the women in the world, Amy would cry at such a moment. But her eyes were dry, and there was a curious look in them when she answered.

"I don't want any other man. I'm happy enough with you."

He shook his head, determined not to show impatience.

"You haven't been happy for many years, neither have I. Let us be honest with each other; our paths have separated and they will never run in the same direction now. I cannot live the life of a squire buried in the country. You aren't suited to the life at Court."

"I have never had the opportunity to find that out," Amy said quietly. "You did not want me with you, Robert, and I have been content to stay away. I am not complaining. I told you, I am happy enough as things are."

"Well I am not."

If she was going to argue, he thought angrily, then there was no use employing gentle language.

"I want a divorce, and I demand that you agree. I won't be held in bondage to you; I want my freedom!"

Amy Dudley looked at him. "So this was the important business you wrote about," she said. "And I suppose you thought it would be settled by tomorrow so that you could ride back to the Queen and tell her it was done."

"What the devil are you saying!" He sprang out of his chair and stood over her glaring down into that white, oddly determined face.

"You said we should be honest. People have been gossiping about you and the Queen for months. Why don't you tell the truth and say that you want to cast me off so that you can marry *her*!"

He had no idea how the truth had come into her stupid head, and he no longer cared. At that moment it seemed as if the sickly woman sitting in front of him, showing signs of independence for the first time in her life, were the sole obstacle to his marriage with Elizabeth.

"You can tell her," Amy's voice was trembling at last, "that she has taken you from me in spirit, and in body. You are always with her and never with me. She is the Queen and I cannot fight her. She wants you now, and therefore I must stand aside and give you to her as if I had no rights at all. But I won't, Robert. You may tell her so. I will not divorce you."

For a moment he thought he must have imagined it; Amy could not be serious—she had never refused him anything, never defied him in the ten years of their marriage. . . .

"I thought you loved me," he burst out. "In God's name, what are you trying to do, ruin me out of spite?"

"I do love you, Robert. I love you more than life itself— I've always loved you. That's why I cannot give you to another woman; as long as I'm your wife you may grow tired of her and she of you, and then you may come back to me."

She crossed to his chair and knelt beside it, her hand gripping his arm, the tears running down her face as she looked up at him.

"I only live in that hope, Robert—that one day we will be as we were. If I let you go as you ask, I should lose you for ever.

I cannot do that. I will not do it. And she will not blame you; you won't be ruined."

"I will," he said. "You don't know the Queen; if she is thwarted. . . ."

"No," Amy said. "No, Robert, it's no use. I'd go to the Tower rather than do what you want."

"Oh would you!" He wrenched his arm away from her and stood up. "You may well go there, Madam, if you persist in this."

"I know that. I know what she can do to me; God help me, I even know that you'd encourage her. But you're my husband; that's all I have left. Until the day you return to me; and I know you will, whatever you feel now. You'll come to love me again as you did before."

"Love you!" Dudley almost spat the words at her. "I never loved you! You think a stripling boy's daydreams of bed were love? You bored me to death within a few months —in bed and out of it. You stupid, vapid little babbler—why God's death you never even bore a child! Look at yourself— you have no beauty, no wit, no graces. Love you! I cannot bear the sight of you."

"Don't, Robert—I beg of you, don't wound me like this— don't be so cruel. . . ."

She was sobbing, clinging to the empty chair. She dragged herself upright and seized his arm again.

"I love you . . . believe me, that's why I am refusing you . . . I love you, whatever you do or say."

"Then don't stand in my way," he answered fiercely. "Don't keep me from what I want most in life. I can marry the Queen, Amy, I can be the most powerful man in England, if you will be sensible and agree to a divorce. I can give you money, lands, anything you want—why I'll feel more fondness for you than I ever did, if you will dissolve this farce of a marriage. Show that you love me! Do what I ask of you and let me go!"

Slowly Amy Dudley shook her head.

"No, Robert. Go back to the Queen's bed which is so much warmer than mine. But you will only lie in it as her lover. You'll never be another woman's husband as long as I live."

There was no sound in the room for a moment. When Dudley spoke his voice was dangerously quiet.

"That is your last word?"

"Yes." It was a whisper. One word, spoken so low that he could hardly hear it, and it sounded the final defeat of all his hopes. He felt the grip of her fingers, holding his arm so tightly that the pressure pinched his skin. He suddenly wrenched it free, and in the same movement his hand swung back and he struck her across the face with all his strength.

He heard her cry out, and the sound of a fall as he turned away. Then the door crashed behind him. When he reached his own room he sent his body servant away and flung himself down on the bed, his head in his hands.

He sat for so long that he lost count of time, until the chiming of a clock in the next room roused him. He had been thinking, slowly and deliberately, his rage purged out of him by that violent blow. He loosened his doublet, kicked off his shoes and lay flat on the bed in his clothes. Within a few minutes he had fallen asleep. He had made up his mind what he had to do.

The next morning Mrs. Odingsell reported that my Lady was staying in bed; she had fallen in her room and badly bruised herself. Mrs. Owen was with her. Anthony Forster sent his wife up to commiserate, and formed his own conclusions when she told him that Lady Dudley had been crying and trying to cover a black eye and a swollen cheek. He was a foxy man, with sandy hair and beard, and pale green eyes which never softened. When he went to Robert Dudley that morning, he noticed the evident signs of bad temper; Dudley was sallow and heavy-eyed as if he had slept badly. He was dressed in cloak and boots, ready to leave as soon as Forster had made his report. He was able to give a very satisfactory account of Dudley's finances, but his master was still scowling and walking up and down; Forster was sure that he had not been listening to a word.

He had only been in his service for two years but he knew Dudley very well. He was not deceived by his genial manners when all was going as it should, or by his generosity or his wit. He had always suspected that Lord Robert would be a savage if he were thwarted, as savage as his father and as unfeeling as his domineering mother. And Lady Dudley had thwarted him, and been given a beating for it. Forster saw no harm in such chastisement; it was not uncommon for the highest born to ill-use their wives if they felt like it, and he had nothing but contempt for Amy Dudley and admiration for Robert.

"Do you know why I told you to report to me?" Dudley turned to him abruptly.

"To give an account of your affairs, my Lord."

"To give an account of them and to draw up a financial settlement for my wife after our divorce!"

Forster said nothing, but his quick mind came to the truth in a few seconds. He had always believed the rumours of Dudley's liaison with the new Queen; but this meant that the latest and wildest rumour of their impending marriage was also true. And that was why my Lady Dudley was upstairs nursing a black eye. . . . She had objected to being put out of the way.

"I am sorry to hear of it, my Lord, for your sake and her Ladyship's," he said. "What arrangements shall I make?"

"None!" Dudley snapped at him. "My wife refuses to free me. You see the unhappiest man in England before you, Forster!."

He sat down, watching his treasurer. Forster owed him everything. He could throw him out into the gutter if he failed to take the hint which he had decided to drop him, and he knew that Forster knew it.

"I have no love for my wife," he said slowly. "Nor has she for me. But out of spite she is determined to keep me from someone who is too exalted to name. This great lady has honoured me with her affection, Forster, and if I reject it, I must bring ruin upon myself and those dependent upon me. I shan't be able to keep you in my service much longer. I shall not have wealth or preference or power to employ you, after I return to Court."

"One moment, my Lord."

Forster went to the door and opened it quickly. The hall outside was empty. He looked through the window and saw no one in the gardens under them. He came back and his thin mouth curved in a slight smile.

"In a house full of women, one must make sure of privacy. We are alone and cannot be overheard. What do you want me to do?"

# Chapter 4

WILLIAM CECIL was so distracted with worry that he could hardly work. His usually precise, calm disposition was in such a ferment that he twice wrote an error in his instructions to the English ambassador at Brussels and had to destroy the paper and begin again. The hot weather disagreed with him; he slept badly at the best of times during the summer, and the Queen's conduct had become so impossible that he was ungallantly reminded of the Gadarene Swine and their rush to self-destruction.

Elizabeth ignored the commonest conventions governing the conduct of a respectable unmarried woman and spent hours shut up alone with Robert Dudley. It was incredible but true that, according to the information of Cecil's snoopers, watching through cracks in the door and holes in the tapestries, the gross liberties Lord Dudley took with her person were always curtailed at the last moment. The Queen still preserved her virginity, if not her modesty, but her reputation was being ruined by the association.

She had told Cecil to mind his own business when he reproached her; he had picked his words with the utmost care, stressing the harm done to her good name by what he described as her innocent lack of convention, and hinted that her numerous foreign suitors might be offended by the scandals linking her name with a subject. And a subject of somewhat ignoble birth, who already had a wife.

Elizabeth had replied by laughing in his face. Her conscience was clear in her own sight; she assured him that the subject in question was more dear to her than the opinion of Princes she had never seen, and that if she could ignore the clacking of evil tongues, so could he. Dudley was not her lover. Cecil had been about to say that he might just as well be, but she changed the subject.

Her conduct was bad enough; it shocked Cecil, whose neat mind regarded it as illogical and depraved, but he lived in terror that her nocturnal indiscretions would lead her either to submission to the scoundrel or else to the marriage he was obviously plotting.

The climax came when Dudley left for Cumnor, making no secret that his purpose was to secure a divorce from Lady Dudley. When he returned he hedged about the outcome, saying that his wife was ill and unable to discuss the matter yet. Cecil, and everyone else who knew the circumstances, supposed that he had been refused, and the most terrible rumour of all began to circulate. The Queen and Dudley intended Amy Dudley's death. Death by poison. Death by assassination. The foreign ambassadors' reports were full of it; the atmosphere surrounding the Court sizzled like a lighted fuse, inexorably burning towards the explosion of scandal which would blast Elizabeth off her throne. Inwardly Cecil raged at his idol for so soon showing feet of more than mortal clay. He had imagined her to be above the weaknesses of women, proof against their fleshly temptations and their emotional instability. He saw her in the Council Chamber, clever, dispassionate, far seeing, and could not believe that she was about to murder a simple country gentlewoman in order to take a self-seeking pimp into her bed and make him King of England.

But he could not allay his fears, because she would not let him. He could not talk to her on this one subject, by far the most important and the most dangerous at that time, however close they were on things connected with the State. He threw down his pen in despair.

Her throne was trembling under her; nothing could keep her on it if anything happened to Amy Dudley and she married Amy Dudley's husband. The whole country would rise against her, and the Queen of Scots, still smarting from English interference in her kingdom across the Border, would descend upon them with the full support of France to claim the English throne. And not even Philip of Spain's Francophobia would make him protect the interests of a woman who had connived at murder to satisfy a personal lust.

" Sir William! "

" What is it? "

One of Cecil's private couriers stood in the doorway, covered with dust.

" I've just come from Cumnor, Sir. Lady Dudley is dead.

She was found at the foot of the stairs with her neck broken this morning."

Cecil found the Queen in her Privy Chamber. She was seated in the middle of a circle composed of Mary Sidney, who was Dudley's sister, Kate Dacre, and several young gentlemen of her household. They were all laughing, Elizabeth holding both hands wide in illustration of some story she had been telling them.

He stood without speaking, looking at her until one by one the heads turned and the laughter died away, and at last she saw him.

"Cecil? What are you doing here. . . ?"

She saw the accusation in his eyes, and the colour of his face; it was as white as his collar. In the two years of their association she had never seen him look at her like that, as if he hated her.

In a moment she stood up.

"Leave us! All of you!"

The rest of them dispersed like leaves before a gust of wind, bowing and curtsying and backing out. When the door closed and they were alone, Cecil still did not move towards her.

"What are you standing there for? What is the matter? Jesus, man, have you gone dumb?"

"I wish that I had," he answered. "I wish I were both deaf and dumb and blind, Madam, before I saw a day like this one."

Elizabeth stepped close to him. She was very pale, but her eyes glittered and her thin lips were set like a trap.

"I asked you once what was wrong. I shall not ask again!"

"Lady Dudley has been murdered," Cecil said.

She spat out such a quarter-deck oath that he was startled. "Murdered? What are you talking about—are you sure?"

"Quite sure. My courier has just reported it. She was found at the foot of some stairs with a broken neck. I came to tell you before the whole world hears the news."

"Who did it?"

She had not turned away from him; there was no sign of guilt or discomfort in her white face: it might have been sculptured from stone instead of flesh and blood. The unfathomable eyes, so black and opaque in spite of their brilliance, stared into his without a flicker. But then she was a mistress of control;

57

no secret, no emotion escaped her unless she meant to show it. If she had killed Amy Dudley with her own hands she would look at him as coolly as she was doing then.

When Cecil did not answer, she said slowly: " Did Robert kill her? "

" You would know that, Madam, better than I."

" Are you suggesting," the voice stabbed at him like a dagger, " that I had any knowledge of this woman's death? Is that what I see in your face, Cecil? "

He turned away from her suddenly, sickened with her and himself, his anger already changing to despair.

" What do you see in your own heart, Madam? What will the world see? That is what matters! Lady Dudley is dead, and dead by foul means, that's obvious. What will you do now—marry him, as everyone prophesied you would when he was free? "

" You must be mad to talk like this. I shan't listen to you, and be thankful I shan't hold your impertinence against you. Cecil, you may go! "

" No, Madam, I can't go. Not until you tell me what you mean to do. I can't be dismissed like a subject this time, for I cannot let you destroy yourself and your country and your friends without telling you what you are doing. Before the God who made us all, Madam, swear to me that you did not know this was going to happen! "

" Before God, I knew nothing about it. I give you my oath, as Queen of this realm, that my way with rivals is not to remove them by pushing them down a flight of stairs. If I wanted Amy Dudley's life, I have a perfectly good executioner who could take it for me. I might do that if the need arose, but never this. Are you satisfied; do you believe me? "

" I believe you. And I ask your pardon."

He fell on his knees in front of her, overcome with relief. He knew she was innocent of the low, cowardly murder of a defenceless enemy. He should have known her better; Dudley, for all his open braggadocio, would resort to the methods of a sneak thief, because he was a sneak thief. There was an inherent, noble courage in Elizabeth which had nothing to do with compassion, but was incapable of committing a major crime under a despicable covering.

Human life and human suffering meant little to her; he knew that; but her own Royal, ruthless nature acquitted her of the crime of Amy's murder, simply by the manner of it.

"How do you know?" she said, recalling him to reality. "How can you be sure that it was not an accident?"

"Even if it was," Cecil answered, "the world will still say that Dudley caused her death, through an agent. No, Madam, it was no accident; the courier told me enough to be sure of that. The stairs are not steep enough. It's more likely someone threw her over the banisters; the fall would certainly kill her."

"How could he have done it," Elizabeth muttered, more to herself than to Cecil. "How could he have been such a criminal fool as to kill her. . . ?"

"I'm not concerned with him," Cecil said roughly. "I'm only thinking of you and the position you are in. If Dudley murdered her, and if it is proved against him . . . you know what must be done."

"I know." Her back was towards him; he could see her hands wrenching at the long silk scarf which hung from her sleeve, pulling and twisting in the attempt to tear the material to shreds.

"I know what must be done. And I'll do it. Send him to me, Cecil. And make the summons public."

When she was alone, she gave a violent wrench, and the silk scarf ripped down the middle. She was trembling with shock— with rage and fear which overwhelmed her now that Cecil had gone and she had wiped his mind clear of suspicion against her. She had fallen in love—a little—perhaps a great deal. She had given herself to a man—not completely, but far beyond normal limits. And this was the result. A murder. . . . And the cause of it all was her supposed lover, the man who had taken her so seriously in his ambitions or his desire, that he had killed his own wife. . . . And in that moment of devastating truth she admitted that ambition was the motive controlling Robert Dudley. He had murdered Amy Dudley; she knew that as surely as if she had witnessed the crime. But he had killed her to be King of England. Not for love or for lust or for any other reason. He had a handsome body, a persuasive tongue and magnetic charm, but no heart. And no brain either, she said suddenly out loud. No brain at all, to do what he had done and think he could succeed, could put his bloody hands on her, and jeopardize her throne and her life by a scandal of his own needless making.

She rang for her women, and hurried into her robing room.

When Robert Dudley came to his audience, he found her standing in the middle of the Presence Chamber, dressed from head to foot in black.

He had been down at the archery butts behind the Castle, practising with a crowd of onlookers, when Cecil himself delivered Elizabeth's message. Dudley had walked back to the Royal apartments whistling and swinging his doublet as if he had not got a care in the world. He knew there would be a scandal and he expected Elizabeth to make a scene. He had had several hours to rehearse what he was going to say and do, because his personal servant Blount had already told him of Amy's death.

He had expected trouble, but he was unprepared for the expression with which the woman, whom he thought so much in love with him, met him as he came and knelt to kiss her hand.

No hand was offered him; the fierce, stony, black eyes glared at him. Her whole face was pinched and cruel; she looked suddenly ugly and almost old. He knew as he looked into that face that, if she were pressed too hard, Elizabeth Tudor would be capable of anything. And for the first time he felt a queasiness in his stomach which was very like fear.

"What have you done, you unspeakable fool?"

"Done? Madam, I come here in answer to your order and you almost spit on me. . . ."

"I wouldn't waste my own spittle. . . ." Her voice was as harsh and ugly as her expression. "You know why you are here. Don't try and lie. Your wife is dead, my Lord!"

"I know," he answered coolly. "I heard early this morning, and I sent Blount on to find out what had happened, since it seemed she had some kind of accident. Did you expect me to grieve, Madam? I'm no hypocrite and I doubt if you'd have been pleased to see me weeping tears over another woman."

To his surprise she made a gesture of contempt and turned away from him.

"By God, you're as vain as you're stupid, if that were possible. You commit this crime and involve me in it and have the temerity to talk on personal levels about jealousy and other women? Do you think I care about such trifles at this moment? Do you think I am a treacherous, trivial fool like you?"

Dudley's lips tightened.

This was not the kind of scene he had imagined; there were

no tears, no questions, no signs of any emotions except anger and contempt.

"What crime, Madam—what do you mean?"

Elizabeth sneered as she spoke. "Don't waste my time and your own. You killed your wife. Don't argue and don't deny it. You killed her. That is not important. Understand that, my Lord Dudley, your life and her life and the lives of fifty like you do not matter a tinker's curse. What does matter is the scandal which affects *me*. The world will say that I was your accomplice, and I could easily lose my throne if my guilt were believed.—This is your crime. And by the God above, I'll see that you expiate it."

He was losing all the way; he had been defeated before he spoke, accused, judged and condemned by the one person for whom he had committed the offence. The woman who had told him to come back to her when he was free—who had dangled the prize of the most brilliant marriage in Europe in front of his eyes—was now cursing and threatening him for having followed her hints to their logical conclusion.

"And if I did do it," he said, "what of it? I love you; loved you more than you ever loved me, it seems. She wouldn't let me go; she swore she'd keep me bound to her forever. I didn't tell you this before. She said you had taken me from her, but you'd never have me for anything but a lover as long as she lived. That was her answer when I went to Cumnor!"

"And yours was to have some hireling throw her down the stairs," Elizabeth remarked.

"I've admitted nothing!" he retorted. "But if I did do it, you of all people should support me. Because it was done for love of you!"

She went and sat down in the high-backed chair by the fireplace. He stood where she had left him; his handsome face slowly losing the angry colour which had blazed into it. Through one of the communicating rooms he could hear the distant notes of a lute; someone was picking over the strings, improvising on an old love song. The whole scene: the room, the sunlight streaming through the windows making patterns on the wood floor, and lastly the figure in black, relaxing in her chair, watching him as if he were a stranger . . . it was all unreal. More unreal than the flash of imagination which overtook him and showed him Forster stunning Amy, before he heaved her unconscious body over the banisters.

He put his hands to his eyes suddenly to shut it out.

"What is the matter, Robert—conscience?" Elizabeth's voice mocked him. "You gambled. You gambled high, but you lost."

"What have I lost, Madam?"

"You killed her for nothing, my poor Robert. I will never marry you now. I could not, even if I wished. You will always be tainted with her blood, even if you are acquitted. I feel that will be a worse punishment to you than anything the law may inflict on you. Don't come any nearer."

He stared at her, his hands held out to touch her fell to his sides.

"What law . . . what are you saying?"

"My law," Elizabeth answered. "The law which requires punishment for crimes of murder. For your own sake, Robert, I hope it can't be proved against you. For if it can, I shall send you to the scaffold without a moment's hesitation. You are under arrest, and confined to your own house at Richmond until this matter is resolved. Leave Richmond or attempt to disobey me and you will find yourself in the Tower."

In that moment he would gladly have struck her as he had struck Amy, but he did not even clench his fist. If she had leant forward and spat in his face he would have stood there motionless, not daring to retaliate. At that moment Dudley learnt the most important lesson of his life: that Elizabeth was not a woman like other women. No matter what they did together in their private intercourse, she was immune from liberties which she did not actually invite. The man who forgot that would be struck down without mercy; indeed he would need to be a madman to attempt it. If the Tudors were famous for anything, he thought suddenly, it was for the ease with which they abandoned their friends and their lovers.

He bowed to her, and walked out of the room.

A week after Amy Dudley's death, the inquest opened at Abingdon. Robert had sent his confidential servant and kinsman Blount down to Cumnor to find out what he could, and Blount had reported a curious tale of how Amy spent the last morning of her life. In her entourage there were her maid and the women, Odingsell and Owen and Mrs. Forster; they all told how their usually mild mistress seemed distracted and ordered them to go to Abingdon Fair and leave her alone in the house. When Mrs. Odingsell protested, she had insisted with some violence; at her request they left her at Cumnor, and on their return they found her dead. That was Blount's story, and he saw to it that it was repeated through the county and the jury told beforehand that Lady Dudley had forced her attendants to leave her alone and seemed in a disordered state of mind that morning.

No one could suggest a reason for such behaviour, except the sinister explanation that she intended to commit suicide. There was another explanation, which only Robert and his financial agent knew. Forster had told her that Robert was coming to discuss a reconciliation, but that his visit must be kept secret because of the Queen's jealousy. It was a condition of his coming that she should send everyone away. And while she waited for Dudley, Forster trapped her in the empty house. But the truth would never be known, for Forster remained in the background, while the crowd of women argued and contradicted and blamed each other, and Blount encouraged the God-sent rumour of suicide. From Richmond, Dudley wrote urging him to sift the matter to the bottom, confident that the truth was safe with Forster, and that whatever Blount discovered he would cover up by bribes. It was a clever move; it seemed as if Dudley were searching harder for the culprit, if there was one, than the Queen's justices. But in those few days he paced up and down his rooms at Richmond like a wild animal in a cage, unable to be near Elizabeth, whom he completely distrusted, forbidden to go down to Cumnor and take a hand in the enquiries himself or see Forster or do anything, but trust to others. And if they failed him, if Forster had overlooked anything or Blount blundered, Elizabeth would sacrifice him on the altar of her own reputation. He knew that without any doubt, and the knowledge terrified him. Often he cursed her, often he spent hours remembering her half-promises, her kisses, her sudden spurts of sensual greed, the favour she showed him and the way she flaunted that favour in the faces of those who hated and opposed him most. And yet she had turned on him with the ferocity of a tiger, when she thought her own interests endangered. She had fondled his cheeks and caressed his hair and then told him that she would cut the head off his body. And meant it. She was not shocked by what she thought he had done to Amy; that was a revelation of her character. If he lost his life it would only be because he had involved the Queen in the crime.

He had to clear himself, once and for all; Blount must secure a verdict from the Abingdon jury which would remove suspicion from his name. He instructed him to take the dangerous course of approaching the jurors directly.

But Blount's efforts were in vain; so were his bribes. The jurors were countrymen who had known Amy Dudley well; her reputation for gentleness and charity defeated Robert's purpose. Yet rumours and suspicions were not enough to alter the known facts, and no proof of murder could be found. The most obvious verdict, and one which would have exonerated Dudley, was suicide. But the Abingdon jury refused to stain the memory of a popular and kindly lady, and thus condemn her to a suicide's unsanctified grave. They returned a verdict of death by misadventure. Robert's neck was safe, but he knew, when he received the news from Blount, that he would never be cleared of the suspicion.

On the 22nd of September Amy Dudley was buried at the Church of St. Mary the Virgin at Oxford. Two days later, Robert received permission to return to Court.

Elizabeth put the Court into mourning for Amy Dudley; she denied herself the pleasures of dancing and music until after the funeral, and conducted her work with the Council in a tense and awkward atmosphere. Robert had been acquitted, and it was known that she intended to recall him. Cecil, after the initial outburst when he heard of the murder, now received her full confidence, but he was the only one who knew her mind. They had talked frankly, Elizabeth wondering as she did so how she could discuss the needs of her own nature with Cecil whom she had always considered sexless and dull. But she discovered that he understood the vagaries of human feelings as well as he did the policies of state. She wanted Robert back because she was unhappy and restless without him, and she had not found a replacement in his absence; she was not, she insisted, a wanton unable to forgo her lover, but a lonely and isolated woman who needed the attentions of a man. Cecil nodded; he asked her quietly how far that need would lead her, and she told him calmly, that it had reached its limit. Whatever people said or thought, she would as soon marry Dudley as her own Tower hangman, bloody hands and all. The world would accuse her of wanting marriage; it was already doing so, while Amy's body settled into its grave. But he had her word of honour that it was not so and never would be. She gave him her hand, on the evening Dudley returned and before she saw him, and Cecil kissed it gravely.

"Don't think too hardly of me," she asked him.

It was extraordinary how she depended upon this curious, clerkly man, so humourless and pedantic and so brilliant. . . . It was extraordinary how close they had become in the last few weeks, when there was not a voice raised in her defence anywhere in her own kingdom or outside it.

"If I were a man, it would seem natural enough, Cecil."

"Marriage is the only natural thing for women, Madam," he said gently. "Until such time as it comes to you, and I pray to God it will before long, then this arrangement has my support if it makes you happy. Not the man; I don't trust him and I have never hidden that; but so long as he pleases you and keeps his place, I have no quarrel with him. But when the time comes to get rid of him, I shall be ready to do that too."

"I'm sure you will," Elizabeth laughed. "But I'm my father's daughter, Cecil. I do my own despatching. Try and quiet my Council; stop them chattering like a lot of old hens and tell them I am not one who thinks the world, or anything else, well lost for love."

When he had gone she rang for her ladies. Kate Dacre and Robert's own sister Lady Mary Sidney came from the next room where they were always on call for the Queen's bell. She sat at her dressing table while Mary Sidney brushed and curled her hair and pinned it up in a net of silver thread sewn with pearls. She pointed to one of the armful of dresses Kate held out for her; it was a long stiff gown of black taffeta, with a velvet petticoat heavily embroidered in diamonds and silver. An eight-row collar of pearls as big as beans was fastened round her narrow neck, and shone in the hollows above her breast. She bit her lips while the two women pulled in her metal corselet until it pinched her waist to sixteen inches, and then stepped into the dress. When they had finished she looked at herself in the glass, watching her reflection, pale and aquiline, the red hair shining like fire through the silver net. She turned, and the jewels encrusting her dress flashed with a dozen lights. Robert said she was beautiful; there were moments when she was softened by flattery and believed him when he described the melting quality of her charms. But not now. The figure in the looking glass was brilliant, like an icicle, glittering, like a diamond, splendid and elegant and supremely Royal. But the rounded prettiness, the warm contours of womanly beauty were not hers. She picked up a long fan of white ostrich feathers, smoothing the plumes between her hands, imagining her meeting with Robert. He would be uneasy, prepared to be contrite or injured, whichever pose suited her mood the best; he would probably try to make love to her and she would enjoy repulsing him with scorn. She knew all about his frantic efforts to secure a favourable verdict over Amy's death. She smiled unkindly, thinking how he must have fingered his handsome neck while the issue was undecided. He had taken her for granted; he had thought that he knew her mind and could precipitate her into doing what he wanted on the strength of her moments of weakness with him. He had not known then that no one was her master because she was completely mistress of herself. But he knew now. He had escaped with his life and come hurrying back like a dog that hears its master's whistle. He would probably hate her for it; it would be the test of her power over him if she could hold him in spite of it, if she could reduce him and threaten him as she had done and show him that she was ready to throw him aside like a worn-down shoe and yet make him admit that he was nothing without her.

Elizabeth was too acute not to know that there was an element of fierce unkindness in her intentions for Robert, but not even she quite realized how close to submission she had come to him, and that this subconscious knowledge was the cause of her resentment and her determination to humiliate him. She only knew that he must be humbled, humbled more deeply than on the day when she tossed his love back in his face and threatened to execute him. Her love for him, her need or whatever it was, had brought her to the edge of catastrophe; she could not forgive herself for that, though she made light of it to Cecil. And she could not forgive Robert either—for killing his stupid wife and causing her this crisis, or for being so indispensable to her happiness that she had to recall him two days after the funeral.

"Mary, send your brother in to me. I feel I should comfort the grieving widower."

Mary Sidney curtsied and then went quickly into the ante-room where Robert had been waiting for the past hour. He came to her and kissed her. He had always been fond of his sister in a selfish way, but they had become more intimate

66

than at any time in their lives since they entered the Queen's service.

"She'll see you, Robert. But be careful, I beg of you."

"How is she?" he asked. "What kind of reception will I get?"

Mary Sidney shook her head.

"A sharp one, I think. I don't know what she feels—you know her, it's impossible to know what she'll do or say from one moment to the next. But she's not trembling with anxiety to see you, I can tell you that. Step carefully; a wrong word now and she might banish you for good!"

Dudley's face darkened. "I've no need to be careful. I'm proved innocent; she owes *me* an apology after the way she treated me!"

"If you really mean that," his sister whispered, "then turn round and get out of the Palace as fast as you can. Don't see her if you're not prepared to crawl upon your knees!"

His eyes narrowed, and then he shrugged and patted her shoulder.

"I've crawled before, Mary. I can do it again if I have to; we Dudleys have a great facility for starting on our knees and ending head and shoulders above everybody else."

He turned away and walked towards the room where Elizabeth was waiting.

## Chapter 5

A T dusk on the 14th of August, 1561, a galley moved slowly out of the mouth of Calais harbour, its oars dipping in the grey seas, a light wind whipping the white pennants, and the Standard with the arms of France flying from the masthead. It was a French ship, its graceful hull painted a dazzling white, its poop-deck gilded and hung with velvet awnings, and at the poop-rail the Dowager Queen of France stood staring out through her tears at the receding coastline of the country where she had spent her childhood and known her happiest years.

Mary Stuart was eighteen years old, but she had been Queen of Scotland since childhood, Queen of a wild and barren country where her father's death had begun a long and savage civil war. The little Queen was sent to her mother's home in France for safety, while her mother had remained behind to struggle with the rebels. Mary had seen very little of her mother. She remembered her as a very tall woman with a commanding presence, a typical Frenchwoman of a militant courageous character, as proud and ambitious as all the family of Guise who were virtually rulers of France.

Mary had been very happy in France; she grew up in an atmosphere of indulgence and admiration as her grace and charm outstripped her years. She was an exquisite child and she became a beautiful girl, gay, quick tongued, supremely sure of herself. There was no reason for self-doubt when every person said how fascinating she was and every mirror bore them out. She was fêted and spoiled by her uncles, the Cardinal Prince, the Grand Chancellor, the immensely powerful Duc de Guise, and dozens of other relatives, all of them rich and influential. Mary's was a world of music and enjoyment, of hunting and dancing and learning the arts required of a Princess already gifted with every personal and material advantage.

When she married, she married the future King of France, and her sickly young husband spoilt and indulged her as completely as her uncles. Unlike most egotists, Mary was naturally kind. She pitied the boy, so obviously wasting with disease and hurrying his end in the effort to ride as well as his bride, to dance and feast until the small hours, buoyed up by the hope that he would one day consummate his marriage. But he came to the throne and died within a year, and his widow was still a virgin. She wept for a companion, almost a brother; but she knew nothing of him as a husband, and in her heart she had never wanted to find out. If she was kindly, she was also infamously proud; proud of her splendid birth, proud of her health in an age when so many were as delicate as her poor Francis, proud of her good looks and her countless friends. Whatever she wished for, God placed in her lap; she had been brought up in the unshakeable conviction that her right was to rule over kingdoms as well as men's hearts, and the kingdom which attracted her most was the one possession which had been withheld from her so far.—She was also the rightful Queen of England, a far brighter prize than the damp, insolvent Scottish inheritance which she could only remember with difficulty.

Her young husband had repeatedly promised to get England for her and to lay it at her feet as the supreme tribute of the love he had been incapable of expressing in a normal way. Mary had dreamed of that entry into London at the head of an army of Frenchmen and loyal English Catholics. In her youth and assurance she spoke of Elizabeth Tudor with contempt; she and her friends made fun of the usurper sitting, as they imagined, so insecurely on her throne. Mary had quartered the English arms and styled herself Queen of England while she lived in the gilded security of France. And then, suddenly, Francis died. She was no longer Queen of France, merely a widow with a hostile mother-in-law, who had made life so uncomfortable that Mary turned with gratitude to Scotland. Scotland might be unknown, but at least she would be Queen in her own right instead of a cypher in the Court where her young brother-in-law Charles was King and the Dowager Queen Catherine de' Medici enjoyed the power. Mary was naturally courageous. Life had never taught her to be frightened of anything or anyone, or presented her with a problem which her own charm and her family's influence could not easily overcome.

After weeks of preparation she was setting out at last, to take possession of her Scottish kingdom so recently torn by civil war and now in the grip of a fierce religious reformation.

Mary was very tall, taller than the Lord Eglinton, who was Bishop of Orkney and a famous sailor, taller than the Lord High Admiral of Scotland, Lord Bothwell, both of whom were escorting their Queen on the voyage and were standing beside her on the windy poop-deck as she looked on France for the last time. She was tall but very slim, with the narrow proportions and delicate bones of a much smaller woman, and the tears she shed accentuated the extreme pallor of her face. It was a strange face with a high forehead and a long, well-bred nose; the hair which curled round her ermine cap was a very dark red, and her slanting eyes were hazel. The face was elfin and yet beautiful; everything about her was expressive, from the sensitive mouth to the movements of her hands when she spoke. Eglinton, who was more of a pirate than a priest, admitted that the Scots had the loveliest woman in Europe as their Queen, and then wondered dourly whether they would appreciate it. It was difficult to be near such a completely feminine creature with her unnatural air of delicacy and her boyish high spirits without being drawn to her. At least as a woman, if not as a Queen. But he could not imagine her as a ruler, sitting in isolation on a throne, symbolizing the Divine law of Kingship to that unruly pack of blackguards who would be waiting for her at Holyrood Palace. Her mother had been as tough as any Border Lord, but the girl's father was a poet and a dreamer as well as a King, an aesthete who had given his daughter her breeding and her pride as well as this precarious throne which she was so determined to occupy. From personal feelings, Eglinton wished her well, but he wouldn't have gambled a week's privateering on her chances.

Bothwell watched her without appearing to do so. He was short and very powerfully built, with the bowed legs of a man who had spent more hours on horseback than on foot, and at twenty-three he had an infamous reputation for piracy, Border raiding and personal debauch. He had followed the Queen's party in the recent war, and done her mother such good service that Mary trusted him implicitly. It was a situation that intrigued and irritated him. He had no respect for women and less for a sovereign who was a woman; it was certain that he felt no pity for the youth and inexperience of the girl he was taking back to Scotland to face the stormiest country in Europe and to attempt to tame a nobility who were notorious for regicide. He knew enough about Mary and her humiliation at the Court where her mother-in-law Catherine de' Medici reigned, to understand why she had been rash enough to leave France and entrust herself to such an uncertain future. She had spirit and she had beauty, and he was interested in those, but it was an interest which he insisted was a base one, grounded in self-advancement. If she prospered, he would do well. If she failed, his enemies would dismember him in property and limb. Therefore he was the Queen's man. He saw her wipe her eyes, and immediately one of her ladies, four of them all named Mary like herself, rushed forward with an elegant silk handkerchief. It was a flimsy, useless thing, trailing fine lace. He took the white linen scarf from his neck and handed it to Mary Stuart without a word. She took it and for a moment their fingers touched.

"Thank you, my Lord."

She spoke English with a strong French accent; he wondered how her insular Scots people would like that, or the musical voice. A pleasing voice, more suited to a lady's chamber or a gentle duet at the virginals than the uproar of a Council Chamber. She would never be able to roar. She would never be able to make herself heard at all where she was going. If they managed to escape the English ships which Elizabeth Tudor had sent into the Channel to intercept them, and arrived in Scotland at all. . . .

The English Queen had refused her cousin a safe conduct because Mary had not ratified the Treaty of Edinburgh, made with Scottish Lords who were in revolt against her at the time. He had been surprised when he heard of Mary's answer to Elizabeth's ambassador Throckmorton. With or without Elizabeth's permission, she would set out to claim her right as Queen of Scotland. If the Queen of England succeeded in capturing her on the journey, then she might do her pleasure and make sacrifice of her. It was an undiplomatic answer which acutely embarrassed the English Ambassador, but its tactlessness appealed to Bothwell who never used a soft word when he could substitute an insult. She had a habit of speaking her mind, and a knack of choosing the right word when she wanted to be rude. It was the arrogance of youth which trapped her into referring to her dreaded mother-in-law Catherine de' Medici as a banker's daughter, and Catherine had made her pay for the sally when Mary's young husband died and she was no longer Queen Consort. She had been unkindly funny at Elizabeth's expense when the scandal of her affair with Lord Robert Dudley was the talk of Europe a year earlier.

"The Queen of England is going to marry her Horse master who killed his wife to make room for her."

Perhaps the price of that remark was the presence of a fleet of English ships in the Channel. It was not always safe to be witty in France; it would be much less safe in Scotland, where the Lords were not particularly gifted with a sense of humour. Was she a fool, he wondered? How did she compare with that other Queen, her cousin by blood, still sitting firmly on her throne in England, having kept her lover Dudley beside her without marrying him, apparently stronger after three years on the throne than when she came to it. . . . If Mary Stuart were like her, he had thrown the right dice for once. . . .

Slowly the galley eased into the open sea, its sails filled by a rising wind. The young Queen remained on deck, surrounded by her ladies and her three uncles, the princely, brilliant Guises, while Eglinton and Bothwell, neither of whom liked each other, drew together as outsiders, their plans for a quick voyage frustrated by the Queen's order that the galley slaves were not to be whipped to increase their speed.

It was a sign of sentimentality which dismayed them both. It might well have delivered them to the English, as Eglinton said between curses, except that the Lord always protects fools and innocents, and sent down a thick Channel fog which enabled them to glide the long way round and land safely at Leith on the 19th.

Elizabeth looked up from the chessboard, one hand poised with a knight. She had played three games with Dudley, and won two; she was about to checkmate him when the Earl of Sussex appeared in the doorway. He pulled off his cap, and knelt.

"Your Majesty's pardon, but I've come from Portsmouth!"

"Come in, Sussex, come in." She put the knight down on the board, and got up without looking at Dudley. Over her shoulder she said: "Checkmate, my Lord. You owe me twenty gold pieces. Now, Sussex, what is your news?"

The Earl looked quickly at Dudley, and hesitated. Elizabeth's hand waved impatiently.

"You can speak in front of Robert. I have no secrets from him."

"Our fleet has returned, Madam. But without the Queen of Scots. Her ship escaped us in a thick fog."

"Damn them!" Elizabeth exploded. "Damn them and their fog. . . . When did she land and where?"

"At Leith, Madam, a week ago. But we captured two of her baggage ships, with all her horses and most of her possessions. It's a rich prize."

"But not the one I wanted," she retorted. "Robert, get me some wine. . . . Horses and trinkets! She landed at Leith, you say? Isn't that a devil of a place?"

"No worse than the rest of Scotland," Sussex answered. "But worse for the lack of those horses and trinkets you speak of. She made no triumphal entry into Edinburgh; the best they could find for her was a knock-kneed old hackney, and the Reformers sang psalms under her window all night!"

To the relief of both men, the Queen laughed.

"By God, what a welcome! Was she well received?"

"I have no details, Madam," Sussex temporized. She was amused by the humiliation of her rival; she would be less amused if he were to tell her that Mary Stuart had survived it with humour and charm. He would leave that task to Cecil; she accepted bad news from him with a better grace than from anyone else at Court.

"Sir William Cecil may have our ambassador's report. He will know more."

"Thank you, Sussex; send him to me. Come and dine at my table later; I want to hear all the news of yourself since you've been out of my sight. I've missed you."

She always said that, Dudley thought, and they always believed her. She had a genius for making men feel important.

"What are you thinking, Robert?" She was looking at him over the edge of the golden wine cup. She may have lulled Sussex by laughing over her failure to capture Mary Stuart, but he was not deceived. He knew that in spite of her calm she was furious, and very anxious.

"I was wondering what good it would have done if you had taken the Scots Queen," he said. "You couldn't have kept her here—you have no excuse."

"I don't need excuses. My cousin would have remained my guest, driven on to my coast by storms, or rather fog—until

73

she ratified the Treaty of Edinburgh and renounced all claim to my throne."

Dudley shook his head.

"She might have refused for a long time, Madam; too long for that diplomacy to last. Then what?"

She sat back, balancing her cup between those narrow, lovely hands, and shrugged.

"I'm tired of talking politics, Robert; I shall have my fill of them when Cecil comes in a few moments. Come back to me later and we will finish our chess. But pay the twenty pieces you owe me before you go."

It was a rule that the Queen should be paid on the spot when she won; it was also a rule that no one asked for her debts. He counted the money out on to the table and then kissed her hand, hiding the chagrin he felt at his dismissal. It had taken him twelve months of superhuman patience, tact and abject submission to regain the favour he had lost after Amy's death. He no longer argued or pressed his attentions on her unless she invited them. Though she made much of him in public, for the pleasure of focusing romantic speculation on herself, as he suspected, she often rebuffed him irritably when they were alone, but he made no comment. He could not afford that luxury, and he knew it. The lesson of the past year had been a hard and bitter one, but he had learnt it.

He bowed to her and went out.

When Cecil came he found her sitting by the chessboard, studying the pieces which were arranged as if she were going to play.

"We failed," she said, without looking up. "Sussex has just told me."

"It was ordained," the Secretary answered. "No one could expect such a fog to come down at this time of year."

"You talk like those putrid Calvinists; ordained be damned! God doesn't alter the weather to suit Mary Stuart and thwart me—He has better things to occupy Him. I hear she made a poor showing on her entry into Edinburgh. Is that true or was Sussex lulling me?"

"Partly true and partly lulling," Cecil answered, taking the seat opposite to her. "She had no horses and no jewels, but she took the people's fancy, and was well received by them."

"You heard this from Randolph?" Elizabeth looked up at him.

Cecil shook his head. "No, Madam; ambassadors' reports travel too slowly for my liking; I have other observers in Scotland with faster pens. They wrote to me the day she arrived."

"Is she as beautiful as they say?" Elizabeth asked him. "Is that why she was welcomed?"

"Beautiful and well advised. She came into the country like a fugitive, entered her capital without proper accoutrements and listened to speeches of welcome telling her to abolish the abomination of the Mass, and she gave the same smile to everyone and said she was well pleased."

"She *is* well advised," Elizabeth's lips compressed. "How long will she conceal herself do you think? Or is it possible that she'll forswear her religion and conform with the Calvinists?"

"If she does, she is less dangerous to you. The malcontents in England are not likely to support one Protestant Queen against another. Her strength in claiming the English throne lies in her Popery."

"In that and her legitimate birth and her Tudor blood. Oh, Cecil, if we had only captured her. . . . But we failed, and now we stand like this, she and I; two Queens on either side of their frontiers, like the pieces on this board. The White Queen and the Red. We have our Knights. There's you, and my Lords of the Council, and my nobles who would lose all they have won under a Catholic sovereign, and the Bishops, each longing to burn the other for the good of their immortal souls. . . ."

"Her Bishop is John Knox," the Secretary interrupted. "He is on our board. And her Knights are her bastard half-brother Lord James Moray, that snake Lethington who'd sell his own mother, Ruthven, who'd *hang* his, and many more of the same kind. She is eighteen and half French, and she knows nothing of Scotland or the Scots."

"All men have the same vices, whatever their nationality," the Queen said slowly. "If she offers them the conquest of England with all the plunder that implies, her Knights and Bishops will fight as hard for her as mine for me."

"They will not win," Cecil said. "They would have less chance of making any move at all, if you would take a husband, Madam, before the Queen of Scots takes one."

Elizabeth stood up suddenly.

"Do you think I had overlooked that factor? I'm not a fool, Cecil, or an innocent at state affairs. My well beloved cousin has quartered the arms of England and styled herself Queen

75

of England since the day my sister Mary died. She has left France where she was only a King's widow and counted for nothing, and gone to that battlefield of a country to become a Queen in her own right. And above all, to step closer to my throne; that is the one she wants to sit on. She may be eighteen and all the rest, but she's got ambition in her blood. This is no simpering girl, content with needlework and books; I only wish it were. If she has this mettle in her, the pieces will move on that board, and they'll move before long. If I marry, you say—marry, marry. . . . Rather let us think about her choice of husband and leave mine alone! "

" She is considering Don Carlos," Cecil said.

Elizabeth struck the table and leant on it, her eyes narrowed at the Secretary.

"Philip of Spain's son and heir! A sadistic imbecile whom even his own family admits is mad. But she considers him, and with enthusiasm! Because he would bring the might of Spain and the armies of Spain as his bridegroom's portion! That is the measure of her. By the living Saviour, my stomach turns at the thought of him, and I'm not squeamish when it comes to the needs of the State. But not Mary's; no, she doesn't balk at him, nor at the King of Sweden who really *is* a lunatic. . . . She'd open her covers to an ape, if it would help her take the Crown away from me."

" The King of Spain will reject the match," Cecil reminded her. " He knows it could mean war with us. Others will see the same danger; if necessary we can make that plain to the Queen of Scots herself."

" We go too fast, Cecil," Elizabeth complained. " My head aches. Caution is necessary now; extreme caution, until we see how she progresses. She knows I am her enemy, as I know that she is mine. We will send friendly words through Randolph, and I shall suggest that we have a cousinly meeting in order to smooth out our differences. She will not agree, and if she does, I will get out of going. We will play chess, my dear Cecil, and move our pawns a little, but nothing more until *she* makes a move."

The interview was over, and Cecil knew that however much he argued, the Queen had decided on the course of her immediate policy, and nothing would alter that decision. As he walked back to his own apartments he thought that her favourite word was caution. It was an unfeminine word, with its suggestion of a careful, premeditated mind; it warred with the idea of a child of Henry VIII and of the rash and wanton Anne Boleyn.

But there was a great deal of the crafty, tortuous grandfather, the first Tudor King of England, in Cecil's mistress. She symbolized the coming struggle for her throne with the pieces on her golden chessboard, and he knew that she would play her deadly game with Mary Stuart with the icy calculation which won her every match. He knew, just as clearly as she did, that the arrival of the other Queen in Scotland preluded a period of the most acute personal danger Elizabeth had ever known. Every disaffected Catholic in England—and, thanks to Cecil's Act of Settlement, there were thousands of them—every petty noble with a grievance, and every great peer with ambitions which the Queen had left unsatisfied—all of them now had a focal point for their rebellion, the rebellion which had not yet come. Much as he hated Mary Stuart, his hatred fed by her detested religion, much as he affected to despise and minimize her, he had no real knowledge of her as a woman. She might be headstrong and foolish and unable to hold Scotland for more than a few months, or weak and full of empty threats; she might be consumed with ambition as Elizabeth judged her. Only time would answer that question, and time, as Elizabeth often said, had been a good friend to her in the past. Cecil instructed one of his secretaries to draft a letter to the envoy Randolph, ordering him to show a friendly face to the new Queen and her supporters in Edinburgh.

In England all was quiet; the expected storm between Elizabeth and the Queen of Scots was dissipated in a flow of affectionate letters and the exchange of Maitland of Lethington, the man Cecil had called a snake, for Randolph as an emissary to the English Court. The two ships were returned to Mary with her treasures untouched, and Elizabeth suggested a meeting of the two Queens at York. Her letters were brilliant; they were dignified and persuasive and they held out real hope of an arrangement which would consolidate Mary on her throne by Elizabeth naming her as her successor if she died childless, thereby removing the only cause of enmity and suspicion between them.

In Scotland the atmosphere was much less restful. The Earl of Arran had led a band of armed men into the Queen's private

77

Chapel when she was attending Mass, and her half-brother, Lord James, and his servants had driven him out with drawn swords. The Earl of Bothwell, Mary's staunch supporter, had been exiled from Edinburgh to appease the jealousy of his fellow Lords and to prevent him avenging the insults of Arran and others in a bloody clan war in the streets of the City itself.

Lord James, sullen and envious of his beautiful sister's position as sovereign, had to be flattered and cajoled to keep his suspicions at bay and induce him to protect her; the violent Papist-hater John Knox roared of the rule of Whores and Jezebels from the public pulpit and received a temperate summons to the Palace of Holyrood to explain himself instead of the committal to a dungeon which Mary longed to send him instead.

In those first months the hot-tempered, incautious girl who had been so tactless in France and so confident in her own power to charm her enemies, displayed astonishing forbearance in the face of every kind of frustration and encroachment on her life as a woman and her powers as a Queen. She sat meekly at her Councils, sewing and listening to her half-brother and the other Lords deciding for her; she endured the ranting of Knox to her face, and only gave vent to her feelings in tears. She cried a great deal in private, but in public she was gentle and moderate and patient, without seeming weak. Her charm was her only weapon and in spite of her youth and her inexperience, she knew it and used it to the utmost. She was a novelty to these rough and ruthless men, and she knew that too. They did not understand her, but most of them were too naturally shrewd to overlook her altogether. Slowly she began to win some of them, and to gain the people's admiration. While Knox and the Reformers chilled their congregations with threats of a Catholic persecution, led by the idolatrous Queen, Mary went out of her way to show tolerance to a religion which she hated and which had declared war to the death on her own Faith. There were no burnings for heresy, no laws introduced which diminished the tyrannical power of the Kirk and its Elders, and no invasion of French troops to compel heretic Scotsmen to behave themselves towards their Queen. Her religion, accent and upbringing were different from theirs, but she rode among them in Highland dress, danced their reels and ate their food, and tried to show that in all essentials she was one of them. In spite of the disapproval of Knox and others who were going to find fault with her whatever she did, Mary gradually introduced an atmosphere of elegance and culture into her Court. Musicians and poets gathered round her; there were gay balls in the bleak rooms of Holyrood, its walls covered with fine tapestries and silks from France, and the dour Scots Lords found themselves entertained by a lovely gracious sovereign who seemed anxious to show equal favours to them all. There was peace, disregarding the occasional outbursts of violence on the Border towns and the riots in the City between rival clansmen, and the more serious of these were put down by the Queen's men, supported by the citizens. It seemed as if law and authority were gaining the support of all but the most hardened ruffians in her kingdom, and it was becoming less safe to insult the Queen's faith and the Queen's habits because of her increasing popularity with all classes of society.

There was no whisper of scandal against her or any of her ladies; Queen Mary and her four Maries, daughters of the noblest Scottish houses, lived lives of extreme circumspection. It delighted her subjects to contrast this with the ugly scandals issuing from England, where the self-styled Virgin Elizabeth was surrounded by flatterers and suitors, and permitted the most sinister of them all, the infamous Dudley, to come into her bedroom and hand her her chemise while she was dressing.

The Catholic Queen of Puritan Scotland subdued her passion for fine clothes and dressed in sober velvets, covered to the neck, while the fashion set by Elizabeth exposed more and more of the unmarried female bosom to the gaze of men in England. If the English loved Elizabeth because she appeared among them like a gorgeous peacock, covered in jewels with her pale face painted and her hair puffed and curled out over her head, the Scots were proud of the grave and modest mien of their own beautiful sovereign. There were now two eligible Queens in Europe, and though she was far less powerful, Mary was the younger and the healthier of the two. She was nineteen and unsullied in virtue, with a valid claim to the throne occupied by a woman with a dubious reputation, ten years seniority and allegedly poor health. The man who married Mary might well find himself King of both countries. Mary was disappointed when her meeting with Elizabeth was postponed and finally put off indefinitely. She was distinctly curious to see the writer of those friendly letters whom men like Bothwell and her brother James said was as cunning as a serpent and never to be trusted. Privately she considered Elizabeth a vulgarian, and excused her by pointing out that her mother was an adventuress from the trading classes. Her morals were her own affair, though Mary deplored the display she made of them. Her protestations might well be genuine; in her growing confidence Mary thought they stemmed from fear, and was already prepared to be generous and wait until Elizabeth died of one of her frequent illnesses before she made her claim for the English throne. Her lack of insight was infectious; it was bred in pride and the conviction that mere craft never triumphed over blue blood. Her nobles began to swagger, thinking with envy of the rich spoils of England, which they only sampled when they raided the English Border, and the defeats in the bitter Anglo-Scottish wars which might be redressed with Mary as their figurehead. They liked her because she rode well, and showed spirit; they obeyed her because she requested, and then only on matters where it cost them nothing to agree. Occasionally her justice had to be executed against someone they wished to destroy on other counts and they rallied to the business with enthusiasm. There was no such thing as loyalty to the sovereign in the sense that Mary knew it, but she began to forget that and be deceived. The Divine Right of Kings, enforced with such bloodshed and terror by Henry VIII, had never penetrated to Scotland where the attitude to the throne was one of envy for the temporal power and accession to it by murder or force of arms was a natural process. The ruler was not God's anointed, tinged with the same mystic quality as the Pope himself; the King was only the strongest and toughest of the Lords, and he remained King until a stronger came and overthrew him.

Mary did not see this, though she had been warned of it and acted as carefully as she did in the first year of her reign with that warning in her mind. But gradually the reality became obscured in the triviality of homage and surface power. Her brother seemed content enough; she supposed he no longer grudged her the throne because she had made him Earl of Movay and given him the first place in her Council; she thought she had won his loyalty forever when she arranged the marriage he wanted by using her influence with the Earl Marshal of Scotland, who had previously refused to give his daughter to a bastard, even a Royal one. She was too straightforward and too generous to realize that Lord James took her favours, the love-match among them, and felt no gratitude because they came from her.

When a scandal threatened her, she acted with devastating courage, and with a revealing lack of mercy. The young poet, Chatelard, had come in her entourage from France. He stayed in the bleak, unfriendly country because he fell madly in love with the Queen; and he allowed his sense of Gallic romanticism to delude him into hiding under her bed, in the wild hope of becoming her lover. Such a thing could be done in France, where it would have been conducted with finesse and Queens and great ladies shared their beds judiciously with whom they chose. But not in Scotland. The intruder was arrested, tried by the Queen's order, and condemned to be publicly beheaded. The sentence was carried out in Edinburgh before an immense crowd, with Mary watching from a galleried window. Unlike Elizabeth, who now kept Robert Dudley in a bedroom adjoining her own, the Queen of Scots forfeited, for the sake of her own honour, the life of a man she genuinely liked, though she fainted outright when his head was struck off. Her popularity soared; even Knox's venomous tongue wagged in vain when the axe fell on Chatelard, and the spectators delighted in a bloody spectacle where the victim was a foreigner and a Frenchman as well. The pawns were moving slowly on the chessboard, but they had left no opening for Elizabeth, and in October 1562 death seemed likely to remove the Red Queen from the board and end the game.

For the second time in her reign, Elizabeth had gone to war. Her first intervention in Scotland had been so costly in men and money that it left her with a rooted aversion to armed interference. It was easy for the Councillors, men like Sussex and Hunsdon and even Cecil, to argue in favour of troops. Men were always ready for war and less ready to cope with the bankruptcy which followed. The conflict in which she was finally persuaded to take part was raging over the Channel in France, where the Catholic and Huguenot parties, headed by the Scots Queen's uncle, the Duke de Guise, and by the Prince de Condé respectively, were engaged in a bitter and bloody battle in which neither age nor sex was spared. Nothing pointed out the powerlessness of the French Crown more plainly than its inability to stop two of its most powerful nobles from plunging the whole country into a savage religious war. For some time Elizabeth remained inactive, waiting as usual while the hotheads round her fumed for action, determined to avoid committing herself until she saw which side was going to win. It was argued that a Protestant ruler could not stand idle while her co-religionists were slaughtered; if the Guises won and Protestantism was wiped out in France, there might be no end to their ambitions. The result of a Catholic victory might be a religious invasion of England, aimed at setting the Catholic Mary Stuart upon Elizabeth's throne. And if that happened, which of the other Protestant Princes would give Elizabeth aid, when she had refused help to Condé and the Huguenots? Cecil was the most insistent upon intervention; his religious prejudices were backed by a sound political reasoning, and though she felt no sympathy with his conviction, she agreed in principle with his policy. When a truce in France was broken and the fighting began again she gave the order to negotiate with Condé and send English troops. She drove a merciless bargain with the hard-pressed Huguenots; they were forced to surrender Havre to the English in return for a subsidy and English troops to garrison the port, and Havre was only a hostage for Calais, lost in the disastrous campaign waged by her sister Mary Tudor. She went to war against her will, but with the determination to squeeze the last drop of profit out of it for England. When she received the bill for the expedition, she was unable to hide her displeasure with Cecil whose advice was responsible for the plunder of her exchequer by merchants and shipwrights. She blamed Cecil for the war, and particularly for the expense, and the Secretary blamed Dudley for the Queen's coldness towards him.

Dudley had become a useful scapegoat. He was everywhere with Elizabeth, and more influential with her than ever before. The relationship was a permanent scandal and even its nature was open to question. There were persistent and alarming rumours that Elizabeth had secretly married him. And not even Cecil dared to ask for a denial. She had developed a habit of absenting herself from Council meetings, making her will known to him beforehand, and if her decisions were questioned, she either vetoed the alternative in writing, or else made a brief appearance which immediately reduced them to obedience. As she tamed her Lords, so she had tamed Robert Dudley until he had moulded himself into exactly the man she wished him to be; courteous, tactful, splendid in bearing and behaviour and completely subservient to her in everything. In return she seemed to have given him her confidence, and, what was stranger still, a higher degree of affection than he had enjoyed at the beginning of their extraordinary love affair. Cecil often watched him in amazement, trying to reconcile what he knew of the man's unscrupulous, self-assertive temperament with the perfect courtier he had become. Elizabeth's favour made him many enemies, and she astonished Cecil and others who knew her reverence for money, by pouring a fortune into Dudley's hands. He confined his interest to pleasing the Queen, to amusing her and flattering her, and presumably to playing the lover when they were alone. It was a distorted picture, and no one could get the two of them into perspective no matter how closely they watched or how much they knew. Cecil's spies reported the old scandals until he was sick of hearing them, but some of the impetuosity had gone from that love affair, if indeed it could be called that, and a far stronger and more dangerous tie was creeping in to take the place of a mere sensual attraction. Now it seemed as if she felt able to trust the man as well as love him, and Cecil could not restrain his hatred of him. He often came to an audience, as Sussex had done a year before, and found Robert sitting with her, and to Cecil's fury he stayed through the interview; sometimes Elizabeth actually called on him for an opinion. There were times when the whole Council said he might yet be Consort of England, and once Sussex had shouted out that however much he loathed the man, he loved the Queen enough to stomach Dudley if that was the only means to get an heir for England. It was a fantastic, infuriating situation which had become a permanent feature in the life of the Court. And there was nothing he or anyone else could do about it.

By the beginning of October, the Prince de Condé had agreed to the terms of Elizabeth's treaty, and a force of English troops were ready to embark for Havre. Cecil retired to his own house to recuperate from the protracted strain of many weeks, and the Queen, accompanied by Dudley as usual, went on a strenuous hunting party. They returned to Hampton Court at four in the afternoon when the light was failing. It had been a long chase, and the Queen's kill, two bucks and a deer, were being brought back on a cart behind them. She reined in her horse to a walk instead of galloping home as she normally did, and complained that the weight of her crossbow had made her arms ache. She looked pale and very tired. When they dismounted she held on to Dudley's arm for a moment, and pressed her hand to her forehead.

"I've got a damnable headache," she said. "I've felt far from well all day."

She had insisted on taking a bath that morning; bathing was regarded as an unpleasant necessity and very dangerous to health, but Elizabeth was as fastidious over personal hygiene as she was about bad smells; she bathed frequently, sometimes in wine, which was supposed to bleach and purify the skin. No one had been able to stop her going out into the cold October air so soon after that perilous bath.

Dudley turned to his sister, Mary Sidney, and beckoned for her to help the Queen. He was alarmed by her colour and her hand was hot and dry.

"Take Her Majesty upstairs, and make her rest.—Why don't you lie down, Madam, and send for Doctor Hughes. I'll wait outside your door till I know you're comfortable and sleeping."

She walked up the steps to her rooms, feeling as if every stair was a mountain; her head had begun to throb so violently that she could hardly see, and her limbs were trembling as she walked. Her ladies undressed her, and she was almost lifted into her bed, shivering with ague, and complaining at the same time that she was burning with heat.

"It's that bath," Lady Dacre wailed, "I begged Her Grace not to go out if she insisted on bathing . . . and now she's caught a chill."

A whisper from the bed told her to hold her tongue and get the doctor; not Hughes who was a fool with nothing in his medicine bag but a cluster of leeches, but that new German physician Hunsdon recommended. "Jesus," the strained voice said, "I feel as if I were lying in boiling oil! Get me something to drink!"

When Doctor Burcot came he did not waste time in preliminaries. He went straight to the bed, pulled back the velvet covering and felt her forehead and her pulse. He bent closer, examining her eyes and feeling the texture of her skin again. When he straightened he looked down into the thin face, the cheeks already sunken and bright red with fever.

He cleared his throat.

"Madam, you have smallpox."

Someone in the shadows of the bed gave a frightened gasp

and quickly smothered it. The sick woman could feel rather than hear the instinctive movement of recoil from the women in her room.

Smallpox! Her confused brain, sliding from sleep to twilight consciousness, digested the terrible diagnosis, and with the remains of her strength she croaked at the squat, pompous figure of the German doctor standing by her bedside, defying him as if he were the dreaded killer and disfigurer itself.

" Get that knave out of my sight! "

They were her last conscious words. She sank back into a sea of alternating heat and cold, tossing and moaning, fighting a devouring fever which rose higher as the hours passed.

Cecil was brought from his home, the other Lords assembled, a hush of terrified expectancy settled over the sprawling Palace, while the Queen lay in her bedroom, and the Court physicians who had replaced Burcot said that it was certainly smallpox, and that the Queen would die as the spots had not come out.

For five days and nights the vigil continued, and when at last she opened her eyes, Elizabeth saw a blur of faces gathered by her bed. She recognized them one by one—her Councillors —Sussex, with tears streaming down into his beard, Cecil, grey and haggard, Arundel and Warwick and Northampton. All staring down at her, her death reflected in their eyes. She turned her head with difficulty and saw a woman kneeling in the shadows, crying. She thought lightheadedly that it must be Kate Dacre, poor, silly, faithful Kate, weeping over the mistress who had so often bullied her, and whom she truly loved.

She looked in vain for one more face, for the dark eyes and the pointed beard, and the single, dazzling pearl she had given him to wear in his ear, and did not see him. Where was Robert . . . had he deserted her. . . ? No, in her extremity of illness, Elizabeth refused to believe that he had done that. He had not left her; but she was dying and unable to protect him, and already his enemies had shut him out. She knew enough about Royal deathbeds to believe that. Robert would suffer when she died. They all hated him, and she was the cause of their hatred. She had set him up to please herself, selfishly and without caring how many enemies she made for him.

Her life was ebbing and she knew it, she knew that the illness had ravaged her system to the point where her spirit was ready to abandon it completely, and she knew, by looking into the

85

eyes of the men standing close to her, that her death was probably a matter of hours. And in that moment, already separated from the mortal power which had been the mainspring of her life, the human softness in her overcame all other feelings; she felt a pain of fear for the one human being that she had come to care for almost in spite of herself and of him: Robert, heartless and unworthy in so many ways, yet so strong and magnificent in his manhood, who would be so helpless, helpless as the child she had never borne, when she was not there to protect him.

"I have a request to make of you, my Lords."

They came closer and then she knew she must have only whispered. It was a feeble chance, a sentimental straw she tried to catch at the last moment, and her knowledge of human nature made her despair of its success. But if they loved her at all, if there was pity in them, they might see her last agony and respect the wish she was going to express.

"I want you to grant my Lord Dudley a pension. . . . I recommend him to you. I would have you choose him as Protector of the realm if I should not recover. He is a man who can be trusted. . . . Come closer still."

The effort was taxing her so much she felt she might be slipping back into that stormy sleep of unconsciousness; her will forced her receding senses to hold fast, and the hoarse, trembling voice went on, making the last, desperate plea for the safety of Dudley.

"I have loved him above any other man," they heard her say, "but I swear before God that nothing improper has ever passed between us. . . . I commend him to your care, as you love me. . . ."

The Earl of Sussex fell on his knees, crying as openly as Katherine Dacre.

"It shall be done, Madam," he promised. "I give my word."

"She can't hear you," Cecil interrupted. "She has fainted again."

He was trembling with fear. In spite of her energy he knew she was constitutionally frail: the disease was devouring the last of her strength. She lay in the bed as if she were already dead. . . .

"Where is that cur Burcot? The others have failed, we must try him; where is he?"

"The Queen insulted him," Mary Sidney came forward from

the head of the bed where she had been standing, half-hidden by the curtains. "He has refused to return and attend her."

"Leave that to me." Sir Philip Carew was the Queen's cousin, a kinsman of the Boleyns. He turned and ran out of the room.

Slowly they left her, some looking back at the slight figure in the bed, so thin that the outline of her body hardly showed under the bedclothes, her fiery hair lying damp and tangled with sweat all over the pillow. The Queen was dying. They were all ruined. They went into the Council Chamber to debate who should be named as her successor. She had a cousin, Lady Catherine Grey, sister to the hapless nine days Queen Jane. Catherine Grey was in the Tower, for having secretly married and borne two sons. She was a stupid, arrogant little ninny, but she was a Protestant and the only person they could think of; no one mentioned Mary, Queen of Scots. They did not dare.

Within two hours Carew had kept his promise. Doctor Burcot rode into the Palace courtyard, and stamped upstairs to the Queen's room, cursing and grumbling in German.

When he refused the second summons to the Palace, Carew's servant threw his cloak and boots at him, and with a dagger at his back, Burcot was forced to dress and ride with them. When he came to Elizabeth his professional feelings overcame his pride. He grunted with contempt at the heavy covers which had been drawn back to ease the heat of her temperature, and ordered her women to build the largest fire possible in the grate. A mattress was laid in front of it, and a length of red cloth brought up from the linen rooms. He made them lift the Queen out of bed and on to the pallet in front of the fire. He wrapped her up in the cloth himself, and when she opened her eyes he gave her a drink and told her to finish it; it would help her sleep. He was unable to resist saying, crossly: " Almost too late, Madam, almost too late! "

Within two hours he returned to the patient and picked up one hand which was protruding from the crimson covering. It was covered with angry spots.

"The infection is out," he announced. "The Queen will live; keep her covered in that manner and she may escape disfigurement. And keep the curtains drawn. Sunlight will only cause scars."

In cottages and great houses all over England, the cure for the dreaded smallpox was the same. Red curtains or a red petticoat shielded the patient from the rays of the sun; it was a feeble attempt to avoid the hideous pitting and scarring which made survival almost more terrible than death.

By the evening the Council received a message that the spots had appeared all over the Queen's body, her fever was sinking and the immediate danger to her life was over. They could hardly believe it at first. The rough plans for proclaiming Catherine Grey were quickly torn up, and a gentlemen's agreement was reached to keep all knowledge of the frantic choice of a successor from the ears of Elizabeth. She was going to recover; even those who hated each other drank mutual toasts of relief, and Cecil suggested that prayers of thanksgiving should be offered as soon as the Queen was safely convalescent.

A week later Doctor Burcot allowed the Councillors to visit the Queen. But Dudley went to see her first. He knelt by the bed, and took her hand in his, and for a moment he was so genuinely affected that he could not speak.

Mary Sidney had told him of Elizabeth's recommendation to the Council; he had been astonished and then almost shamed when he heard of her suggestion that he should be made Protector. He was genuinely touched by her effort to exonerate him for their relationship and to placate all the enemies she must have sensed were gathering to attack him.

"Dear Robert . . . It's all over, and I'm not even marked."

It was a miracle; she was unbelievably thin and frail, but the disease had not left a scar on her face.

"If you were as pocked as my old nurse, I shouldn't care," he said. "As long as you lived . . . that's all I prayed for, night and day."

"I know," Elizabeth smiled, "I know that you did not desert the sinking ship either. You stayed outside my rooms when another man in your boots would have been half-way out of England. I thank you for it. I kept remembering my sister's death, and wondering whether all my friends were hastening to find a successor, just as they hastened to me. My good Sidney told me you never left the Palace."

"Nobody left you," Dudley said.

"There's always the point that they had no particular place to go," she murmured, "but that does not apply to you. I tried to secure a good pension and a position for you, but I fear you won't get either now."

'They had no particular place to go. . . .' How well she knew them all. And how well she must have known him to be

88

able to make him get down on his knees for the first time in countless years and pray to God to let her live. Now he could say it and believe it was true, without reservation, almost without self-interest.

"I love you, Madam."

"I know," she said. "I wanted it so, and so it is. You will find me grateful, Robert."

He remained by her bedside, one thin hand held in his, until she fell asleep.

It was early December and the Palace of Holyrood was so bitterly cold that Mary Stuart spent her time in one of the smaller ante-chambers, her writing-table drawn close to the big open fireplace where a heap of logs threw out a scorching heat. But it was still cold; the far corners of the room were freezing, and a strong draught stirred the heavy tapestry covering the walls. The Queen wore a dress of dark red velvet, its sleeves and collar lined with miniver, and a sable rug covered her knees. She was aware that her brother James Moray disapproved of her furs and her refusal to freeze to death in the big Council Chamber. She had a suspicion that he considered it unpatriotic to suffer so obviously from the Scottish climate. He was a tall, dark man, with a grave expression which was becoming increasingly dour. He seldom smiled and she had never heard him laugh.

"Lethington's despatches came this morning," she said. Her accent was still painfully French after nearly two years. "Queen Elizabeth has fully recovered from her illness . . . unfortunately."

James frowned.

"Surely you don't wish your cousin dead, Madam?"

"And what did she wish me, when she sent a fleet to search for me on my voyage here?"

Mary was finding it more difficult to be tactful with him lately. He never forbore to point out to her what he considered errors of judgment, conduct or speech, and, in her growing confidence, the Queen showed her irritation more and more.

"The question of the English throne is only delayed again, when it might have been settled by an act of God. Naturally, my dear James, I am disappointed, and I am honest enough to say so. Lethington says her life was despaired of for several days; and for weeks afterwards everyone was frightened, she was so weakened. He tells me that if she had died the rumour is that her Council proposed to proclaim her kinswoman Catherine Grey as Queen. He says no mention was made of me."

"It pains me," James said slowly, " to hear you lamenting another Crown when you wear the Crown of Scotland. I would advise you not to show your eagerness to others, Madam; we are a proud race and no good at taking second place. I will not repeat this, but others might."

"If I were Queen of England, as well as Scotland, don't you know what it would mean to you? " she asked him. She knew he was greedy and ambitious; she knew that no one would claim more from her in power and spoils than James if she ruled over England, but it infuriated her when he would not admit it. It put her in the wrong, as if she had no right, no divine sanction by blood, to unite the two kingdoms.

"Power is not my God," he answered sharply, stung by the implication of her remark which put him in the same category as that unprincipled robber, James Bothwell, and others like him. They would follow the devil into hell to fill their pockets, but he was not one of them. He was a man and the son of a King; that King's failure to marry his mother was responsible for his position as a bastard, taking bounty from a mere sister, when the Crown should have been his. Other men would have been tempted to take it from her, and when she first came to Scotland it would have been easy. He had resisted that temptation; he had helped her and supported her loyally against his inclinations, defended her idolatrous religion and made a show of brotherly affection which he had not really felt in his heart. She was in his debt, not he in hers; she owed her life to his sense of honour.

Suddenly she smiled and held out her hand to him.

"Come, my brother—let's not quarrel! We have the same high blood, you and I, and the same temper. You know I love you dearly and would give you anything; I never meant that you would wish to take."

"I am not quarrelling," he said. He ignored her hand and saw it go down to her side again. "But I find my position very difficult. I wasn't brought up in France like you; I may have the same high blood, as you describe it, but only one side is Royal and that's not enough. I want to be a loyal brother to you—God is witness of that—but I cannot share your passion for advancement. Keep the throne you have, guard it and guard yourself, and leave England alone. No one wins who plays against Elizabeth Tudor. That's all I shall say to you."

She still smiled, but he could not be sure whether it was feigned. She had a stubborn character in spite of her meekness. She called him dear brother and mended their disagreements, but sometimes there was a light of wilfulness, almost of anger in her peculiar slanting eyes which made him doubt her friendliness.

"Then we'll talk of something else," Mary answered gently. "My suitors—there's a good subject! The Countess of Lennox, as Lethington points out, is another blood cousin of mine, and she has a son who is unmarried. Lethington thinks he might be a likely candidate."

"You mean Henry Darnley," James said. He was better informed than she thought. "He's in England, and am I correct in supposing he has a distant claim to the English throne?"

"Oh, very distant," Mary dismissed the most important factor as if it meant nothing. "Lethington says he is well favoured and young. His mother would welcome the match."

"No doubt," he said sourly. "If she were allowed to make it. I can't see the Queen of England permitting a kinsman and a subject to marry you and so strengthen your ambitions. I think Lethington is a fool to mention it."

"That's one thing Lethington is not," she countered. "And you know it, even though you don't like him. He is not a fool. He knows the kind of husband I need, and if he recommends Darnley, there must be something in the man. As for Elizabeth, what right has she to stop me? Every candidate I suggest, she vetoes for me. The Spanish Prince, Don Carlos—— No, that would mean an unfriendly alliance with Spain and she would be forced to protect herself. The King of Sweden—the same excuse. . . . The King of France——"

"Your own brother-in-law," he pointed out. Her cold-blooded attitude to marriage always affronted him. It was indecent for a woman to consider a husband as a dynastic loss or gain; that was a man's privilege.

"Oh, James," she said wearily, "what of it? I was never poor Francis' wife in anything but name. But no, my cousin refuses that more violently than the others. She promised to meet me, but that promise came to nothing. She promises to name me as her successor if I do this or don't do that; I'm growing tired of her interference. I wonder that since the Scots are so proud, they don't resent it too! What does she imagine? That I shall stay a withered virgin like herself, without sons to come after me? "

" That cannot be," her brother answered stiffly. " You must have a husband to guide you. But it must be the right husband, chosen for the right qualities, not a fool who may be able to further your ambitions."

" We said we wouldn't speak of that," she reminded him, and the hostile gleam flashed at him for a second and was gone. Her smile reappeared. " I won't detain you, James; but I like to discuss everything with you first. You know I depend on you so much."

He kissed her hand and then her cheek, and bowed as he left her. When she was alone she threw the rug off and stood up, her lips compressed, her slanted eyes half closed with anger.

She must have a husband. By God, he was right! She must have a man to stand between her and her half-brother and her nobles and somehow rescue her from this maddening life of encirclement, this masquerade as Queen where everything she did or said was subject to the approval of others. It was somewhat better now than at first; she had more freedom, she had made many friends, she was loved a little for herself and a great deal for what she represented: the chance of engorgement of their rich enemy across the Border. But she did not love the Scots or their country; she could not. She could not spend her life hemmed in in this bleak and wretched kingdom, when a land of freedom and enlightenment, with a large population of her own faith, rich towns and splendid Palaces, lay within reach. In England she would be a Queen as Elizabeth was Queen. She had tried to love Scotland, but the terms of Scotland's love were the negation of everything she had been taught regarding the rights of a sovereign and the necessities of a cultured existence. It was cold and humourless and half civilized. In her frustration and despair she paced the little room imagining how easy it would be to love an English kingdom and transform herself into an English Queen. Her mind returned to Lethington's despatch. In spite of his reputation as an unscrupulous opportunist, Mary liked Lethington; he was a shrewd man with a dry sense of humour which she found refreshing, a cynic but a polished cynic, who often looked at her with a gleam of amusement in his light eyes as if he could see beyond the quiet demeanour into the depth of her ambitious and incautious spirit. He had watched her closely in the first months of her reign in Scotland, and she knew she had won his respect by her tact, or rather her dissimulation. They shared not only a sense of humour but also a conspiracy to outwit her enemies. He hated the rude, ranting preacher Knox, despised her brother James, and was confessed agnostic enough to be indifferent to her religion. Once he had decided to support her, he had given her excellent service. He had no patience for fools and no intention of choosing a losing side. Lethington saw her possibilities, and he had decided that with the right advice and a little luck, his Queen might well unite England and Scotland under one Crown.

He wrote a great deal about her cousin Elizabeth, for whom he had a healthy respect. He admitted to his mistress that her rival was a clever, devious personality who appeared to be absolute ruler of her kingdom, with power that made Mary hot with envy. She was a consummate actress, and an equally accomplished liar; she protested her friendship for the Scots Queen, and sighed sentimentally over the prospect of a meeting between them, which she herself had frustrated. Lethington further reported that she had no religious feelings whatever; her private taste inclined towards Catholic ritual; she liked music and ceremony and candles, but on those of her Catholic subjects who refused to attend the established services, she levied fines which were ruining them financially. As a result, many had capitulated rather than be reduced to penury. She had no scruples, but she dreaded war. Mary was comforted by this; she mistook it for a sign of weakness and rejoiced in her own high spirits which would welcome a romantic campaign. Elizabeth's attitude smelled of the counting house and the middle-class caution which Mary so heartily despised. Lethington thought the English Queen unlikely to marry; she was said to be barren, which explained her position as the mistress of Lord Robert Dudley. If Mary waited, and avoided antagonizing her cousin by a foreign marriage, Elizabeth would eventually name her as her successor. When that was done, the situation could be reassessed. But he emphasized, in every letter he sent back from England, that Elizabeth was a formidable opponent, backed by some of the cleverest men in Europe, with Sir William Cecil at their head.

Formidable, Mary repeated that word to herself, trying to

conjure the living woman from all the accounts she had heard of her. Ruthless, deceitful, able to impose her will upon those men whom Lethington considered so exceptionally wise and strong. A gifted musician, a beautiful dancer, passionately fond of dress and openly acquisitive about jewels and treasures. (One of the safest ways to Elizabeth's favour was a valuable present, articles of clothing included.) She spoke three languages fluently and translated the Classics like a University scholar, indeed better than many of them. But she was still a bastard, the daughter of a common adventuress who was beheaded for adultery and incest. She was not beautiful like Mary, or truly Royal, with the blood of the Stuarts and the majestic Guises running in her veins. She was a heretic and an usurper, and all her cleverness could not outweigh these disadvantages when it came to a clear choice between the Queen of Scotland and herself.

In spite of Lethington, in spite of James, in spite of everyone who warned her and looked dubious, Mary's confidence in her own destiny was stronger than ever. She could review her two years in Scotland and tell herself that England would be easy after such an apprenticeship at ruling the unruly.

She picked up Lethington's latest despatch and began to re-read the remarks on Henry Darnley.

At the end of that year, English troops were in occupation of Havre. Having committed herself to war, Elizabeth ordered a vigorous policy. Cecil was restored to favour by one of her disconcerting reversals; she sent for him, remained alone with him for three hours, and appeared at Court the next day leaning affectionately on his arm. If she was cool at times it merely sharpened his wits and improved his work with a little healthy anxiety; when she welcomed him back, he fell under her influence more completely than before. His subjection was a slow process, but it was as absolute as her dominion over Dudley. He loved his wife and his growing family of children; he could never explain the particular mixture of fascination and uncertainty which bound him to Elizabeth.

But in March of 1563 the war ended in France with the capture of the Protestant Prince de Condé and the murder of the Catholic Duc de Guise. The rather ridiculous figure of the Regent, Catherine de' Medici, suddenly emerged from the political shadows in a different shape. The neglected wife, the foreigner with nothing to recommend her except the fortunes of her Florentine banker's family, put an end to the war in France, and revealed a sinister ability. Her first action was to unite the forces of the Huguenots and Catholics against the English troops at Havre. It was a clever move; religious differences were forgotten in patriotic hatred of the hereditary enemy who had taken advantage of a private French quarrel to make claims on the soil of France, making Calais their objective. Elizabeth's soldiers had done no fighting for Condé; they now found themselves besieged by Condé's supporters in concert with Catholic troops, and a long and bitter engagement began, in which the English fought with courage and tenacity. Anxious and enraged at the setback, Elizabeth now encouraged her armies as fiercely as she had first resisted their embarkation, and she drew Cecil closer than ever into her confidence. But her efforts and the fighting qualities of the Havre garrison were defeated by a deadlier enemy than the French. Plague broke out in the port and soon a hundred men a day were dying, with twice as many sick. There was nothing to do but accept the peace Catherine de' Medici offered, with the final renunciation of all claims to Calais.

Plague came to England with the remains of the army and raged through the population, turning London into a charnel house. Starvation followed, with the usual aftermath of looting and violence, and the sickness spread from the towns to the villages all through the summer, until the cold and damp of the autumn ended the infection.

War had brought nothing but defeat and financial difficulties, exactly as Elizabeth had foretold when pressed to declare it. But she neither turned on Cecil and his friends, nor shifted the responsibility in the eyes of her people. Nothing was said, but her Council knew her well enough to understand that the man who next suggested war would lose his place on the Council, if he did not lose his head.

The Parliament which was summoned to vote money for the war had taken the opportunity to remind the Queen of her late illness and to petition her to name a successor or else marry and provide an heir. They were joined in this by the Lords. Elizabeth answered gently, refusing to commit herself until the grant was given, and then, in phrases expressing motherly affection, rejected their plea. She refused to name an heir to her throne on the assumption that she might yet marry, though if she did it would be from a sense of duty and against her personal inclinations. As usual, she had answered this particular question in a way which allowed her petitioners to hope, and which, at the same time, committed her to nothing beyond vague generalizations.

When she returned to Whitehall Palace after the end of the Session, she sent for Cecil. He knew when he came into the room that she was in a furious temper.

" Well, and are you satisfied now? "

He shook his head.

" Madam, I beg you not to be angry with me. I was not responsible for the Petition from the Commons. I know it angers you, but they only expressed the wish of all of us who love you."

" Who love yourselves," she retorted. " So much for Parliament and money grants! I'll see them damned before I let them meet again. Sit down, for God's sake. . . . Why must I be harried and worried like a dog with a pack of hounds after me, all yelping on the same note? Marry, marry. . . . Or else dig my own grave and declare a successor! "

" If you did name your heir it might put an end to all the difficulties," he said slowly. " If you marry, then that nomination will be set aside. As it is now, nothing is settled; one serious illness like the last might be the end of you, Madam. And you would leave England at the mercy of every adventurer with a drop of Plantagenet or Tudor blood."

" There are no Plantagenets left," Elizabeth reminded him. " My father killed them all. . . . As for a successor, are you so anxious for the Queen of Scots? *She* is my heir! "

" Catherine Grey is a claimant, so is the young Darnley."

" Catherine Grey isn't fit to rule over a pigsty, and you know it. As for Darnley . . . that drunken fool? My God, Cecil, how could you! Now listen to me. You are my friend and I love you; and you love me, is that not so? "

" You know it is," he said.

She came and sat down beside him and put her hand on his sleeve.

" I am not afraid for myself. I am not afraid of invasion or an attempt upon my life; I would risk these at any time if it was necessary. But I am afraid of civil war, of bloodshed and factions and the effect of human greed. I will not bring all this upon my people, which is what naming a successor would precipitate. Do you really think that Catherine Grey or Mary Stuart or anyone else would wait until I died before they came to claim the English throne? Are you as stupid as those clods in the Commons to talk about a civil war after my death and then purpose the sure means of starting one while I'm alive? "

"Then marry!" he burst out. "Choose a husband! God's life, choose Dudley if you must, but marry and have a child and put an end to it all!"

"I may yet," she said, but she had turned her head away from him. "The prospect has never appealed to me. I saw enough of marrying with my father. . . . I like it less and less as the time passes. But I may do it, if I can force myself. If there is no other way. . . ."

"You would be happier," Cecil said earnestly. "You'd have someone to share your burdens."

"I like my burdens," Elizabeth replied. "They're not burdens to me. The last thing in the world I want is to share them with anybody. Cecil, I tried to explain to you once, three years ago, that I don't long for masculine support in the business of governing. I need you and Sussex, and the others, but that is different. We work well together, there's trust and goodwill between us all. It would not be like that between husband and wife. There's no such thing as joint sovereign, only one ruler. And I am that one. As for Dudley, I appreciate your desperation in suggesting him, but I like him best as he is."

"There will never be peace or quiet of mind, so long as Mary Stuart is across the Scottish border and only your life safeguards the throne of England. We'll have an invasion of French or Spanish or some other troops, depending on whom she marries, and all your avoidance of war will come to nothing."

"I have thought of that," she said. "I think of very little else, if you wish to know. And there you have your answer. My marriage can wait, hers apparently cannot; she is negotiating with so many men it makes me blush! Marry her to the wrong one, my dear friend, and who knows how our problem may resolve itself. In fact our crafty Lethington, in a despatch of his last year, mentioned a possibility which was so ludicrous I couldn't believe my eyes when you showed me the copy. You remember who he suggested to her! Henry Darnley!"

Cecil's pale eyes blinked for a moment, as if a sudden light had flashed into them.

"I saw the cypher copy of his last letter to her," he said.

"He has been approached by Darnley's mother. He says the boy is ready to escape to Scotland if the Queen of Scots will consider him. I thought it would enrage you, Madam, and you've been made angry enough for today. I meant to tell you later."

For a moment Elizabeth looked at him, her dark eyes, half hidden by the heavy lids, more prominent since her illness had wasted her face. No light touched them, but the corners of her lips began to curve in the amused, rather cruel little smile he knew so well.

"Cecil, my dear, clever Cecil, sometimes you are not so clever after all. Now I tell you what we shall do. We shall have our supper here, you and I, all alone so that we can talk. And then I shall tell you why I am not at all angry about Master Darnley and his ambitions to see Scotland. No, not angry in the least."

# Chapter 6

I T was early spring, and the Hertfordshire countryside was very green. The weather was warm after a fiercely cold winter, there had been no rain for several days, and many of the trees and hedges were in bud.

The Queen had moved from Whitehall Palace to stay with her maternal cousin Lord Hunsdon on the estate which she had given him out of Royal lands. Hunsdon itself had been her father's hunting box; he and Anne Boleyn had often stayed there and hunted over the flat Hertford country, and Elizabeth herself had spent some time there as a child. The small house had been re-built into a splendid mansion with elaborate gardens boxed in with yew hedges, and with rockeries, fountains and statues and little paved walks, similar to the beautiful stylized gardens at Hampton Court. Lord Hunsdon was already very wealthy; he could offer Elizabeth a magnificent suite of rooms in his new house, with an enormous tester bed made especially for her visit and hung with valuable Flemish tapestries.

The Queen liked travelling; she was not deterred by the appalling roads or the discomfort of a protracted journey with a long wagon train rumbling behind her. Dudley, as Master of the Horse, was responsible for her transport and the safe arrival of all her personal plate, dresses, horses and servants. Removing Elizabeth from London to Hunsdon, a distance of thirty miles, was a complicated and detailed operation, like transporting a small army with supplies, but Dudley was so efficient an organizer that she was encouraged to travel further and more often than any of her predecessors. She was especially fond of Hunsdon, because the hunting was excellent, and also because she had an affection for her cousin. It was a peculiar affection, and it included her other maternal relatives, the Careys. They were connected through the Boleyns and, though distant kin, they were all that remained of her family, and a sentimental quirk, quite alien to her rational and self-sufficient spirit, entitled them to a place in her inner circle of favourites.

She had left on a hunting expedition that morning, taking Dudley with her as usual and a company of fifty ladies and gentlemen. She felt very well and exhilarated, freed from the routine of Council meetings and audiences; only the most urgent despatches were sent to her from London, and no courier had disturbed her for three days. It was a successful hunt; the Queen's grey horse led the field, and the Queen's arrow brought down a magnificent five-pointed stag which Hunsdon had saved for her visit. It was a happy, informal morning, full of sport and excitement, and the company gathered for a picnic under some beech trees.

Servants had already arrived by wagon, bringing the food and the cutlery in baskets, and the Queen lunched with Dudley and two of her ladies a little apart from the others. She sat on a heap of cushions, with a white linen cloth spread on the ground, her own cup-bearer and steward in attendance, and ate chicken and lark pie, and several kinds of salted fish, with ale or wine to drink. She laughed a great deal with Dudley, and took a forkful of sugared ginger off her own plate to feed to him.

Elizabeth leant back against the tree trunk, and held out her hand to Robert. He kissed it and held it when she tried to draw it back.

She smiled at him, a mischievous contented smile.

"There will be more scandal," she said, "but I don't care. What a magnificent day it has been! Do you know, Robert, it makes me wish I were not a Queen but just the wife of some country gentleman, and able to spend my life like this!"

"It's all well enough for one day or a few days," Dudley laughed at her and leant back until their shoulders touched. "But you are a Queen by nature, Madam, and all Queens like to play milkmaid now and then. But not for too long. I know you—you'll be restless and irritable by the end of the week, longing for Cecil to come padding in like an old tabby cat, full of some crisis about Scotland or France."

"Cats are all the more dangerous because they're quiet. And Cecil is no tabby."

"And no tiger either," he retorted.

He only ridiculed the man because he knew he was a person to be feared. He hated him even more because he had never been able to influence Elizabeth against him. She had made

Dudley a Privy Councillor, given him a valuable monopoly on the import of wines which brought him enormous wealth, and he was admitted into many governmental secrets, but there was one impenetrable barrier between them and that was the power of William Cecil.

"There are quiet tigers," she reminded him. "They don't all strut through the forest like you, my Robert, or bellow like old Sussex. Tiger is a good description of Cecil. I shall remember it."

She picked up a sweetmeat from the little gold dish made in the shape of a galley, with Cupid at the prow. Robert had given it to her as part of his New Year gift. He had also given her a splendid set of ruby buttons and a pair of Spanish leather gloves, tanned to the softness of velvet and covered from knuckle to wrist with her cypher in diamonds and pearls.

She loved sweets; there was always a dish of them by her bedside, on the backgammon board or the chess table, and even on her table when she was in Council. Violets, roses, cachous covered in sugar and marzipan. She ate and drank very little, with a rather plebeian taste which preferred the coarse ale to Spanish wine, but she was as greedy as a child for anything sweet. She watched Robert for a moment; the shade of the beech tree dappled the ground around them with patterns of sunshine and shadow, and the patterns shifted with the movement of a slight breeze.

"Talking of crisis and Scotland and France," she said at last, "I have a proposition to make to you. I might be able to give you that status you have wanted for so long. Are you interested?"

He turned to her quickly, and the grip of his fingers made her wince.

"If you mean what I hope," he said. "If status means marriage with you. . . ."

"You have always wanted to marry a Queen, haven't you, Robert?" she said lightly. "Well how would you like to marry one at last?"

"What do you mean, Madam? There's only one Queen I have ever wanted."

"You can't have me." Elizabeth withdrew her hand and sat upright. She had sent Lady Knollys and Lady Warwick out of hearing; the servants had gone to their own food. "We are agreed about that, aren't we?"

"I'm not," he said. "I never have been; I never will be. I only know better than to mention it to you unless you do. When you spoke like that a moment ago I thought you had changed your mind."

"I change my mind a great deal," she admitted. "That is a woman's privilege, and damnably useful it is at times. But my mind won't change on that count. My aversion to marrying you, my Robert, is as strong as my love for you. Never be in doubt about either. But if you want a Queen as a wife, why not the Queen of Scotland?"

She saw the surprise and then the anger on his face.

"You are mocking me," he said. "I must beg you not to, Madam; it's a sore subject and I have no sense of humour for it."

"On the contrary, I am quite serious. My cousin needs a husband; unlike me, she is only too anxious to lose her independence. I can't think of anyone who would restrain her ambitions and serve my interests better than you, if you filled the place. What do you say, Robert? If you cannot be King of England, Scotland is not such a poor consolation prize—and she is said to be very beautiful."

He gave an angry laugh.

"I doubt if she'd thank you for the suggestion. You forget I have a murderous reputation, so foul that you wouldn't marry me, and even more foul in her eyes because I am supposed to be your lover. I have never seen Mary Stuart, but I hardly think she'd welcome your leavings."

"I think she'd welcome anything if a promise of the English succession went with it. Sit back, Robert, and don't lose your temper. Supposing the idea appealed to her, what would your answer be?"

"My answer," he said coldly, "is 'no'. You must find another means of getting rid of me."

"Why is it 'no'?" she persisted. "You would have great power, equal sovereignty, if you were clever with her. . . . Why, Robert, you could be a King!"

"Because I am so unmanned through you that I'd rather stay here as a pet dog," he said. "Find another candidate, Madam. I won't accommodate you."

"If you were really unmanned, Robert," Elizabeth told him softly, "you would have said 'yes'. And that would have been a foolish answer because I have no intention of letting you marry her or anyone else. But I may ask you to play at it for a while. Will you do that for me? "

" Play at it? " He stared at her and then suddenly shrugged. " You are beyond me. You put the idea forward, tempt me with it, and then tell me I had no freedom of choice anyway."

" On reflection you would have seen that. But first impulses are more valuable than decisions. I am glad you refused. But I shall want you to play at it, as I said. I intend suggesting you as a candidate; firstly because I know she will be outraged, as you pointed out. Then I will sweeten the suggestion with a lot of promises, and at the same time I shall violently oppose another person who is on her list of suitors. It is only an idea, and it's a pity to spoil a lovely afternoon by talking about intrigue, but I cannot do this unless you help me."

" Who is this other candidate? " he asked her. " And why should you put me forward as the alternative to him? "

" Because it might be the one way of making her choose him. Who he is does not matter yet."

" Was this Cecil's idea or yours, Madam? " He helped her up, and the Queen smiled coolly into his face.

" Cecil knows nothing of my real reason. Don't credit him with this idea, it is entirely mine. He will think you are pursuing your ambitions and that I am being over-trusting of you. A lot of people will warn me that if you marry Mary Stuart you'll join her in an attack on my throne. You must be prepared for it and bear it patiently. You must bear a good deal in the next few months, but remember two things. You are not going to Scotland. And you must not be surprised when I pretend that you are."

When the hunting party returned to Hunsdon, Elizabeth said that she was tired and needed rest. She changed out of her dusty riding clothes after inspecting the carcase of the big stag which Lord Hunsdon promised to have skinned and the head mounted for her, and which she then presented to him as a memento of her visit. She dressed in a long robe of crimson brocade with a collar and sleeves trimmed with sable and a little half hood of black velvet, edged with the same fur. Her ladies lit wax candles, part of the luxury her cousin provided for her, since the tallow lights smelt unpleasantly strong, and the Queen sat down at the virginals to play and amuse herself, having dismissed her attendants. She liked solitude when she wanted to think; she often played for hours in an empty room, apparently absorbed in the music, while her mind worked out some tangled problem, separating the threads and re-weaving them into a pattern of her own.

Mary Stuart would reject Robert. Any woman proud of her lineage and her reputation would take the suggestion as a gross insult, and she knew from Randolph in Edinburgh and Lethington in London, that the Scots Queen was very sensitive about both. Just as Mary had tried to judge Elizabeth, so the Queen imagined her rival, as her fingers moved over the keyboard of the virginals, bringing the beauty of a galliard by Herriot to life in the still room.

Mary had done very well, and her life in that barbarous country must have been gall to a spoilt and spirited girl who had been taught to regard her position as inviolate. She had gone from a life of cushioned unreality in France, where her least wish was a law to her uncles and her foolish husband, and survived three years of nominal rule over a pack of undisciplined ruffians and a scruffy, loud-mouthed clergy with no respect for their superiors. She had not made one false step, but Elizabeth's instinct insisted that the credit was mostly due to her advisers. The Guises were masters of diplomacy and intrigue; they had obviously primed their niece how to avoid the dangers implicit in her sex and her religion; and men like Lethington and presumably her bastard half-brother, James Moray, had guided her along the difficult way of concilia-tion when she might have been tempted by ignorance and temper into a trial of strength with her nobles and her heretic Church.

Unlike Elizabeth, whose childhood had been a succession of upheavals and humiliations, Mary had not learnt the hard lessons of craft by long experience and personal error. She had been told how to avoid mistakes, which was a disadvantage because the only way to learn was from the consequences when one made them. She was not naturally deceitful; Elizabeth had divined enough naïveté in the letters she received to know that when Mary was intriguing she did it badly and with many witnesses. She was ambitious and proud and full of a mediaeval belief in the Divinity of Kings which had somehow survived the monotonous murders of so many of her Scottish ancestors. She probably suffered from the delusion that her sex protected her from that hazard, and as she looked out at the darkening view from her window Elizabeth remembered her mother, who might well have seen it from a room in the demolished hunting box, and smiled contemptuously.

Mary was not evil, in the sense that Elizabeth understood evil. She was not cruel, like some of the English ladies of rank who had their servants thrashed and branded for petty theft. When Chatelard's head was cut off in front of her, Mary fainted. But she had ordered the execution, and the episode with the poet had done more than anything else to raise her in Elizabeth's estimation. Provided that she had killed the man from policy and not from any fatuous regard for sexual virtue. She had no lovers, and her suitors were encouraged at a strictly political level, but Randolph reported that she had great charm over men; some of the roughest of the Border Lords were making fools of themselves trying to be gallant.

What kind of woman was Mary Stuart? Would she possess that quality of judgment and acumen without which no woman could hope to rule over men? Would she see beyond the apparent blunder of suggesting Dudley as a husband for her, and look into the motives behind the motives? Would she see what manner of man the alternative was, before she committed herself to him through pride and a mistaken idea that she would be defying her interfering cousin?

Would she really be so headstrong and lacking in judgment, as Elizabeth believed and was prepared to gamble on, as to manoeuvre on behalf of Henry Darnley? Darnley. Her hands struck one of Herriot's bright chords, musical and clear as running water. Darnley had Royal blood and an ambitious mother whom Elizabeth personally hated. But he was a stupid, bad natured youth, with a private taste for drink and vice and nothing to recommend him beyond charming manners and a handsome face. He was the sort of man that she would have kicked aside with her foot at the very age when she was involved with the Admiral. At fifteen she would have seen through him. But she had always had that faculty. She had known in her heart that the Admiral was an adventurer, ready to despoil a child in the pursuit of his ambitions, even though she loved him. She had known what Robert was too, though she had loved Robert, and still did. Robert had refused to go to Scotland because he had been taken unawares; he had got into the habit of loyalty to her, and habits did not break down in a few seconds. But if he went to Scotland and acquired a young and beautiful wife, her own remark might have come true, and Robert, the faithful lover and loyal suitor, was not so faithful or so loyal that he might not have marched against her as the husband of the Queen of Scots. It was possible to see men as they were and yet to love them. But her one hope was that Mary would *not* see through Henry Darnley, if and when he reached Scotland, as Elizabeth intended he should at the right moment. For if she recognized him as a degenerate and a coward, she would know that such a man would not survive in Scotland, and nor would she if she were to become his wife.

All the mistakes Mary had avoided, Darnley would make for her. If only Mary could be tricked into marrying him.

The sound of Elizabeth's playing drifted out into the corridors, where some of the house servants had gathered to listen. The stately music reached its climax, the climax of the Scottish Court dance, the Galliard, and when the last notes died away, someone said reverently that the Queen's Majesty played like an angel.

Maitland of Lethington had not even blinked; privately Elizabeth admired his self-control. He had listened to her astounding proposal without allowing a sign of surprise to cross his face. It was not a handsome face in the strict sense of the word but it was pleasing, with an intelligent eye and a neat little beard under a rather humorous mouth. He was a clever man, and she liked him; he was polished in his manners, and she liked that too. She also liked him because she knew from the letters to Mary which were intercepted and copied, that he admired her in spite of himself. They were sitting under an artificial awning made of lattice work entwined with flowering shrubs and foliage erected outside on the terrace of Greenwich Palace. The river flowed past them further down, its waters reflecting the light of torches from the barges moored by the jetty. The Queen had invited him to an evening reception, followed by a banquet and a masque. She had left the Great Hall, accompanied by Cecil, and with Lethington on one side of her and the Secretary on the other, she had just suggested Robert Dudley as a husband for the Queen of Scots.

They were very close, their faces lit by the torches burning in sconces against the walls; her dress glittered in the shifting light; it was so stiff with jewels and so heavily panniered that he wondered how she was able to move in it.

On these occasions she looked more and more like the effigy of a Queen, so stately and over-jewelled that she literally dazzled the eye. She had a wonderful sense of the theatrical; she was clever enough to sacrifice mere feminine charm to achieve an effect of glittering majesty. She looked ageless and remote; her deliberate personification of power was inhuman and rather frightening. Lethington could not help regretting his own Queen's warm, informal personality. It attracted many, but it also placed her within reach of her enemies. He could not imagine John Knox arguing with Elizabeth Tudor and reducing her to tears.

"Madam, you surprise me," he said. "I know your affection for my sovereign but I had no idea it could lead you to such self-sacrifice. How could you bear to part with someone who is so dear to you?"

"Nothing is dearer to me than friendship between your Queen and myself, and peace between our kingdoms," Elizabeth answered. "My affection prompts me to offer a man whom I know from experience would make my cousin a most worthy husband. The whole world knows that I would have married him myself, if I had a mind to marry anyone. There is no higher compliment I could pay her than that."

Cecil moved in his chair. "You know Lord Robert. He is able and loyal; Her Majesty would give him a title and endowments suitable to the husband of your mistress. I can heartily endorse her suggestion, and I know that it comes from her heart."

"I'm sure it does," Lethington smiled. He was already imagining the rage and incredulity of Mary when he wrote to her; for a moment he shared her anger at the presumption of this damnable woman and her smooth-tongued Councillor to dare suggest that tarnished adventurer as a possible husband for the Queen of his country. But he gave no sign. He did not really believe that either of them were serious.

"The whole difficulty between our two kingdoms could be solved by such a marriage," Elizabeth continued. "My fear, and it's one I have never concealed from you, my Lord, is that a foreign Prince may win my cousin and prevail upon her to enter into an alliance against me. I don't doubt her good faith, but I fear her youth and the weaknesses of women where their affections are involved. An unscrupulous Scottish Consort could do irreparable harm; not only to our mutual peace but to my cousin's prospects of inheriting my throne. An Englishman of noble birth and excellent qualities like my Lord Dudley would ensure Queen Mary a happy domestic life and a firm liaison with me. I should be happy to name her my successor as a wedding present. You may tell her that."

Lethington nodded. It was in fact a serious proposal as well as a gross impertinence, couched in terms of open blackmail.

"I shall be happy to inform my mistress immediately. Naturally she will encounter one doubt, Madam, which has already occurred to me. Lord Robert is known to be deeply attached to you; would he be willing to transfer his affections elsewhere? My Queen is a gentle lady and anxious to make a marriage that is based on mutual love as well as policy. For this reason, I fear she may doubt the wisdom of your proposal."

Elizabeth smiled.

"My cousin is reputed to be the most beautiful Princess in Europe; my Lord Dudley is certainly a handsome man in the prime of his youth. The sight of her would be enough to banish all sentimental thoughts of me from his mind. Believe me, my Lord, I've given much thought to this and I cannot see a better solution. Let me tell you something—I once drew up letters patent to create Robert Earl of Leicester, did you know that?"

"Yes, Madam," Lethington glanced sideways at the impassive Secretary. "I also know that you changed your mind and cut the document to pieces instead of signing it."

"This time, I should sign it," she answered coolly. "I have my father's temper, you know, and poor Dudley's patent was presented to me after a quarrel. The earldom was a personal token of my gratitude for his good service. I withdrew it for my own reasons—you know how changeable women are, my dear Lethington, and I'm no exception. But nothing would please me more than to honour him as high as your mistress could wish. He shall be Earl of Leicester, and you shall propose him as my official candidate for my cousin's hand. I shall write and personally recommend him to her."

"My Queen will be overwhelmed," Lethington murmured. He wondered how he could restrain Mary from replying to that personal recommendation in terms which would result in war. It would be all the more difficult since she was seriously interested in the suit of Henry Darnley. He had seen Darnley several times, thanks to the persistence of his mother, Lady

Lennox, and he had been able to tell Mary that Darnley was extremely good-looking and with pleasing manners. He also described the Countess of Lennox as a troublesome and ambitious old virago, who would have to be left behind in England if the marriage were seriously considered.

As for Robert Dudley, he knew him well and disliked him intensely. He had always suspected that William Cecil shared his antipathy, and he could only suppose that he supported this extraordinary suggestion in order to get him out of England and break his influence with the Queen.

He saw that Elizabeth had held out her hand to be kissed, which was the signal for his dismissal. It was as pale and cool as marble, her exquisite fingers were not spoilt by rings, except the ring she had accepted at her Coronation as a symbol of her marriage to the State.

When he left them Elizabeth turned to Cecil.

"He'll have to convey the message," she said, "and I think he believes it's serious. He also believes that she will be furious."

"He has a secret appointment with Darnley and his mother again tomorrow," Cecil said quietly. "The Countess sends him messages every day."

"When the time comes, I'll send that old harridan to the Tower," she snapped. "It will convince my dear cousin how angry I am at the marriage and it will give *me* immense satisfaction."

"How can you be so sure this plan will succeed, Madam?" Cecil asked her. "What will you do if she swallows that bribe about the succession and accepts Dudley?"

Elizabeth laughed. "You know very little about women, my dear Cecil. Madam is growing mighty confident; she has come to the point where she is intriguing to marry one of my subjects behind my back—that's a step forward after all her tact these past two years, and she has a high stomach, all the Stuarts are as proud as Lucifer. Robert himself gave the answer when he said she'd hardly take my leavings. That miserable Lennox pimp has Tudor blood; that will be his marriage gift to Mary, and more likely to appeal to her than any promises of mine. If she did agree to Robert, I should simply refuse him permission to leave England and the negotiations would come to nothing."

"I am relieved," Cecil said dryly, "to hear that you wouldn't consider the marriage as a last resort. That has tormented me all the way through."

"You don't trust Robert, do you?" she said. "And you don't trust me either, to suppose I would keep anything back from you."

"Do you trust him that far?" Cecil retorted. "Do you think he could be sent to Scotland to be tempted into invading England, and not fall?"

"No." Elizabeth stared out to where the lights were flickering along the river. "I trust no man that far, except you."

"How can you love a man you do not trust?" he said softly. "How can you keep him by you, turning you from the thought of other men, how can you honour him and lavish presents upon him, knowing that he is unworthy of you?"

"How can you ask that question when you are married and you don't know what it means to need another human being? Robert has many faults; God knows I hear enough about them, but I don't want a man of saintly principles, I want a good companion, a good dancer, a good horseman, a prop to lean on, even if in fact it's he who does the leaning. . . . I can give you a dozen answers to that question of yours, all of them true and none of them the right one. Robert is ambitious and shallow; he hasn't your brain or Sussex's honour, or Hunsdon's chivalry, but in his way he loves me and he needs what I can give him. That is something *I* need, and I can have him on my terms and trust him just as far as it is fair to expect of any man, when I am neither his mistress nor his wife. Now go in and send him out to me."

Three people were sitting in a small room in a house not far from the Royal Palace of Whitehall; the curtains were drawn, closing out the evening sunlight, and there were no servants to wait on them. The wine was poured by the younger of the two men, and the second man watched him closely while he listened to the Countess of Lennox praising the virtues of her son. Lady Lennox had a harsh voice and a domineering, mannish attitude; she sat like a man with her knees spread wide under her skirts and her hands resting on them, leaning forward to impress the Scottish envoy with what she was saying.

Her rather coarse and florid features, with the darting green eyes and the hard mouth, were in complete contrast to the rounded good looks of her son. Lethington took the glass from his hand and thanked him.

Henry Darnley was so tall that he had to stoop low over Lethington's chair. He was very fair, with hair that curled like a child's, and bright blue eyes; if the face was too smooth, without beard or moustaches, the figure was undeniably graceful and slim. He had an air of refinement and good breeding which made his relationship to that gross, blustering woman difficult to reconcile, though the precious Tudor blood flowed in his veins from her.

Lady Lennox was the daughter of Henry VII's sister, therefore granddaughter of Owen Tudor and blood cousin of Elizabeth. She was also the blood cousin of Mary Stuart.

"There isn't a better match for the Queen than my son," she declared. "Look at him, my Lord—is there a better favoured young man in Europe?"

Lethington caught her son's eye and exchanged a smile. He noticed that Darnley had blushed and looked uncomfortable while the Countess made her appraisals of him, as if she were trying to sell a thoroughbred horse.

"Nobody doubts your qualities, Lord Darnley," Lethington turned on him. "And your maternal pride only does him justice, Madam," he added.

"There are only two obstacles to the marriage that I can see; firstly my Queen will not make any promises without having seen your son, and secondly, the Queen of England has made Dudley Earl of Leicester and apparently believes that my Queen is prepared to take him as a husband. Under those circumstances, I don't see how your visit to Scotland can be arranged openly, and there can't be a contract without a visit."

"The whole world is laughing at Queen Mary," Lady Lennox snapped. "God knows how she can have allowed Elizabeth to go so far with this ridiculous proposal, raising that scoundrel to the peerage and telling everyone that he is going to Scotland as her personal token to the Queen. If I were Mary I would have torn up the letter and returned her the pieces as an answer."

"That was the Queen's first impulse," Lethington explained patiently. "She is fully sensible of the insult which has been offered her, and it has strengthened her determination to marry without the approval of Queen Elizabeth. But as the best candidate is your son, who is here in England, it has been necessary to pretend to take the suggestion of Dudley seriously, until we can arrange for Lord Darnley to flee the country. When he is safely in Scotland, my Queen will make her decision and show Queen Elizabeth exactly what harm that monstrous proposal has done her."

"I would go at any time," Darnley interposed. "I am not afraid of Elizabeth."

"My son is no coward, as you can see," his mother said. "He has my stomach, my Lord. I'm perfectly sure that when Queen Mary sees him the match will be made—I've had trouble enough chasing the women away from him since he was sixteen."

Again Darnley looked modestly embarrassed; it was an expression that suited him. There was nothing in the frank blue eyes to show that a dull headache pulsed behind them, or that his limbs were stiff after a night spent in one of the lowest brothels in Cheapside. His mother had certainly defeated the eligible young ladies who had made advances to him, but she was ignorant of the conquests he made among the servant girls and prostitutes. He preferred to keep his amusements secret from her; it was bad enough to live under her eye, to be bullied and cursed and cajoled by turns, and generally kept in the position of an overgrown child. Her voice grated on him; he hated the loud tone which never softened; he shrank when it became an angry bellow, and hurried away to the wine cupboard and drank to calm himself and to give himself the feeling of courage and self-confidence which was lacking whenever he was sober. And he was not sober very often now. The strain of the intrigue to marry him to the Queen of Scotland had driven him deeper into debauchery; he lost himself in sexual excesses which were already tinged with vice, and in an alcoholic daze he dreamed wild dreams of independence in Scotland, free of his mother's domination, married to a young and beautiful woman who could realize all the Countess's ambitions for him without his having to achieve them for himself. In Scotland he would be his own master; he would be important and powerful, and he shared his mother's opinion that Mary Stuart would find him irresistible. Most women were attracted to him; so were men. He could see that even the astute Scots ambassador was impressed. He had played the part of a dutiful, accomplished son so skilfully that it was easy to lie and posture in his relations with everyone else. Only in the wretched bawdy houses, accompanied by a few companions of the same tastes as his own, only there did the cruel, immature, bullying nature show itself. He was able to pay for the bruises, the smashed furniture, the wanton destruction that climaxed his entertainment and to swagger out into the world, feeling that his spirit was as impressive as his body.

"My husband might be able to go to Scotland," Lady Lennox was saying. "Our estates were sequestered under the late reign, and it would be a valid excuse to go there and try and get them restored."

Lethington nodded. "Quite possibly. But if your husband went, how would that help Lord Darnley?"

"He could send for him," she said. "If the Queen refused permission, he'd have to slip over the Border without it. We could do it easily; leave all that part of it to me."

"We." Lethington looked blandly into her face; he wondered how he could persuade Darnley to leave his mother behind.

He stood up.

"Lady Lennox, we've had a most profitable talk. My Queen asked me to convey her warm good wishes to you when she last wrote; she also entrusted a message for Lord Darnley, which I must deliver before I leave you."

As the Countess made no move to go, he added, "The message is for him alone. I can't give it, even before you."

When the door had closed behind her, Lethington turned to Darnley. Both men sighed at the same moment and then laughed.

"I never saw King Henry of England," the envoy said, "but I imagine your excellent mother bears a strong resemblance to him!"

"So I believe," Darnley answered pleasantly. "I'm not sorry I don't share it; it's quite enough to have the blood without the temper or the manners. What was the message, my Lord —I'm desperately eager to hear it."

"The Queen said that she was anxious to see you as soon as it could be contrived. She feels sure that her cousinly affection for you will be strengthened by a meeting, and she assures you that whatever public display she makes in this business of the Earl of Leicester, her heart is totally disengaged, and waits upon your coming."

Darnley bowed; he was inwardly feeling so out of sorts that his emotions were easily touched and Lethington saw tears in his eyes.

"From the moment you gave me that locket with her portrait," he said slowly, "I fell in love with her. Tell her that I shall come to Scotland; tell her that if she doesn't choose to marry me I shall still remain there to serve her in the humblest capacity she cares to name."

"I will tell her," Lethington said. He was suddenly touched by the boy; impressed by his sincerity, moved by the simple nobility of his words. He could imagine him beside Mary, both of them superbly tall and slim, with the same fine-bred look about them, both going out to conquer in the glory of their youth. . . .

"If you marry my Queen, care for her," he said. "She will need you, my Lord Darnley. There isn't a nobler Princess in Europe."

"I know that," Darnley answered. "I only want to be worthy of her."

Lethington left him then; he went out of the house by a back stairs used by servants and returned in a plain coach to his own lodgings outside the fashionable river area. He had no idea that Cecil had spies among the servants in the Lennox household, and that every visit he made to them was known to the English Government. He felt completely satisfied that if Mary married Henry Darnley she had made the best choice among the Princes of Europe.

The newly created Earl of Leicester was at his post in the Queen's ante-room. He stood a little apart from the crowd of people who were always gathered there hoping to catch the Queen's attention when she came out. He had altered in the last few months, as if the title Elizabeth had bestowed upon him had carried several years with it. He was more handsome than before, his figure pared down to muscle and bone by exercise, and his clothes were richer and yet more subdued than in the days when he first found favour and had money to squander on himself. His doublet was cloth of silver, the buttons were freshwater pearls edged with diamonds, and there were more diamonds in the hilt and scabbard of his sword. He wore a ruff of starched and double-pleated linen and the white cloth made his face darker skinned and his eyes blacker. It was no longer the face of the rather raffish adventurer, obviously on the watch for an opportunity to advance himself. Now it was stamped by self-confidence and pride; the eyes were haughty and inclined to stare. The Earl of Leicester, immensely rich, increasingly influential, a Privy Councillor, a Knight of the Garter, owner of estates in the country and valuable land close to London, the man being groomed for marriage with the Queen of Scotland and heiress to the English throne, was the successor of the upstart Robert Dudley, the culmination of a life devoted to ambition and the restoration of his lost fortunes.

But Elizabeth was his existence; Elizabeth was his title and his wealth and his entire significance. Without her he would have ceased to exist within a matter of days. He had made love to her and resisted her and fallen into the mortal mistake of treating her like other women; but when that phase was over and the correct adjustment made, he had found his position not only secure but in no way unmanly. It was possible to live as he did in permanent submission to the will of a woman only when that woman was Elizabeth and consequently so far above her own sex and its frailties that it was rather like serving a spectacular King.

The part of their relationship which now seemed strained and artificial was the most intimate; he instinctively felt it incongruous to embrace someone of whom he was fundamentally afraid. He wondered whether she shared his uneasiness; it was only an exercise in mutual frustration, and he suspected that she found it as unsatisfactory as he did, because the occasions when she indulged in amorous play were more and more infrequent.

Instead there was a greater warmth and intimacy in the purely platonic gestures of affection. He felt genuine love for Elizabeth when he held or kissed one of her hands, or helped to lift her from her horse; he had begun to take a fanatical pride in her achievements as if she were an extension of himself. They had entered a conspiracy to outwit the conventional world and make her unique among Queens as well as among women, and she was determined that they should remain together on their own peculiar footing and on their own agreed terms. He came into her rooms when she was dressing; not to indulge in liberties as their enemies imagined, but to help her choose her clothes for the day. He had a keen eye for what was both majestic and becoming. He picked out her largest jewels, suggested wider skirts and bigger ruffs, encouraging any fashion which made her outstanding. She was the Queen; she must never be mistaken for anything else whatever she was doing.

She was not only his consuming interest but his sole occupation. He was busy every moment of the day attending to her personal needs and her public necessities; he sat at the Council Chamber with her, escorted her when she went out, joined her hunting parties, and was never excused from a single evening's entertainment. It was widely accepted, even before the creation of his title and his expected marriage, that the way to the Queen could only be opened by Dudley. Cecil never asked favours for anyone.

He had played his part in the marriage farce with Mary Stuart as faithfully as she had demanded of him, though there were times when he needed her reassurance that it was all a trick, so convincingly did Elizabeth discuss his suit to the Scots Queen. And at those times she laughed and stroked his hair, and whispered that she meant to rivet a great chain round his leg with her own hands, just to make sure that he never left her. . . .

He had more enemies than at any time in his life; his earldom had emphasized the fact that he was no longer a bedchamber companion but a man of power and increasing substance whose voice counted for something in the government of the country. He was hated and courted at the same time; everyone who met his eye in the ante-room made him some acknowledgment, including some of Elizabeth's highest born and haughtiest nobles. The one exception who never looked at Robert or spoke to him if it could be avoided, was the Duke of Norfolk. He too was in the ante-room and his expression implied that the Queen's favourite, standing within five feet of him, did not exist.

He was a tall, thin man, with the prominent Howard features, and an intelligence which was chiefly occupied in the contemplation of his own importance. He was further elevated by close blood relationship with the Queen for the previous Duke had been the uncle of Anne Boleyn. They were a curious family, unscrupulous and mediaeval in their outlook; the uncle had not hesitated to sit as chief judge at the trial of his niece and to pronounce the sentence of death upon her. The present Duke lacked his ferocious predecessor's cunning; he had once condescended to tell Dudley some time earlier that unless he withdrew from the Court and ceased distracting Elizabeth from her foreign suitors he would be removed by the swords of his superiors.

Elizabeth had ordered both men to apologize and forbidden the duel which Dudley proposed to fight with the Duke, but they had remained mortal enemies.

The door of the Queen's room opened and her page of the bedchamber called out: "The Earl of Leicester to the Queen's Majesty!"

Everyone turned and looked as the Earl went in; only Norfolk remained quite still, his eyes fixed on a point on the opposite wall.

Elizabeth was dressed for the evening reception; she dined in public once a day, and then attended a play in the Palace Great Hall, or joined her Court in the dancing which she loved.

She wore a gown of brilliant emerald green, with a petticoat of white satin embroidered with emeralds and pearls; the same jewels were round her neck and blazing in her hair.

She held out both hands to Robert and he kissed them.

"They say Venus came out of the sea," he said, "and looking at you tonight, Madam, I believe them. You should never wear anything but emeralds."

Elizabeth laughed; he could see that she was in high spirits; her pale face was flushed and she stood back, giving him time to admire her costume.

"Then you know what present to give me next. I will wear nothing but emeralds, my fond Leicester, unless you should happen to choose rubies or diamonds instead! However, this time I have something for you. Come here."

She brought him to the cabinet which stood against one wall, and unlocked it herself. When she opened the door he saw a magnificent goblet shining in the recess. It was made of gold, the lid and rim were studded with diamonds, and engraved with his crest, the bear and ragged staff.

She held it out to him, smiling.

"A loving cup," she said. "For you, my Robert, as a reward for playing the lover to someone else."

"I cannot thank you," he said after a moment, "there aren't enough words in the English language. My beloved, I have never seen anything so magnificent in my life."

"It's a compensation," Elizabeth closed the cabinet door and relocked it. He knew that she kept a fabulous ruby in one of the drawers. The jewel was too big to wear, but she liked to take the huge stone out and look at it. It was destined to be set in the Crown when she could be persuaded to part with it. "A compensation for not marrying my cousin in Scotland," she continued.

"You mean the negotiations are broken off?"

"Not yet, but it's only a formality now. That's why I sent for you. Alas, my love, she has decided to resist your impetuous siege, and give her heart to someone else. The Earl of Lennox has just asked permission to go to Scotland. I have given it, and I'd wager that little goblet of yours that his son Darnley will sneak after him in a matter of days. She is about to spit you out, and swallow the true bait."

"Thank God for it," he said quickly. "I wish them joy of each other."

"We'll drink to that."

There was a silver jug of wine already set out for them; he poured some into the splendid goblet and handed it to her.

"No other woman will ever put her lips to that cup," he said.

"Not to the cup of the owner." Elizabeth sipped slowly and he drank from it after her. "Here's health to the Queen of Scots, and health to her bridegroom, may she see nothing beyond his blue eyes! It's my confident hope that she won't; other women haven't, and from all I hear she's so bent on spiting me that she'll fall on his neck the first time they meet."

Dudley looked at her and slowly shook his head.

"I'm no match for you; God knows I can't see how you could let her marry a man with a claim to your throne, however distant. The whole world will say she's outwitted you."

"We'll see what the world says after a year of marriage to that pup," Elizabeth retorted. "We'll see what her nobles and her Reformers say when they find their Consort in the Edinburgh brothels."

"How do you know this when Lethington doesn't?"

"It's my business to know what anyone does who has a claim to my throne, however distant," she mocked. "Cecil has eyes and ears in every Palace and bawdy house in the kingdom. Darnley keeps his pleasures secret, but there are no secrets to be kept from me. He'll ruin my cousin once she gives him rein. There'll be no invasion of England with Darnley riding beside her unless she wants a drunkard in the saddle. I'd go further and say that her nobles will probably murder him before the year is out! "

"You always win, Madam," Robert said slowly. "I know you so well and yet I don't know you at all. There isn't another woman in the world who could have made such a plan and manoeuvred her enemy into carrying it out for her. By God, England should be proud of you! "

"And proud of Cecil, too. I thought of it; he helped me to execute it every step of the way. And he never doubted its success."

For a moment Leicester's face darkened.

"You told me I was the only one who knew."

Elizabeth patted his shoulder.

"I had to say that; knowing how jealous you are of him, I knew you'd make difficulties if you thought he was a party to it. Come now, Robert, take me out into the ante-chambers; I must see Lethington tonight and pretend to be uneasy about Lennox's visit. And I shall find a few words for the Countess of Lennox; they'll be the last she'll hear from me before I put her in the Tower."

At midnight on February 13th, 1565, the people of Edinburgh were brought out of their beds by a strange and terrifying phenomenon. The empty streets were filled with the sound of fighting, as if a ghost army were engaged in combat. There were cries and the clash of swords and the echo of hooves in the deserted squares and alleys, under a freezing cloudless sky. The next morning John Knox climbed into his pulpit at St Giles Cathedral to point out that the phantom omens of war and disaster coincided with the arrival of Lord Henry Darnley in the City.

## Chapter 7

THE two cousins, Henry Darnley and Mary Stuart, met for the first time on February 17th as guests of the Laird of Wemyss. It was deliberately informal because the Scots Queen did not wish to commit herself and give open offence to Elizabeth until she had met the man of whom Lethington spoke so well. They were both nervous; Darnley was unnerved by the presence of his father who blustered and behaved as if the match had already been made; Mary fidgeted and changed her dress twice before she was satisfied. Her feminine vanity was determined to make a personal conquest, for this was the first of all her suitors who had presented himself in person. She had been too occupied with policy to permit her emotions to become involved with any man on an intimate basis; she had no experience of masculine love beyond the sad, abortive relationship with her first husband and the hideous incident with Chatelard which ended on a scaffold. She came to meet Darnley dressed in one of the elegant, severe black velvet gowns which enhanced her graceful figure and exquisite colouring, with a long scarf in the scarlet tartan of the Royal Stuarts pinned from her shoulder to her waist like a sash. The reports of Lethington and his father had not prepared Darnley for the effect of her beauty as she came towards him down the long, cold room in Wemyss' house. He stood very still, his fair face flushing with nerves and excitement. He knew a great deal about women but he had never seen one that moved like the Queen; he had never seen such a complexion matched by that extraordinary hair, as warm and burnished as the autumn leaves on a beech tree, or the brilliant eyes where the same changing colour was repeated. She was certainly the most beautiful and the most unusual woman he had seen in his life.

Mary had not expected him to be so tall. When he was described as handsome, she had no idea of the impression of grace and youth which would meet her that February day.

"Welcome to our kingdom, my Lord. It gives us great pleasure to meet with you at last."

Darnley bowed deeply over her hand and kissed it.

"The pleasure and the honour is mine, your Majesty. You must pardon my confusion; I find that I meet not only the Queen of Scotland, but the Queen of women."

The gallant compliment came easily to him; he had been trained at the Court of one of the most sophisticated sovereigns in Europe. He spoke to Mary as all courtiers addressed his own Queen, Elizabeth. The Queen smiled, and her eyes softened, as if the sun had caught them, changing the hazel to green and blue.

She was prepared for the sort of young men who surrounded her in Scotland, men who had youth and vigour to recommend them, but none of whom matched this divinely handsome, charming youth whose admiration showed so plainly on his face. Mary had never been in love with any man in her life. She was twenty-four, a widow and a virgin; in spite of her training and her rough experience of the past four years, she was as fatally romantic at her father. Within twenty minutes of meeting Henry Darnley, she was lost.

He made an official appearance at Holyrood two days later, and it was obvious to the delighted Lennox that his son was going to be the next King of Scotland. Others, like Murray and Ruthven, a supremely evil man who could never endure the sight of innocent affection without reducing it to his own loathsome level, watched the Queen's courtship of her cousin with suspicion and resentment. For it was Mary who was in love and in pursuit. Her infatuation with Darnley irritated the jealous Scottish Lords, who saw nothing admirable in his English manners and his extravagant clothes; their own sons were more manly, stronger, more truly Scottish than this lanky, pallid youth, with his simpering compliments and affectations. It annoyed them to discover that he was a capable horseman and athlete; he was too exhilarated by his own success and the attentions of Mary to need drink or debauchery to bolster his self-esteem. He had won such an easy victory, and at first he was still rather overwhelmed by the charm and beauty of the prize; he showed only the best side of his character, especially to those most anxious to detect a flaw in him, and to Mary he seemed incapable of a fault.

But soon his unwholesome appetites began to dwell upon the prospect of physical possession, and Mary's ignorance inflamed his vanity with the desire to arouse passions which had never woken in her. The poisonous inferiority which festered beneath his polished exterior became suddenly obsessed with the idea of completely subjugating his cousin; this was instantly fused with his personal ambitions which he imagined could be indulged without hindrance from anyone and with her ardent complicity.

With her, too, he was clever, being gentle and refined in the initial stages of their relationship; it gave him a perverted satisfaction to reverse his normal mode of conduct until the time came when he would be entitled to use her as he liked. He watched her headlong, helpless infatuation with him and preened like a peacock. By the time his conceit had got the better of his caution, Mary was too blind with love for him to notice anything.

Fundamentally she was a creature of emotion, though the emotions had been schooled by necessity and the discipline imposed on a Princess of Royal blood. Men like Lethington and her Guise uncles had been able to muzzle her temper and moderate her pride only so long as her personal passions were left sleeping. But now Darnley woke them; Ruthven spoke poisonously of her lust, sneering at her insistence on an early marriage. And if it was love that Mary felt, it was the lust of Darnley which began to permeate the atmosphere between them, offending even Lethington who loved her and had hoped for so much from the match.

By the summer the real implications of Darnley as Consort were obvious to everyone except Mary. He was so swollen with self-importance that he began insulting her Lords, taking particular delight in baiting the dour, sensitive Lord James, whose resentment of his sister was inflamed still more by the arrogance and pretensions of her future husband. He took liberties with the impeccable ladies surrounding her for the pleasure of seeing their embarrassment on their mistress's behalf. There were times when the Queen saw him emptying his glass and lolling rudely in his chair, his face flushed and disagreeable. She made his youth an excuse; he was only nineteen and probably homesick, and if his head was a little turned, then she was to blame and not Darnley.

As soon as she sensed opposition, her pride fastened on to the marriage with the obstinacy for which the Stuarts were famous. She had found a man she loved who was of Royal blood, perfectly suited by inheritance and upbringing to be her husband, and those who attempted to dissuade her or speak against him only seemed to be trying to thwart her happiness.

Lethington was the first casualty among her friends. He blamed himself bitterly for his part in bringing Darnley to her notice and he almost tore his hair in despair when he realized that Mary was incapable of recognizing a mistake and retreating from it while there was time.

If any members of the Reformed Church were prepared to accept the marriage, Darnley alienated the mildest of them by flaunting his Catholicism and encouraging the Queen to do the same. The English ambassador Randolph wrote to Elizabeth that Lord Darnley was making so many enemies that Mary might yet be forced to abandon her intentions, and Elizabeth chose that moment to order Darnley and Lord Lennox to return to England under pain of her displeasure.

As if she had only just realized what Mary was going to do, Elizabeth wrote her a personal letter, calculated to irritate the most patient recipient, warning her not to attempt to marry an English subject without her permission, and protesting that the Earl of Leicester was ready to travel to Scotland and offer himself without further delay. Mary's answer was to proclaim Darnley King of Scotland and marry him in Holyrood Chapel on July 29th. The resentments, anxieties and jealousies which had been smouldering in the hearts of Lord James and his associate Protestants, the powerful Duke of Argyll, the Earl of Rothes, the Lords Glencairn and Boyd and many others, were fanned by the conduct of Darnley into open rebellion within a few months. Their influence with Mary was overridden in a way that gave them no alternative but to overthrow their enemy by violence and compel the Queen to give them the religious assurances which had always been the condition of her reign and their support.

They were no longer received at her Court; their advice was ignored, their possessions endangered by the new King who was fond of threatening to annex their lands. And the Queen who had managed them all so cleverly, especially her half-brother at times when he had less cause for complaint than at that moment, now lost her temper in an interview where the bitterest reproaches and accusations were exchanged between them. She had never liked him, and now she felt strong enough to show it; he and his friends were meddling in her affairs and criticizing her husband, and much of her vehemence was due to the fact that the passionate love-match had developed a frightening and distasteful aspect which she hardly dared admit to herself.

She parted from Lord James with the injunction to obey her as his sovereign, or she would forget the treatment due to him as her brother. By the following spring, James had mustered a force of armed men, in company with Argyll and many of the other Protestant Lords, and refused Mary's order to submit.

The Queen replied by recalling Lord Bothwell from his exile, and gathering an army which she placed under his command. Urged on by Bothwell who was longing to revenge himself upon Moray and his enemies, and by Darnley who saw the whole issue as a God-sent means of removing the last restraint upon his conduct to the Queen and his interference in the country, Mary declared her brother and his followers, traitors and outlaws, and ordered her army into the field against them.

It was a particularly fine summer in England. Elizabeth woke in her room at Windsor Castle to a succession of warm and lovely days, days full of peace and serenity, where her ordered, prosperous kingdom seemed to laze under a benevolent sun, and she amused herself by reading the reports of the war and turmoil in Scotland to Cecil as they sat together on the terrace of the Castle, looking down on to the town below.

They shared the success of their plan like two lovers, entranced with the secret; they spoke the same language and almost thought the same thoughts, united by an understanding which had suddenly reached a state of perfection. Cecil had come to the point where he considered her ability almost inhuman; certainly he had forgotten that he had ever mistrusted her or feared weakness because she was a woman. His work obsessed him, but his work and his relationship with Elizabeth were indivisible; he could never imagine himself conferring with another sovereign, even the idea of a King was repugnant to him, though he still disliked the principle of feminine rule. To Cecil, she was above comparison. His devotion to her was more passionate in its intensity than any fleshly love. She exhilarated his spirits, literally exalting him in his own eyes because of the trust she placed in him and the extraordinary satisfaction he derived from their intimacy. She could torment him or flatter him or disconcert him, and she did all three, but she gave him the feeling that he held a particular place in her heart which was founded on his own merits, and that in that place he was unique. His wife had once complained that she had lost him more completely to the Queen than to a mistress. Cecil had not spoken to her for a week, even after she apologized.

He was jealous of the younger, gayer men who surrounded her; he regarded their attempts to flatter her as an insult. The suggestion that anyone less than a King or a King's heir should dream of marrying her infuriated him, and he was furious that afternoon when they sat playing chequers on the sunny Castle terrace. He had been prepared to tolerate Leicester in the role she had allotted him; he had restrained his objection to the title and to the money she gave him on the assumption that it was part of her intrigue against Mary Stuart. But only three hours earlier Leicester had come to his room and made a plain proposal that he should advise his marriage to Elizabeth as the final coup to the disaster of Mary's union with Darnley. If Elizabeth married and bore children, that would dispose of the Scots Queen and her claim and leave her completely at the mercy of her enemies. Cecil had not trusted himself to answer directly. He temporized, controlling his anger and suspicion, and Leicester left him imagining that he had been clever in approaching his principal opponent first.

" You seem very distracted, Cecil. It's your move."

He pushed his chair back from the table and looked at Elizabeth.

" I was thinking that the Archduke Charles of Austria might be worth considering, Madam."

Elizabeth sighed in exasperation.

" Not another husband for me, for God's sake. I've told you I don't intend to marry. If you want one reason, remember my cousin across the Border—marriage hasn't brought her much benefit! Now get on with the game."

" As much benefit as it would bring you if you married Robert Leicester," he said suddenly.

Elizabeth's eyes narrowed.

" What the devil are you talking about? "

" He came to me today and suggested it; he seemed to think you might agree. His whole tone was so confident that I was thoroughly alarmed. I thought all that matter was settled between you."

"So did I," she said sharply. "Page, take this board away! Now, what exactly did master Robert say to you?"

"He said I should counsel you to do it. He said you should have a husband and heirs, and he proposed himself. I gave no answer one way or another. I had to ask you first."

"By the God above," she said, "his earldom has gone to his head . . . he's heard too many state secrets and now he thinks to direct an intrigue of his own. . . . How dare he mention such a thing to you behind my back!"

"He said you'd be wise to choose him," Cecil continued, deliberately goading her temper. "I did point out that you were not in such desperate need of a man as he seemed to think."

"I'll leave him in no doubt of it." She stood up suddenly; her face was white with anger. "I shall find my Lord Leicester and perhaps remind him that I can put him back in the dust where he was when I found him. You may leave me, Cecil. I will have no master here and only one mistress. If he has forgotten that, I shall have to teach him all over again."

Leicester listened to her for the first half an hour without losing his temper. He hardly spoke because she gave him no opportunity to interrupt her. She began with calm, the kind of deadly, acid calm which disguised a state of furious temper. She asked him how he liked his new estates and his even newer title; she remarked on his rich clothes and pointed out the pearl earring she had given him. She appraised him and his possessions like a man reminding his mistress of the payments made to her, and then suddenly the quiet, sarcastic voice rose to a shout, and she told him she had a good mind to strip him naked like the beggar he was and throw him out into the Windsor streets. If he dared to approach Cecil or even think in his miserable heart of marrying her again that was exactly what she would have done with him.

He had never seen her so angry; her face was ashen and her eyes were blazing through the narrowed lids. No past quarrel had been as bitter as this one. He was pale himself, and a nerve in his cheek was throbbing. He had no idea how he had stood and listened to her insults without striking her. But he knew that he would never dare, as he had not dared the day she placed him under house arrest for Amy's murder. He was afraid of her, but he was not naturally a coward.

"You deny me everything," he burst out, using the only excuse he had. "Not only marriage but the rights of a man with a woman who says she loves him! Give me those, and I won't think of marriage to get them! You taunt me with the things you have given me, as if that was compensation for sitting at your feet like a trained dog. May I remind you, Madam, that my father was the Duke of Northumberland when you were still plain Lady Elizabeth!"

She moved so quickly he was taken by surprise; her right hand caught him across the face so hard that he stepped back. For a moment they stood close, glaring into each other's eyes, quivering with hatred like two animals waiting to spring.

"The crows picked your father's head," she spat at him.

"As they picked your mother's," he retorted. As he said it, the thought raced through his mind that he had ruined himself with those five words. But she did not strike him again as he half expected. She stared at him and then her eyes opened wider; they were cold and empty; suddenly without rage.

"No man in England would have dared say such a thing to me."

"No man will soon dare to say anything to you but what you want to hear. But don't count me among them. I make an honest proposal to marry you, and you spit at me like an adder. Take one of your foreign suitors, marry some half-wit German who'll climb into your bed as a duty, and treat you as King Philip did your sister! Take anyone you like, and by God I wish them joy of you!"

She turned her back on him deliberately; she scornfully, almost casually, dismissed and sentenced him at the same time without turning round.

"You are exiled. Go to your house at Richmond. *My* house, which I gave you. Stay there and think on your presumption and ingratitude."

When the door closed and she was alone, Elizabeth turned slowly as if she were tired, tired and much older than her thirty-two years. She went to her chair of state, the tall-backed chair covered with carving and gilt where she received official visitors in her Presence Chamber, and sat down in it in an attitude of despair. The room was unnaturally quiet; the bright sunshine streamed through the lattice windows, making patterns on the floor. Elizabeth leaned back against the chair; her head ached—just like her sister when she was upset, she thought irrelevantly. Mary was always tormented with pain of some kind; toothache, headache, pains that ran through her limbs, and above all the pain that nagged at her heart, the pain of memories and of loving a husband who did not love her.

For the first time in her life Elizabeth felt the onset of emotional pain, keener and more terrifying than mere physical agony. She sat with her hands gripping the arms of her state chair, and felt the oppressive silence of the empty room with all its grandeur and the symbolic shadow cast by the velvet canopy over her head.

Robert had gone. Robert had tried to intrigue with Cecil— what a fool, she thought contemptuously, what an ass's head he must have to play those tricks with the Secretary—he had actually tried to resurrect the old conflicts and problems and tempt her to jeopardize her independence. Just when their relationship was really satisfactory and she could indulge her affection for him without stint, when she could parade to the world as a woman with a dozen suitors and one constant lover, without having to commit herself with the men abroad or the man at home beside her—at the moment when she had been enjoying the most peaceful and relaxed period in her reign, Leicester—or Dudley, she corrected herself angrily—Dudley had to dare make an issue of his ambitions, bringing all her old suspicions and conflicts to life. She repeated his crimes to herself, trying to revive her anger as an antidote to the quiet and the loneliness which closed in upon her in the lofty room. He had gone into exile, with the last sting of her reminder about the Richmond estate in his ears. He was gone and she was right to send him; but he would never know how that insane remark about her mother's execution had saved him; it had brought them to the same level, a man and woman quarrelling all the more bitterly because of the closeness of the ties which bound them. In her own way she loved him; Elizabeth's cheeks were wet with tears. It was years since she had cried last, and she could not even remember the occasion —she thought it was her first night as a prisoner in the Tower when life had seemed so sweet and death so revolting and inevitable. Now she wept for Robert, and for herself, because she was the Queen and she would never marry him, and she was still a woman whom her position condemned to send him away and punish herself more than she punished him.

" Madam."

She raised one hand to shield her wet eyes, and quickly wiped the stains of tears away. Lady Dacre was standing in the doorway; she curtsied and fidgeted shyly.

"Madam, I have been searching for you everywhere. . . . My Lord Sussex begs an audience; he has received news from Scotland."

Elizabeth leant forward and said very loudly and distinctly in a voice Lady Dacre hardly recognized, it was so hoarse and choked:

"You can tell my Lord Sussex to go straight to hell. And take the whole of Scotland with him."

James Stuart, Earl of Moray, stood in the smallest ante-chamber of the Queen's Palace at Greenwich, warming his hands in front of the fire. It was a cold, sombre room, with stone floors and heavy tapestries and curtains, which closed out what little was left of the dull October daylight. The mist rising from the river had pearled the window panes; it was a different kind of cold to the bitter Scottish climate which never affected James like this miserable pervading dampness which made the clothes he wore seem chilled and clammy.

He had been in England for nearly a month after fleeing from Mary's forces over the Border. The rest of the rebel Lords were in England with him, but not in London. He had been elected to go to the Queen of England and reproach her for not sending them the men and money she had promised and to remind her of her obligations to them. She had encouraged their rebellion against Mary; her agents had made it clear that a successful overthrow of their Queen would place Elizabeth in their debt and she was ready to give them material support. She had sent some money; enough to raise their hopes but too little to have much effect. When Queen Mary's soldiers defeated them and chased them across the Scottish border in a running fight, the rebels fully expected the Queen of England to declare herself and send them reinforcements. Instead James received a note forbidding him to approach any closer to London and to wait on the Queen's pleasure.

He was not accustomed to such action from a woman; he had never been given an order by his sister Mary until he actually raised arms against her, and it never occurred to him to obey Elizabeth and stay away. Women did not command men, whether they were Queens or not. Certainly no woman commanded him. He set out at once for London and presented his petition to see the Queen.

As the shadows outside the windows lengthened, Moray began to walk up and down the narrow room, his hands behind his back in the attitude which his sister Mary knew so well. He had never been kept waiting by her and she was his sovereign, not a foreigner like this woman. . . . Mary had always been polite and considerate as befitted her membership of the inferior sex; he could still hardly believe that she had so far debased herself as to mount up and ride after him like a man with a pistol in her belt. She had no sense of fitness; possibly she felt impelled to make up for her miserable husband's cowardice by the unseemly display of masculine spirit. Whatever the reason Moray felt no admiration for her, only hatred; hatred because he had challenged her at last and she had met his challenge and beaten him soundly on his own terms. She had spurned his advice and given herself to a contemptible libertine who drank and whored behind her back; but he did not pity Mary, because he considered it a just retribution for her own obstinacy. He pitied himself instead; his fate was to stand by while a woman degraded the Crown and abused the rights of her subjects, a woman so unfit to be Queen that she had fallen under the influence of a young chamberer whose appetites she couldn't even match after a year of marriage.

At that moment the doors opened. Behind the figure of Elizabeth's Gentleman Usher, Moray saw a room full of light and people.

"Lord Moray to the Queen's Majesty!"

He stepped into the Presence Chamber, finding himself facing a semi-circle of men; two of them dressed in the fashion he recognized as French. He knew instantly that they were official representatives, he knew that the others were Councillors or noblemen, and he saw them all in a second before he came face to face with the Queen of England.

She was dressed in black; deep black, unrelieved by any colour except the rainbow flash of some enormous diamonds which clustered on her breast, catching a festoon of pearls. He had not been sure what to expect; she was much older than Mary, his sister, who also wore black, but never looked like that. She was extremely pale, but it was a pallor he could only associate with stone, a stone face with hard black eyes and narrow lips, painted bright scarlet. A face which was sculptured, too cold and sharp for beauty, not in the least like the Queen his sister, who was so feminine and lovely. He had never seen a woman who looked like Elizabeth Tudor with her extraordinary piercing eyes and her outrageously red hair.

"How dare you come to London when I forbade it!"

He felt the colour coming into his face. A dry voice interrupted after that single, ringing sentence.

"It is customary to kneel in the presence of the Queen."

The speaker was standing very close to her; he was a quietly-dressed man with round shoulders and a face which was prematurely aged. He had the keenest green eyes that Moray had ever seen in his life. They bore him to his knees like points of steel.

"Don't chide him, Cecil. Don't you know the Scots have no respect for Majesty? My Lord Moray here is in rebellion against his sovereign, our own dear cousin Queen Mary. By God, my Lord, I wonder you show your face before me with such a crime on your conscience!"

"It is no crime, Madam, to rebel against tyranny."

His voice was shaking with anger; he was so unprepared for the attack that he could not think of anything to say after that one retort, and some instinct bit back the obvious reference to her own promises and subsidies to the rebels.

There was something in her face and in the faces of the men beside her, which warned him not to say that.

"M. de Foix——" the Queen turned to one of the Frenchmen and pointed at Moray. "You are my witness that this audience has been forced upon me. I forbade Lord Moray to enter London.

"You are a traitor, my Lord. You have led a rebellion against your lawful Prince and I assure you, that as her cousin and sister Queen, I do not succour Queen Mary's enemies."

Moray knew at last what she was doing. This was a play, arranged for the benefit of the French who must have known she was encouraging Mary's rebels. She was making him the scapegoat and he had to accept it. If he betrayed her, he read the promise in those reptile eyes that he would never leave her capital alive.

"My friends and I have rebelled against the excesses of her husband, Lord Darnley, Madam. The Queen dealt fairly and was fairly treated until she made this marriage."

"Husband and wife are indivisible," Elizabeth said coldly. "In any case, it is not for a mere subject to examine the conduct of his Prince. You are a rebel, Lord Moray. You owe the same allegiance to your Queen's husband as to the Queen herself."

"He will be the ruin of Scotland, and the Queen!" Moray exclaimed bitterly.

"You are not the saviour of either," Elizabeth's eyes gleamed at him. "You have broken your oath of loyalty to your sovereign. You have defied my express command and dared to present yourself brazenly before me. I warn you, my Lord, you may find yourself a prisoner in England, instead of an exile. Now, gentlemen, if you will leave us, I desire to question Lord Moray more closely about the affair in Scotland and the part he has played in it."

Moray stood up and watched the French ambassador kiss her hand and walk past him with a look of contempt; the English Councillors saluted her, including the man she had addressed as Cecil, the man who had told him to kneel. He was interested to see the most famous of her advisers—interested and surprised at the insignificance of his appearance.

They were alone at last and then Elizabeth turned to him.

"Well done, my Lord. You took your rating like a man. I'm sorry I had to deliver it, but I think the French ambassador was impressed. We must make sure our alliance is a secret."

"It is almost a secret from us too," Moray said sourly. "We waited for the soldiers and the money you promised us, and nothing came. We flee to your protection and you try to avoid seeing me. What am I to tell those who sent me, Madam?"

"Tell them," her voice grated, "that they should have picked a better mannered spokesman. Watch your tongue, my friend; I'm not Queen Mary! As far as my promises are concerned the explanations are due from you. You began this rebellion, and you bungled it. You ran like a pack of curs from my cousin when she brought a few troops against you, and you have the impudence to expect me to throw good money after bad. Tell your fellow rebels this; the best thing you can all do is to make peace with my cousin and try to redeem your failure by some other means. I will intercede for you; if you utter one word of our dealings on your eventual return to Scotland, I shall advise Queen Mary that the best way to kill a long serpent is to cut off the head. Farewell, Lord Moray. Be thankful that she is your mistress instead of me. She may be persuaded to forgive you."

She turned her back on him and walked out of the room into her own apartments before he could answer. As he left the Presence Chamber a page approached him.

"Sir William Cecil sent me to conduct you to your horses, my Lord."

Moray followed him without a word. He found himself in a small courtyard, and was about to protest that this was not the way he had entered Greenwich, when the page pointed out a magnificent chestnut gelding, its rein held by one of four mounted gentlemen.

"Sir William begs you to accept this mount; your own has been too hard ridden to take you on the journey back. These gentlemen of the Queen's household will see you safely on your road, my Lord."

Moray nodded, his practical mind evaluating the splendid horse and its equally fine equipment. It was the first indication that Elizabeth's powerful Secretary was his friend.

Leicester was still exiled from the Court; he had moved to his own very luxurious house at Wanstead after an interval, and his life was not as isolated or as dull as Elizabeth liked to imagine. He had many visitors because no one believed that the Queen would keep up their quarrel, and it was a good opportunity to ingratiate themselves with the Earl against the time when he returned to his former position of power. He hunted and held evening parties, and he complained steadily that his separation from the Queen was affecting his health in the hope that she would hear it and relent. He gave no sign of the intense resentment he felt for the way she had treated him and for his present humiliating position. No word of reproach or complaint escaped him, but inwardly he was convulsed with rage and anxiety. Elizabeth made no move, showed no sign of recalling and forgiving him. The time passed and Dudley's nerves grew ragged and his sense of grievance increased. He heard that she was gay and surrounded by men eager to take his place, and that she spoke of him contemptuously if she mentioned him at all. He had no redress, no means of revenge and he had never thought of taking a mistress. He could satisfy himself at Wanstead or anywhere else without risking discovery;

there were women in his household who had accommodated him at some time or another and been paid for it afterwards by his steward, but for the last six years he had never made love to a woman of his own rank.

He could hardly believe that the woman who lay beside him in his bed that autumn morning was truly flesh and blood. In the half light she was almost a parody of that other woman who had given him so much and then ruthlessly snatched it all away; red hair, dark eyes, the same rather deep voice, but softer, more voluptuous, less commanding, and the face was different. It was a round face with smooth cheeks and a pretty nose instead of an imperious beak, a face that was sensual and feminine. He knew her quite well; that was what surprised him when she first made advances; he had talked to Lettice, Countess of Essex, many times at Court and thought her an attractive woman who was probably as light as her reputation. When she came among his many visitors he was pleased; when she accepted his invitation to stay and dine, he was not suspicious. When she suddenly came into his arms and offered to comfort him for Elizabeth's heartlessness, he had responded before he realized what he was doing. She was charming and it was impossible to rebuff her advances without ill-grace, and now he was Lady Essex's lover. She turned over and smiled at him; she had a curious slow smile like a contented cat.

"What are you thinking, Robert?"

"I was wondering what will happen to us when the Queen finds out."

"There is no reason why she should," Lettice Essex said. "There is no reason why anyone should know. We were discreet last night, we can go on being discreet."

"Go on?" Leicester raised himself on one elbow. "God's death, aren't you even nervous of her?"

"Terrified—if she discovers anything. But then my husband wouldn't be pleased with me either. But I still want to go on, my dear ungallant Robert. I am quite dementedly in love with you, and I have been for some time. This was my first opportunity to get near you without Her Majesty's proprietary eye watching every move, and it was a marvellous success. I think you'll agree to that." She touched his cheek with one finger and her eyes shone at him in the half-light.

"I don't think you'll turn me away," she continued. "I think you are man enough to enjoy yourself without trembling at the mention of a woman who won't perform the same little services for you herself, legally or otherwise."

"How are you so sure?" he asked her, wondering why he made no attempt to stop her hand in its cunning caress of his face and neck. He did not love her; he was too obsessed by Elizabeth to feel any tenderness for another woman, but he was not incapable of desire, and Lettice was not a bought relief. She was experienced and she had a natural talent for sensual practice.

"How do you know what the Queen refuses and what she grants?" he demanded.

Lettice laughed outright.

"Oh, dear God, how vain men are! I never thought she was your mistress for a single moment when everyone was tongue wagging and scandalizing. I just could not see Elizabeth Tudor like this. And now I know that I was right. You are woefully out of practice, my Lord. You will be so grateful that I found you, after a while."

She leant over and kissed his mouth. He should have stopped her, but after a moment he returned her kiss. When he fell asleep later, she slipped away to her room.

She joined his other guests that morning, and then returned to London. She had arranged to come down again within three days on the pretext of visiting a cousin who lived close to Wanstead.

That evening Leicester composed a long and humble letter to the Queen asking for her forgiveness. It was the first time since their quarrel that he had approached her personally; he had done something which he knew she would never forgive, and he felt able to humble himself, because he had injured her and intended to continue doing so. Once again he had fallen into a basic error of judgment when he supposed that the love of Elizabeth, the generosity and the trust and the marks of affection which he received without stint, meant that she would ever wake beside him as an ordinary woman. At that moment of honest reflection he admitted that even if he had never disposed of Amy, there was something in Elizabeth that placed her beyond the reach of a mundane relationship, something over and above the normal feminine requirements from which Queens were not expected to be immune. He saw her at last as curiously isolated, not only by her own choice but by the circumstances of her life and her own character. She could not share, much less submit. She had always been alone; she had paid lip service to her stepmothers and her sister Mary without loving any of them even when she was a child. He remembered her so clearly as a little girl, ready to play with anyone who asked her but never really joining in. He was the only one who had come close to her then. They had played together and fought like uninhibited little animals, and the ten-year-old Princess admitted him to an intimacy never achieved by anyone else. He had come close to her again when they were adults. But not close enough. If she hadn't been Queen of England, she would undoubtedly have been dead. There was no middle course for Elizabeth. He knew then that he would never marry her; but his mistake had been human and his attempts were not as presumptuous as she made them out. Only she was strange; strange and unpredictable until one accepted her as different from other women and ceased expecting her to think and feel and act as if she were fallible and sensual and human like Lettice Essex.

He no longer resented having to write that letter, admitting his faults and begging to be taken back. He was suddenly reconciled to the future and he could see it clearly for the first time in years. He would go on living for Elizabeth, taking from her and giving exactly what she asked in return. He would be powerful and honoured and safe with her as long as he did what she wanted. And on the other side of his life he had already admitted the necessity of someone like the Countess of Essex.

# Chapter 8

THEY were reconciled, as everyone, Cecil included, expected they would be. Elizabeth was so obviously unhappy and so difficult to deal with that her Ministers were driven to intercede on Leicester's behalf. She was softened by his letter of abject apology, but she indulged in the luxury of postponing his forgiveness a little longer until he feigned an illness and asked to be readmitted to her favour as he feared that he was dying. If the Queen saw through the ruse, she pretended to herself as well as to others and hurried down to Wanstead to revive the invalid. She found him sitting in his room, dressed in a bedgown, with his personal physician persuading him to try and eat. The doctor and his body servant were sent away. Nobody dared to smile when he emerged an hour later, fully dressed and in the best of spirits and took the Queen for a long ride round Wanstead Park.

He was surprised and shaken, when he returned to his duties at Court, to find a particularly handsome young man had entered her circle of intimates during his absence and established himself so firmly that Leicester was unable to oust him. Sir Thomas Heneage was several years younger than Elizabeth, but he was witty, intelligent and amiable. He played cards well, but not too well, so that the Queen always won; he danced gracefully, and was an accomplished musician. He was good enough at all these things to compete with Leicester, and his presence at the evening receptions and the hunting parties gave Leicester the chance to sneak into Lettice Essex's bed whenever he could escape the Queen's vigilance, and he justified his infidelity by pointing out her familiarities with the younger man. He did not know how far the verbal love-play went between them; he wondered in agonies of jealousy whether Heneage enjoyed the intimacies which had once been his privilege, and which were never invited again after his return. He hated Heneage and he hated Lettice when she tormented him with gossip about Elizabeth and her new favourite. He quarrelled as savagely with his mistress as he used to do with the Queen, but he returned to her again and again because no woman had ever given him such flattering proof of his own manhood, and, faced by Elizabeth's unbending frigidity, he was in desperate need of that proof. They were reconciled but it was an uneasy peace, poisoned by suspicions which were not only on his side as he supposed; Elizabeth was sharp-tongued and irritable with him, pettish if he showed the least sign of independence, affectionate within her chosen limits and then cold as ice. He could feel that a storm even more violent than the last was gathering over his head and he felt helpless to avert it. It was about to break when Elizabeth decided to visit his sister, Mary Sidney, who had apartments at Court but no official post, because she had caught smallpox after nursing the Queen through the disease and was terribly disfigured.

Elizabeth was tired and tense when she came into Lady Sidney's room. She had a sudden urge to seek out someone whom she could trust to defend Robert, someone to whom she could pour out her bitterness and suspicion and know that they were nearly impartial in as much as Mary loved her brother and had loved her Queen enough to carry the marks of it forever on her tragic face. Even at that moment it hurt Elizabeth to look into the ruin of her beauty, at the ravaged features, made uglier still by the contrast of her large, luminous brown eyes.

"My poor Sidney—you shouldn't stay shut up in here; it's a clear day—perfect for riding. I shan't visit you for long, and then I order you to go out and take some exercise—enjoy yourself a little!"

Lady Sidney smiled.

"I'm very happy where I am, Madam. And happier still that you always find time to come and comfort me. God bless you for your goodness. Even my own husband is too occupied to waste more than an hour or so looking at this face; and I don't blame him."

"Well I do!" Elizabeth snapped. She made a note in her mind to remind Sir Henry Sidney not to neglect his wife if he valued his place at Court. "And anyway today I come to you for comfort," she added, sitting in the chair Mary had drawn up for her.

"Your Majesty could never need comfort from me," Lady Sidney said gently. "But you know I'd give my life for you if you needed it."

"You gave your fair looks," Elizabeth said slowly. "That's more than life from a woman. I do need you. I need you to answer me one question with absolute truth and without fear. Will you?"

"Ask it, Madam."

The Queen turned round and looked at her.

"Is Robert betraying me with Lady Essex?"

There was a moment of silence before Mary Sidney answered.

"Why do you ask me that question, Madam?"

"Because you are the only person I can trust not to say 'yes' because they hate Robert, or 'no' because they're afraid of me. Is he?"

"Yes," Lady Sidney said quietly. "Yes, I believe he is."

"I knew it." Elizabeth got up; she stood in the middle of the room, her hands clenching into fists. "Now I'm going to ask you another question, no—two questions. Why did he do it, and what in Jesus' name am I going to do with him?"

"He did it," his sister answered, "because you gave him too much opportunity. Robert is very proud, Madam, especially so where you're concerned. He always thought you'd marry him; he used to say so and I used to tell him not to be a fool; but he would have it. He would have it that you loved him and would make up your mind one day. Now he knows you never will—so I suppose he fell a victim to Lettice at a weak moment, and he feels free to deceive you because you have disappointed him. I'm not excusing him; God knows I haven't much sympathy with infidelity; and God knows how many beds Henry has been in and out of since I caught the smallpox. But you asked me why, and I have told you what I think. Truthfully, Madam, and not to spare Robert."

"And what do I do?" Elizabeth asked her. "Can you tell me that too?"

"No." Lady Sidney shook her head. "I could only compare you with myself, Madam, and that would be ridiculous. I know how unhappy I should be without Henry, even though I see so little of him. So I have chosen the lesser of the two evils and I accept him as he is. What you do, depends upon how much my brother means to you. And whether it is possible for someone like you, Madam, to take the easy way of an ordinary woman, and look through your fingers as I do."

"How much does he mean to me?" Elizabeth repeated the words slowly. "If I could answer that I'd know so many things. . . . I was wretched when he was at Wanstead. I had Tom Heneage and half a dozen others and a life so full I hardly had time to sleep, but I was bored and I was lonely. I could tear his eyes out when we quarrel and we only quarrel when he tries to marry me and force me into something which I know is impossible and disastrous for us both. He is an ambitious man, your brother. I wouldn't give a farthing piece for my own life if he was ever in a position to dispute for my crown."

"Our father was the same," Mary Sidney said. "He pursued power as some men pursue women; sometimes I think the letch is stronger. Robert is what you say, and more; I know him very well and he is just like father. They could both beguile the birds off the trees when they wanted to be charming, and they could cast off their own flesh and blood to further their ambitions. My other brother, Guildford, married a Queen of England, and they cut off his head an hour before hers. I used to remind Robert of that too. But Robert will never threaten you, Madam, simply because you are too strong and too clever to let him. You can afford Robert, and others like him, you know that, and he knows that. He knows that he is no match for you, and perhaps that is another reason why he likes to see himself through the eyes of a stupid harlot like Lady Essex."

"You advise me to look through my fingers," Elizabeth said at last.

"I advise you to suit yourself, Madam. If Robert means happiness to you, then keep him. After all, very few women love saints, or want them. If you can cast him off and not regret him, then do that. But give me your word that you will never tell him you discussed it with me. If he knew I had answered that first question of yours as I did, I believe he'd kill me."

"He will never know," Elizabeth said. "So I'm afraid he will never be as grateful to you as he should be. If I hadn't talked to you, I think I would have certainly sent him to the Tower in the end. Now, I shall—look through my fingers."

She came forward quickly and resting one hand on Lady Sidney's shoulder, she bent and kissed her ravaged cheek.

"I am doubly your debtor, my dear Sidney. I thank you with all my heart."

"It was good of you, Sir William, to provide me with such a fine horse."

Cecil shrugged at Lord James sitting opposite him; they were alone in Cecil's private rooms at Nonsuch Palace, the favourite country residence of Henry VIII before he acquired Hampton Court, and a retreat which Elizabeth used during the early spring.

"A small gift, Lord Moray; I'm not much of a horseman myself but I'm a competent judge."

"I feel you are that at everything you undertake," Moray said slowly. He had been looking hard at Cecil for the last ten minutes without being able to extend his judgment of him any further than when he saw him first in the Queen's ante-chamber. Quiet and deliberate in speech and manner, dressed as soberly as Lord Moray himself, yet resistant as steel, and probably as sharp if he were roused.

"I do my best," Cecil answered pleasantly. "I serve an exacting mistress, my Lord, who spares neither herself nor her servants. The Queen of England expects efficiency; I try to see that she receives it from me at least."

"She is very fortunate," Moray said sourly. The story of his reception and the rebuke she had administered had travelled through Europe, thanks to the French Ambassador; Moray could never forgive her for that deliberate humiliation, but he hated her more for the acidity she showed him when they were alone. He abhorred her; he particularly abhorred his position as an exile in her country, and he also disliked the country and the people. He hated the weather, the laxity in speech and morals which was evident everywhere among all classes of society; there was a hotch-potch of religious observance, differing in every parish, an overpowerful middle class and an aristocracy devoted to the flesh pots and so effeminized by their Queen's pernicious vanity and influence, that he swore he could hardly tell the men from the women. He longed, with almost physical pain, for the clean, bleak air of Scotland. But he had not yet found a compromise with his half-sister Mary.

"I wish to God the Queen of Scots showed the good sense of Queen Elizabeth," he said. "But then she would never have married that cur and found herself in her present position; at the cur's mercy, without my support and the support of my friends whom she drove out of the country!"

"We hear that she is pregnant," Cecil remarked. That news had prompted him to invite this unprepossessing Scot to Nonsuch for a private talk and a reassessment of the situation.

Moray nodded.

"She is, and God knows what the offspring of such a match will be; that is if the rumours are untrue and the child *is* Darnley's."

The pale eyes narrowed for a second.

"What rumours, my Lord?"

"If you haven't heard them," Moray said bitterly, "I may as well repeat them in their less lewd form. My half-sister is very fond of music; it's a habit which always distressed me, but it was the result of her education in France. She kept her private musicians and two years ago she engaged an Italian as one of her singers. His name was Rizzio; you never saw an uglier creature, crooked as a stick and sly as a rat. I needn't tell you that my Lord Darnley singled him out for special attention. The Queen had lost all her powers of judgment or even decorum in those early days; whoever my Lord Darnley favoured was immediately admitted into her circle."

"Am I correct," Cecil interrupted, "if I say that Queen Mary has a secretary called Rizzio?"

"The same man," Moray said grimly. "He has insinuated himself so far with her that she has placed him in that office, and shows him such tokens of friendship that my Lord her husband now hates him as heartily as he once liked him."

"And the Queen, your sister, now dislikes her husband as much as she once loved him, I hear," Cecil said.

"Providence has punished her," Moray said with satisfaction. "She sees him at last as all the things I warned her; a drunken lecher without respect for God or man. I hear he has treated her shamefully in spite of the child."

His tone implied that whatever Mary was suffering, it was no more than she deserved for rejecting his advice.

"Then she should be ready to recall you, my Lord," Cecil suggested.

"Ha!" Moray gave a short, angry laugh. "You misjudge my sister if you imagine that policy plays any part in her government! She is as vindictive against me and the other Protestant Lords as ever—adamant against our returning to Scotland. She listens to nobody and nothing now but the dictates of her own intemperate nature and the advice of that Italian snake. Maitland of Lethington was no friend of mine but even he has no influence over her any more. So now the time has come for other methods. And that's why I have come to you, Sir William, because I believe that you are friendly to us, and that you should know what is going to be done."

"I'm flattered." Cecil betrayed no excitement; he folded his hands calmly. "What *is* going to be done? " he asked.

"We've been in contact with Darnley," Moray said abruptly, "or rather he has been in contact with us. Like all curs he wants someone else to bite his enemy for him. He has let it be known that he is prepared to abandon the Queen and join with us. His price is the removal of David Rizzio and his own proclamation as King of Scotland. Our friends in Edinburgh— and by God they've grown in the past year—are prepared to carry out the business and restrain the Queen until I return to Scotland. I need hardly assure you that neither she nor Darnley will be allowed absolute authority; my sister may be permitted limited powers as Queen—he will be lucky if he remains as he is."

"My congratulations," Cecil said. "When you speak of the removal of Rizzio, I presume that you intend to dispose of the Catholic faction in Scotland at the same time and establish the power of the Protestant nobility once and for all."

"We do," Moray said. "My first action will be to insist that my sister's child shall be baptized in the Protestant rite."

"It would have to be, if it is ever to succeed to the throne of England," Cecil murmured.

The child was an insuperable barrier to Moray's ambition to seize the throne from Mary; Mary was going to be deposed, he was sure of that in spite of Moray's empty words about a limited power. They were going to kill Rizzio and "restrain" her, and then he felt suddenly quite certain that when Moray had returned and established his own power, Mary would be quietly poisoned before her child was born.

"I must tell the Queen," he said. "But I shall put less emphasis on the measures which you intend to take against your sister, even though they are temporary, of course. The Queen shall be told of Rizzio's removal and your return, and I know she will give the plan her blessing. Personally, I shall pray for its success. Keep in touch, my Lord, keep in close touch."

"You shall know the time as soon as I do," Moray promised. They shook hands, and Cecil came to the door with him. As soon as the Earl had gone down the corridor, he went immediately to the Queen's apartments.

"You don't suppose," Elizabeth said frowning, "that they would do any injury to the Queen herself?"

Cecil shook his head. "Oh, no, Madam, you needn't fear that. Once her favourite is removed and her brother and the rest are back she will simply have her power curtailed, that's all. And if Moray establishes the Protestant party in supreme power and rears the Queen's child in the true religion, most of our dangers will be over."

"I don't trust that sour Scot. Bastard by birth and by nature —that's my opinion of him. I believe he'd like to kill Queen Mary, only of course he wouldn't dare. He knows, doesn't he, Cecil, that whatever my enmity towards her, I wouldn't agree to a sovereign being put to death by subjects? You made that clear, didn't you?"

"Without possibility of doubt, Madam," Cecil said. "Rizzio will be removed, as he described it; there will be a bloodless revolution and reconstitution of power, and the Queen will emerge from it unharmed; and harmless to you, which is the main point."

The Queen walked away from him and looked out of the window. The park at Nonsuch was wilder, less formalized than the gardens of her other Palaces. It was still only an elaborate hunting lodge. She had once mentioned a stay at Nonsuch as part of the programme mapped out for that meeting between her and Mary which was never intended to take place. She knew how her cousin enjoyed the chase, she could see the words in her own letter, written so many many months ago; the game at Nonsuch was the most plentiful in England. . . .

"It is now February," she said suddenly. "When will this thing be done?"

"I should think by next month," Cecil answered. He stood, waiting for his dismissal; after a few moments he coughed to remind her that he was still there.

"Thank God," Elizabeth said abruptly, "that I have no brother and no husband. You may leave me, Cecil."

A supper party had been arranged in the Scots Queen's

private cabinet for the evening of Saturday, March 9th, 1566, and Mary had been in good spirits all day, as excited by the prospect of a convivial evening as if she were going to a sumptuous party. She had refused to allow Darnley to join her. Was it really possible that only a few months ago she had been incapable of denying him anything, and now he had only to make a request however trivial and she instinctively objected . . . ? Tonight she intended to enjoy herself, the sight of Darnley was anathema to her, the good-looking face she had so often caressed and admired was only a smooth mask, lit by the cunning blue eyes. When they weren't narrowed with ill-temper or heavy with the onset of his disgusting bouts of vice, they were bleared with drunkenness. Everything which had first attracted her now repulsed and frightened and irritated her until she could hardly bear to look at him or sense his presence in a room.

He had struck her and cursed her and betrayed her with common prostitutes; when she refused his outrageous demands for lands or money or vengeance against someone driven to insult him, he had whined and cajoled and then bullied her until she fled from him and locked herself weeping in her own room. Her pregnancy had weakened her; she was sick and nervous and apt to cry very easily. Without the kindness and the understanding of her secretary, David Rizzio, Mary felt she would have lost her mind. He was always so calm, a curious attribute for a member of the ebullient Italian race; he had a rare facility for finding the humour in a situation, however irksome it appeared, and turning her despair into smiles. Above all, he was gentle and she took refuge in that most precious quality, so different from her husband's brutal hectoring. Rizzio was a friend rather than a servant; he was ugly, but he had the expressive brown eyes of his race, and they gazed at her with the soft adoration of a faithful dog. If he was less intelligent, less manly, coarser in manner than befitted a man in his position, Mary was too emotionally disturbed to be able to judge either Rizzio, or the situation she had created, in its true perspective. She was desperately unhappy and desperately in need of solace from the ruin of her personal life, a ruin for which she blamed herself with hysterical despair. She clung to the Italian with fanatical obstinacy; she paid him extravagant marks of favour, and so far forgot her dignity as to express her feelings for him in her letters to her French relatives. These feelings were devoid of the sexuality of which her enemies accused her. Her experience with Darnley had refrigerated Mary's instincts to the point where they were permanently damaged. The essence of her dependence upon a man of such inferior quality and appearance was the absence of physical attraction.

She had worked hard that March day, receiving petitioners in the Palace Great Hall, huddled in her fur cloaks and rugs in the freezing, vaulted chamber as tall and cold as a cathedral. She had spent a trying hour and a half with Lethington whom she no longer trusted because he was suspected of supporting her treacherous brother's rebellion. Their old intimacy was gone; it was a strain to talk to the man she had once counted her friend and to see him watching her with a cynical half-smile and answering her with cool reserve. She had disappointed Lethington, and he had not forgiven her. She was too proud to follow her impulse and burst into tears and admit it and beg him to help her. The Lords Morton and Lindsay were at Holyrood, and their presence made her uneasy. They were not friendly to her, nor to Darnley; she could only suppose their loyalty lay with the brother she had exiled and was refusing to recall because she did not trust him either and knew him to be incapable of forgiving her for their quarrel. But now, at the end of the day, she could look forward to a pleasant supper with Rizzio and her friend the Countess of Argyll. She had ordered some of the French delicacies, which were usually omitted in case her stout Scots took offence at their Queen's foreign habits, and some excellent Spanish wine. She had chosen her cabinet because it was small and comparatively warm, with some of her personal treasures in it. After dinner they might play cards, or Rizzio could sing and play to them if she felt too tired to gamble.

The Countess of Argyll was a tall, angular woman with a tongue as sharp as vinegar; she was older than Mary, but they shared the same sense of humour and there was something appealing about the young Queen, burdened with her despicable husband and beset with troubles, which aroused the Countess's affection and made her one of Mary's loyalest supporters. For the Queen's sake she was prepared to tolerate Rizzio.

He had made a mat of himself for the Queen to tread on, and by God, the Countess said to his detractors, it was a change from all those who were only too eager to trample on her.

It was a gay meal; Mary's appetite rose with her spirits; she and the Countess laughed at Rizzio, who told several amusing anecdotes about his activities that day. He was in the middle of a story when the door was wrenched open. Rizzio's voice stopped; he sat staring into the doorway with his mouth open and a look of terror spreading over his face. Mary hardly realized how they came into the room but it seemed as if it were full of men, armed men, in breast plates, with drawn swords and daggers, and Darnley was among them, his face flushed, swaying slightly as he stood with his legs apart to keep his balance, and his naked dagger in his right hand.

Mary rose, her chair scraping, one hand drawing her tartan scarf over her breast and her defenceless womb, imagining in that blind moment that the weapons of death were for her.

"In the name of God, what are you doing here?" Even her voice sounded unreal, but it was like a signal. Three men rushed at Rizzio and he sprang out of his chair and came to her side, his hands dragging at her skirts; he was screaming in Italian. She saw that one of his attackers was Lord Ruthven, wearing armour over his nightshirt, the pallor of death on his contorted face. His was the first dagger that struck Rizzio, and the wound bled on to her skirt. She saw Darnley come to her and aimed a useless blow at him. He caught and held her wrists, and the others had hustled the Countess to the other side of the room where they held her with a pistol at her breast. Mary heard her own voice crying out, and the room was full of dreadful sounds, the grunts and snarls of men who had become animals in their attack upon their victim, and the victim, pitiful in his cowardice, shrieking for the helpless woman to protect him. She tried to bite Darnley's hand, and suddenly one of the Lords whom she recognized as Morton jabbed a cocked pistol repeatedly against her side.

"Hold your tongue or I'll blow you and your brat to hell . . ."

There was a convulsive tug at her dress and then she closed her eyes, her senses failing at the sight of Rizzio being dragged by his arms and his jacket, still howling like a wounded jackal, his blood making pools on the floor.

When she opened her eyes, there was only Darnley and the

Earl of Lindsay in the room. She had a wild impulse to spit straight into her husband's face; she stopped because she remembered the child and knew that if she did it he would knock her down.

"He's dead. . . . He's dead at the bottom of the stairs and bleeding like the pig he was! " She saw Ruthven's face, shining with sweat, the eyes glazed as if he were drunk or sodden with lust, and he was staring at her, wiping his dagger on his sleeve.

"One word from you, and you'll join your dirty little lover. . . . Cry out," he hissed, his breath on her face until she shrank even though it was against Darnley. . . . "Make a to-do, my Lady, and I'll cut you into collops. . . ."

"You killed him," she said. "You filthy murdering dogs! "

To her humiliation the last words were broken as she began to sob and cry hysterically, shaking so violently that Darnley pushed her towards a chair.

"Control yourself," he mumbled at her. "The cur is dead, no harm is meant for you. Your rooms are surrounded; what was done was by my order; my good friends here have avenged my honour. If you behave sensibly, Madam, I'll see that nothing happens to you."

Ruthven was laughing, and taking long drinks out of the jug of Spanish wine. The others were back in the room, dishevelled and muttering and looking at her sideways. At that moment the City tocsin began to ring. The tocsin only sounded in moments of civil crisis. Someone must have heard that she was in danger and gone out to warn the citizens and bring them to her defence. She made a movement towards the window and was flung back into the chair so violently that she cried out.

"Stay where you are," Morton shouted, and the pistol was rammed into her again until she fought it off with her hands in the effort to protect the child he was trying to injure.

"You! " he turned to Darnley. "Go to the window." Darnley obeyed him, his movements unsteady.

"They're streaming into the courtyard," he said and his voice was shaking. "There are hundreds of the people, and they're armed."

Mary could hear them shouting up, demanding to know that the Queen was safe, demanding to see her. She saw the murder in Morton's face and the hand of Ruthven creeping to his knife, and stiffened in her chair.

Darnley turned round, his face pasty with fright. "Someone gave the alarm," he stammered. "They want to see the Queen or they'll attack the Palace."

"Well they won't see her," the Earl of Lindsay snarled. "Unless they catch her body when we throw it to them over the wall. Tell them to go home, you fool. Go on, damn you, open the window wide and tell them she's safe and they're to go home."

Mary could hear Darnley shouting above the clamour which rose to the open window; he was telling them the alarm was a mistake and she was well and trying to sleep, giving them his word as her husband that no harm had come to the Queen or the prospective heir, telling them to return to their homes. When she heard the window shut the sounds of the crowd were already diminishing as they turned and began leaving the courtyard. After a few moments there was silence outside; Darnley stood awkwardly in the middle of the room, looking from one to the other of the Lords. He was sober now; and she could tell that he was afraid of more than the mob which had dispersed. He glanced at her and she saw with hysterical horror that there was some kind of appeal in his eyes.

The Countess of Argyll had been released; she knelt by Mary's chair rubbing her hands, repeating over and over again that she must keep calm and remember the danger of miscarriage. It was her insistence that finally moved the Earl of Lindsay to tell her to take the Queen into her bedroom; but it was Morton who refused to let the Countess stay with her. Mary heard the key turn in the outer door. For the next seven hours she was alone, in the room where Rizzio had been stabbed to death.

They expected her to miscarry; during the early hours of Sunday morning she began to scream with such effect that some of the armed men placed on guard all round her apartments were heard muttering and the Earl of Lindsay went in to her and reported that she was holding her side and looked likely to lose the child. As a great concession the old Countess of Huntley was allowed to come and attend her, and the Countess was astonished when the ashen, delirious woman who fell weeping into her arms, suddenly whispered fiercely that she was not as ill as she appeared, and to tell her what had happened outside the Palace. Mary's eyes, reddened with tears and sleeplessness, lit up as if electrified when she heard that both the Earls of Huntley and Bothwell had escaped from Holyrood on the night of the murder and were preparing to rescue her. While the Countess undressed her and persuaded her to go to bed, the two women whispered. Lady Huntley was ordered out again, but she returned to her own house where Bothwell and her son were hiding with the news that the Queen was alive and unharmed, and prepared to take any personal risk or stoop to any measure to revenge herself. The plan she had whispered to Lady Huntley was the seduction of her husband into helping her escape.

"And that, Madam, is the whole sorry story." Sir Nicholas Throckmorton had given a personal account of the murder of Rizzio and the subsequent events to Elizabeth in her private room at Greenwich. Cecil and Leicester were with her; the two familiars were so utterly unlike and yet it was difficult to imagine the Queen without one or both of them beside her.

"They killed him in her presence," Elizabeth repeated. "And they used violence against her . . . and you say Darnley *held* her!"

"He did." Throckmorton nodded. "They're all trying to deny the details now, saying no one laid hands on the Queen and that Rizzio was pushed into another room and murdered there out of her sight.

"But I have heard from eye witnesses that her clothes were covered in blood and she was shut up for seven hours in the room where the stabbing was done, without even a woman to attend her."

"And her Lord husband helped them, and held her by force." Elizabeth swung round to Cecil, her eyes blazing. "By Jesus, I'd have taken the dagger out of his belt and stabbed him to the heart with it!"

"She paid the penalty of her own folly," Cecil remarked, and to his surprise she rounded on him angrily.

"Oh, for God's sake, hold your tongue for once . . . *You're* pleased with this business, we all know that."

"Not really, Madam," he said quietly. "I have no interests except yours; I have no room for sympathy with the Queen of Scots however pitiful her position. And it is a good deal less pitiful since she's escaped and placed herself under the protection of the Earl of Bothwell."

"She has the Tudor blood," Leicester broke in, "and the Tudor wit, too, to persuade that miserable clown Darnley to abandon his friends and help her get away."

"She must have nearly choked on her own gall to speak to him without spitting in his face," the Queen said. "I doubt if I could have done it, and God knows I'm mistress enough of myself! "

"She promised him a full reconciliation," Throckmorton explained. "She must have pointed out to him that he was as much a prisoner of the Lords Morton and the rest as she was, and persuaded him that his only hope of safety lay in escaping with her, before they decided to murder them both. She saw her brother, the Earl of Moray, when he returned to Edinburgh the day after the murder, and she completely deceived him with tears and pleas for his protection."

"And she has gone to Bothwell," Elizabeth said. "What kind of man is he? "

"Not much better than those who burst into her room that night. A Border ruffian, with more brain and a better education than most. He's been loyal to her mother and to her for most of his life—he's about thirty-two years old, I suppose. He's a bitter enemy of Lord Moray's and he hates Darnley. The Huntleys are a powerful clan and they are with him; so too is the Earl of Rothes. She sent for him and he has deserted the rebel Lords and gone over to her in exchange for a complete pardon. With these men behind her, she may yet get back her power; more especially since the other Lords who returned with her half-brother are quarrelling among themselves. But she's shown no sign of vindictiveness for the outrage committed against her. It may be that her spirit is broken; but she still carries the next Stuart heir, and that's weighing heavily in her favour."

"Nine women out of ten would have miscarried on the spot," Leicester remarked. He glanced across at the impassive Cecil, wondering how much he had known of the plot and its intention before it was carried out. More than he had told the Queen, he thought suddenly. Much more. Cecil never showed his feelings; he had a face like a mask. But it was too expressionless, too guarded. He had thought Mary would be dead, and he was deeply disappointed. And he was disconcerted by the attitude of his mistress towards her mortal enemy.

He was finding her sympathy for Mary difficult to reconcile

with all the poisoned shafts of diplomacy that Elizabeth had
personally loosed against her; and none more lethal than the
bridegroom who had just behaved with such infamy that even
Leicester was shocked. He allowed himself a slight smile. For
all his genius and his ability with men, Cecil was still very
ignorant at times about the functioning of the female mind.
It was satisfying to know that all clever men have a blind spot,
and Cecil's was an extraordinary inability to see one vital
characteristic of the mistress he otherwise understood so
well.

Cecil would talk about the disasters which had befallen Mary
Stuart since her marriage and in the next breath begin his
constant urging of Elizabeth's own marriage. And he would
see nothing incongruous in his arguments, or realize that her
natural antipathy to male domination was permanently justified by her cousin's example. She would never marry; Leicester
knew that and he was content. She indulged in flirtations with
Heneage and a new gallant called Christopher Hatton who
flattered her and wrote her impassioned love-letters, but
Leicester was certain that their relationship with her was as
sterile as his own. Passion was dead in Elizabeth if it had ever
truly been alive, and looking back upon the stormy, frustrated
period of their early lives, Leicester now saw the amatory
dabblings at their real value. A relationship based upon the
senses was certain to be the most ephemeral any man could
enter with her because the head and not the body ruled Elizabeth, and she was normal enough to sicken of preliminaries
which she was emotionally incapable of carrying to their right
conclusion. She enjoyed flattery, but she was not deceived by
it; she enjoyed her unique independence more than anything
a man could give her, but she was feminine enough to amuse
herself by pleasantly deceiving the deceivers. She knew that
he was Lady Essex's lover; she had remarked quite calmly
one evening when they were dining together that she understood the appetites of men, but preferred not to have the
participants under her nose. And she considered the Countess
to be a particularly rank smell which must not come to
Court.

That was all; he nodded without saying anything and their
conversation continued as before. Lettice was furious, and perhaps a little piqued that the Queen should accept her position
as his mistress so lightly, and at the same time refuse her the

excitements of attendance at Court. He had offered to end the liaison, but she surprised him by refusing. They met frequently in spite of the ban, and in spite of the objections of Lord Essex, who was conveniently away in Ireland for long periods. And they were happy together. Her sensuality amused Leicester; she reminded him more and more of a soft little cat, with the cat's sheathed claws. She was a witty, amiable companion as well as a lover; he relaxed in her presence like a man sitting peacefully in the sun, after being buffeted by the high winds and sudden squalls of temper, the constant air of tension and stimulation which epitomized his life in the company of Elizabeth. He could not imagine existing without the Queen; he would have been equally miserable without Lettice as an antidote.

On June 19th, 1566, Mary Stuart gave birth to her child at Holyrood Palace. It was a son, and the little Prince entered a world which belied the violence and upheaval which had threatened his birth a few months earlier. The Queen suffered abominably, but her brother Lord James, the loyal Earls of Huntley, Mar and Crawford, and Argyll were staying at the Palace with her, all apparently reconciled. The men who had killed her secretary and threatened her own life were exiles under pain of death, and the chief conspirator who had betrayed his wife and then his friends, moped in his rooms, forbidden to attend the birth of his child or to torment Mary by intruding upon her. He was lost, and Darnley knew it. She had tricked him with promises, playing upon his cowardice after that dreadful night, until he believed that Morton and Ruthven were about to murder him, and that if he redressed the wrong done to Mary and escaped with her, they should begin their lives again with everything forgiven.

Now he realized that she had lied to save herself and that the hatred of the Scottish Lords of all parties who knew what he had done was only matched by the mortal enmity of Mary. He had no friends, no one whom he could trust or who would trust him, and when he heard that she had borne a son, he broke down and wept with pity for himself.

He had thought that he knew Mary; he knew she was quick tempered and mercurial and inclined to act upon impulses of love or hate, but she had become a stranger, a cold, embittered woman who treated him with withering contempt. She had welcomed her treacherous half-brother, James, back into her favour as if he had done nothing to encompass Rizzio's murder; she had pardoned her enemies right and left with the exception of those who had actually been in her room that night, and the result was his own horrible isolation. When she looked at him out of those narrow changing eyes he knew that he was doomed, as he had doomed the miserable Italian. It increased his agony that he had no idea what form his punishment would take or when it would fall on him. And his teetering brain, unbalanced by drink and debauch and cruel inferiority, added a wild jealousy to his fear, when he saw the look in Mary's face when she spoke to the Earl of Bothwell. Bothwell had taken her on his own horse the night they escaped from Holyrood; Bothwell had been beside her ever since like some menacing bird of prey outlined upon a highland crag. The male dominance, the rough, ruthless personality of the man who had remained loyal to her from the beginning of her reign, seemed to fill the whole Palace, as his men filled the City. All that was left to Darnley was the intuitive sense of self-preservation, and it warned him that Mary was in love with Bothwell, and that Bothwell knew it. Every look and gesture betrayed her infatuation with the man.

The others seemed unaware of the atmosphere between them. In the rejoicing over the Prince's birth and the entertainments for his christening, when the treacherous Elizabeth of England stood godmother to her rival's son, everyone seemed blind but Darnley, and no one would listen to him. They dared not, if they wished to keep in Mary's favour. And Mary was acting with diabolical cleverness, typified by the gesture in asking her deadly enemy to stand for her child. She had forced the English Queen into the position of her friend, and united the Catholic and Protestant factions in Scotland round the throne which now had a male heir.

By September Mary had summoned her brother and her Council and asked them plainly how she could secure a divorce from her husband who was so repugnant to her that she could not bear him to be in the same room; and the same brother and Council offered their sympathy and, some said, offered to save her the trouble of legal wrangling by putting him to death. The Queen had forbidden it, but he did not believe her; he spoke of leaving the country and she forced him to come before the Council and retract the threat. He knew it was only because he might make trouble for her abroad, or go to England and beg Elizabeth to forgive him. Mary could not allow him his liberty until she divorced him or the Lords had disobeyed her injunction and murdered him.

He was too discredited to be able to take advantage of the fact that these same Lords—Lord James in particular—were becoming as jealous of the Queen's favour for Bothwell as they had been of Rizzio, and to warn them that Mary only wanted to get rid of him and replace him with the Earl. He sank into the apathy of complete despair when his wife pardoned the actual murderers and allowed them to return on Christmas Eve. The apathy developed into sickness, and the sickness into smallpox. He lay in a house outside Edinburgh, a lodging chosen for him by the Queen who insisted he keep the infection away from the little Prince James. He was feverish and ill and haunted by fear and his fear brought him cringing to the woman who had once loved him so blindly. There was no other heart he could hope to touch. If he was dying, Darnley wanted to see her and be forgiven. It was one of the few genuine emotions he had ever felt. Mary came to him reluctantly, because her brother said she must for appearance sake. Another advocate of wifely forbearance was the Earl of Bothwell. And because Bothwell urged her to go to him, the Queen went, and allowed herself to be wept over and begged for forgiveness until the heart she had managed to steel in implacable hatred, was touched with pity for the wretched wreck of a man lying in the bed, his disfigured face covered by a velvet mask. It was over between them; she made no secret of that, but she spared him the lash of her contempt and indifference. She was kind, and much of her leniency was due to the hope that he was going to die and free her without further complications.

She left him to attend a Ball at Holyrood, and he went to sleep wearing a ring she had given him as a token of her forgiveness.

At three in the morning the house of the Kirk o' Fields blew up like a firework under a massive charge of gunpowder, and Darnley's body, half naked and dead by strangulation, was found lying in the garden.

"What a fool!" Elizabeth said. "What a criminal fool!" Leicester shrugged. "You can't expect all women to be as clever as you, Madam. And you did say you would have stabbed Darnley to the heart when you heard of the Rizzio murder."

They were walking up and down the gardens at Whitehall Palace. It was spring but bitterly cold; the sky above them was the colour of lead and the river flowing past the parapet wall was swollen by rain. But the Queen insisted on a daily walk, and, wrapped to her chin in sables, she paced up and down the paths, followed by Leicester who was obliged to adopt her habits. Two of her ladies, Kate Dacre and Lady Knollys, trudged behind them, too far away to hear the conversation and too cold and uncomfortable to talk to each other.

"If she had killed the wretch then and there no one would have blamed her," Elizabeth said. "If she had divorced him, the whole of Scotland and all of Europe would have supported her. But to make an open show of her hatred for him and her preference for this Earl of Bothwell and then have him blown up when he's sick and helpless. . . . Jesus, she must have gone out of her mind after the childbirth!"

"How fortunate," he mocked, "that *I* didn't marry her. She might have lit a bonfire under me!"

Elizabeth nudged him sharply.

"Be thankful I saved you from your own ambitions," she retorted. "By God, by this piece of folly she's lost all my sympathy, for what it was worth. I can just see Cecil rubbing his hands and saying that she's doomed by her own idolatry and I shan't have the heart to make fun of him. The mists of that damned country must have poisoned her brain—what can she hope to gain by this that couldn't have been got by patience for just a little longer?"

"You would know that best, Madam. You've always seen into her mind better than anyone else; you saw into it so well that you knew she'd marry Darnley in the first place and ruin herself as a result. Did you also foresee how it would end for him?"

"I neither thought nor cared," Elizabeth said. "Dead or alive he was always worthless; the world is well rid of him. The point which has escaped you, my dear Robert, is that Mary is once more a widow, and if by some miracle she avoids the consequences of this murder and finds a suitable culprit, she will be in need of a husband again, and the old problem is revived."

156

" Randolph said that Bothwell was the culprit," he reminded her.

"Then she will have to punish him. As I would have punished you, for a much less heinous crime than killing a King Consort."

Elizabeth turned and began to walk back. The ambassador in Scotland had last written three weeks before, describing the tumult which had broken out in Edinburgh after the explosion. Public sympathy, always ready to change like the wind, had suddenly taken the side of Darnley. His violent death had shocked the nobility and the people into forgetting the appalling ordeal he had inflicted on his wife a few months earlier. There was talk of a Papist plot, always a reliable bogey with which to frighten away impartial judgment; talk that the Queen was directly responsible for or at least aware of what was going to happen; rumours that her brother, Lord Moray, had threatened to lead another rebellion and depose her in her son's favour unless she allowed him the right to find the murderer and punish him according to the law. But public opinion agreed on one point; the murder had been done by one man, and that man stood at the Queen's right hand, as arrogant as ever and as favoured as ever, with his clansmen filling the streets of the City like an army, ready to strike down his enemies and establish him as the power behind Mary and her throne. The Earl of Bothwell was guilty, and regardless of the Queen's personal feelings and the wrongs she had suffered from Darnley, she was expected to abandon Bothwell and bring him to trial. Her fate depended on her decision, and Randolph gave his opinion that she would find it a better risk to deliver the Earl than support him against her entire kingdom and everyone in it.

"We'll go in," the Queen said. " I see those two behind us shivering like a pair of plucked fowls. Look, by God, there's Cecil coming to meet us ! "

The Secretary was hurrying up the path towards them, holding a cloak round his shoulders in competition against the stiff April wind which blew in from the Thames.

They stopped, and Elizabeth said quickly, "Nothing but an earthquake or news from Scotland would bring you out of the Palace today, Cecil. Which is it? "

" The last, Madam. I have just received a despatch from Randolph."

Elizabeth's eyes narrowed on the Secretary's face.

157

" Queen Mary has acquitted Bothwell," she said.

Cecil smiled one of his rare, slow smiles in which there was a frightening lack of humour.

" She has married him," he said. " And an army led by the Earl of Athol and all her nobles is marching out to destroy them both."

## Chapter 9

I T was June, 1567, and a warm sun blazed down over the rough
ground of Carberry Hill, splashed with the bright colours of
yellow gorse and budding heather. Mary Stuart raised her
hand and wiped her forehead which was damp with sweat. She
had sat for almost an hour on her horse, watching the disposition of the rebels' troops on the ground below, occasionally
seeing Bothwell riding through the thinning ranks of their own
men, cursing and threatening and exhorting, and she watched
it all with the calm of someone who has lost all hope. Her wan,
dull apathy had made Bothwell furious in the past weeks; he
had told her bitterly that he had sooner spend his time with
any hedge drab who could laugh and show a little animation
than sit opposite to her looking as if she were walking in her
sleep. The more Bothwell shouted at her, the less she responded.
Her spirit had been broken at last, and broken by the man she
had believed to be her only friend and with whom she had
fallen in love when she rode away from Holyrood after poor
David Rizzio's death.

Darnley had been right when he believed she meant to marry
Bothwell. She had suffered enough from weaklings, and the
strength and determination of her new champion had deluded
her into thinking him as safe as the others had been false. She
had imagined that they were a match in spirit and courage;
she was so grateful for the security he had given her before
the birth of her son that she believed herself in love for the
first time in her life. She knew he had murdered Darnley and
she did not care. The force of her own feelings made her reckless; she repaid Bothwell's loyalty with extravagant marks of
favour and affection. When he came to his trial in Edinburgh
and packed the hall with his clansmen, she ignored the protests
of his enemies that he had secured his acquittal by force. In a
few weeks she had forfeited the sympathy of her people and
her nobles by her defence of Bothwell, but with some remnant
of caution, she refused to marry him until the public clamour
had subsided. If she trusted the Earl, he had not trusted her.

On her way to visit her son at Stirling, he had met her with a troop of soldiers and escorted her to his own Castle at Dunbar with the excuse that he was protecting her from being kidnapped by their enemies. And at Dunbar, where she was helpless, Bothwell had come into her room the first night and locked the door and violated her.

The mental shock, more than the physical indignity, had broken her spirit; Bothwell's assault succeeded where the murder of Rizzio and the whole miserable history of her marriage to Darnley had failed.

And she had failed Bothwell. The beautiful, imperious Queen, who had promised the fulfilment of all his ambitions, was finally committed to the marriage he demanded, but not because she loved him, for she hated him and he saw her hatred in her red-rimmed eyes, forever avoiding his; not because he had aroused her passion as he had hoped, though he had subjected her to alternate caresses and brutality in the attempt to do so; but only because she was pregnant as a result of his outrage. He hated her for that as he hated her for her shivering inexperience. Stripped of her Royal estate, Mary had grossly disappointed him. He had left her after a few days at Dunbar and consoled himself with the wife he intended to divorce. He did it to insult the Queen, whom he blamed for making promises she could not fulfil; the circumstances in which he had claimed that fulfilment and her previous experience with a drunken degenerate made no difference to him. He had proved himself a ferocious, merciless animal, exactly as his enemies had described him to her all along, but if he no longer wanted the woman, he was determined to have the Queen. He had ruined her, as he pointed out, swearing his foulest oaths to try and shake her into anger or retaliation or anything but the sick resignation which goaded him beyond bearing; she had to marry him or bear his bastard and thereby resign her throne and be committed to her half-brother's mercies. And she knew what to expect from *him*. . . .

She gave her consent to that marriage in a voice that made him want to strike her; and he brought her back to Edinburgh in state, escorted by his clansmen, and married her on a brilliant spring morning.

They made a show of unity; she was so low in pride and so physically ill that the least sign of humanity might have driven her to Bothwell once again, but he showed none. He was coarse

and vile tempered; he cared nothing for religion but forced her
to marry him in the Protestant rite. The same morning she was
heard to cry out for a knife to kill herself. But she was committed to him by the marriage which had condoned his
abduction; they could not count upon one friend, and their
natures prevented them, even at the last moment, from counting on each other. He could not forgive her for being a
reproach; he was incapable of humbling himself by admitting
that he had ruined her and himself; she could not go to him
because her fear of his treatment was only equalled by her
anxiety to hide it from their enemies. Moray and Morton and
Lindsay and the rest saw Bothwell raised to the height of power
through his marriage to her. They had killed Rizzio because
they were jealous of him; they were ready to kill Darnley if
Bothwell had not done it for them. Now they had exchanged
a humble secretary and a drunken weakling for the one man
who was strong enough to crush them all if he were given time.

And so, less than two months later, she waited at the head
of a dwindling army to do battle with three-quarters of the
nobility of Scotland. There was no hope of victory; there was
no hope of anything. The rebels held her baby son; they
demanded that Bothwell should be surrendered to them and
the Queen place herself under their protection. Their couriers
assured her that she would not be harmed. Bothwell was insisting upon fighting; the French ambassador had ridden out to
try and mediate; he had urged her to submit, saying her cause
was hopeless and that everyone knew she had been imprisoned
and forced into marriage with the Earl. Her only hope was to
surrender to her nobles and trust their affection for her when
they heard in detail how she had been mistreated. And she
knew that Bothwell would never agree to such terms and go
unarmed to his enemies.

He was like a wild animal, defiant and snarling at bay. He
had no fear of death in battle; but he had told her plainly that
he would kill her and himself before he fell into the hands of
Lord James and his supporters. Her brother was in France; it
was typical of him to leave the rebellion to be fought by others.
When it was successful, he would return, protesting his
innocence. He was responsible for the revolt, he was the
organizer, the brain behind the ruffians she could see below
her. And he had promised that she would not be harmed.
Perhaps he meant to keep that promise. It was her only hope;
161

she felt so sick that she swayed in the saddle. If they fought they died—she and Bothwell and the child she carried—fought and died for nothing, without even the memory of love between them. And suddenly Mary did not want to die. She was sick of blood and pain and futility, and she was only twenty-five.

She turned to one of the clansmen standing by her and sent him to find Bothwell. He came after some delay, scowling and sweating in his heavy steel breastplate.

"Their troops are round the back of us," he said shortly. "All this parleying was just a feint to strengthen their position while we talked. I told you to send that damned Frenchman away!"

"We cannot win," Mary said slowly. "The men are deserting; there are less and less left to us every hour."

He began to swear and pull out his sword and she touched his arm suddenly.

"If they give you a safe conduct, will you abandon this battle?"

"What?" he stared at her, his dark eyes narrowing against the sun. "Don't talk such madness; they want my head and they'll have to come and get it. I'll kill that cur Morton if it's the last blow I strike on earth."

"If they let you go," she insisted, her voice strained and trembling, "I will surrender to them. I am the one they want most. Du Croc says I shan't be harmed. I beg of you, James, I beseech you, listen to me."

"Listen to you!" he laughed bitterly. "I listened to you long enough, Madam, and now see where it has brought me!"

"I don't want it to bring you to your death. Blame me if you wish; God knows I blame myself, but what is done cannot be altered now. We were friends once, before all this; I truly loved you once, and I am carrying your child. For that child's sake, I want you to escape."

He looked at her and for a moment he caught her arm, not unkindly but to give her support. He couldn't believe that she meant what she said; she would surrender if he could go free. Even at that moment his insane pride rejoiced at the idea that he had conquered her in spite of everything, that, even if he despised her, she cared for him. . . . Women had always cared for him, no matter how he treated them, they came whining back, asking for more. All women except the Queen whose attentions had driven him to disaster, and then proved that when it came to a trial of power and strength, her title was only an empty echo against the men and money of her brother and her nobles.

"Let me send down to them," she pleaded. "And if they grant your life, we will lay down our arms."

"How do I know you will be safe?" he asked, and suddenly ashamed of his relief, he looked away from her.

"They have given their word for that already. James could not break it publicly. No harm will come to me."

It was late afternoon when the rebel Lords gave their assurance. As Lord Lindsay said, once they had the Queen safe, Bothwell would not get very far.

The sun was sinking when Mary said goodbye to him for the last time; her face was very white under the red light as he stood awkwardly in front of her, anxious to get away and torn by a feeling of shame and anger and regret that could not find expression. In his own way he had loved her, in a way that was ruthless and ambitious and predominantly lustful. He could not come nearer to telling her so than by saying he wished it had been different and hoped that she had forgiven him for what had happened at Dunbar.

"I wanted to marry you," he mumbled. "And I thought you might be persuaded against it if we delayed. I did what seemed the only thing to make up your mind for you. It's an old Border method."

"It was the wrong one, but I believe you thought it right," she said wearily. "There's nothing left for us but forgiveness now. I do forgive you from my heart."

"We can still fight," he said, but she was not deceived. He wanted to go, and she longed to be free of him now that she knew he was ready to abandon her, free even to depend upon her brother James. It was not possible to sink lower than she had done in courage or in hope.

"Farewell," he said abruptly. "I will be back, and I swear I'll help you if you need it."

She watched him mount and spur his horse into a gallop back over the ridge of the hill; then she began to ride slowly forward towards the rebel forces.

It was so unusual for Elizabeth to attend a Council meeting, that when Cecil told the other members to expect the Queen, they knew it would be a difficult session. They were all standing by their places round the long polished table, with the canopied chair at the top; the Duke of Norfolk, the Lords Leicester, Hunsdon, Sussex, Bedford, Sir Nicholas Throckmorton and Sir William Cecil, and Cecil had a pile of papers stacked with his characteristic neatness just in front of him, placed edge to edge, with a sheaf of clean parchment; a stand of freshly cut quill pens, and ink and sanding paper were laid out before each Councillor. It was his duty to write down the Queen's comments and keep the minutes of the meeting. He had been hoping that Elizabeth would leave the guidance of the Council to him as she normally did; in that way he felt there might be a chance of altering her attitude to the fate of Mary, Queen of Scots, at that time held as her brother Moray's prisoner on the island castle of Lochleven. She was under the guardianship of her deadly enemies, the Douglas, and lucky to have lived through the ordeal of her parade through the streets of Edinburgh after her surrender at Carberry Hill, where the crowds had yelled for her blood, and besieged the house where the Lords had lodged her, screaming that she should be burnt alive as a witch and a whore. . . .

Elizabeth had reacted with volcanic fury to the reports of the brutality, indignity and ill-usage to which her sister Queen had been subjected, after receiving promises of humane and honourable treatment from those who held her captive. And it was this obstinate defence of Mary's Royal immunity which had so far prevented Moray and the others from putting their prisoner to death. The Council which was waiting for her had been called to point out the folly of her attitude.

"Make way for the Queen's Grace! The Queen's Grace to the Council!"

They could hear the shout of her gentleman usher; they were all turned towards the door when at last it opened and Elizabeth walked quickly through into the room. Every back bowed. The Queen wore a stiff skirted gown of pale cream satin, lined with gold tissue; the soft, shimmering colour blended with her hair and was repeated in the little yellow cap, the edges sewn with pearls and topaz.

"Greetings, my Lords." She spoke briskly, and inwardly Cecil's spirits drooped. He knew that clipped, businesslike tone and the mood it indicated.

She sat down in her chair of state and began to pick sweets out of the gold bowl.

Cecil cleared his throat and began to ask the Queen's consideration of a proposed amendment to the local judiciary system in country parishes. It was a futile trick because she interrupted him in the middle of the second sentence.

"You don't need my opinion for such stuff. Get to the real business. The Earl of Moray has asked for another assurance that he has nothing to fear from me if he executes Queen Mary."

Her dark eyes swept round the line of faces.

"That is the question, Gentlemen. And here is my answer, which it will be your pleasure to convey on my behalf. The day any rebellious subject takes the life of their lawful Prince, on any pretext whatsoever, an English army marches into Scotland."

"Madam," Throckmorton leant towards her, "we all know your merciful nature, but there's surely a point where mercy and policy cease to meet. The Queen of Scots is your mortal enemy. She has claimed your throne from the day your sister Mary died and has continued to claim it ever since she arrived in Scotland. Nothing has changed her attitude. If she regains her throne in Scotland and, knowing the country as I do, it's not as impossible as it seems in spite of her conduct, she will be as dangerous to you as ever, perhaps more if she finds another man fool enough to marry her and engage in her ambitions. I beg you, Madam, on behalf of your Council and all your people, to allow Lord Moray and the other Lords to do what they want. Let them try the Queen for Darnley's murder and execute her. We shan't have peace as long as she lives."

There was a moment's silence before Elizabeth answered him. She knew that he spoke sincerely and without personal malice towards the Queen of Scots. It was a natural and just solution to Throckmorton who was not as bloodthirsty as her cousin Hunsdon or the Earl of Bedford, or as basically unchivalrous as Leicester. They all thought she was being obstinate and sensitive to world opinion; Cecil thought she was being sentimental and was positively sad in his disappointment in her. They saw nothing wrong with killing a sovereign, because they were all commoners.

"It is not my habit to give explanations," she said at last, "but I know the affection you all have towards me, and I don't wish you to think it is taken lightly. My Lords, this once I will open my heart to you. I want no record of this written, Cecil; let it stay in your memories. Before my grandfather, Henry VII, came to the throne, it was the custom of English Kings to take the crown by force. Civil war, tyranny and terrible crimes were the result of that precedent; in fact our country was no better than Scotland. The Tudors have changed that; with our dynasty kingship has gained a sacred place in the hearts of subjects of all degree. I can come and go amongst you all because I know there is not a man among you who would put his poignard into my heart, because I am your Queen and as your Queen my blood is sacred. It was this ideal, this truth, which prevented my sister from putting me to death when so many advised her to do so, using all those arguments you have employed against the Queen of Scots. I was her heir and of the Blood Royal. So, God help us, is Mary Stuart to me. If I stand by while those ruffians send her to the scaffold, I have stretched out my own neck and bared my own bosom. If I, as Queen of England, admit the right of a Prince's subjects to judge and try and condemn their Prince, then my own precedent might well rebound upon me. I do not admit Moray's right. I have spoken to you as a Queen and now I tell you that as a woman I abhor the treachery and brutality with which he and the other scoundrels have treated a defenceless woman who is carrying a child."

"She connived at Darnley's murder," Sussex pointed out.

"If she did, she is only guilty of poor timing and worse planning—I will not allow you to sit there and pretend that such a cur deserved anything other than death for his conduct towards her. Conduct towards his Queen, more than his wife, I would remind you. Besides, it is not proved, and I fear it troubles my conscience very little. I will not set an example to the world by abandoning the Queen of Scots to a judicial murder. Nor will I close my eyes to poison—tell Moray that too. And if the time comes when she can regain her throne, she may only regain it with my help and on such terms that she will never perplex us again. That, surely, is a better alternative and if we are patient it may come about."

She held out her hands palms downward across the table. Her coronation ring shone in the light.

"I have been Queen of England for ten years, my Lords,

and my hands are not stained with any man's blood. I will never sully them with the blood of a fellow Prince who comes of the same stock as myself."

There was nothing to be said after that. The Council agreed that her warning should be sent to Moray, and the subject of Mary Stuart was superseded by the Queen's pressing need of finance. For the last ten years Elizabeth's exchequer had been unsteady; national bankruptcy was her nightmare, and the fear of it drove her to drastic economies which were always aimed at those extravagances sacred to her male advisers, to wit, the fleet and the army. The intervention in France had squandered millions of her carefully hoarded Treasury gains; now the great financial houses in the Netherlands were unwilling to hazard more money for England, who might well be overrun by Spain once the Netherland rebels had been finally defeated. And final defeat was something Elizabeth would not consider. It was all very well, she broke in angrily during the meeting, to talk about Mary Stuart who was shut up in a Scottish Castle without men or money or hope, when their real danger lay in a huge Spanish army of veterans across the Channel, who might well be launched against England at any moment.

If Philip put down the revolt in the Netherlands, he would be the first power in Europe. If they had forgotten Philip of Spain in all this blabbering about a woman, she had not. She had never forgotten Philip, even when she was most anxious about Mary Stuart. He had a long memory and a slowly mounting score to settle. He had been held back, forced into pretending friendship for her by factors which were known to them all: the fear of her possible marriage to a French Prince; the equal fear of a French-inspired attack upon her to put Mary Stuart upon the throne; the necessity to keep English trade flourishing in his Netherland kingdom. He had only to be sure she would not marry a Frenchman, that Mary was no longer eligible as a French cat's paw, and that the best way of keeping trade intact with the Netherlands was to swallow the other half of the business, and then they would all be lost.

They needed money. They needed it primarily to send to the rebels and keep that costly, terrible war going as a distraction and a drain upon the resources of Spain. When Sussex suggested sending troops the Queen sprang out of her chair with a string of oaths, and asked him whether he wanted a war with Spain at this moment, or was he so old that he was tired of the rigours of living?

There would be no troops; no open offence; only lies and procrastinations and more lies, and as much damage to the power of her dear brother-in-law as they could do him without being actually found out. That was what she wanted, not an old man's blustering. When they could think of a solution, Cecil could come and tell her.

She swept past them down the room and the door banged behind her. The Council gathered their papers and reseated themselves with a sigh of relief. As the Queen had baulked their wishes over Mary Stuart, Bedford and Hunsdon and even Sussex, still very red after her rebuke, returned to the old problem of her unmarried state and insisted that both the danger from Mary and the greater danger of activity from the Spanish enemy were the consequences of her obstinate refusal to marry and safeguard her throne with an heir. She was demanding money to finance the Netherlands rebellion, but as soon as they approached Parliament for the grant, Parliament would re-open the issue of her marriage. The time would come, Bedford said angrily, when the Queen would fail to placate them with excuses. Leicester remarked dryly that no doubt the Queen was prepared to intimidate them instead, and the meeting ended in general agreement that there was no way of circumventing her wishes. Mary Stuart would have to be protected and Parliament would have to be persuaded or squeezed into granting more money. As they left, Cecil heard the Duke of Norfolk mutter under his breath that he wondered why the devil they bothered to hold a Council meeting at all.

By the winter of 1568 the position was static; the men surrounding the Queen of England were nervous and discontented, convinced that her policy of inaction would have fatal results and the money granted by Parliament, after an angry encounter with the Queen over her professed virginity, would not be sufficient to meet the national need and leave anything with which to put heart into the rebels in the Netherlands. The King of France was hinting that he might place troops at the disposal of Mary's few supporters in Scotland, free her and restore her to her throne, with the obvious sequel of invading England while they had the opportunity. Moray's answer was a threat to execute Mary the instant a French fleet was sighted off the coast of Scotland. But no troops sailed for Scotland and Mary lived on in her prison at Lochleven Castle, where she had miscarried of twin sons. And if her cousin Elizabeth exasperated her advisers without losing their loyalty, Mary repeated her feat of winning some men to her by personal attraction while she turned the rest into mortal enemies.

The sickly boy who had been her first husband had loved her as deeply as his capacity would allow, and even the blackguard and rapist Bothwell had felt some stirring in his soul which drove him to the course of violence which had ruined them both. Now another boy fell under the enchantment of the young Queen who was a prisoner in his family's castle. Willie Douglas was only fourteen and he had been brought up to regard his sovereign as an adulteress, a Papist and a witch. It was an alarming picture which immediately showed false when the Queen came under his roof and he saw the supposed wanton conducting herself with gentleness and piety under the most unchivalrous conditions. When she miscarried the boy heard his relations rejoicing, expressing the wish that she might die. He undertook duties in her quarters and saw the Queen nursing a right arm which was black with bruises after a visit from Morton and Lindsay, who departed with the act of abdication they had obtained only by holding her down and forcing her hand to guide the pen. He saw a great deal, and Mary knew he was watching. She was in the same mood of reckless desperation which had given her the courage to escape from Holyrood with Darnley; extreme danger sharpened her wits to a high pitch of cunning which unfortunately flagged under less tense conditions. She had at last recovered from the betrayal of Bothwell and the horror of her experiences immediately after surrendering. She was free of the burden of his children, and her health had returned. She was prepared to use any means of escape that offered, and the means was the young cousin of her captor who was obviously in a romantic daze and besotted enough to do anything. She laid siege to Willie Douglas' loyalty as carefully as a general undermining a fortress. Men had used Mary, and now she used the young Douglas, and to such purpose that before the trees were in bud round the moat at Lochleven, she had crossed it in a small boat and was on her way to raise her Standard and rally her supporters against Moray for a final battle.

The battle took place in May at Langside, but it was less of a battle than an ambush; her old friends the Hamiltons and the Gordons came forward, and laid down their lives in a terrible defeat which turned into a massacre. There was no time to try and reach the coast and escape to France; there was no time to do anything but avoid the capture which would certainly end in her death, and Mary turned her horse from the scene of carnage and disaster and rode across the border into England to take refuge with Elizabeth.

"Now that we have her," Elizabeth said, "we must keep her. She cannot return to Scotland; Moray would kill her and I cannot let him do that."

"She is asking," Cecil pointed out, "to be sent to France. What answer can we give to that request?"

The Queen looked at him and shrugged. "Any answer we choose, my dear friend. We have sheltered the fugitive. I saved her life and my conscience is not going to prick me if I compel her to lead it here where I can see that she does me no harm. She will not be allowed to go to France and stir up trouble there, or to do anything but stay in England. As my guest—or my prisoner, if she decides to be difficult."

It was impossible to foresee Elizabeth's reactions; Cecil was only too grateful she had not thrown her arms round her cousin's neck and welcomed her like a sister when she first arrived in the country. Mary had come into the North of England in nothing but the clothes she wore, and sent a request to her Royal relative for a few necessities while she made her way to London. And suddenly Elizabeth had changed, almost before the eyes of the men who had heard her defending, even sympathizing with Mary a few weeks before. The pale, rather peaked face had grown thinner and whiter, and the black eyes were very narrow, like the mouth. Elizabeth stood in front of them like a fox taking scent, as taut and pitiless as a vixen finding a wounded terrier bitch in its lair. She answered Mary's plea for clothes by a bundle of dirty petticoats and a length of torn velvet, and forbade her to proceed any closer to London without her personal permission.

She was never allowed to forget the presence of the Scots Queen, even though Mary was many miles away in the North, for Cecil brought her reports of demonstrations in Mary's favour among the people and described how the Catholic nobility and gentry were busy making the fugitive's lodgings a place of pilgrimage. He did not comment; there was no need to stress the personal affront to Elizabeth which was the result of Mary's presence. He knew his mistress, and he knew that her jealousy of her people's love was even greater than her jealousy in personal relationships. She had often used the affection of her subjects as a weapon against her Council and her Parliament; when she overrode the wishes of both bodies, she could appear in the streets on her way through the country and point to the cheering crowds who surrounded her as the answer to her critics.

Now they were cheering someone else, a younger, lovelier woman who was already invested with an aura of romantic tragedy. Elizabeth's contact with her people was confined to that portion of her country which was staunchly Protestant. She knew within weeks that she could not rely upon the same loyalty from the population in the North where the old religion still survived in spite of the legal repressions which had been in force against it for the last ten years. Religion was no excuse to her; it was pointless for Leicester to tell her that men were more influenced by a Queen they could see than by the decrees of a sovereign known only by name. She was too angry to be reasonable and too realistic to be lulled by logical explanations. He had an alternative suggestion which was in the minds of Cecil and her other Councillors but which they dared not propose: why not agree to the pleas of Lord Moray's emissaries and return Mary to the vengeance of her Scottish subjects. And there were moments when Elizabeth swore that if Mary were dead, by whatever means, it would be worth the censure of the world to be rid of her, and rid of the internal cleavage her presence had already revealed. But if the Scots were clamouring for the surrender of their enemy, the ambassadors of France and Spain were always at Elizabeth's elbow, seeking her assurance that she would not betray the trust her cousin had placed in her. France offered her asylum and Philip of Spain promised to be responsible for the Queen of Scotland if she were surrendered to him. When the French were informed of his interest in the heiress to the English throne, they made it clear that they would prefer Mary dead at the hands of her own rebel Lords, if Elizabeth could not keep her out of mischief.

And that was Elizabeth's answer. It reminded her of the chess simile she had used to Cecil once, some years ago, when the board was just set out and the pieces seemed evenly matched in the game between them. With the White Queen in their hands, it was checkmate. Threats from France or Spain could be quietened by the simple means of holding Mary to ransom. Elizabeth refused the request of Moray and countered it by promising not to let Mary go to France or Spain, and she dispensed with the pretence that her cousin was a guest by ordering her forcible removal to Bolton Castle where she was taken from the shelter of the Catholic North and placed under the care of the Earl of Shrewsbury. And in December of that year Elizabeth solved her monetary troubles by seizing ships sailing through the Channel with cargoes of bullion destined for Spain.

There would be no war, she maintained, when some of her Council came clamouring to her, accusing Cecil of responsibility. Spain was now paralysed for lack of money; Philip could protest and bluster as much as he liked. There was nothing he could do but add the seizure to his list of grievances, and wait for his revenge. When the reckoning came, if it came, she would be strong enough to meet it in the open. The men who were most afraid of war with Spain were those who had most to fear from a Catholic revival, the men who pressed for the death of Mary Stuart, for marriage with a foreign Prince, for any measure which they thought would safeguard their own interests against the risks inherent in a woman's political juggling; and since they dared not criticize the Queen, they found a scapegoat in her Secretary and principal adviser, William Cecil. He was already too powerful for Norfolk's peace of mind, while Bedford and Hunsdon and Sussex were all jealous of his wealth and his growing power.

None of them believed that Elizabeth meant to marry anyone. Nor would she allow the Scots to dispose of Mary Stuart who was royally lodged at Bolton Castle and busy winning the confidence of Lord and Lady Shrewsbury. And at twenty-six, in excellent health and openly determined to escape and secure her rights, Mary Stuart was obviously destined to survive Elizabeth. Her bitterest enemies decided to insure against the future by secretly negotiating with her.

If Mary were married to an Englishman, then their position would be secured. The candidate chosen, by birth and by his own willingness, was the Duke of Norfolk. Norfolk had seen Mary at Carlisle and was sufficiently stupid and vain to be completely captivated by her and to forget the formidable character of the other Queen he had sworn to serve. He had always been influenced by nobility of birth, and there was no Princess in the world whose blood was more illustrious than that of the young woman confined at Bolton. He belonged to the old order of English feudal aristocracy where women had always been the pawns of men, and he had never relished the autocracy of Elizabeth. In his heart he regarded her as a parvenue and a bastard with a lashing tongue and an unseemly disregard for the superior breed of men. The winning, dignified, yet feminine Mary was infinitely more appealing, and the prospect of uniting himself with such a woman and sharing her dazzling birthright, drove all fear of Elizabeth out of his mind. He was so confident and so limited in his vision that he tolerated the presence of his hated enemy the Earl of Leicester among those implicated in the plot.

Leicester had joined because he was afraid, and for the moment the fear of others infected him and swayed his judgment. Panic is the most contagious of all human emotions, and the fears of Sussex and Arundel, neither of them weaklings, brought him to the point where he believed that Elizabeth was about to be overthrown by a Spanish invasion, or else succumb to a sudden illness and be replaced by a Catholic Queen who had a grudge against them all. Throckmorton was among the conspirators and he reminded Leicester of his own tenuous position, of the constant humiliation which his pursuit of Elizabeth had brought him, and then asked bluntly whether he were prepared to lose his head for her after she was dead, or have the courage to make a provision for himself. Leicester baulked at Norfolk, but they told him roughly that there was no choice. He could buy Norfolk's tolerance by complicity, and Norfolk's scruples were waived by the assurance that the plot could not succeed without Leicester who must be persuaded into it to stop him betraying it to the Queen. The Spanish ambassador was informed of their intentions, and through him the King of Spain gave the project his blessing.

In her quasi-confinement at Bolton Castle, Mary declared that she was deeply in love with the Duke and ready to marry him as soon as her escape could be arranged. She made the declaration in cold blood, and she was prepared to carry out the promise and give herself to any man who could help her. Passion and feeling were dead in Mary; they had died the night

James Bothwell came into her room and robbed her of her womanly dignity, and her natural sentimentality had withered like the gorse on Carberry Hill the day her ravisher and husband, whose unborn child she carried, rode away to freedom and left her to the cruelties of her enemies. She could give her heart because she no longer had one; but she did not let Norfolk or Shrewsbury or any of the other Englishmen involved with her see that, for purely political ends, she was more bloodless than Elizabeth had ever been. Her pleas to meet Elizabeth had been refused on the pretext of the charge of murdering Darnley which her subjects had brought against her and substantiated with copies of impassioned love-letters she was supposed to have written to Bothwell, proving her an adulteress and a party to the crime. These letters were not only forgeries but copies of forgeries; to anyone who knew Mary the letters were palpably false, but they served the dual purpose of blackening Mary's reputation and excusing the English Queen from accepting her and hearing her side of the story.

They had been shown to the Council and to certain privileged peers, including Norfolk, all of whom affected to believe them and expressed their horror. Elizabeth was publicly shocked and privately cynical.

The early days of 1569 were a time of acute strain for Leicester. He felt uncomfortable with his fellow intriguers; he could not quite trust the men with whom he was involved or believe that they could succeed in the second part of their design which was to impeach Cecil for treason. He still hated Cecil but he was so close to Elizabeth and knew her mind so well that he often lay awake and thought that the whole scheme would end in disaster foundering on her invincible will and her uncanny aptitude for turning everything to her own advantage. She would fight hard for Cecil; she was ruthless and exacting, but she had never yet abandoned anyone who served her faithfully.

Fear had brought Leicester into the intrigue and fear kept him in it, long after his confidence in its success had begun to fade.

It was Lettice Essex who persuaded him to betray the conspiracy and the conspirators to the Queen before it was too late.

They were dining together at his new house on the Strand;

it was a magnificent mansion surrounded by a park and gardens which had just been completed, and staffed by his personal retinue of several hundred servants. Lettice often stayed there with him when the Queen allowed him leave of absence from the Court. She was his accepted mistress; they lived an almost domestic life when they could arrange to be together, and he had begun to tell her more than most men told their wives.

"For the last ten minutes you've been playing with your food," she said suddenly. "And if you lose your appetite, my love, then I know something serious is wrong; what is it?"

He pushed back his plate and made a sign for his steward to remove it. When the servant had gone and they were alone, he leant his head in his hands, staring moodily in front of him.

"What is it?" Lettice asked him. "Tell me."

"You were right," he said suddenly. "You told me not to join this intrigue with Norfolk and I wouldn't listen to you; now I only wish to God I had. Every day I feel more certain it will fail; every time the Queen looks at me I wonder if she knows, and if she doesn't, what will she do to me when she finds out!"

"She's fond of you," Lettice said. "She may forgive you. But you were so confident when you began—why have you changed?"

He moved irritably. "I don't know; it sounded clever enough. Make an insurance against the Queen's death, get rid of Cecil who's eating up lands and power for himself. . . . I think that was what really trapped me. I'd give anything to see him humbled. But the Queen is in better health than she's ever been lately; there's no move from Spain, there's no move from anyone. And I feel certain now that the whole damned scheme will founder. She will find it out, or Cecil will. And even if she doesn't and we succeed, there's something else I don't like." He paused, groping for the right words, knowing how jealous Lettice was of his feelings for Elizabeth. "I don't trust Norfolk," he went on. "If he marries the Queen of Scots he may aim for the throne with her."

"And that would mean overthrowing the Queen," Lettice said slowly. "They would have to put her to death, wouldn't they, Robert?"

"Yes," Leicester muttered. "And I want no part of that."

Lettice Essex watched him for a moment. She knew him very well, as well as that other woman from whom she had stolen him; she knew that he was unscrupulous and ambitious and primarily in love with himself. He had many faults and few compensating virtues, but she loved him enough not to wish him any different. And because she loved him and understood him, she knew what it meant when he shrank from harming Elizabeth.

"You still love her, don't you?" she said at last. "No, Robert, don't deny it! It's not like our love, but it is there."

"It won't save me if she finds this out," he interrupted. "I am the one man above all the others that she'll rend to pieces when she discovers what I've done. Why didn't I listen to you, Lettice? Why did I ever get involved with these fools?"

"What's done is done," she answered quickly. "If you think she'll punish you, you're probably right. There's only one way to make sure that she doesn't."

She left her chair and came and knelt beside him. He put his hand over hers, and she felt that it was shaking slightly.

"How?" he asked her.

"By betraying the whole business before it is too late. Go back to Whitehall and tell her everything. It is your only hope."

For a moment he hesitated; for a moment he weighed the chances, imagined the consequences to the other men who had trusted him, and how many enemies he would make once it was known what he had done. And then he imagined Elizabeth if the intrigue miscarried and he had said nothing.

"Go," Lettice whispered. "Go now, and don't hesitate. Who will come forward to save you if things go wrong? No one, I tell you. I love you, and I'm not blinded by false loyalties to anything or anyone but you. Confess everything to the Queen and you'll be safe. If you don't tell her, someone else will."

He stood up and they embraced; he realized at that moment that he was very much in love with her. He kissed her with real tenderness.

"I won't wait," he said. "I'll ride to Whitehall now. God keep you, Lettice, and pray that all goes well."

Elizabeth had been very quiet while he told her. She had sat in her chair, embroidering, occasionally looking up from her needlework frame into his flushed and anxious face while he talked of his fear and his doubts and the influence which had been brought to bear on him by the other conspirators.

The recital did not do him credit. When he had finished she still said nothing; the silence in the room became unbearable. He went on his knees beside her chair.

"Madam, I beg you to forgive me."

"So first you betray me, and now you betray your fellow traitors. Tell me, Robert, what made you confess?"

"I was afraid for you," he stammered. "I kept wondering whether you would be safe if the marriage took place and Cecil was forced out of office. It seemed a wise plan at first . . . a sort of safeguard . . . then I thought Norfolk might try to go further still . . ."

"And make an attempt to remove me along with Cecil," she finished for him. "A reasonable conclusion; I'm surprised it took so long to occur to you."

"Believe me," he begged, "believe me the moment it did, I made up my mind to warn you."

"Would Bedford have agreed to that?" she asked him, "and Arundel and Throckmorton, who's such a stout Protestant? Were they prepared to dethrone me in favour of Mary Stuart and Norfolk?"

"No," he said desperately; he was so frightened by her calm, almost casual reaction to the plot that he began to tell the truth. "No, it was Cecil they aimed at, not you. But once these things begin, when you have a claimant like her married to the first noble in the country, anything can happen."

"How true." Elizabeth leant back and looked at him. "But what would have become of you when I was gone, Robert . . . I expect you thought of that too, in your anxiety for my safety?"

He only shook his head. "I warned you," he said unsteadily. "I beg of you to remember that."

Elizabeth stood up.

"I shall remember, Robert, and I am flattered that you were more afraid of me than of Norfolk and the rest."

"That's not the only reason," Leicester came towards her. He caught her hand; but it was cold and lifeless.

"God knows, and so do you, I'm not an admirable character; but if I have one feature that redeems me from your absolute contempt, it is my love for you. Whatever I am, that has never changed and never will. I couldn't stand by and risk anything happening to you. I risked your anger instead, and that's no small hazard."

He faltered. Her face was white, as expressionless as a mask; it told him nothing of her thoughts as she looked down at him.

So Robert had intrigued against her. He had lied to her for months, and most of his explanation was a lie in the attempt to excuse himself and minimize his responsibility. But he had told the truth when he said that the plot might go further than he had supposed. He was untrustworthy, but she had always known that. He was vain and ambitious, but his vanity and his greed stopped short of agreeing to her death. He had confessed to her from several motives, but at that moment she believed that concern for her safety was the main one. When she was desperately ill with smallpox, the same inconsistent loyalty had kept him beside her, now at a moment of equal danger he had shown in his own way that he loved her still.

"You can arrest me now," he said at last. "It's no more than I deserve. But say that you forgive me first."

"Arrest you?" To his astonishment she laughed.

"I'm not going to punish you, Robert. If you want forgiveness you can have it. I don't feel inclined to play our little comedy of rift and reconciliation yet again; this matter is too serious. I'll pardon you now, but on one condition."

"Name it, Madam! Anything, anything in the world." He had begun to kiss her hand; there were tears of relief in his eyes.

"Promise me that you'll join every plot against me in the future, then I can watch its course from the beginning. Nobody shall know you told me about this one, except Cecil. He may trust you more after this. I could get it out of Throckmorton in ten minutes if I sent for him, but I think I'll squeeze the truth out of the eager bridegroom. Norfolk shall tell me. And when he does, he'll go to the Tower."

"The best place for him," Leicester said quickly. "And the Queen of Scots?"

Elizabeth's face hardened. "Something must be done to dissuade her from making trouble; I must think, Robert. I know what Cecil will advise—return her to Scotland and let her brother execute her."

"It's good advice, take it," he urged. "She has repaid your shelter by intriguing against you, she deserves to die."

"For that matter, so do you and all the others." Elizabeth sat down and pulled the embroidery frame towards her. "That isn't the answer, Robert; I'm not going to salve your conscience

178

by putting a sovereign to death, even indirectly. Leave me now, I want a little time to think."

" And you have really forgiven me? " he insisted.

She glanced at him; if her smile was cynical it was also strangely sad.

"I have forgiven you, Robert. I'm afraid it has become a habit."

She sewed for some time when he had left her. She was an exquisite needlewoman; as a young girl she used to work for hours, straining her eyes to make presents for her sister Mary and her brother Edward when she had no money to buy something suitable. Like music it soothed her nerves and cleared her brain, and she was thinking fast and clearly as she sewed. She was not surprised by Robert; old habits died hard, and he was born with a passionate care for his own skin. They had all begun this intrigue to protect themselves, thinking she might die, or Spain would invade, doubting the wisdom of her policy even though she had never been proved wrong through the last ten years. Frightened men would stoop to anything; even those like Robert, who loved her in his own worthless way. They were all jealous of Cecil, who was braver and shrewder than any of them, and they made him the scapegoat for their own lack of confidence. She had spent those ten years in building confidence, steadying her throne and stabilizing her country, and there had been no whisper of discontent until Mary Stuart crossed into England. She had plunged Scotland into civil war, her crown was stained with the blood of her husband, the Hamiltons and Gordons had perished in thousands defending her; the villainous Bothwell was now a prisoner of the King of Denmark where he had sought shelter, because his association with Mary had made him worth holding to ransom. Everyone connected with her had suffered, and the same sinister pattern had begun to form in Elizabeth's kingdom now that she was in it. Plots and betrayal and fear. And finally bloodshed would follow, as Cecil had prophesied from the beginning. She would not kill Norfolk or imprison the others. She would send him to the Tower and hope that he had learnt the lesson without having to lose his head as well. She would try and avert the violence which her instincts warned her to expect, and she would continue to hold Mary in spite of Cecil, because she dared not let her go. But she too must be taught that intrigue would be followed by consequences.

Elizabeth went to her writing-table and wrote out an order for Mary's removal to Tutbury Castle. It was a damp and gloomy mediaeval building, buried in a desolate part of Staffordshire, and uninhabited for many years. It was also one of the strongest fortresses in England.

# Chapter 10

THE first armed rising in favour of the Queen of Scots came from the North, and the revolt was an offshoot of the intrigue to marry her to Norfolk. The Catholics in the North were seething with discontent; the Reformation had taken root in the centre and south of England, but the ancient religion flourished in the more inaccessible part of Elizabeth's kingdom, where it was supported by the two nobles most powerful in land and seniority next to the Duke himself. The Earls of Northumberland and Westmorland were staunchly Catholic, and they were too influential to be terrified into apostasy by Cecil's government. For ten years they had kept a truce with Elizabeth until the woman they believed to be the rightful Queen of England came over the Scottish border as a fugitive. Her charm, her beauty, and her professed piety were like a match dropped in straw. But it was a clumsy intrigue, and Mary made the first of many errors when she suggested that it should be supported by a landing of Spanish troops from the Netherlands. If Northumberland and Westmorland were guilty of rash judgment, Philip of Spain was not; he agreed to support the rising, but only when Mary had been released from custody and Elizabeth assassinated. The negotiations were conducted through a Florentine banker called Ridolfi, an amateur meddler who entirely overlooked the efficiency of the English Government's spy system.

The rebels were so ignorant of the character of Elizabeth and her advisers and so out of touch with the temper of the majority of her people, that they believed the whole country would welcome the substitution of Mary and the re-establishment of the Catholic faith. When Norfolk was arrested, the Northern Earls gathered their followers, proclaimed Mary Queen of England and set out for Tutbury to rescue her. Elizabeth was at Windsor when she heard the news from Cecil; she summoned her Council, and placed her own cousin, Hunsdon, at the head of a force which was to proceed north and engage the rebels. Huntingdon and Sir Ralph Sadleir were sent to Tutbury to remove Mary further south to Warwickshire; the Lord Admiral Clinton was to lead a third army from Lincolnshire, and the Earl of Warwick recruited troops from his own county and proceeded to join Hunsdon and Sussex at York. Elizabeth's calm and courageous attitude in the crisis prevented panic among her Councillors; the measures to meet the rebels were agreed within a few hours; counter-proclamations drawn up and circulated, and any servants or contacts of the traitors were arrested and questioned. It was an agent of Ridolfi's who revealed the extent of the plot and the complicity of Spain. Cecil had taken the precaution of watching the ports for some time; he had noted the activities of the Florentine and set a watch upon his servant, Bailly, who left for the Netherlands and was imprudent enough to return with papers compromising himself, his master, Mary and Norfolk and the King of Spain. Bailly was arrested and taken to the Tower. Cecil interrupted Elizabeth one afternoon when she was sewing with her ladies to show her the results of the interrogation. Bailly had been tortured after refusing to confess; but stretched on the rack he had screamed out the key to the cypher used by Ridolfi and the names of all those concerned in the plot.

While the Queen and her advisers unravelled the details in London, the armies gathered to overthrow her in the North had marched through four counties without gaining a single recruit from the common people, and without rescuing Mary Stuart. The expected uprising never took place. The Earls and their men, weary, dispirited and unnerved by rumours of the strength of the forces Elizabeth had sent to meet them, rode through silent villages and towns, watched by hostile crowds who listened to their proclamations and then dispersed. The majority of the English people remained loyal to the Queen; they were indifferent to the dynastic claims of Mary Stuart and to the restoration of a religion which had ceased to be preached or practised effectively for nearly twenty years. They knew little of Mary except that she had brought trouble and bloodshed to Scotland and had lost her throne as a result. The benefits of Elizabeth's rule were evident in flourishing trade, employment and peace.

They turned their backs on the rebellion, and at Tadcaster the Earls of Northumberland and Westmorland halted their dwindling troops and gave the order to retreat. By January, they had been driven to the Scottish Border, and took refuge there with the supporters of Mary. In the same month her half-brother, Lord James, was assassinated in an act of private revenge and Lennox, Darnley's father, became Regent for his infant grandson, King James. The Earls and the Catholic Scots were immediately engaged in a bitter and internal fight with the new Government. But in England the rebellion was over. The two leaders were in exile; the Scots Queen was closely guarded at Coventry by men who were ordered to kill her if she tried to escape; and Norfolk was imprisoned in the Tower.

Most of the rebels had been hunted down and captured; hundreds of Catholic gentry and thousands of their followers were prisoners, waiting for the Queen to decide on their punishment. When that decision was made Elizabeth proved for the first time that she was indeed her father's daughter.

No one had ever thought of her as cruel; Cecil and Leicester, who imagined they knew her so well, were surprised and secretly appalled at the fury of vindictiveness which she displayed towards her enemies when they were in her power. She sat in her Privy Chamber at Whitehall Palace, facing the members of her Council and in dead silence told them how she proposed to deal with traitors.

"For eleven years," she said to them, "I have ruled with mercy. Not long ago I held out my hands to some of you and boasted that they were clean of my subjects' blood. Now some of my subjects have shown that they do not appreciate mercy; they preferred my cousin with her stained reputation and record of misgovernment, and they asked the aid of Spanish troops to put her in my place. They failed, thanks to the loyalty of most of my people and of all of you, my Lords. Now they shall pay for that failure, as their fathers paid for the Pilgrimage of Grace, when they rose in revolt against my father, King Henry."

Most of the men listening to her remembered that religious rebellion, the last attempt to rescue the Catholic religion from the violent persecutions directed by Henry VIII. And they remembered that he had drenched the North in blood as a reprisal.

The Queen's voice continued. It was harsh with anger, and there was a savage expression in her black eyes.

"No one possessing land or wealth is to be executed. They will ransom their lives with their last penny. As for their followers, one man out of every ten is to be hanged."

No one answered for a moment, and then Hunsdon moved forward.

"I beg to advise your Majesty," he said, "that my Lord Sussex suggested the opposite course. He proposed punishing those who by birth and education should know better than to rebel against you, and to show mercy to their tenants and men at arms. These are ignorant peasants, Madam, only following their landlords. How can it be just to hang them—so many of them," he added, "while the nobles and gentry escape?"

"We are not living in the Middle Ages," Elizabeth retorted. "These ignorant peasants as you describe them must learn that their first duty is to me. It will be just to hang them because there is nothing to be gained by giving them their lives. If they are not loyal from love, my Lord, they will be loyal to me from fear. Sussex may be a good general but he's a poor lawyer. If we execute the landowners, the Crown has no claim on their property. I want their property. They raised the rebellion and by God I'll see they pay the cost of it. Tell Sussex to proceed with my orders at once."

"Does this decision include the Queen of Scots, Madam?" Cecil spoke at last. It was inconceivable that hundreds of Englishmen were to die, while the real culprit was not even mentioned.

Elizabeth's mouth tightened angrily.

"She is not my subject; she is not bound to me by any law but a sense of her own honour. If you propose to badger me about punishing the Queen of Scots, then I can answer you once and for all. She will be more strictly imprisoned, but nothing more can be done against her."

"And Norfolk, Madam?"

She turned to answer Leicester. He had always hated the Duke. This was his moment to revenge himself upon the man who had insulted and ignored him for years and repeatedly accused him of betraying the initial intrigue to the Queen.

"I sent the Duke to the Tower for trying to make a marriage without my consent; I spared his life because he promised never to write or communicate with the Queen of Scotland again. The evidence taken from Master Ridolfi's papers proves that he broke his word and was party not only to this rising, but to a Spanish invasion and my assassination. You all know that, my Lords. Once more, I showed mercy and I was rewarded by betrayal. Norfolk shall be tried for treason; if you find him

184

guilty—and I think you will—then he shall be executed. By rights he should hang like a dog with the others. Does that satisfy you, my Lord Leicester? "

He smiled blandly at her.

" If it satisfies your Majesty," he said.

Eight hundred Englishmen of low degree were hanged by her personal instructions. The North of England was polluted by the corpses hanging from gallows in every town and hamlet; villages were razed; the estates of the rich were sequestered and their owners rotted in dungeons long after their ransoms had been paid. Elizabeth punished her people with the jealous fury of a woman revenging herself upon an unfaithful lover. She had prided herself upon her people's love; she travelled up and down the country, to towns and universities, showing herself to them and inviting their loyalty. She had ruled them wisely and made them richer and more prosperous than ever before, and she could not forgive or forget that a section of them, though they had not been visited and courted, had turned on her in favour of someone else. She took her revenge and her conscience never stirred. It was all the more extraordinary to her Council that when she had signed away the lives of hundreds without pausing, she could not order Norfolk's execution.

They had tried him and found him guilty, and expected her to sign the death warrant. She accepted the verdict with pleasure, spent the evening dancing with Sir Thomas Heneage and playing cards with Leicester who lost a large sum of money to her. She was in such a good temper that she offered to waive the payment till the next day. Everything about her was brilliant and untroubled, from her choice of a new dress shining with cloth of silver and pearls, to the familiarities she showed both her favourites, laughing and teasing them in turn. When she awoke the next morning and Cecil came with the warrant for Norfolk's execution she refused to sign it.

She was sallow and her eyes were deeply circled. She looked suddenly so ill and strained that Cecil was alarmed. When he placed Norfolk's warrant in front of her, her hand took up the quill, inked it, and then paused. Death did not trouble her, torture did not disgust her. They had wrenched every limb out of the wretched Bailly's body to make him reveal Ridolfi's cypher and Elizabeth had listened to the account of the questioning and even seen the tremulous cross made by the victim on his confession because his hand was too crippled to sign.

But during the night the thought of beheading paralysed her imagination. It gave her a feeling of hysteria, almost of suffocation; she had lain awake, trembling and sick. The image of her mother and her first lover, the Lord Admiral, was blurred by time; the former was submerged in her subconscious but it rose like a witch at the words of incantation. They expected her to cut off Norfolk's head. She could have had him hanged, or tortured or burnt; the most brutal methods left her indifferent, neither stimulated by pain like some women she knew—in France they fought to see an execution—nor moved to compassion by suffering. An enemy was an enemy, and her heart was a stone concerning their removal. It was the method which horrified her, and it was the last privilege left to a gentleman that he should die by the axe instead of the rope.

Suddenly she screwed up the warrant and threw it aside.

"I have changed my mind," she said. "Find another way to kill him, or else he must be pardoned. I can't sign this."

"Madam . . ." Cecil stared at her, amazed. Pardon Norfolk; he could hardly believe that he'd heard what she said. No one had been more vehement in their demand for the Duke's execution than Elizabeth, who now refused to authorize it.

"You can't pardon him," he protested. "He's a proved traitor!"

"Then hang him!" She spat the words at him, and her right hand swept the warrant, the pens and ink and papers off the table. "Poison him, do what you like, damn you! But don't worry me with this, don't stand over me like some old grey-bearded ghoul. . . . I had no sleep. I'm tired," she said desperately, holding her head. "I'm ill, Cecil, can't you see? So leave me alone."

He watched her pass into her bedroom, leaning on Lady Dacre, saying again and again, "I'm ill, my head aches, I'm ill."

He told the Council that she refused to sign, and those who had not seen her supposed that she was moved by mercy. Cecil did not repeat her suggestion that he should find another means. He knew that whatever her reason it was not the result of pity, but he was lacking in the sensitivity to see that for once Elizabeth was looking back instead of forward.

For the next two months he presented the warrant in vain, but his failure was Leicester's success. When she was ill or disturbed he was the only one who could comfort her, the only one she would permit to see her looking tired and unpainted. And in his arms, with her head against his shoulder, Elizabeth spoke of the past and the nervous terrors she had undergone since the day she had refused to sign the warrant.

She could talk to him about the Lord Admiral; listening to her, soothing and stroking her hands, Leicester saw the glimpse of Elizabeth which no one had seen but her childhood attendants; emotional, with nerves strung like fine wires, pursued by phantoms in the mind, and affected by them in her rational conduct.

"I hate him, and I want him dead," she said. "I meant what I said to Cecil. Find another means—anything. But why should the method affect me, Robert? Why should a beheading paralyse my will, make me physically ill so that I can neither eat nor sleep?"

"Because it brings back memories," he suggested gently. "But they are only memories. You did not kill the Admiral; you must kill Norfolk. You must pick up that pen and say to yourself that you are going to sign and it will be done before you know it."

She sat upright and he wiped her face with his own hand-kerchief. Without her stiff dresses and her jewels, with her hair hanging loosely round her shoulders, Elizabeth looked strangely young, much younger than her thirty-seven years. Her pale skin was unlined, the fine bones and the proud nose would keep the illusion of youth longer than for most conventional beauties. It was peaceful and strangely touching to see her sitting up in the enormous bed, and to hold her without passion, almost as if they were both old and had lived together for many years. Lettice was right when she said he loved Elizabeth. He had found tenderness and loyalty late in life; they were virtues that she had forced upon him. He raised her hand to his lips and kissed it.

"I am going to send for that paper, and you are going to sign it while I'm with you. And then you are going to get up and dress; the sun is shining and your horses are dying for lack of exercise."

Late that afternoon Cecil received the death warrant with the Queen's signature on it, and was told that she had gone for a ride with the Earl of Leicester. On 2nd June the Duke of Norfolk was beheaded on a newly erected scaffold on Tower

Hill. He died with courage and with dignity, after months of cruel suspense; he wrote a simple letter to the Queen he imagined had been loath to execute him, apologizing for his treachery, and insisting that he had never intended her personal harm. The news of his death reached Mary Stuart at Tutbury; she had been brought back to the Castle as a punishment and installed in apartments where the walls ran with damp and the roof leaked, and the pale summer sun filtered through narrow windows which were fitted with bars. Already suffering from rheumatism from her previous stay there, she was too cold to get out of bed; when Lord Shrewsbury told her that Norfolk had been executed she collapsed, weeping and hysterical, refusing to eat or be comforted. She embarrassed him by insisting that her cousin Elizabeth had only spared her from execution because she intended her to die from the conditions of her imprisonment. Shrewsbury was unable to deny it convincingly because he thought the same himself. He was not a cruel man, and within limits he was influenced by the charm and attraction of his prisoner.

"If you would only stop plotting against the Queen, Madam," he said awkwardly, "if you would only resign yourself to living in England and give her your promise not to intrigue for your escape, the Queen would deal generously with you. I beg of you, for your own sake, write to her and give your word."

"Resign myself!" Mary sat upright. Her face was swollen with tears, the lack of fresh air and exercise had sallowed her famous complexion, and her hair fell lankly down to her shoulders, uncombed and wild.

"Resign myself to a life of imprisonment! I came to her for shelter and I find myself in a dungeon in England instead of in Scotland! 'If I give my word she will deal generously with me'—ah, how easy it is for you, my Lord, to talk of resignation to such a life, because yours is half over. I am twenty-seven—I am the Queen of Scotland and your rightful sovereign—she should be where I am! If I give my word to Elizabeth that I will renounce my freedom and my rights, live like a nun, with my women and my needlework, betray my birth and forgo my inheritance, then she will send me to a pleasant place to die my living death!

"Well, I will never do it; I will plot and strive for my freedom as long as I have breath, or until she kills me. I could forgive

188

*that*, Jesus is witness that I would almost welcome it, rather than this existence, this misery. . . . But I will never condone her deceit and ease her conscience by saying I am content with what she has done to me, just for the sake of a dry room and permission to sit in my gaoler's garden! You can write the letter yourself, my Lord, and tell her that. Tell her she has murdered Norfolk and slaughtered her people for nothing, because I will never let her rest! "

She buried her face in the pillows and sobbed, and Shrewsbury left her. He liked her and he sympathized, but he longed to be relieved of his responsibility. If she escaped, Elizabeth would blame him; if she died in his custody the world would suspect him of causing her death. And the night before his wife had asked him bluntly what he would do if he received orders from the Council to resolve their problems by poisoning his prisoner. He thought of the distracted woman, shut up in her unhealthy rooms, with a lifetime of imprisonment before her; in his opinion she would be better dead, but he had no intention of providing that release if he could help it. He took her advice and wrote to the Council the same evening and begged them to find another custodian.

Cecil was alone in his room at Hampton Court; the candles were burnt down to their sockets on the table where he was sitting, but the room was already light enough to see without them and the birds outside his window were singing in the first sunlight of the spring morning. He had left the Queen's Masque in the early hours after an urgent message whispered by one of his secretaries. He was sure she would not notice his absence; he played no part in the frivolous side of her life and he lacked the nervous energy which enabled her to dance till dawn and then work through the day without sleep. But he had not slept that night; he had sat at his writing-table and opened the paper which was given to him, and after reading it, he sent his secretary to bed. He was a calm man with unshakeable nerves and no temperament; even at that moment he showed no sign of alarm or surprise, his first thought was to keep the contents of that piece of creased and dirty paper secret from everyone until he had decided what to do and how to tell the Queen.

It was spread out in front of him, and the big Papal seal at the end of it was clearly impressed with the triple tiara and the Keys symbolizing Peter's guardianship of the Kingdom of Heaven. It was a device Cecil had hated all his life, and it had not been publicly displayed in England for eleven years. The top of the document was torn where it had been ripped down from the Bishop of London's door at St. Paul's. He had read it so often in the past two hours that he knew every word in it by heart.

'The Sentence Declaratory of the Holy Father against Elizabeth, Pretended Queen of England and those heretics adhering to her.'

The Pope had excommunicated her at last. After eleven years of patience, perhaps of hoping for the compromise which Cecil knew would never be reached through a Catholic marriage or anything else, the Pope had declared Elizabeth an outlaw to the Christian world, a bastard and a usurper, a persecutor of the true religion whose Catholic subjects were absolved from their oath of allegiance. The friends of Elizabeth were the enemies of Rome, automatically sharing the anathema pronounced against her. It was now the bounden duty of every Catholic in the country to dethrone her if they could.

None of the Council had anticipated this; they had fallen into the habit of regarding the Pope as a distant and impotent enemy who was too weak to take the initiative against them, content to ignore the systematic destruction of the Catholic religion in the hope that the process would be halted by her death and the accession of her cousin Mary Stuart. But Elizabeth had not died; and she was holding her successor a prisoner who might be put to death at any moment. And if Mary died, the infant King of Scotland, reared in the blackest Protestantism, was the inevitable ruler of England. If Mary had stayed in her own kingdom, or been executed before she had time to foment a rebellion, the Pope would not have taken this irrevocable step. Now he knew the only hope of maintaining the Catholic faith in England was to drag Elizabeth off her throne in favour of Mary, and that was the purpose of the excommunication. This was his blessing to the martyrs of the Northern rebellion, and his encouragement to all revolts in the future. It was also a direct invitation to the other Catholic powers in Europe to invade England in a Holy War. Someone had posted the Bull at St. Paul's; even if they discovered the culprits and punished them with all the ferocity of the law, it had been seen by too many people to be suppressed, and there would be other copies smuggled into the big towns throughout the country.

Cecil had been sitting there for nearly three hours, wondering what steps to take and how to protect Elizabeth from the consequences of the sentence in her own kingdom.

"They told me your lights were still burning. What is the matter, Cecil?"

She was standing in the doorway, still dressed in her masque costume, glittering with jewels, the painted and plumed headdress swinging from her wrist.

He stood up and hesitated, and one hand covered the glaring crimson seal.

"I didn't want to disturb you, Madam. I thought you must have gone to bed."

Elizabeth pushed the door close and walked towards the table.

"I was enjoying myself. You should copy me sometimes and wear yourself out with pleasure instead of work. Take your hand away and show me what you are hiding."

He gave her the paper without answering and she stood reading it, the golden mask and headdress of Diana, Goddess of the Chase, hanging still from the ribbon round her right wrist.

"Too late for Northumberland and Westmorland, but timely enough for the future," she said. "I am a bastard and a usurper and whoever takes my throne or sticks a dagger in my heart does a service to God. The same sentence was levelled against my father, and he died in his bed."

She threw the Bull of Excommunication back on to the table.

"It was different in your father's day," Cecil said at last. "There was no Catholic claimant to his throne but his own daughter Mary. Tyrannical and wicked as she was, she would never have rebelled against him."

Elizabeth laughed unpleasantly. "She wouldn't have lived long enough to try."

"France was quarrelling with Rome," he continued. "They are allies now. Spain was in no position to invade, Germany was in upheaval, the Protestant movement was too strong all over Europe to permit anyone to carry out the Pope's excommunication against your father. Your father gambled and won, Madam, thank God. The odds against you are much heavier."

"Only in one direction, Cecil, and for all these years that

direction has never changed." She sat down facing him, and raised her hand when he tried to speak.

"Not Mary Stuart—she is an obsession with you, but she is far less dangerous to me than my dear brother-in-law the King of Spain. I am excommunicated—very well. She is my successor, but France will not attack me to put Mary on the throne because they know I will kill Mary when the first French ship is sighted in the Channel. We have crushed one rebellion at home, and we will crush others when they come. We have the best spy system, the most deterrent punishments that have ever been devised, and we have the principal conspirator under our supervision. If we know Mary's secrets we will know the secrets of our enemies in England and abroad. I am not afraid of Mary; I am afraid of Philip of Spain. You talked about his father, the Emperor. He was occupied with Germany then, Philip is occupied with the Netherlands now. But he will not be tied down there for ever. And Charles V was a politician; his son is a fanatic. When the time comes, he will try and carry this out," she pointed to the Bull. "He was once King of England; he hates it, as much as he hates me. He would like to do here what he is doing to the Netherlands—not for the worship of God, but for the worship of Philip. There is no distinction between the two in his mind. He will not attack me to make Mary Stuart Queen in my place; I've told you that so often I'm tired of repeating it. He is not going to spill Spanish blood to give France a half-share in this country. So long as we keep her alive, we are safe from him."

"He engaged in the Ridolfi plot," Cecil reminded her. "He promised troops and money then, why not now?"

"I didn't say he wouldn't promise," Elizabeth corrected him. "He will promise anything if it will make trouble for me, but I don't think for a moment he has any confidence in that foolish woman's ability to succeed in any plot she undertakes. God above, you know Philip—you dealt with him while my sister reigned—do you suppose he has anything but contempt for a woman in the first place, much less one who has lost her throne through marrying a drunken bawd and being ravaged by the man who killed him? Ah, Cecil, she may touch the hearts of many, but she will no more draw Philip into her lists as champion than she could seduce you! When he attacks me, it will be to take England for himself."

"We should ally with France," the Secretary urged. "We

should send Mary Stuart back to Scotland, and let the Regent execute her, and you should marry a French Prince. Catherine de' Medici is not so bound by Rome that she will refuse the chance of the throne for one of her sons."

"She is bound by astrology, not Rome," Elizabeth said dryly. "I am aware of that. But if I listened to you and sent Mary to her death, a Spanish force would be sailing from the Netherlands before I could marry a French Prince or anyone else."

"The time may come when we cannot keep her as a hostage any longer," Cecil said slowly. "You talk of her as an asset, Madam; but now this has come, I tell you her hand will be behind every assassin's pistol or dagger that can be hired! We may have the best spy system, but we must make Catholics traitors and execute them for treason and not for religion. We will hang, draw and quarter the man who posted this and any of his fellows we can find. The same must be done with priests and with those who hear Mass. We must make their religion an act of disloyalty, punished by the utmost penalties of the law for traitors. The two must become synonymous in the eyes of your people. We must quench this religion until no vestige of it remains—that is your only hope of safety. But to do it finally, we will have to put Mary Stuart to death with the rest. You can lop off the branches of a tree but it will not die till you hack at the roots. And that day will come, Madam. It must, however you resist it."

"When it does, and if it does," Elizabeth answered him, "we must be ready for Spain. Now I am going to bed."

The Bull was traced to a Catholic gentleman named Felton, who refused to betray his associates under torture, and made an attempt to mitigate the Queen's anger against his family by bequeathing her a valuable diamond ring as he stood on the scaffold. The Queen was assured that he had suffered the full rigours of the appalling sentence, put the ring on her finger and admired it, and infuriated Cecil by giving Felton's widow a personal dispensation to have Mass said in her house for the rest of her life. Religion was not mixed with her motives; Felton had been tortured and dismembered for politics, and Elizabeth saw no reason to begrudge his wife the consolation of her faith. She was savage and ruthless and adamant; there was no mercy in her when her power was threatened, but nothing Cecil or Sussex or even Leicester could say made her a hypocrite or a bigot. It was the Secretary's secret grief that his mistress had so little feeling for religion in her soul.

She often wore the ring given her by Felton, and she had bought Mary's fabulous rope of pearls from the late Earl of Moray at a third of their price; they were always round her neck. She dismissed the Bull of Excommunication with the remark that the Pope was trying to lean out of the Vatican and spit across the ocean, and she paid out two thousand treasured pounds to the Scottish Regent for the Earl of Northumberland, who had been made a prisoner, and had him executed at York. Then she wrote a personal letter to Catherine de' Medici, her good sister of France, and hinted that she was willing to reconsider marriage with her unmarried son the Duc D'Alençon.

Elizabeth was thirty-seven, her suitor was nineteen. Shrewd and cunning as Catherine was, she was obsessed with power, power for herself and her children, and it was just possible that the Virgin Queen of England was prepared to marry and safeguard herself after the recent rebellion and the Papal sentence, which Catherine blandly ignored. For once she fell foul of her own greed; Mary Stuart wrote impassioned letters complaining of her treatment and her danger and trying desperately to involve France in an intrigue on her behalf, but there was no response. The marriage negotiations opened, and Elizabeth could be sure of French neutrality as long as any hope of self-interest remained.

In spite of his experience of past courtships, Cecil was unable to resist the temptation to take Elizabeth's overtures seriously; he had never abandoned his hope that the Queen would overcome her scruples and take a husband; he longed to see her with a child and he was sufficiently desperate to support a bridegroom who was a Catholic and still in his teens. He disapproved of Elizabeth's familiarity with men, but he regarded it as a sign of susceptibility to the more regular relationship instead of the empty substitute it really was. He could not see how a woman could be content with flattery, flirting with Leicester and Heneage and Sir Christopher Hatton, all of them young and distinguished by physical attractions, without secretly yearning for the felicities of marriage. It was his one blind spot, and it led him into the same error as the Dowager Queen of France. It was always possible that Elizabeth meant what she said when she talked about marriage, and his enthusiasm infected her Council who wasted as much time over the negotiations as the French. Elizabeth did not disillusion any of them; it rather amused her to deceive Cecil a little —he was so seldom wrong about anything. But she did not pretend with Leicester; he was not concerned with this new suitor whom he knew would be rejected like all the others, but he was mortally afraid of losing his own comfortable position of favourite to younger men like Hatton, who deluged the Queen with love-letters and presents exactly as he had done when he had hopes of marrying her years before. He was jealous, and he exaggerated his jealousy to please her. She was becoming very vain, a common symptom in women approaching middle age, and the satisfaction of her vanity was an exhausting and uncertain occupation. He could never afford to be tired or depressed or anything but a mirror to reflect the Queen's mood; if he relaxed in his role of adorer, Hatton or Heneage made up the deficiency, and Elizabeth retaliated by encouraging them and snubbing him when he competed. It was a hectic life, bedevilled by the caprices of a woman who seemed to become less predictable as she grew older, who danced till the small hours and hunted all the afternoon and yet always seemed to be working with Cecil and her Council. Leicester was also nearly forty and he grew tired long before she did. He escaped to Lettice with increasing affection and relief, and left Elizabeth to his rivals because he could not endure the pace she set without an occasional respite. He had a great many enemies, but Cecil was no longer active among them. After his betrayal of the Norfolk plot, the Secretary had intimated that there was a permanent peace between them instead of a truce. He had shown himself loyal to the Queen and Cecil was prepared to forgive him his riches, his influence and his arrogance on that account. He was a fixture who would only be removed by a husband, and he now caused less scandal than the conduct of Hatton and half a dozen others. He accepted Leicester and Leicester no longer resented him. When Elizabeth made Cecil a peer and gave him the title of Lord Burleigh, Leicester was the first to congratulate him. There was only one supreme power in the country and that was the Queen; he was content to share what remained with William Cecil.

The marriage negotiations dragged on; Elizabeth showed enthusiasm one moment, and maidenly reticence the next; so great were her powers of dissimulation, so brilliant was her acting, that the French ambassador saw nothing ridiculous in the nervous scruples of an experienced woman of almost forty over the character of the bridegroom who was now twenty-one. Neither side betrayed impatience over the lapse of months which had spun into two years. It was not uncommon for a Royal marriage to be agreed upon after a year or more of bargaining by both parties. Nor was it incongruous when the Queen spoke wistfully of children. She was as slim and active as a girl; her handsome features defied an analysis of her age, and since she had adopted the fashion and wore a variety of wigs in different styles, it was impossible to detect a grey hair. Certainly her health was delicate. She ran high temperatures, suffered from violent stomach upsets and was inclined to hysterical outbursts of tears and temper. But there was no reason to suppose her incapable of bearing children, and if she died in childbirth, then Queen Catherine's grandchild would be the ruler of England. And the French would be less scrupulous than Queen Elizabeth about executing Mary Stuart and securing the infant its inheritance.

In February, 1572, the Treaty of Blois was signed between England and France as a preliminary to the marriage contract. It was a defensive treaty aimed against Spain; both countries were bound to send troops in the event of an invasion by a third and to abstain from interfering in Scotland. It was a triumph for Elizabeth's diplomacy and, more significant still, it ignored the existence of that other protagonist whose mother had been a Guise, who was still held a prisoner in England and still writing hopeless letters to France reminding Catherine that she was proposing to marry her son to an excommunicated usurper.

Elizabeth's fears were calmed by another outbreak of revolt in the Netherlands, more violent than the first. Earlier she had opened her ports to hundreds of Flemish refugees, most of them skilled craftsmen who enhanced native trade; now she released as many as wished to volunteer to fight in their own country, and at the same time expressed her regret at the rebellion to the Spanish ambassador, promising absolute neutrality.

Again her policy was vindicated, but it was a cautious policy based on making as much trouble for the Spanish as possible without direct intervention. Elizabeth wanted to avoid war with Spain at any cost, but the young King of France was persuaded that at last the moment had come to interfere and sweep Alva and his troops out of the Netherlands and annex the country for himself. His adviser was the Huguenot leader Coligny who wanted a religious war on behalf of his fellow Protestants, and for the first time Catherine de' Medici's advice was over-ruled by her son.

Consumed by possessiveness for her son and fear for her own power, the Queen Dowager decided to murder her rival while he and the heads of the great Huguenot families were all gathered in Paris.

Elizabeth was out riding when a courier delivered the despatch from her ambassador in Paris telling of the massacre of St. Bartholomew's Eve. She stopped her horse and broke the seals and read through it slowly. Her first reaction was incredulous horror, followed quickly by astonishment that Catherine de' Medici, whose intelligence she respected, could have committed such an appalling blunder. She had bungled the murder of her enemy Coligny; the assassins had wounded but not killed him, and the Queen Mother had been forced to arrange the wholesale murder of the Huguenots within twenty-four hours of the attempt, to prevent them taking their revenge upon her. The wording of the despatch was almost as violent as the event it described. She knew the ambassador in Paris; his name was Francis Walsingham and he belonged to the increasing sect of dismally Puritan reformers whom Elizabeth instinctively disliked. He was more anti-Catholic than Cecil at his worst, and when he wrote of the hideous brutalities committed in Paris on that day, he spared the Queen no details. Men and women and children, even babies at the breast, had been dragged into the streets and slaughtered; their homes were looted and burnt, the city was running with blood and the Seine carried hundreds of mutilated corpses. Not only the Queen Mother and her son and their Court were responsible for what Walsingham described as the greatest crime next to the Crucifixion; the common people of Paris had joined them and after them the people of France. In every town and village, the populace were murdering the Huguenots. He called Catherine de' Medici the female anti-Christ and prophesied the downfall of the nation which had shown itself capable of such atrocities. But in his indignation, in Elizabeth's opinion, Walsingham had completely overlooked the salient point. Public outcry would force her to drop her marriage negotiations with France. She rode on slowly, still holding the despatch under her arm, and none of her companions asked her what was in it. They knew it must be serious when she gave the order to turn back.

On reflection, Catherine de' Medici had retrieved her initial mistake as well as she could. Coligny was dead and the whole Huguenot faction which had threatened her power and rent France with religious wars, was destroyed root and branch. Horribly and cruelly—Elizabeth winced, remembering Walsingham's descriptions of the murder of little children—but nonetheless destroyed. And the French people had participated in the crime. The Queen Mother had ineffably blackened her name and the honour of her country, but she had made France a first-class power for the first time in a hundred years. She would have to express her horror, and she was horrified, Elizabeth admitted, not only by the needless cruelty to the innocent, but by the mismanagement which made it necessary, and she would have to pretend aversion to the marriage. But only for a time. The negotiations could be shelved, but they must not be closed.

It might be easier if she recalled that hothead Walsingham from his post and sent someone more politic and less religious to take his place.

She refused to receive the French ambassador for fourteen days, and then gave him an audience dressed in the deepest mourning, accompanied by her Council and ladies and gentlemen, all of whom were dressed in black. She made her public disapproval plain to the satisfaction of her people and her Government, and wrote one of her brilliant, involved letters to Catherine de' Medici expressing horror, grief and censure in the correct proportion. But she also intimated with great delicacy, that when her sorrow for her co-religionists had faded, the French Prince might be allowed to revive his suit.

The Earl of Shrewsbury had not been relieved of his duties as guardian of the Scots Queen. His letter was shown to Elizabeth who remarked that the safest custodian was one sufficiently unmoved by his prisoner to want to be rid of her, and ordered him to remove Mary to Sheffield where she was kept in a suite of rooms which were dry and comfortable by comparison with Tutbury. The Earl had said her health was bad, and the Queen was very anxious to keep her alive. It was a wish the English

Parliament did not share. Protestant fury at the French massacre was concentrated in an attack on the Catholic Queen who was a prisoner and in a position to pay for the crimes committed by her fellow Catholics. Parliament met and demanded the head of Mary Stuart for her part in the defunct Norfolk plot; when the Queen refused them, they put forward a Bill by which anyone of any degree or station could be executed for treason against the State. Elizabeth vetoed this proposal. She had no doubt that there would be other plots and that if such a Bill reached the Statute Book, Mary's head would fall within twelve months. She refused in the lofty language which never failed to stir the emotions of those whose wishes she was frustrating, and within a year she judged it safe to re-open the marriage negotiations with France. This had such a disturbing effect upon the mind of King Philip of Spain that he sent his ambassador on a special visit to Elizabeth to protest Spanish friendship and make sure that her intentions of a matrimonial alliance with the French were only a political feint.

The courtship began once more; the question of the Queen's marriage was discussed in every tavern and in every great house throughout the country; romantic speculation was focused on the Queen, and it was noticed that the Queen showed signs of enjoying the attention for its own sake.

But while Elizabeth began the game of marriage with a man she had never seen, another marriage took place within forty miles of her own Palace at Whitehall.

The Earl of Essex had died in Ireland where he was performing his duties as Governor with the brutality and oppression customary in that obstinately Catholic and independent country. On 20th September Leicester married his widow.

The new Countess of Leicester held out her left hand and admired the wedding ring on her finger.

" Even now I cannot believe it," she said. Leicester pulled himself up on the pillows and laughed. The bedroom at Wanstead was full of the bright autumn sunshine; it was nearly noon and no one had disturbed them. The marriage had been performed in secret at his private chapel, witnessed by Lettice's father, Sir Henry Knollys, who had left immediately after the ceremony. He was a member of the rising sect of Puritans and he had never approved of his daughter's mode of life or of the scandals which resulted from her choice of the Queen's favourite as a lover. He also strongly disapproved of the lover. When Lettice was widowed, he made it clear that Leicester must marry his daughter or he would petition the Queen to intervene and place Lettice under his control.

Leicester never considered losing Lettice for a moment; he agreed to the marriage on condition that it was kept a secret, and on that autumn morning he awoke feeling strangely contented, and far less frightened of the results of discovery than he had imagined. He watched his wife with amusement and tenderness as she stood by the side of the bed in her satin bedgown, admiring her wedding ring and smiling at him. He was always amused and a little envious of her sensuality. She was unashamedly in love with warmth and food and bodily pleasures, with a quick wit and a lively mind which prevented her capacity for indulgence from becoming a bore to herself or to him. He could never understand how he had once compared her to Elizabeth just because they both had red hair.

"Come here," he said. "A bride's place is with her husband. Come and show me your ring, sweetheart, and let me prove to you that you are truly married."

The Countess laughed. "Oh no, my Lord—I've had proof enough of that already. How will you treat me now that we are married? Will you be a gentle husband, or will you be a roistering old boor like poor Essex. . . ."

"If I were, you'd undoubtedly serve me as you served him," he retorted. "And I prefer to have you happy—and faithful. Why did you say you couldn't believe it a moment ago?"

"Because I suppose it is the final proof that you have given up all hope of the Queen. And for all these years I have never been sure of you until now."

"Women are never convinced," he said slowly. "You know that I love you, but sometimes you are as bad as she is—asking and demanding and setting traps for me."

Lettice came and sat on the side of the bed; she took his hand and suddenly kissed it.

"I do not demand and I do not set traps," she said. "You would never have borne it from anyone else but the Queen, and I knew that. I love you, and you love me, and if she makes you turn somersaults to please her, that is not my fault."

"I know," he answered. He leant his head against her breast.

"I'm very happy, Lettice. I can go back to Court now and dance on a high wire like all the others and know that I have you hidden in my life and that no one can take you from me."

"You speak sometimes as if you hated her," she said softly. "But you don't, Robert, even if you think you do. You are only jealous because there are other men around her with the same ambitions you once had yourself."

"They won't gain any more than I did," he answered. "She'll play the devil with them, just as she did with me, loving and smiling one minute and snarling the next. No man will ever have her now. When I first tried for her there was a chance, but a meagre one as I look back on it, and that has gone. The Queen is changing, Lettice; she changes before my eyes. You are always saying that I love her still, and I pay you a compliment for your intelligence when I admit it. But what manner of love it is I'll never know. How does a man love lightning, or riding at high speed over rough ground? How does he feel when he kisses the hand that strokes him and remembers how it struck him in the face. . . . I'm no poet or perhaps I could describe it. I leave that to Hatton, he's the rhymester now. I tell you this: the Queen is less of a woman than she ever was, and more than a woman in her need of men. She works and she governs—by God, her conduct at a Council leaves me breathless, no King could be more forceful when it comes to policy! She drinks in her power as if it were wine, and it has gone to her head like wine. She lives and breathes for her power. And her only relaxation is to pretend to herself and to others that all she really wishes is to be counted like a woman. Until her will is crossed. Then the mask falls. I've seen what lies behind it and there is no husband in the world who would survive a contest. So there will never be a husband. There will only be men like Hatton and the others, seeking what they can get from flattery, and one man like me, who stays because I dare not leave and could not keep away from her if I did."

"I think," Lettice remarked at last, "that I am a remarkable woman to hear such a discourse from my husband and not stab him with jealousy."

"You are a remarkable woman, my love, and you will never stab me on the Queen's account." He was smiling again and she settled into his arms.

"I don't want the part of you which belongs to her," she

whispered. " I love what I have, and we'd best make the most of it, before she sends a message ordering you back to Court. When does the French Prince's envoy arrive in London? "

" In a week; his name is Simier—he's Alençon's chamberlain. He'll stay for a month or so and then nothing will come of it. Are you hungry, Lady Leicester? Shall I ring for food, or will you dine a little late today? "

" I shall dine late for a week," Lettice answered. " And so will you, my Lord."


William Cecil had relinquished the post of Secretary to the Queen. As Lord Burleigh he became her Chief Minister, and with his usual foresight, he presented his own candidate for the vacant post which was the second most important after his own. The Secretary was with the Queen night and day; he dealt with her correspondence and was in a position to shape the policy of her Government if Elizabeth trusted his advice. The wrong man in such a place of privilege might cause havoc with Burleigh's work. The right one could only complement it, and there was no one whose ideas were more in sympathy with his own than the late ambassador to France, Sir Francis Walsingham. They waited together in the Queen's ante-room.

" I have told Her Majesty that she can rely upon you for discretion and sober judgment," Burleigh repeated. " I have praised you to her so highly that she will certainly give you the appointment unless you spoil your own chances."

Walsingham was a tall thin man, with very piercing eyes of a peculiar green and a narrow mouth which never smiled. It was the face of a fanatic, harsh and uncompromising and perpetually at war with what he referred to as the powers of evil. This description embraced every interest and adherent of the Roman Catholic Church throughout the world.

" If you tell me the pitfalls, I shall avoid them," he said. " I have dealt with Her Majesty by letter, but I hear she is capricious; it is a common failing among women and I am not incapable of dealing with it, my Lord."

" Then take care not to speak to the Queen in the tone you have just used to me," Burleigh said sharply. " If you want this position you must not hector the Queen, or contradict her, or advance an opinion which conflicts with hers. You must be humble without fawning, alert and truthful when she questions you, you must be able to tell her where every piece of correspondence is, and exactly what you dealt with last. You must not betray bias of any kind, and above all, refrain from religious controversy in matters of State. The Queen is a devout Protestant but she is quite out of sympathy with your extreme views and expressing them will only irritate her. I have learnt to muzzle my own tongue and you must do the same. Never forget that she is the Queen, and that while she must be treated courteously as a woman, she does not suffer from a woman's failing. Do not, Sir Francis, show your contempt for her sex; you will quickly find that Her Majesty is an exception."

Walsingham nodded; there was no time to answer because the Royal Page summoned them, and he walked behind Burleigh into the Privy Chamber.

He had not seen Elizabeth for nearly two years, and he had become used to dealing with Catherine de' Medici whose sluggish eyes never rested on his face when she was speaking. He was therefore unprepared for the penetrating stare with which Elizabeth met him.

He was also unprepared for the silence which lasted for a full minute before the Queen spoke after Burleigh had presented him.

" Sir Francis Walsingham, you may kiss my hand. And you, my dear Burleigh, may leave us. I prefer a man to speak for himself."

Sir Francis kissed her hand and bowed a little deeper than he had intended. But he resisted the impulse to look away; he had never seen such an odd contrast as those jet black eyes set in the pale and painted face. There was an enormous pear-shaped pearl in the middle of the brilliant red curls which he noticed with distaste were artificial. He did not approve of wigs; he did not approve of any of the female vanities which were evident in the jewels and scent and the lavish cosmetics used by his Queen.

" I need a replacement for Lord Burleigh as Secretary," Elizabeth said. " He has strongly recommended you. So strongly that I can hardly believe in the existence of such a paragon of virtue. Can you fill the post, Sir Francis? "

" I believe so, but that is for you to say, Madam."

" I am quite sure that he has told you what to say to me and how to conduct yourself. You are to forget every word of it. I don't want someone else's puppet as my Secretary. Whatever you are I shall find you out in time, so it had better be now.

You may sit down, Sir Francis, and we will talk. And I want to hear your own voice and not Burleigh's."

He sat on a low stool facing her; he would have preferred to stand. He wondered whether she knew this and had offered him the seat to put him at a disadvantage; she looked down on him shrewdly from her chair.

"Tell me, whom do you consider the greatest enemy of England?"

She had asked for an honest opinion and Walsingham gave it to her in spite of Burleigh's warning.

"The Papist Church, Madam."

"I see. And which of the offshoots of that Church would you say was the most dangerous?"

He did not know it but if his answer was the Queen of Scots he would lose the post.

"Spain."

There was a moment of silence. Elizabeth leant back in her chair, and suddenly she smiled.

"Master Walsingham," she said. "You are the first man who has shown that he can see beyond his nose. Spain is our danger; the rest, my cousin of Scotland, the English Papists, France, all of them are secondary to the real enemy, and we have not done battle with him yet. Now, what is the situation in the Netherlands—how is the rebellion faring?"

Walsingham frowned. "Badly, Madam. The Duke of Alva is a master of repression, his troops are the best disciplined in the world and he is a man without mercy or scruple. Our Protestant brothers are dying for their faith in thousands, but they still fight on. The unhappy country runs with blood; they are in terrible need of help from us."

"They shall have help," Elizabeth said. "I am sending what money I can spare, and God knows it's little enough, and somehow I shall squeeze out more, but I will not go beyond that; I dare not. We are not ready for war."

"Nor is Spain," he countered. "So long as her best troops are needed in the Netherlands and her Treasury is being bled to keep them there, she cannot attack. We are safe from Spain for the moment, Madam, and that brings me to another point. You asked me to speak with my own voice and with your consent I'll take you at your word. We've talked of the enemy abroad, but I believe the time has come to deal with the enemy in England."

204

"Go on," Elizabeth nodded.

"I know your reluctance to punish the Queen of Scots for her crimes against you, and against humanity," Walsingham spoke slowly. "I must admit, Madam, that I agree with Lord Burleigh and all your Councillors that your clemency is a mistake. But if you will not proceed against her, now is the time to cut down her adherents. While I was in France, a Jesuit seminary was opened at Douai with the sole object of training English traitors to be priests. These men will return to England to try and revive their religion and to foment plots against you. Their numbers have increased since the proclamation of your law making it an act of treason to say their Mass or take the cloth of Rome. They are dangerous and fanatical, and they are not deterred by the fear of death."

"Several have already been caught," the Queen interrupted him. "What are you suggesting—if a man doesn't baulk at being hanged and disembowelled alive, what more can be done with him?"

"Nothing. But mete out the same punishment to any Englishman or woman who shelters him or fails to betray him if he is hiding in their district. The Papists in England are a dagger at your throat, Madam. You have been too soft with them for too long. Fines and a few executions are not enough. They must be hunted down and destroyed."

"You are a religious man I see," Elizabeth remarked, and he flushed at the sarcasm. "But if you are to serve me, you will not confuse dogmas with politics. And you will not suppose that I confuse them either. I tell you, as I have told Burleigh, that I don't care whether a man says his prayers in Latin or English and I don't think the God he's praying to cares either. But if the man who prays in Latin is a menace to my throne, then he will have to change his language if he wants to live to pray at all. Half the men bleating about Papists and wanting me to cut their throats were Papists themselves in my sister's time. I know that you were not among them," she smiled slightly at him. "You're of the same mettle as these Douai priests, whether you like to be told so or not. But it's a mettle I respect, and I would have it on my side rather than against me. You are a man of sense, Master Walsingham, and also a man of vision. If I leave the problem of these Catholic exiles to you, how will you deal with it?"

"I will set spies in France and spies in every port in England.

I will found an army of informers who will nose out every traveller coming to this country, every stranger in the villages and towns, every son of known Papist families who reappears at home. I will offer rewards and pay them, and we will have our prisons full within a few months."

" Informers are expensive; so is the spy system you propose," Elizabeth said. " I cannot afford it."

Walsingham looked at her. She saw the cold fanaticism in his pale green eyes and thought that in spite of his abilities, she would never like him.

" I can afford it, Madam. I am a rich man, and I will pay the expenses out of my own pocket."

" I can see that Burleigh has sent me the right man," she said. " Your duties begin tomorrow."

She held out her hand.

" Farewell, Master Secretary."

# Chapter 11

S N O w fell at the beginning of February, 1579, and it covered the park outside Mary's prison at Sheffield so deeply that there had not been a visitor to the house for nearly twelve days. The house itself was bitterly cold, and the Queen's rooms were covered in tapestries and hangings, and Shrewsbury had moved one of his best beds and much of his furniture into her apartments; she was as comfortable and as warm as he could make her.

She had grown attached to the Earl; she was even glad of his wife's company and she bought the Countess's favour with flattery and little gifts. The Countess was an incredibly tough and energetic woman, obsessed with money and possessions; she reminded Mary of a foul-mouthed man. When she was in a good temper she joined her prisoner and amused her by repeating the current slanders about Elizabeth, and after so many years fighting that elusive personality and always losing, Mary listened to every word spoken against her with enjoyment.

The Countess described her passion for clothes and the outrageous fashions she adopted; she made fun of Elizabeth's musicianship, her dancing, her habits at the table, and most of all, her flirtations with the men at her Court. Leicester was an old scandal; she no longer allowed him to come into her room and help her with her underclothes, but she shut herself up with Sir Christopher Hatton and indulged in practices which the Countess hesitated to describe. But she overcame her diffidence and laughed outright when she saw the Queen of Scots blushing.

" And now," she said, " she has taken M. Simier as her new playfellow. If you can imagine a woman so depraved, Madam, that she misconducts herself with the man sent to negotiate her marriage! "

"I can't," Mary said coldly. She could not imagine any woman wanting the physical attentions of a man. She wondered whether Elizabeth's disgusting appetites might have been checked had she been shut up in that room in the keep at Dunbar Castle when Bothwell came. . . . She closed her eyes for a moment and tried to dismiss the memory. He was dead; he had gone mad in his prison and spent the last years of his life chained like an animal to a stone pillar, pacing up and down in his own excrement, tearing at his flesh and raving about the past. She had loved him and then hated him as bitterly as she knew he had hated her, but she could never imagine the agonies of that terrible imprisonment without being glad that for his own sake he had escaped from his torment in death.

So many men she knew had died; the power they had wrested from her had brought death to her brother James, to the Earl of Lennox, Darnley's father, to Lord Mar, who was poisoned by his successor Morton. She could see Morton at that moment, standing beside her with his pistol pressed into her side the night they murdered Rizzio, looking like an incarnation of the Devil with his red hair and beard and his eyes blazing with blood lust and hatred. He was still Regent of Scotland, tutoring her miserable little son in the heretic religion and teaching him to revile his mother's memory. Morton had survived, but the others had paid their debt to her like Bothwell. She nodded while Lady Shrewsbury went on talking; she was telling her how the Frenchman, Simier, had begun the negotiations for the marriage of the Duc D'Alençon by behaving as if he were the suitor.

"He's an ugly little creature, but she's so vain she couldn't resist flattery from a monkey! He writes her love notes every day and sends her presents and sighs and dances attendance morning, noon and night. By God, they say in London that if any man can bring her to marriage it's this one—he's playing the lover so skilfully that when they substitute that pock-marked Alençon, she's so bemused she'll hardly notice."

"I think it's all a trick," Mary said. "I don't believe my cousin will marry anyone, she's far too wise. And too old," she added. "At forty-five she has no hope of bearing children, and that would be the only reason for a match. She has left it too late to disinherit me by that means. The French are being duped, my dear Countess, and God knows I've written telling them so often enough!"

The Countess was not interested in politics and she could see that Mary was about to change the conversation from the

208

topic of Elizabeth's sexual indiscretions to her political motives. She did not like Mary; she only talked to her because it gave her a feeling of superiority to entertain her with scandal, and to revile the other Queen whom she hated because she was actually afraid of her.

She was fundamentally jealous of any woman who was young and still as beautiful as Mary Stuart and capable of rousing sparks of chivalry in her own dull husband. She could see the signs of depression which afflicted Mary sometimes for days and if she was going to sit there and weep and talk about her own tiresome and hopeless fortunes, the Countess was not going to keep her company.

"If you will excuse me, Madam, I have letters to write."

"Of course." Mary managed to smile at her. She was sick of the creature, sick of her loud laughter and her revolting tongue. She would be glad to be alone. The Countess curtsied and went out.

The room was very quiet; her little spaniel lay stretched out in front of the fire asleep, and the panel of embroidery she had been working on for months was just out of her reach. She was too tired to get up and fetch it, and disinclined to disturb her lady-in-waiting, Mary Seton, who was resting in another room. Seton had been with her all through these weary years, sharing the discomforts and the frustrations of her imprisonment, ready to console and encourage her and nurse her when her health broke down and her spirits failed. Men had betrayed and exploited her, but women, like Seton, and the others who looked after her, had shown her nothing but unselfish loyalty and love.

It would be Easter soon. Another year had passed, less rigorous than the previous two, but paralysed by inactivity. She was well housed, and she enjoyed the benefits of her French dowry so that she lacked nothing that money could buy, and her gaolers were generous. She had women to care for her and a secretary to help with the correspondence which occupied most of her time. She read and wrote and sewed and prayed and the days ran into one another followed by the months and the long, dragging years, and she only lived on her hopes and her resurgence of energy to try and procure her own release and the restoration of her power. Without that objective, she would probably have died, or lost her mind like Bothwell. It was a temptation to live in the past, however terrible it had been, and she was only saved from completely retreating into it by her obstinate obsession with the future. She was still in her thirties and she was still alive. France would not help her, because French interests were involved in this matrimonial farce which was taking place in London; but there was always Spain. She wrote frequently to the King of Spain, urging him to act on the Papal sentence and come to her rescue. Spain was her principal hope, and the sympathy of the persecuted English Catholics was the second. Someone would rescue her; if she had managed to touch the hearts of Scotsmen in her adversities, if she could soften Shrewsbury and win over the English servants in his household so that they went out of their way to do her little services, then some day a man bold enough and strong enough would be found to release her.

She looked up at the sound of a knock.

She called out, and the door opened; it was Shrewsbury's ward, Anthony Babington. He was a slight, gentle youth of sixteen, fair-haired and blue-eyed, and he was always finding an excuse to come to her rooms. Mary smiled at him.

"Come in," she said. "What can I do for you, Master Babington?"

In many ways he reminded her of that other youth, Willie Douglas; he had the same shy way of looking at her, and the same habit of blushing when she spoke to him. The old Earl and the beardless boy, suffering the pangs of calf-love—they were the sum total of her champions.

"I came to see if you wanted anything, Madam."

The Babingtons were an old and wealthy Catholic family; rich enough to survive the fines levied on them for their religion and wise enough to avoid political activity.

"There's nothing I need, thank you."

Anthony Babington came closer, hoping for an invitation to sit down. Sometimes the Queen let him sit by her and asked him questions about himself. Once he had found her crying, and lain awake for nights imagining how, if he were older, he might have taken her in his arms and comforted her and told her that he had arranged for her escape. The imagery was so real that the boy had almost felt the wind whipping his face as they rode away from Sheffield to join the army he had raised for her defence. In his waking dream, Mary rode pillion behind him with her arms round his waist.

"I could exercise the dog, Madam, if you liked."

She smiled and shook her head. "He's comfortable as he is; the snow is thick outside. He might take cold and so might you. But if you want to do me a service, move my embroidery frame over here."

She changed the thread in her needle, and held out her hand for the silks. For a moment their fingers touched and she felt that Babington's were trembling.

"You are very kind," she said gently. "I would ask you to keep me company but I know that Lady Shrewsbury is uneasy if you see too much of me. You are young yet, Master Babington, but I would not be the cause of trouble to you. Next time, you can stay a little if you like."

He went down on his knee beside her, and on an impulse, Mary gave him her hand.

"If ever you want me, Madam, if there is anything I can do for you now—any letters or messages or anything, you have only to ask. I am your servant for as long as I live. And one day, I swear before God, I will do you a real service."

She felt the pressure of a warm and clumsy kiss upon her hand, and then he turned away quickly and rushed out of the room.

Jehan de Simier released the Queen of England's hand. Whenever he kissed it he lingered; he knew how to change an act of homage into a caress. When he looked into the face of Elizabeth he conveyed his wish that he might have been kissing her mouth instead. He was short and he was ugly, but his irregular features and his bright black eyes were an essential part of the peculiarly aggressive virility which he possessed. He was a wit and a courtier, with exquisite manners, but everything about him suggested a man of fierce sexuality and reckless temper. He had been sent to England to persuade a hesitating woman to marry his master Alençon, and he proceeded as if he were suing for himself.

He had been prepared to flatter a middle-aged spinster who was pretending to virginal scruples which disguised a scandalous past, but within a few days he had changed his opinion and his approach. The Queen of England was unique. She was not a beauty, but she was handsome; she had a mind as sharp as any man's, relieved by streaks of outrageous feminity. She looked at him and through him as if she could see exactly the kind of man he was, and did not mind. He spent his first audience telling her that Alençon was madly in love with her, and ended by saying boldly that he was falling a victim to her charms himself.

Elizabeth had laughed in his face. He would never forget that laughter; it was full of mockery and full of provocation. He had opened the campaign on personal grounds, and she challenged him to win it on the same level if he could.

"If you were the suitor, M. Simier, I should feel myself in terrible danger."

"If it were me, Madam," he retorted, "you would have married me two months ago."

She had given a reception at Hampton Court, and they were sitting side by side in the Long Gallery, watching her ladies and gentlemen in waiting dancing a pavan Elizabeth moved her feather fan in time to the music. Her dress was white, and her shoes and underskirt were scarlet satin; she wore a necklace of enormous rubies and pearls, and a bandeau on her hair covered in the same jewels. The hair was a wig; her own was greying and brittle, the result of years of crimping with hot irons. Her lips were painted red, and her thin brows outlined with pencil. In his first report back to Alençon, Simier had remarked on the whiteness of her skin and the slender proportions of her figure. She was almost too thin for his taste. He often wondered about the old scandals of her entertaining the Earl of Leicester wearing nothing but an open dressing robe. She neither looked nor talked like a wanton, but there was no curiosity and no hypocrisy in her eyes when he made physical advances to her. If the improbable happened and she married Alençon, she might be a technical virgin, but Simier knew that such women devoured their men in the act of submission. It was a pity, he thought privately, that he was not the bridegroom instead of the proxy. She would never be happy unless she was mastered, and he had never failed except once. He had failed with his wife with whom he had foolishly fallen in love and even more foolishly treated with gentleness and indulgence. As a result the lady had betrayed him with his brother. Simier had avenged his honour by having his brother murdered and poisoning his wife. The Queen of England knew that too, and there was no shadow of surprise or revulsion in her eyes when he paid her compliments and caressed her hand with his lips.

"Will you dance with me, Madam?" he asked her. He had

seen the Earl of Leicester watching him, his jealousy showing plainly on his face. He had made the same request and been refused a few minutes before.

Elizabeth glanced at him and smiled. The smile was mocking.

"You are quite determined to make enemies of all my nobles, aren't you, Simier? If I dance with you, I shall offend all those I have refused."

"If I can succeed where they fail, that's their misfortune. They must stomach me, if they're going to stomach my master."

"*I* am the one who must stomach him, and I've been queasy all my life. Come then; play the proxy for him, but I warn you, I expect perfection in my partners."

It was another challenge, and Simier met it confidently. They moved into the centre of the floor, and the rest of the dancers drew back to watch. He was a magnificent dancer; graceful and light, he moved like a fencer, and he was thankful because Elizabeth was the most accomplished performer he had ever seen. For a quarter of an hour they moved and twisted in the intricate figures of the pavan, and the Long Gallery was silent. No one coughed or spoke; there was only the sound of their own steps on the polished floor and the sad, stately music coming from the musicians' gallery. At the end the Queen sank into a deep curtsy, and he went down on his knee to kiss her hand.

When they rose the Court began to applaud. As he led Elizabeth back to her chair he found the Earl of Leicester standing by it.

"The 'Bear' looks as if he's been baited," he murmured, referring to the Englishman by his motto. He knew that Leicester hated him; one adventurer soon smelt out another, and the favourite was afraid.

"He also has a 'ragged staff'," Elizabeth reminded him. "Take care he doesn't strike you with it."

"I pity him," Simier said. "No wonder he is jealous of you, Madam. What will he do when you have a husband?"

"Exactly what I tell him. It's a good precept, M. Simier."

"Not good enough; you never married *him*."

"I haven't married your master either. But if he dances as well as you, I might be tempted."

"Better," Simier retorted. "I am only a shadow of him in everything I do."

"If you are the shadow," Elizabeth answered, "God protect me from the substance!"

It amused her to see Robert glaring at the Frenchman, and not only Robert but half a dozen young men who enjoyed her favour. It was extremely enjoyable to rouse them all to jealousy, and watch them trying to compete with Simier in compliments and attentions. She looked very handsome that night and she knew it; she also knew that she danced better than any of her maids of honour, some of whom were only in their twenties.

She painted and scented and changed her costumes several times a day; she had fewer headaches and felt more energetic than ever and the atmosphere of competition among so many men affected her like a powerful intoxicant. She had become increasingly irritated by the fables of her cousin Mary's beauty and her conquest of every man who saw her; even the wretched tale of Bothwell's rape had been distorted into a legend of romantic passion by the years. So many men had died for Mary Stuart, that she was described as an enchantress, rather than a fool who had bungled everything she touched. No man had died for Elizabeth except the Admiral, and that was long ago and half forgotten. Mary had outlived three husbands and borne a son, and with the onset of physical changes in her body, Elizabeth found herself thinking of her own isolated condition with unreasonable resentment. She had been urged to marry for nearly twenty years, and she had never been remotely tempted after the fiasco of Robert's early courtship, until the arrival of Jehan de Simier. When she was sensible she mocked her own foible, reminding herself that the affair was purely political and intended to fail, fighting the demand of her natural instincts for fulfilment before it was too late. Soon she would be too old for childbirth, too old to offer herself even to a youth like Alençon whose mother would marry him to anyone. Elizabeth had never feared age because she never felt old; she had never wanted children or a husband until now, when both were about to slip out of reach for ever. She had been content, until Simier came and made the phantom courtships of the past into the pursuit of a determined male. He was as strong as Robert was weak; he knew from his own bloody experience what love and passion meant; he had killed his wife for infidelity, while Robert had murdered Amy for ambition. Both men were hunters, but when he said that he had come to trap the lioness, it pleased her more than Robert comparing her to the goddesses of mythology while he sneaked into bed with the Countess of Essex.

If Simier had come twenty years ago, if he were the bridegroom and not the proxy, her life might have been very different. And through his eyes she could still see herself combining her Crown and her womanhood, and for the first time she did not dismiss the idea with scorn or indifference.

And now that she was showing some genuine enthusiasm, all those who had argued and implored her to marry, were finding reasons why she shouldn't. Her people were grumbling; they distrusted the French and feared a Catholic revival if she married Alençon; her Parliament were doubtful and her Councillors mumbled warnings about her health and the risk of having children at her age. They had harried her for years and now they dragged up every humiliating and infuriating obstacle they could think of to dissuade her from doing what she had imagined they all wanted. The author of a pamphlet denouncing the marriage had lost his right hand at her personal order. She vented her frustrations and her wounded pride on the humble offender because she was helpless against the galling advice of her own nobles. She was too old and too delicate and now nobody took her marriage seriously any more, just when she wanted to consider it herself for the first time. And nobody opposed it more bitterly in the Council Chamber and in private than the Earl of Leicester.

"Her Majesty is the most perfect dancer in the whole of Europe," Simier was saying.

"Without doubt," Robert retorted. "But she needs a tall partner to complement her. I hear your master the Duc is shorter in the leg than most."

Simier's eyes glittered, but his mouth smiled.

"Height is not important when he has so many graces, my Lord. And no man alive could hope to match the Queen, whatever his stature—don't you agree?"

"No Frenchman, certainly," Leicester snapped his answer. He held on to his jewelled sword-belt to prevent himself striking the other man across his ugly, impertinent face. He was so angry that he trembled, and his anger was murderous with jealousy and fear. He had not taken the marriage suit seriously; nobody who knew Elizabeth imagined that it would come to anything, until the arrival of this bawdy-eyed adventurer. He might have bewitched her; she was preening and painting and laughing like a frivolous girl engaged in a clandestine love affair, instead of the hard-headed, icy-hearted woman who took everything from her admirers without giving anything of her emotional self in return. Leicester could have killed him for his success. He was beginning to think that he might have to kill him before he beguiled the Queen into promising marriage before she had even seen the bridegroom. If she married Alençon, he would lose his power; there was no room for him and a husband. He looked quickly at Elizabeth and saw the hostility in her eyes.

"You have a sharp tongue tonight," she said suddenly. "Go and whet it out of my hearing. Come, M. Simier; we will go into my Privy Chamber and we will see if you play cards as well as you dance."

"The Queen has lost her senses," Walsingham spoke bluntly. "It is unthinkable that she should go so far as to receive Alençon in this country unless she really means to marry him, and the marriage would be a disaster. A Frenchman and a Papist! I repeat, my Lord, she has gone out of her mind!"

The Secretary had ridden to Leicester House as soon as he heard of the latest development. He admired the Earl and he liked him. He also believed that his influence with Elizabeth was strong enough to check the course of this marriage project before it got completely out of control. They were odd allies, the stern, fanatical young statesman with his Puritanical beliefs and the rich and powerful favourite who owed everything he had to a woman's caprice. Walsingham was a model of efficiency and diligence, sparing neither his pocket nor himself in the Queen's service, but while Elizabeth took full advantage of both, she did not like her Secretary, and did not pretend to; so he haunted Leicester in the hope of learning how to ingratiate himself.

"It's the fault of that damned Simier," Leicester said angrily. "I used to jeer at her old suitors and call them paper courtships, and by God we had nothing to fear as long as they remained a name on some ambassador's lips. This man has made his master live; he's playing Alençon's part for him so well that the Queen is bewitched. Without Simier, the whole affair would fall into ruins. If we could get rid of him . . ." He paused and Walsingham watched him closely. Assassination was a political expedient; it did not trouble his conscience, and one man's life was a trifle compared with the horrors of a Papist consort and an alliance with the country responsible for the massacre of St. Bartholomew.

"The whole country is against it," he said slowly. "The Parliament, the Council, everyone who holds the Protestant religion would agree to anything that stopped this marriage. And Simier will never leave England of his own accord."

"Everything is at stake," Leicester said. "We both know what must be done, Sir Francis. If I take steps to protect the Queen against her own folly, will you support me?"

"With my own sword, if necessary."

"Then leave this to me. Say nothing to anyone, especially to Lord Burleigh. But be ready to come forward with me when the thing is done."

Soon after his arrival, Simier had begun collecting information about his enemies. He paid well and made use of the official spy system of the French ambassador, and after heavy bribing he had discovered that Leicester, his chief enemy and the loudest opponent of the marriage, was secretly married himself. Simier was smiling as he walked through the dark streets towards his lodgings beyond Westminster. The Queen had warned him not to go out alone at night; she said that her city was infested with thieves who prowled in the darkness, looking for single victims or foreigners, or gentlemen in their cups leaving a tavern. He had laughed and promised her, and broken his promise because he liked walking and he liked solitude. He was wondering what moment to tell Elizabeth that her favourite was trying to prevent her marriage while enjoying a clandestine union himself, when two men sprang at him from a dark doorway. He always walked with his hand on his sword hilt; the moment they ran at him and he saw the dull flash of a weapon, Simier drew. Something ripped through his cloak and pierced his arm; he lunged at the nearest assailant, and felt the shock of the blade entering his body. For a moment it seemed that he had impaled his sword and the man's falling body would twist it out of his hand. He kicked the man backwards in the groin, and wrenched his sword out to meet the second of his attackers. But he had fled; the streets were empty except for the figure lying at his feet. He was groaning and Simier knelt beside him. He caught the man by the breast of his doublet, and his hands were wet with blood.

"Who set you on me?" He dragged the dying man on to his knees and shook him. "Answer me, who paid you? Answer, and I'll get you a physician. . . ."

This was no thief, this was a swordsman, not a cut-throat, who would have bludgeoned him from behind with a club and grabbed his purse.

"You've killed me. . . ." The man's mouth was full of blood and Simier could hardly hear him. He shook him again, as a dog shakes a dying rat.

"Answer, and you'll live," he spat at him. "Who sent you to attack me?"

The reply was a mumble; he had to bend to the man's lips to hear it.

"My Lord Leicester's steward. . . . Help me, for the love of Christ . . ."

Simier straightened. He looked into the contorted, pleading face and laughed.

"I'll help you as you would have helped me, friend." He threw the wretch back against the cobbles with a force that knocked the breath out of his body. He brushed his clothes, sheathed his sword and stepped over him without bothering to look at him again.

The next day he presented himself at Greenwich, where the Queen had moved for a few weeks, and walked into her presence with his injured arm in a sling.

When she saw him, Elizabeth went white. She reached his side before he had time to kneel to her, and one hand touched his injured arm.

"In the name of God, what's happened to you! You look as pale as the devil—and your arm—why is it bound up like that?"

"May I sit down, Madam? I rode down here as fast as I could to see you, and my head is swimming like a woman's. I don't want to faint at your feet."

"Wine," Elizabeth shouted to her startled lady-in-waiting. Kate Dacre ran to the closet and brought a fierce oath on herself by dropping one of the silver goblets in her agitation.

"Sit down, here, beside me." Elizabeth guided Simier herself, helping him into the chair. She took the cup of wine and held it to his lips. Without turning round she told Lady Dacre to leave the room.

Simier swallowed the wine, and allowed his head to droop.

It rested on the Queen's shoulder, and her hand was stroking his cheek, while she whispered anxiously asking what had happened, had he seen a physician, and was it a sword wound —she had seen them bandaged up like that before.

"Who were you fighting?" she demanded. He saw that her eyes were full of tears. "Whoever it was, I shall punish him for daring to injure you!"

"I disobeyed you," he said. "I went walking in your London streets last night and two men attacked me. One ran off, and I killed the other. But before he died he told me something. He told me who had paid him to assassinate me."

"What?" He felt her stiffen. "What are you saying?"

"They had been sent to murder me," he insisted. "They came at me with swords and at once I knew they were more than ordinary thieves. The man I killed gave me the name of the true murderer."

"Who was it?" Elizabeth asked the question so sharply that he looked up at her, surprised.

"The Earl of Leicester."

After a moment she said slowly: "The man was lying. Robert would never do that. He would never dare . . ."

"A frightened man is a desperate man, Madam," Simier said. "Lord Leicester must have known I had found out his secret; he was afraid I would betray him to you, and so he tried to kill me first."

"Stop talking in riddles." She withdrew her arm from him and he sat up. "What secret have you found? Wound or no wound, Simier, I want an answer and I want a short one. Tell me!"

She did not look handsome at that moment. Her face was white and peaked and her heavy-lidded black eyes blazed at him.

"He is the strongest opponent of your marriage—not only with my master but with every man who's courted you for years —but he might have a right to stand in your way if he wasn't a married man himself!"

She started as if he had struck her. Her very pale face grew suddenly red and then whitened to a ghastly pallor.

"Who is the woman?" Her voice sounded as if she were being strangled. Simier had never been afraid of anyone in his life but he thanked God that he was not standing in Robert Leicester's shoes.

"The Dowager Lady Essex."

"Are you sure of this—can you prove it?"

"The records are at Wanstead. Her father was a witness."

She turned away from him and he watched her move to the window. For some moments she stood rigid; she had forgotten Simier. No one and nothing existed for her but Robert and the fact of his monstrous deceit—his unforgivable betrayal. She had taken him out of obscurity, permitted him to kiss her and caress her—she felt suddenly afraid that the memories of their old intimacies were going to make her physically sick—she had given him money, raised him to a splendid title and to a place in her Government. She had forgiven him treason and infidelity because she believed in his insistent avowals of love. She had laughed at his jealousy and encouraged it on the same premise, and all the time it had been sham. He had made a fool of her, lied to her, exposed her to the ridicule of everyone who knew the truth, and if Simier could find it out, it must only be a secret from her. He had married his mistress. She could excuse his lust, but never, never the love he must bear that other woman to have married her and relinquished Elizabeth forever. From the window she could see the roof of an old tower, a grey brick extravagance built by her father and now used as quarters for her guards. The Tower of the Miraflore, built by an infatuated man for the woman he loved. Her own mother, Anne Boleyn, had lived there once. For the first time in her life Elizabeth felt as she imagined her father had, when he ordered the execution of the wife who had betrayed him. The Miraflore. The bare and empty symbol of a spurious love affair. To his astonishment Simier heard the sound of an hysterical, furious laugh. She went to the door and dragged it open. Two of her Gentlemen Pensioners were on duty outside.

Her voice rang out into the corridors beyond them.

"Arrest the Earl of Leicester! Take him to the Miraflore; tell him he will leave there on the next tide for the Tower!"

When she came back Simier rose from his chair, and she frowned as if she had been faced by a stranger.

"You had better have your quarters in the Palace," she said curtly. "I'll send my own physician to attend that arm."

She walked past him before he could answer and shut herself into her bedroom.

She was in bed and she was ill and no one could get near

her. Her women went through their duties, silent and nervous; she threw a glass of cordial at her Mistress of the Robes when she suggested she should see her doctors, and swore that if one of them admitted Lord Burleigh or Walsingham or anyone else into the room, they should go to the Tower. She cursed with a fluency and obscenity that would have shocked a man, and then suddenly fell on her pillow and began to cry hysterically. She told her women, and anyone in the next two rooms who could hear her shouting, that she would have Leicester's head cut off and sent to his wife as a wedding present. At two in the morning the Earl of Sussex forced his way past her ladies and came to the side of her bed. Leicester was under guard in the Miraflore; his clothes were packed up and a barge was waiting to take him up the Thames on the morning tide; a message had been sent on to the Governor of the Tower of London to expect him and admit him by the Traitor's Gate.

The Council had met in her absence, and it was decided that Sussex was the best person to brave her interdict and go and see her. Burleigh was useless in calming her rages; Walsingham would only infuriate her; her cousin Hunsdon doubted if she would listen to him. They remembered that they had sent Sussex to her many years ago to try and injure Leicester; she might remember that when he came again to save him.

He was an old man now, trusted and privileged, and known for his courage in speaking the truth.

"What the devil are you doing here? Who dared to let you in?" Sussex knelt before he answered.

"See me alone, Madam. Grant me that one favour for the sake of all my years of love and service. No one admitted me— I forced my way. Hear me first and punish me later if you wish."

Elizabeth leant back; she was exhausted with the force of her own anger, her head ached and her eyes were red and smarting with sleeplessness and tears. She loved Sussex; he had always been true to her and he had never asked a favour for himself. She was suddenly glad that he had defied her and come in. She could talk to Sussex in a way that was impossible with Burleigh, who had so much brain and so little heart, or with a younger man who must never be asked for his pity.

She turned to her ladies.

"Get out—all of you. Sit on the bed, Sussex; you're the only

221

man alive that I can trust to come in here and not boast that he's seen my grey hairs. Have you come about Leicester? Don't answer—I know it! He's married, did you know that? He's married that harlot of his after all these years, and made me a laughing stock before the world. . . ."

"I know, Madam," he answered quietly.

"Why did no one tell me?" she demanded. "Why did I have to hear it from that Frenchman first?"

"Those who heard rumours didn't want to hurt you," Sussex said gently. "Robert Dudley was not worth your tears at any time; he isn't worth them now."

"You always hated him," she exclaimed. "Oh God, how true your instinct was! I should have listened to you, Sussex—I could have spared myself this vile humiliation. . . ." She began to cry. "I'll execute him; by the living God I swear I will. No man shall betray me and mock me and live to boast of it!"

"I said he wasn't worth your tears," he answered. "He's worth nothing, as I tried to tell you from the beginning. I am only here now because I care for you, not for him."

"Then I'm right to do it," she flashed at him. "You will support me?"

"I will support anything you do, Madam. But I beg you to think of your own reputation and do nothing of the kind. Killing that dog will not hurt anyone but yourself. It will only show the world how much his treachery has stung you. People will laugh then, and those who don't laugh will say you are a wanton, murdering an unfaithful lover. Forgive plain words; they only come from love. You are the Queen of England. You cannot take a man's life because he marries. You cannot even imprison him, because it's not a crime."

"How can you plead for him—you've always been his enemy!"

"I am still that," he answered quietly. "As much as I am your friend. I care nothing for him, but everything for you. You are the Queen. You cannot show yourself a weak and jealous woman, whatever he has done to you. You are above Leicester, and Leicester's petty marriage and his petty betrayal of your trust. If you punish him, you fall to his level; you stand equal with the woman he preferred to you."

"Equal with her! How dare you say such a thing to me— every word that you speak hardens my heart against him! I

222

will never forgive him, I will never be satisfied until I have hurt and punished him as he deserves."

"It's still not worth it. Especially if you really intend to marry this young Frenchman."

"Marry?" She looked up at him and her face contorted. "How can I marry—my life is half over. Oh, God has smitten me today—everywhere I look I see the truth, and the truth is nothing but pain and disillusion. Sussex, I know myself at last. I've lain here thinking of Robert's treachery and my own weakness as if I were seeing us both in a mirror. I might have married once, but in my heart I never wanted it. Why should I? I was young and there was no loneliness ahead; I never felt the wish for children or the longing to be subject to a man. I had all that I wanted, and that traitor helped to give it to me. . . ."

She wiped her eyes. "Lately I've wondered whether it were not too late, whether I might find a little comfort with a husband. This boy would be grateful for the match; Simier says he'd cherish me. . . . I've thought of it, and I could feel a temptation, almost a weakness creeping on me. And now nobody wants it. I am too old in all men's eyes except my own. Sussex, Sussex, you've never lied to me? Tell me the truth—do I mean what I feel, and if I did it, what would be the outcome?"

"As I see it," he said slowly, "it is too late, Madam. You cannot demean yourself by taking a youth for a husband. The pangs you suffer now because of Leicester are a pinprick to the humiliations such a marriage might bring upon you after a year or two. And you could not send a husband to the Tower."

Elizabeth sighed; it was a deep sigh as if some caged emotion had been suddenly released. She leant back on her pillows and closed her eyes. Slowly two large tears began to run down her thin cheeks.

"It was a dream, Sussex. It came to me late in life, and now I hear from you what I've been hearing from myself today. It was a dream and I have woken up. I never wanted marriage; I've hated the thought all my life, and now that I'm awake at last I hate it still. The play is over. I shall remain alone."

She groped for his hand, and he took it and kissed it.

"Loneliness is the lot of Princes, Madam. And you are a Prince above all things. I will not ask you now, but I know that you will never do a thing that is unjust or unbecoming

223

to a Prince. You will not dupe yourself with dreams, or lower yourself with an unworthy vengeance. And one old man's heart will go with you to the grave."

She was not going to marry Alençon; she was preparing to receive him and make much of him and carry the farce to the limit of pretence, but she could look forward to the futile ending without flinching or resentment. Looking at herself in her mirror as she dressed, Elizabeth frowned in self-disgust. How low had she fallen, how weak had she become, to consider uniting herself with a man so many years younger and not even handsome, brilliant, or accomplished like any of the courtiers who surrounded her? Her own face stared back at her in the steel mirror; it was thin and the sharp angle of her jaw and the arrogant nose were more prominent; there were deep lines between her pencilled eyebrows; the expression was severe, the eyes were hard and watchful, and the narrow mouth, painted bright red, was sad and looked as if it seldom smiled. It smiled at Simier still, but the laughter no longer reached her eyes. It was a cold and empty face, and it matched the isolation in her heart.

She was alone, and she would always be alone, no matter how she filled her private life with substitutes and fed her vanity on the lies and the false love-play of men who only flattered her in their own interests. She glanced down at her hands; the Coronation ring was too tight to slip over her knuckle. It was the only ring that she would ever wear, and like a wedding ring, she never took it off. It was embedded in her finger now, the symbol of her irrevocable choice of isolation.

She was a Prince, as Sussex said; and she had never compromised with that. Her youth, her feelings, everything had been sacrificed to the establishment of her power, and her power alone sustained her. The fear of ridicule had cooled her fury against Leicester; the knowledge that she could punish him with death was a strange balm to the pride he had injured so deeply. She had forgiven him from motives which she tried to analyse as lofty and generous, and ended by admitting to be selfish and sentimental. She pardoned him because his defection was only the proof of his veniality and weakness, and in her heart she wondered if his lack of good qualities were not the secret of her bondage to him.

She could love an inferior; she could love and eventually forgive anyone whom she knew she could master whenever she chose, and Leicester had never been her match. He had defied her and schemed against her wishes and he was always caught out and forced to beg for pardon. He might steal a forbidden sweet but she could always make him spit it out.

He could not do without her. His craven dependence concealed the fact that she could not be happy without him. He had gone to Wanstead, firmly believing that he was exiled for life, and had fallen seriously ill. His wife had been sent to one of his estates in the Midlands; he too was alone unless Elizabeth relented. She travelled to Wanstead secretly, repeating the same tragi-comic pattern of their frequent quarrels. He offended her and she punished him and had to forgive him when he fell ill. At other times he was pretending, and she allowed herself to be deceived, but the man who got out of his bed at Wanstead was a wreck, his heavy body wasted with fever, his hand trembling.

He fell on his knees in front of her and burst into tears. It was an unmanly exhibition of nerves and cowardice, and for a moment she was stung to angry contempt. As she stood there, listening to his wild excuses, blaming Lettice and her father, blaming the Queen herself for her coldness towards him, stammering about his folly and his ingratitude, the contempt gave way to pity, and pity was an emotion that seldom came to Elizabeth. She had no imagination where other people's suffering was concerned. She refused to picture it or to transpose herself into their place.

She was unnerved by her intense compassion for the unhappy coward kneeling at her feet, babbling as if she were about to take his life. She suddenly saw him as he was when they first met at Hatfield, bold and brave and full of confidence, reaching towards her with both hands in his greed for life. He had been a man then, and she had loved him for it. Twenty years of living in her shadow had turned him into the craven she saw then; she had destroyed him. The enormity of her crime against his manhood excused anything he had done or ever would do to offend her. With the tears streaming down her face, Elizabeth had taken him in her arms as if he were the child she never had, and told him he was pardoned.

On the surface she was as charming to Simier as ever, but he was too acute to ignore the fact that Leicester had been reinstated, his crime forgiven, and too conversant with the female mind not to sense that Elizabeth's attitude had changed. He felt that, in the moment when he thought his success was complete, his whole mission had failed. Even the arrival of Alençon and the fulsome reception she gave him, did not convince Simier. In spite of everything she said and did to encourage the young Duc, the older, more experienced man felt that she was personally indifferent and quite dispassionate. His master overcame his physical shortcomings by an heroic display of gallantry towards the formidable Queen who was old enough to be his mother. He was pockmarked and distressingly short, but he possessed the small man's ebullience. Elizabeth gave receptions for him and exchanged presents and nicknamed him "her frog", and only Simier appreciated that women do not make pets of the men they are going to marry. It was an expensive and protracted farce; but there were no more attempts on his life because the opponents of the marriage sensed they no longer had anything to fear. At the critical moment, Elizabeth refused to allow Alençon the right to practise his religion, and the negotiations came to an end. As a compensation, she sent him to the Netherlands with a large grant of money, and her blessing for the campaign he undertook against the Spanish forces there. The unsuccessful suitor departed to find military glory, and embarrass the English Queen's enemies. He confided to Simier that he was secretly relieved; he disliked England, and the Queen made him nervous. He much preferred the hazards of war.

Lord Burleigh suffered from gout; it was an unfair affliction because he was an abstemious man. He walked with a stick, his left foot thickly bandaged, his hair and beard were white and his stoop was more pronounced. He looked alarmingly old, and the exigencies of his service were increased by the fact that the Queen seemed unable to relax or remit the pressure on her Councillors.

It was late afternoon when he hobbled to her rooms; a page had roused him from a weary doze, snatched when he imagined she had gone out hunting.

Leicester was with her; at her suggestion he gave up his chair for the Minister.

"I know you were resting," she said, "but my Lord Leicester

came with some news just as I was going out. I need your advice, Burleigh. Sit down and ease your leg."

Leicester turned to him.

"Walsingham told me this morning that he has arrested my old protégé, Edmund Campion," he said.

Burleigh nodded.

"He was found hiding in Berkshire," he remarked. "We've known he was in England; he came with two other Jesuits last summer and Walsingham was sure he would return to the University area. There are many Papists there, but more in the North, that's why it took so long to catch him. This is a great coup, Madam," he turned towards Elizabeth. "Campion's defection to Rome was bad enough; his return here as a missionary Jesuit has done more to hearten the Papists in twelve months than all the other renegade priests put together."

"I remember him well," Elizabeth said. She was frowning. During a visit to the University in the early years of her reign, she had received an address from the young Oxford student, and his wit and erudition had impressed her so deeply that she recommended him to Leicester. He had been a gay young man, ambitious and glib-tongued and obviously dazzled by the attentions of the great. His future had been brilliant; he was already famous for his scholastic achievements, and it was many years since the Reformed Church had recruited a man of such outstanding intellect. He was a favourite at Court for a time and considered for the highest ecclesiastical office. He was the last man imaginable to abandon everything and enrol in the outlawed Church of Rome.

"He is in the Tower," she continued, "and Robert suggested that from our point of view it would be better to reconvert him, than make another martyr."

"It would certainly damage Catholic prestige," Burleigh agreed. "So far none of these traitors have recanted. If Campion admitted his error and renounced the Pope's authority, it would be a triumph."

"I should be glad to see it," the Queen said. "I would rather have the loyalty of a man like Campion than his life. Robert knows him well, and Robert thinks that promises of pardon will not move him, but a personal interview might."

"It sounds outrageous to suggest that the Queen should see a confessed criminal," Leicester explained, "but Campion is not an ordinary traitor; he is a famous man, a respected scholar, a leader. He is also very human from my memory of him. He had great regard for me once, and he loved the Queen. If we were both to see him and persuade him, I believe he would retract everything."

"It's worth it," Elizabeth stood up. "No one need know of the meeting, Burleigh. What do you say?"

The Minister pulled himself upright and winced at a twinge from his swollen foot.

"See him by all means, Madam. I agree with Lord Leicester —Campion alive and reconciled to the Protestant religion will be worth more than fifty Jesuits hanging at Tyburn. I will tell Walsingham myself."

They had put Campion in the dungeon known as the Little Ease; it was not much bigger than a hole in the wall and he had been crouched there for four days, unable to stand or sit or lie. When they took him out he had to be carried; he was crippled with cramp and covered with filth. He had been washed and given a ragged suit of clean clothes and something to eat. He sat in a small boat between a guard of four soldiers while they rowed up the Thames in the darkness, his head bowed and his lips moving as he prayed. No one would tell him where he was being taken; he supposed that some members of the Council wanted to examine him, but such interviews usually took place in the Tower and the prisoner answered their questions on the rack. They moored at the steps of a large garden; he walked with difficulty supported by his guards. It was a cool and lovely evening with a brilliant display of stars. He smelled the scent of flowers and shrubs, and blinked as he came through a side door.

"Where am I?"

No one answered him; he found himself standing in front of another door, and when it opened suddenly he covered his eyes to protect them from a glare of light. He had lived in darkness for four days and for the first few moments he had to be guided into the room as if he were blind.

When he could see at last, Campion gave an audible gasp of surprise. He recognized the Queen, though it was ten years since he had seen her last. For a moment the pale face, framed in a blazing crown of red hair and winking diamonds, swam in front of him; he thought, irrelevantly and with pity, that she looked old and hardened beyond belief. Leicester, his old friend and patron, was standing beside her, thicker and ruddier than he remembered him, a middle-aged man in a scarlet doublet with a golden chain round his neck. And on the other side he recognized her former Secretary, the sober, self-effacing William Cecil. His beard was long and white; he looked a kindly, venerable old man.

"I see you have not forgotten us, Master Campion."

Elizabeth was shocked in spite of herself. She stared at the bent and bearded scarecrow and failed to identify the upright, rather dandified young churchman who used to ornament Leicester's circle. Campion stumbled and went down on one knee.

"Forgive me, your Majesty. The light blinded me for a moment; I thought I must be dead or dreaming."

He heard the guards going and the door closing. He was alone with the three most powerful people in England, the three principal enemies of his faith. He was to be judged by the Queen herself.

"You may stand, Campion," Leicester said, "and you have nothing to fear. The Queen and Lord Burleigh and I are your friends; we only want to help you if we can."

Campion stood up awkwardly. His head was clear now, and with a flash of his old wit he thanked them.

"Excuse my clumsiness; my room in your Majesty's prison was tailored for a smaller man, and I am still a little cramped."

Leicester smiled; but the Queen's expression did not soften. She was suddenly irritated by the condition to which Campion was reduced, and angrier still that he could stand there in his ridiculous torn clothes, a young man made old and feeble overnight, and make a joke of what had been done to him.

"You were a loyal subject once," she said sharply. "Why did you betray me, Campion?"

"I have never betrayed you, Madam." His voice was quite steady, almost gentle.

"You are a Papist and a Jesuit, don't you call that treason? Don't you know it is treason to come here as a priest and stir my people up against me?"

"I have never stirred anyone to anything but the practice of their faith. And I would be a traitor to God if I failed to do that."

"It is forbidden to come here," Burleigh said. "You knew the penalty for returning. England is no place for traitors to the Queen."

"England is the only place for Englishmen," Campion turned to him. "And no law on earth can keep us out, and keep us from serving the Queen in the way that is right. I am no traitor to her or to my country. I have always loved both, my Lord."

"If you loved me," Elizabeth said, "you would not join my enemies. I made much of you once; my Lord Leicester gave you his patronage, advanced you and recommended you. You could have been a great man in my kingdom, and you threw it all away to leave your country like a hunted dog and lick the feet of those who hate me. What is your excuse, Campion? You stand here face to face with me, your Queen—now tell me. Excuse your treason if you can!"

"The truth is not treason as I understand it, Madam. I came to the truth in spite of myself; I had been blind for many years, as blinded by ambition and temporalities as I was by the lights in this room when I first entered. I could indeed have been great in your kingdom, and thereby lost my place in the Kingdom of God. I am not a brave man, Madam, nor a strong one. I fought my conscience as long as I could; I was a traitor to you then because I upheld what I knew to be a lie. I am loyal to you now, when I tell you that the Church of Rome is the Church of Christ, and that true Englishmen will come and seek to save your soul, because they love and revere you. The gallows and the rack will not deter that love. Death will not change it. Living they will try for your convertion; dying they will pray for it. And pray for England."

"I have not brought you here," Elizabeth said bitterly, "to listen to a sermon. The Pope has excommunicated me; he has absolved you from your allegiance to me. Now, as an Englishman, answer me this. If England were invaded, whom would you obey, the Pope or me?"

"Before you answer," Leicester interrupted, "think well, Campion."

The Queen was going too fast; she was angered by the spiritual quality of the man. She did not want to hear about the Church of Christ and the salvation of her soul; she did not want to see Campion as a man of sanctity and ideals, however mistaken. She did not live her own life upon that plane and she could not deal with him unless he came down to the level which she understood.

But life was not a bribe unless Campion could be made to value it. He was weakened and ill; aggression would stiffen him but a few words of kindness and friendship might bring his spiritual resolution down in chaos.

"I thought very well of you," Leicester went on. "I was proud of your achievements, and proud to be your patron. I was your friend then, and still am. Reflect, Campion. All that the Queen asks is that you should be loyal—that you should promise not to aid her enemies if they strike against her. Is that so unreasonable? Isn't that being more merciful than you have any right to expect? You came back to your own country expecting death and cruelties and you find this—your Queen and sovereign Prince receives you, and gives you a chance to mend your fault. And promises you a full pardon and a place at Oxford."

He turned to Elizabeth for confirmation and she nodded. Leicester was right. This man was important; he was famous and respected. He must be made to recant, for if he betrayed Rome, hundreds of his fellow English Catholics would follow. Threats were useless. She could see that; she could see with terrible clarity that if Campion left this room unreclaimed, the utmost rigours of torture would not move him. And for a moment she looked at him and wondered, without anger, where he found the source of his strength.

"I will ask very little of you," she said quietly. "I shall not punish you or humiliate you, Campion. All you need do is avow your loyalty to me personally, and make one attendance at the established service. Only one. What you do after that and how you choose to worship God is no concern of mine. I am no persecutor; I have no wish to interfere in any man's religious faith. If all my Catholic people would acknowledge me and reject this edict of the Pope, they could say Mass with my personal blessing. You are a man of note; your example could bring peace to England, you could save many rash and foolish men from death by showing them that it is right to compromise. Give me your hand, Edmund Campion. Swear to obey me as your lawful Queen in the face of all my enemies, and you shall leave this room free and fully pardoned."

She held out her hand to him. For a moment Campion

231

hesitated. It was not a hesitation of purpose; the Queen and Leicester misunderstood it. He wavered, because he wondered whether he could take it when he was about to refuse to do what she wanted. It was strange that he, who had imagined his own weakness, dreading his defection under torture, often lying without sleep during the weeks preceding his arrival in England, should have felt no temptation to yield at all. In theory it was so easy; he had only to disavow the edict of the Pope and go to a heretic service once, and he could live again in his own country, pursue his studies, return to the beloved University, and pass the rest of his life in peace. It was so easy, and he could feel the will of the three people in the room, pressing upon him, urging him to consider and accept. The strongest was the woman, the hard, shrewd-eyed woman who saw nothing beyond the material threat to her power. To her the Pope was a hostile old man, building an alliance with her foreign enemies. There was no link with the humble Fisherman of Galilee, no miracle in the contest fought by the first of all the Popes and the handful of poor illiterate Jewish disciples, against the might of pagan Rome. There was no miracle in their victory, and through them the victory of the Christian faith over the world. It was simple for her to demand the Pope's rejection. It was like transferring loyalty from another King. He could never explain to her that it was impossible to reject truth. And the Pope and his significance in the fierce, greedy, power-ridden world, were an essential part of Campion's truth, and the whole of his truth was a belief in the plan God made for men.

It was sad and at the same time unbearably joyous to realize that, compared to that, Elizabeth had nothing to offer him.

He came and gently kissed her hand.

"I swear to be loyal to you in everything my conscience will permit. But it does not permit me to deny the power of the Vicar of Christ or to attend a service which I believe to be false."

For a moment he looked straight into her eyes; he could see the anger and the disappointment in them. He saw something else. There was a sudden change, an alteration of the light in the black pupils. It was gone in a second, but he saw it. Disappointment, anger—and regret. He had doomed himself, and he had also doomed her, for she would have to deliver him to the workings of the laws she had made.

"Forgive me, Madam," he said gently, and for a moment he looked into her face and smiled.

"On your own head be it!"

She nodded to Leicester and he called out. The guards came back and, as they surrounded him, Campion saw the Queen bite her lower lip and turn away.

"Return the prisoner."

That was Burleigh's voice, very brisk and anxious to get home to bed. They hurried him out of the room and down the garden to the boat. Campion knelt as they rowed back up the black river, and he prayed steadily and with an extraordinary sense of peace.

## Chapter 12

EVERY window in the Queen's room was open but the heat was stifling; the gardens were parched, the paved walks and stone benches were burning to the touch, and no breeze came from the river. It was the hottest summer Elizabeth could remember. She had moved from Whitehall at the first outbreak of the summer epidemics in the City and left Greenwich for Hampton Court. It was her favourite residence; she loved the rich red brick, the spacious courtyards and the airy rooms with their wide views of the river and the parklands. She was especially fond of the herb gardens and spent many hours sewing with her ladies in the shaded arbour, surrounded by the sweet and pungent scent of the shrubs. She was too hot and too irritable to go out that day; the weather frayed her nerves and interfered with her sleep, and perversely she made no concessions in dress for herself or her attendants. She sat close to a window, laced into a gown of violet satin; the bodice was stiff with bead and amethyst embroidery and it clung to her tired body like a suit of mail. Her head ached under an auburn wig; her hair was now too thin and too white to cover with anything but a nightcap, and she fought the signs of age with richer dresses, multicoloured wigs and a mask of paint which took two hours to apply twice a day.

Lady Bedford sat beside her, moving the humid air with a fan; it made Elizabeth hotter, and after a few moments she snapped at her to stop. She snapped at her women; when they made mistakes or irritated her, she boxed their ears. They hated her and feared her, and she hated most of them because they were young, and her old attendants were thinning out. Lady Dacre was dead, and Mary Sidney had caught fever and died only a few months ago. There were young, fresh faces round the Queen; women whom she remembered as children. They simpered and giggled, reminding her constantly of her vanished youth, and enviously watched the young men who clustered round her. As a virgin herself, Elizabeth had begun stressing the value of maidenhood; she conveyed her displeasure at signs of flirtation and her outrage at the mention of marriage. No one was permitted to enjoy the consummation of love which she had renounced for herself, and she monopolized the time and attentions of every man at Court. Since Alençon's departure she felt affronted by the sight of other people's personal happiness and tormented by the suspicion that her position was tinged with ridicule.

She was selfish and demanding and unreasonably jealous, and there were times when she despised her own weakness and her need of flattery, but the illusion of youth and desirability were essential. She could not stand erect upon her pinnacle without them and, even had she really wished to, she was fifty and unable to step down.

She looked across at the youngest and prettiest of her new ladies, Elizabeth Throckmorton.

" Go to the virginals and play something! "

" Yes, Madam." Bess Throckmorton curtsied and sat down at the instrument; after a moment she began to play a country melody which she knew Elizabeth liked. She played very well, but not as well as her mistress; Margaret Knollys had once mastered a piece which the Queen found too difficult and she had never been allowed to open the keyboard again.

Elizabeth's thoughts were diverted from her own loneliness and irritability; she was thinking of her lady-in-waiting's kinsman, Nicholas Throckmorton, handsome and charming, and destined for her favour. She was thinking of the day that Walsingham came to her and showed her papers proving that Throckmorton was a Catholic and plotting to assassinate her and proclaim Mary Stuart Queen of England. Throckmorton had died the terrible death prescribed for traitors, but the intrigue showed a terrifying increase in the number of educated, high-born young men who were turning to the Church of Rome and championing the imprisoned Queen of Scotland.

It was the fault of the Jesuit missionaries and lay priests, who were sneaking into the country in greater numbers than ever. Their fanaticism was re-kindling the embers of the old religion, and the Queen found herself compelled to quench that fire in blood. It was more difficult than ever to preserve the life of Mary, when her Council and her Parliament saw constant evidence of the threat she presented to Elizabeth and to themselves. She had replaced Shrewsbury with Sir Ralph Sadleir, and finally given Sir Amyas Paulet the unwelcome task of guarding the most dangerous prisoner in Europe. Elizabeth personally disliked Paulet; he was a sour, unbending Puritan, a devotee of Walsingham and a man incapable of being corrupted by chivalry. Mary's confinement was as uncomfortable as his vigilance could make it, and since Throckmorton's plot, her correspondence had to be written in his presence and approved, and his methods were so successful that she had no means of secret communication with the outside world. Paulet had sealed her off from her friends in England and in Spain as effectively as if she were dead, and when Mary protested to her son James, then styling himself King of Scotland, she was informed that he had asked for Elizabeth's assurance that his mother would never be released. Elizabeth wondered cynically how she had been fool enough to imagine anything else. Did she believe the ties of filial love bound James, who had never seen her since babyhood, and was thoroughly enjoying himself in her place . . . ? Nothing moved James but his own interests, and the last thing in the world he wanted was the emergence of his famous and troublesome mother to reclaim her throne.

What dream did Mary live in, that she should rely on her son, and fall into a paroxysm of rage and grief when she heard that he was among her bitterest enemies? If there was one thing she had learnt from reigning over men for over twenty years, it was the folly of placing too much trust in them. Friends and relatives, lovers and children—how foolish to attach the heart strings to any of them, when ambition so easily tugged them out.

Elizabeth stared into space through narrow eyes. After all these years she was not yet secure; she was an old woman, and she admitted it, wincing inwardly, and there was no respite from the struggle to keep the power to which she had dedicated her life. She had kept her people at peace; they were better fed and employed than at any time in England's history, and still she could not rest on her achievements and be certain of their gratitude. They followed chimeras; the title of Mary, the religion of which she had made herself the champion, though God knows it was power and not Papistry that Mary fought for—the greatest chimera of all, religious truth, urging a man like Edmund Campion to torture and death, and scores of others after him. They could not be content with bread and peace and comfort, and they were always better men than those who were. Braver and nobler than the fops and opportunists who surrounded her, singing songs and writing poetry in praise of a beauty which she had never possessed even in her youth, but fools in the final judgment, and there was no place in the world for fools.

It was not heroic to try and unseat the best sovereign England had ever had, and Elizabeth made that claim without boasting; it was malicious and ungrateful and she hated them for it, and punished them ferociously when she caught them. Most of all she hated Mary Stuart. While so many of her friends died, her enemy lived on, surviving damp and hardship and epidemics, the beacon light that rallied traitors.

"If she were dead, I might have peace."

"Did you speak, Madam?"

Lady Sutherland interrupted her thoughts and the Queen realized that she must have spoken them aloud.

She stood up and snapped her fingers at Elizabeth Throckmorton to stop playing.

"Send for Lord Burleigh and Sir Francis Walsingham. When they come, you can withdraw."

Burleigh and the Secretary sat down near the window; the Minister's gout had not improved, and he annoyed the Queen by pleading for a leave of absence which she had so far refused. She needed Burleigh; he was cautious and balanced and wise, and there were too many younger men like Walsingham swaying the Council with rash ideas.

"It's so hot, I expect to see the Devil any moment! My poor Burleigh, I imagine you were sleeping again when I disturbed you?"

"No, Madam, it's too hot for that. I was only reading."

"And you, Walsingham?"

"Working, Madam. The weather makes no difference to me."

"Nothing makes any difference to you. I sometimes wonder if you're human."

The Secretary flushed. Whenever the Queen was bad-tempered, she made him the scapegoat. His dignity had never recovered from the incident when he once flatly contradicted her opinion and she took the shoe off her foot and threw it in his face.

"What was the last report from Paulet about the Queen of Scots?"

"He reported to the Council as usual last week. She is in moderate health, protesting daily about the censorship of her

237

letters, and railing against you, Madam. He had no news of importance."

"He has no news," Walsingham interrupted suddenly, "because she is so strictly watched. It was better when we knew what intrigues were hatching by opening her letters. Now she knows nothing and nor do we."

"As you say," Elizabeth said, "she was our best source of information. Thanks to that zealous idiot Paulet it is completely dried up. I have been thinking that her dabblings were less dangerous than her silence."

"If Paulet relaxes, she will suspect," Burleigh said. "We would have to open a channel for her letters without his knowledge. Walsingham, you could find a way of doing that. . . ."

"I was never in favour of cutting her off from the world," the Secretary insisted. "We know she is the Queen's deadly enemy and capable of any crime against her. But, to commit the crime, she must have the opportunity, and to punish it, we must have proof."

"For once," Elizabeth remarked, "you do not go too fast. I survived Throckmorton's plot; the next assassin might not be so clumsy. But if Mary hears of it first, so will we. And if she can be found in concert with my enemies again, it should be possible to punish her as she deserves."

For a moment Burleigh and Walsingham stared at her without speaking. For nearly twenty years she had been urged to kill Mary Stuart, and it was inconceivable that even Elizabeth should have chosen this stifling, uneventful afternoon to change her mind.

"If you mean that you will take our advice at last, Madam, I feel like falling on my knees and thanking God," Burleigh said.

"I'm not sure what I mean," Elizabeth retorted. "Except that I'm tired of my life being menaced in such a woman's favour. I am tired of hearing that she rails against me, who have saved her life for all these years, and that because she cannot spend her years in peace, she denies all quiet of mind to me. I promise nothing, understand that."

"Madam, I beg of you, don't weaken now." Walsingham leant towards her, his hands gripping his knees, his pale green eyes dilated with excitement. "Lift your protection from her. She is a viper, coiled in your breast! Do you think she would suffer from scruples if the position was reversed? You would

238

have been dead years ago, executed or murdered, it's all one to her. Give us your word that if there's one more plot, she'll suffer for her part in it! "

Elizabeth looked at him, her face was inscrutable. If there was an expression in her eyes, it seemed to Walsingham that she was almost bored.

"Find me the plot first, and the proof. Then I will answer you."

She dismissed them, and the two men walked away together down the long, hot Gallery, past groups of courtiers, talking and sitting by the windows, and through the outer chamber where the Queen's personal guard of fifty Gentlemen Pensioners was on duty. Burleigh was the first to speak.

"What is the date today, Sir Francis? "

"July 23rd, my Lord."

"Remember it," the Minister said quietly. "I know the Queen. This marks the end of Mary Stuart."

Mary had been moved again. In the depths of the winter, when her stay in the lethal cold and damp of Tutbury Castle had reduced her to beg Elizabeth for warmer quarters, the Scots Queen was taken to a different prison. Chartley was in Staffordshire; it was a heavily fortified house, manned by a strong garrison under the command of Sir Amyas Paulet, but the rooms were comfortable and well heated and, for the first time in months, Mary was able to get out of bed. She spent long hours sewing with her ladies, or staring out of the window at the barren parklands, drenched with rain. She never laughed and seldom even smiled; she felt ill in mind and body, depressed by a presentiment of death which drove her to the exercise of her religion, but deprived of comfort by the intense bitterness and hatred which poisoned her prayers. Her son had failed her; France and Spain had done nothing to effect her release and the inhuman strictness of Paulet tortured her with inactivity. She had no hope of escape, no means of knowing whether there was one man prepared to work on her behalf, and the sense of desertion, of utter hopelessness, was weakening her will to live.

At forty-three she was bent with rheumatism, unable to walk without a stick, her beautiful figure had thickened, and her hair was white. She was an old, tired, embittered woman, with nothing left of her beauty but the lovely changing colour of her hazel eyes. She had been in prison nearly eighteen years, and for the first time she felt that she would never be free until she died. Her enemies had triumphed over her in life; but in death she might be able to cancel their victory. Some of her servants left her when she moved from Tutbury. It was her last opportunity to send a message to the outside world. Witnessed by her Secretary Nau and Mary Seton, the Queen made her will, and showed it to Nau's assistant who would soon be travelling to France.

"Go to the Bishop of Glasgow in Paris," she said, "and tell him that you have seen this, my final testament, and that I have solemnly disinherited my son James from his right to the throne of England. I declare the King of Spain to be my heir. Tell him to inform King Philip, and say that as soon as I can find a means of getting letters out, I will confirm this in writing."

Now, she thought, staring into the fire at Chartley, if I die, I've given Elizabeth's mortal enemy the right to take her crown. Now Philip will invade her; nothing can stop him. And if he wins, he'll march on Scotland and my wretched son. . . .

She saw Seton watching her and smiled. Poor Seton; Seton who was always anxious, trying to cheer her when she was depressed, soothing her when she gave way to bursts of impotent anger, sitting for hours beside her when she wept and recalled the past. She loved Seton; she loved Nau, and Curle, his junior; she loved the spaniel dogs that sat round her feet and slept on her bed at night. But these were trivial loves, insufficient barriers to the unending agony of her regrets and her frustrations. Their selfless loyalty was a poor compensation for the betrayal of Darnley, and Bothwell and her brother and now her son. Life had been cruel to Mary, cruel in its seeming generosity at the beginning, holding out hopes of dazzling brightness, and quenching them one by one in treachery and violence and blood. She was not resigned or at peace; she could not forgive her enemies, living and dead; she could only console herself with trying to strike them from the grave.

Walsingham ignored the man standing in front of him and went on writing for some moments. He was aware that the other shifted and coughed; when he put down his pen the Secretary stared at him coldly.

"I trust no one saw you come here, Master Gifford."

"No one, Sir Francis. No one knows I left Chartley village; I gave it out that I was ill."

Gifford's brown eyes flickered away from the Secretary's face and fixed on the wall. He had a shifty look, and he was nervous. He had first met Elizabeth's master-spy when he was arrested for Catholic activities, and he had never overcome his fear of him. He was not a brave man, and his convictions were influenced by a natural love of intrigue. He had quickly sacrificed them to save his life, and entered the service of the Queen. He was an ignoble character, but an able spy; he had long since overcome his scruples at betraying the men he had worked with and who trusted him in ignorance of his desertion to the enemy. Walsingham had chosen him as his agent, and he understood that his final pardon depended upon the success of the trap being prepared for Mary Stuart.

"What progress have you made?" Walsingham asked.

"I've opened a source for the Queen's letters," Gifford replied. "I approached Sir Amyas Paulet's steward and he has agreed to smuggle papers in and out of the house in a beer cask which is replenished every week. I told him it was in your service and that his life depended upon his discretion. The first letter was from me, it reached her two weeks ago, and I have her reply with me."

Walsingham read the note; there was nothing in it but an expression of thanks and a warning to be careful. She begged him to write to Morgan, her agent in Paris, and let her have the answer.

"You have done well," he said. "Has Morgan replied to you?"

"He has indeed." Gifford placed a packet on the table. "I opened it, Sir Francis; but no one would know the seal was tampered with."

Walsingham read the letter slowly. He had forgotten the spy standing in front of him; at one moment he gave a little exclamation of triumph, and when he looked up again at Gifford his narrow mouth was smiling.

"We have the beginning of a new plot here," he said. "Sir Anthony Babington has approached Morgan—he begs to know how he can serve the Queen of Scots . . . he has a following of loyal Catholics like himself, ready to spend their lives to free her. All he needs is direction. By God, he shall have it. I know him—he's here in London! Send this letter to Chartley, and make yourself known to Babington. Tell him you are the Queen of Scots' agent, and that you have heard of him through Morgan in Paris. Find out anything you can and impress on him that he must write full details of his plans to the Queen and do nothing till he receives her agreement in writing."

"You can rely upon me." Gifford bowed.

"The important thing is Mary Stuart's sanction," Walsingham said. "We know now that Babington is a traitor; we can lay hands on him at any time. The Queen is the prize I want. Urge Babington to any method, suggest that the assassination of Queen Elizabeth is the only way of saving Mary Stuart. Emphasize that. And make him write to her in such a way that she agrees to it. You understand me, Gifford——" His pale eyes fixed the spy with an expression that made his knees tremble with fright. "If you bungle this, you'll die for your original offence. There's a room in this house of mine where I sometimes question traitors, and I'll see that you visit it and only leave it for the gallows. If you succeed, I'll reward you out of my own purse, and recommend you to the Queen."

Gifford nodded. He was very pale. "I told you, Sir Francis, you can rely on me. I shall do what you say, and you shall have the Queen of Scots as well as Babington. I swear it."

One evening late in March Elizabeth left Whitehall Palace to dine with Lord Burleigh at his house in the Strand. The gardens were crowded with courtiers, and the banks of the river lined with the people of London, all waiting to see the Queen sail up the Thames in her barge. Nothing could stop her displaying herself to the people; Burleigh warned and Leicester begged, reminding her of the danger of assassination and pointing out that the leader of the Netherlands Protestants, William of Orange, had been killed in his own house by an agent of Spain. But the Queen refused to hide herself. The London crowds loved her, and she was not going to become a memory to them or appear through a barricade of armed men as if she were a prisoner in her own kingdom.

She walked through Whitehall gardens, with an escort of eight Gentlemen Pensioners in front and behind, and two torch bearers; it was already dusk, and the flaming lights made her such a perfect target that Leicester followed her with his hand on his sword. Two hundred members of the Court and the household were crowded on either side of the path; they were curtsying and bowing as she passed, and she walked at her usual stately pace, refusing to hurry. A bullet or a fanatic with a knife could have killed her at any moment. Leicester was less reckless about personal danger as he grew older; but though Elizabeth hated illness and dreaded dying in her bed, she had a magnificent, fatalistic courage about being murdered; her bravery was a reproach to him and to many members of the Council who employed food-tasters and slept with armed men outside their bedroom doors since the Throckmorton plot. She looked deceptively young in the torchlight, and her carriage was as graceful and upright as if she were a girl. She wore a dress of white brocade, the stomacher and outer petticoat glittering with diamond and emerald embroidery, a fan-shaped collar of stiffened lace framed her head, and a long cloak of green velvet, lined with white ermine, fell from her shoulders. She smiled and waved, and once she looked over her shoulder at him and smiled, as if she sensed his anxiety. He was thankful when she reached the jetty, and the heralds sounded a fanfare by the barge.

Two other men among the crowd were watching her as closely as Leicester; one was tall and fair, with a rather mild and handsome face; his companion nudged him as the Queen passed within five feet of them. He was pale, with a very dark beard and hair and fanatical black eyes which glowed with hatred as he watched Elizabeth.

"Why do we wait, Babington? Why not strike now—or tomorrow?"

Robert Barnewall was an Irishman, scion of an ancient Catholic family which had suffered bitterly under the punitive expeditions sent to quell religion and rebellion in that unhappy country. He had travelled to London with the express purpose of killing the Queen whose heresy and tyranny had made her in Ireland the most hated of all the English sovereigns.

Like Babington, Barnewall was admitted to the Court by his gentle birth and he was free to stay there as long as he could maintain himself financially and was able to conceal his religion. Babington watched the Queen for a moment before answering. He was not as prejudiced as Barnewall; he was able to admire her dignity and appreciate her courage, and to admit to himself that if she had not been the enemy of his religion

243

and responsible for the death of so many of his friends, he might have loved and served her, and been proud to do so. He was not bloodthirsty or lawless and he had a respect for the person of the monarch which Barnewall could never understand. But Catholic or Protestant, Babington could never serve Elizabeth because she was the enemy of the woman he had loved since he was a boy in his teens. He could see her and judge her with complete indifference, because his imagination and his emotion were dominated by the memory of Mary Stuart. He was blind to every woman and unaware of any purpose but the one to which he had dedicated his life. He was going to release the Queen of Scots, and it was unfortunate but relatively unimportant that the only way to do it was to kill the Queen of England.

"Why are we waiting," Barnewall whispered fiercely. "All the others are willing—Savage has sworn an oath to do it, so have I! What are we waiting for, in the name of God?"

"Queen Mary's reply," Babington said under his breath. "Gifford will have it in a few days."

"Gifford urges assassination, and Gifford insists on delay. The two don't match, Babington. We should strike at once; the longer we hesitate, the greater the danger of discovery. Too many people know of this already; if one tongue wags, that will be the end of us all."

"I will do nothing without the Queen's consent," Babington answered. "Gifford is adamant about that and he is in closer touch than we are."

"She is leaving now," Barnewall nodded towards the barge, its interior lit by blazing torches. The oarsmen stood for a moment, waiting till the figure in the shining white dress seated itself in the bows. The watching crowds along the river banks were cheering. Then the oars slowly dipped into the water; the trumpets sounded again, and the gilt and painted barge began to glide away from the bank and up the river.

"I pray to God it sinks with her," Barnewall said bitterly.

"And I pray," Anthony Babington murmured, "that I see the day my own Queen rides in it in state to her Coronation."

They separated and Babington went back to his lodgings outside the Palace grounds, to see if there was any news from Gifford.

Nau, Mary Stuart's secretary, stood in front of her writing-table and shook his head. He felt inclined to wring his hands he was so agitated. Mary looked up at him. She was smiling and her expression was animated; she seemed to have shed ten years in the last few weeks.

"Madam, I beg you, I implore of you—do not answer that letter!"

The Queen placed her hand on Anthony Babington's long account of the plans he was making to release her and fulfil the vow he had made to her so many years ago at Sheffield, when, as he reminded her, he promised to do her a real service one day.

"Don't be so foolish, Nau. I've been receiving and sending letters out for weeks in perfect safety. The method is perfectly safe. Certainly I'm going to answer this—nothing can stop me!"

"But ordinary mail is one thing, Madam," Nau pleaded. "Letters to France and Spain and communications with your agent are your right, no one could blame you for them, or for complaining about your circumstances. But this man proposes to assassinate Elizabeth! He's made you his accessory by writing such a letter; if you answer it and encourage him, you could be charged with his crime!"

"Only if he is discovered. And you forget, I know Babington. He would do anything for me. Why quibble, my poor friend; as long as Elizabeth lives I shall never be free, and so long as she hangs and quarters Catholics the Catholics will try and murder her. Babington says he wants my authority; supposing I refuse it, or ignore it, and he does nothing, when he might have succeeded! Oh, Nau, Nau, I've lived this wretched life too long to worry about risks. I'll take this chance and any chance that comes, so long as there's hope of freedom."

"Madam, this life is better than death," the secretary said slowly. "I know what it means, because I've shared it with you for many years. And one sentence in this letter could mean the end of everything for you. 'The usurping competitor must be despatched . . . six gentlemen will undertake the tragic execution.' If you took my advice you would send that letter to Elizabeth in London!"

"You are not serious, Nau," the Queen said slowly. "I know that, and I forgive you. I also know how faithfully you've served me; there was no need to point it out. I am in your debt and, God help me, I have no way of repaying you except with thanks. I am a prisoner and alone; if I lose hope and resign myself I shall die as quickly as if I were executed.

"If you love me, Nau, never again suggest that I should betray Anthony Babington or any other friend of mine, just to save myself. Now sit at your table please, and take down my reply."

Nau was right; for the first time in her long and fruitless struggle with Elizabeth, she was staking her own life. Many Englishmen had died for her in the last nineteen years; men she had known and men that she had never seen. They had suffered cruelly on her account, fighting for her and for what she had come to represent, rejecting the worldly success of that supremely successful woman whose triumphs only showed the failures and tragedies of her own misspent life in darker contrast. It was rare for Mary to feel unworthy or to question her own fitness for the sacrifices she inspired. In the few moments while Nau waited to write down her words to Babington, she came closer to genuine prayer than for many years. If Babington succeeded, the waste and the bloodshed of the past would not have been in vain; if she came to the throne of England at last, she made a solemn promise to rule with all the virtues of prudence and justice which her champions expected. If she won, Elizabeth would die, and Mary could not pretend a single scruple. If she lost, then she would suffer with Babington and his followers, and now that the moment of final decision had come, she was no longer afraid of death or of anything but the continuing martyrdom of imprisonment and despair.

She spoke slowly as Nau wrote, asking for details, enquiring about the help of Spanish troops, and then, as the secretary paused, she made the final committal:

"'When all is ready the six gentlemen must be set to work . . . you will provide that when their design is accomplished, I may be rescued from this place.' Now give me the letter, Nau, and I will sign it."

"Well, my Lords, our work is nearly done."

Walsingham looked at Burleigh and then at Leicester. His usually dour face was shining with animation; even his gestures were a little exaggerated. He kept looking at the copy of Mary Stuart's letter to Babington and he was unable to restrain his triumph.

" ' The six gentlemen must be set to work . . .' she has signed her own death warrant with that one sentence."

"I congratulate you," Burleigh said. "You have done a wonderful service, Sir Francis. The Queen will be truly grateful."

"Nobody questions what you have achieved," Leicester remarked quietly, "but I have a doubt about the Queen's gratitude. She has never wanted the death of Mary Stuart, and this letter may force her hand. Don't be too sanguine; she is quite capable of changing her mind and refusing to take action on the strength of one piece of paper."

"I have thought of that," the Secretary frowned. "Though the Queen authorized everything I have done, I am well aware that she may decide to disregard her own instructions. We all know and love Her Majesty but I think we all agree that she is er—somewhat capricious. But this is one time, my Lords, when we must protect the Queen against herself. I propose to amass every scrap of evidence of the Scottish Queen's guilt and lay it before the Council. They, and not I, will insist that the Queen proceeds against her cousin. And I doubt if the Queen herself will hesitate when she sees the proof of Mary Stuart's enormities before her own eyes."

"Where is this proof, and how will you obtain it?" Burleigh asked.

"We will find it in Queen Mary's private papers," Walsingham answered. "I ask your permission, gentlemen, to have them seized and brought to London."

There was a moment of silence, and then Leicester spoke.

"We dare not do such a thing without the Queen's permission. I certainly won't take the responsibility and I doubt if even Lord Burleigh would."

Burleigh shook his head.

"I have sought the death of Mary Stuart for many years," he said quietly, "but I know Her Majesty too well to try and encompass it behind her back . . . she must authorize the seizure. I will approach her, but I cannot do more than that."

"Why not let Lord Leicester try and persuade her," Walsingham suggested. He had never endeared himself to Elizabeth but he had a profound respect for Leicester's understanding of her. Burleigh would be clear and logical and talk to her as if she were a cool-headed statesman like himself. But she was growing more erratic every day, and increasingly apt to act on the dictates of her own emotions. Leicester understood those emotions and knew how to play on them. It was safer to send him than Burleigh. Walsingham was so anxious to bring his project to a successful conclusion that he risked offending the powerful Minister by his suggestion. He was ready to override anyone except Elizabeth herself, rather than see Mary Stuart escape from the trap he had closed over her.

"I agree," Burleigh said. "You go to her Leicester. You know best how to persuade Her Majesty these days. She may listen to you where an old greybeard like me might well antagonize her. Now, Sir Francis, when we have the papers, what do you propose?"

"I propose that we take her secretaries too," Walsingham said. "Have them brought here and I will question them myself in my own house. At the same time we will arrest Babington and his associates and question them—in the Tower. We will disclose the plot to Parliament, and I will compile the evidence against the Queen of Scots and lay it in front of the Queen and the rest of the Council. The rest must be achieved by you, my Lords."

"Have no fear," Burleigh rose and held out his hand; "what you have begun so well, we will finish." He turned to Leicester, "My Lord, will you go to the Queen today, and get a written permission from her and if you can, Sir Francis will see to the details."

"I will." Leicester bowed. "The Queen is expecting me this afternoon. I will ask her then."

It was almost five years since Mary had been allowed to hunt. When Sir Amyas Paulet asked her if she cared to take a small retinue and ride to Tixhall, where the stags were plentiful, she could hardly believe that he was serious. But Paulet had no sense of humour, cruel or otherwise. She could go under his escort, and he gave the permission so ungraciously that it never occurred to her for a moment that the invitation of the Lord of Tixhall was a subterfuge to get her out of Chartley without her destroying her correspondence. She said goodbye to her servants and managed to sit her horse as if she had never had rheumatism and been caged up in her apartments through the whole winter. She was gay and full of high spirits, secretly buoyed up with her hopes of Anthony Babington's success and her joy at the prospect of following the sport which had once been her passion. They rode through the green English country-side, and the Queen set a fast pace in her impatience to reach Tixhall. She had prepared a gracious speech for the owner, and was even a little curious about him. His invitation was an act of true charity and it was also brave. She looked forward to meeting him and finding yet another friend.

But Mary never saw the Lord of Tixhall, and she never hunted the stags which roamed his parklands. At the gates of the house a troop of horsemen met her, and forced her secretaries, Curle and Nau, away from her retinue. Then she saw Paulet's eyes looking at her, full of triumph and contempt at the ease with which she had let herself be deceived. When she tried to ride to the secretaries and cried out in protest, he told her they were under arrest for suspected treason against the Queen of England, and seized her bridle and whipped her horse through the gates of Tixhall. Then she was lifted down and hurried into the house and locked into a small upper room. Some miles away at Chartley, Walsingham's commissioners were breaking open the doors of her writing-cabinet and listing and sealing all her papers. They also packed up her jewels and anything in her personal belongings which were of value, and they took everything to London.

After ten days of close confinement at Tixhall, she was returned to Chartley and it was there that she heard from Paulet that Babington and his friends had been tried and executed.

Sir Amyas stood in front of her with the list in his hand and solemnly read out the names and the sentences passed upon them, while the Queen sat as if she were petrified, refusing to look at him and wishing that she could sacrifice her dignity and put her hands over her ears. Babington and the priest Ballard and a certain Robert Barnewall were among the six who suffered the full rigours of their penalty, he announced, looking up.

"They confessed everything, Madam, in their last extremities. The others were executed the next day, and the Queen's Majesty was moved to mitigate their sufferings; they were hanged until dead. . . ."

Mary raised her eyes to his face. It was hard and grave, and there was still that expression of contempt which humiliated her.

He despised her and he hated her; to him she was a worth-less, perfidious woman, responsible for the deaths of all those men, and she could see that he had read that dreadful recital to shame her with the evidence of her own responsibility.

"God have mercy on them," she said unsteadily. "And on me, for they all died for my sake. I shall remember their courage and their sacrifice when my own time comes."

"It will come, Madam," Paulet said grimly; he was irritated because the Queen was holding her rosary and moving the beads nervously through her fingers. He viewed all evidence of Catholicism with superstitious horror, and he also considered her an unrepentent hypocrite.

"It will come," he repeated. "Your papers betrayed your treason to Queen Elizabeth with Babington and with every traitor who's conspired against her in the last nineteen years. You will be tried, Madam, and condemned, if there is any justice in this world."

"Elizabeth Tudor is not my Queen."

Mary rose, leaning on the arm of her chair; she felt faint and trembling.

"She cannot try me, for I am not her subject; she can only condemn me to an unlawful death and I am ready to suffer that. Now be good enough to leave me."

When she was alone she went to the small alcove which she used as an oratory and fell on her knees, desperately trying to pray for the men who had died so cruelly. The thought of Anthony Babington brought out the floods of tears she had been too proud to shed in front of Paulet; she saw him as a boy of sixteen, very fair and earnest, gazing at her with his eyes full of adolescent love, promising to give his life in her service. And his life had been required of him, accompanied by such physical agony that she shuddered. Nau had been right when he begged her to ignore that letter, and Nau had been tortured and would die like the others. Poor Nau; she had thrown his life away as well as her own. She bent her head on her hands; she felt suddenly too tired and empty to weep. Nor could she pray; the words dried in her mouth. She knelt in silence with her eyes closed, unable to feel or think. For the first time in the whole nineteen turbulent years of her captivity, Mary felt certain of her death, but if she was empty of hope, even of sorrow, she was also untroubled by bitterness or hatred. When her lady-in-waiting, Jane Kennedy, found her two hours later, the Queen was still kneeling but she was fast asleep.

Elizabeth was writing; she had been sitting alone in her Privy Chamber for most of the afternoon, staring at the sheets of paper, writing a few lines and then destroying what she had put down. The afternoon light was gone; her page had lit the candles on her table and withdrawn, and the room was full of shadows. She had sent her secretaries away, refusing to dictate, refusing to see Burleigh or Leicester, or any of the men who had been surrounding her, humming like bees in the past few weeks, all sounding the same, maddening, triumphant note. The proof of Mary Stuart's activities against her was so voluminous she had pushed the pile of documents aside after reading the first dozen. One paper had been specially shown to her. It was a decoded list of all those of her nobles who were secret partisans of Mary. She had read it in silence, her eyes expressionless, and then thrown it on the fire. She was not surprised; she was not particularly enthusiastic to find tangible proof that Mary had been encouraging rebellion and assassination, when they had all been aware of it for years. She was angry and irritable and inwardly furious with Walsingham who was being lauded to the heavens by the Council for his skill in the affair. She had almost forgotten that moment of exasperation at Hampton Court when she obliquely suggested the very plan which had been carried out so successfully. She had wanted peace and security, and all Walsingham had done was to present her with a mass of evidence against her cousin and put her in a position where she had no choice but to put her on trial and execute her.

She had been tempted to ignore it all, but Parliament and her Council would not be fobbed off with autocracy or excuses now. Their enemy was in their hands and they would not let Elizabeth release her. There were times when she had no intention of having Mary brought to trial; the idea of a sovereign standing arraigned before a jury of commoners outraged Elizabeth's sense of what was due to Princes; later, when she felt calmer and able to consider all the factors clearly, she admitted that Mary must be put to death if her own life was to be safe. She talked to Leicester, who used every argument to prick her pride and her feelings in an effort to make her lose her temper and wreak a quick vengeance on the prisoner, and to Burleigh, who had a hundred excellent reasons for doing what she did not want to do. And still she did not want to do it. She hated Mary and she had punished Babington with such ferocity that her hardened sensibilities revolted when she heard the details of his death. She had spared the next batch of prisoners. It was almost as if the force of her human vindictiveness had spent itself in that awful bloodbath when some of the flower of her young nobles had perished slowly before a crowd of hundreds at Tyburn.

Now Mary stood alone, the last of the principals alive, and her death would still the clamour of treason and discontent for the rest of Elizabeth's reign. That was the argument of the short-sighted who refused to see beyond the scaffold to the ports of Spain, where a huge fleet of ships had been gathering. It was Elizabeth's old argument and she was not distracted from it by public hysteria. When Mary died, Spain would attack, and the ships fitting out at Cadiz, and the troops training across the Channel in the Netherlands, were all poised, waiting like an arrow pointed at her throat. Mary's death would loose them at her, and she paced up and down her apartments, cursing Walsingham and her Council and Robert and everyone who was pressing her to kill Mary and expose her country to the inevitable war with Spain. She was in a circumstantial vice, and she was also being squeezed by her own inherent dislike of condemning an anointed Queen to a felon's death.

But there was an alternative, which might stave off the final decision. It would not please anybody except Elizabeth, who had proved over and over again that it was always easy to be bold, but infinitely better to be cautious. If Mary was utterly discredited before the world and especially in the eyes of the religious fanatics in England, it might be possible to let her live.

And so Elizabeth was writing offering her her life. Normally she wrote with fluency; her pen had always been a master weapon, but now it was stiff in her fingers and the words were laboured. Mary had been taken to Fotheringay Castle, the bleakest and strongest of all her prisons, and there the trial would be held and the sentence carried out. She knew what was being prepared for her; her gaolers saw to that. She must be waiting in daily anticipation of death, and Elizabeth could only hope that her spirit would falter when she saw a suggestion of hope. She remembered her own mental state, so many,

many years ago when she was a young girl imprisoned in the Tower, her life threatened by the suspicions of a jealous, ailing sister and the plots of a succession of hotheaded incompetents, determined to compromise her whether she wished it or not. She had been very much afraid because she was young and passionately fond of life; the thought of death had terrified her, and there was nothing ignoble about her fear. Unlike Mary she had not been soured by sufferings and disappointments; she had not been middle-aged and abandoned to despair and disillusion. But even if she had been, if she and not her cousin were at Fotheringay, ruined and helpless, with nothing to look forward to but a twilight existence in one fortress after another, she, Elizabeth, would always choose to hope on and live on.

At last the letter shaped itself into the beautiful phraseology which she could always command. She urged Queen Mary to admit her guilt in the Babington conspiracy.

"If you will do this by letter in your own hand, as Queen to Queen and woman to woman, if you submit to my personal judgment, you will not be tried in any open court in this realm and I will find some means of lenience towards you. . . ."

After a moment she signed it with her beautiful, distinctive signature and suddenly remembered how carefully she had perfected it; it was almost impossible to forge. She had been clever then and careful, not a rash fool like that other woman to whom she was making her last offer of reprieve. In her inner heart she did not blame her for using any weapon, even murder, to try and regain the freedom denied to her for nearly twenty years. She understood it when Mary lied and stooped to pathetic deceits and ridiculous codes that Walsingham's cypher clerk broke down in a few hours; she would have done the same, but done it with greater skill. She could say that to Robert, because she never pretended with him; Robert was a cynic and they understood each other. And, thank God, she thought angrily, as she sanded and sealed the letter, Robert did not regard her as a semi-divinity, too wise and exalted to suffer the pangs of doubt or conscience, and too rarefied to admit that she was tolerant of many human crimes. If Mary wrote out and signed a confession, she would be comparatively harmless. The kind of men who went to their deaths at Tyburn for a religious ideal would never shed their blood to put a coward and an admitted murderess upon the throne of England. She could purchase her life at the expense of her honour, but as Elizabeth rang her bell and gave the letter to her Secretary to send to Fotheringay by special courier, she had a premonition that the price was too high.

In her apartments at Fotheringay Castle, Mary Stuart read the Queen of England's letter, and as she read her pale face flushed with anger. Her ladies were watching her, hoping that the letter contained some message of hope. Jane Kennedy spoke at last:

"Madam, what is it? I beg of you tell us, we are dying of anxiety."

Mary turned to them and smiled; it was a bitter, sardonic smile.

"The Queen of England offers to pardon me if I confess. If I admit myself guilty of all the crimes she charges me with, if I throw myself upon her mercy, she will save me from this commission of judges and spare my life."

Nobody answered; none of them, knowing Mary as they did, even dared to suggest that she might give serious thought to the letter.

"You see, ladies, I can live if I betray myself and all those brave men who have given their lives for my cause. Queen Elizabeth must think me as base and crooked as she is herself," she added quietly.

"Get me some paper and pens and ink. I will answer this now. The courier who brought it can return with my reply."

It was a short note, the wording was polite but uncompromising, as if she were addressing a stranger.

She could not beg Elizabeth's pardon for crimes which she had not committed. She had no intention of answering the English Commissioners or accepting their judgment, because she was a sovereign and only accountable to God. She wished her cousin well, as she had always done, and ended by forgiving her for the twenty years of unjust confinement she had suffered. The message was sent back to London and when the Queen had watched the courier riding away from her window, she went back to her oratory to pray.

On October 11th, the Commissioners arrived at Fotheringay and Mary was brought before them in the Castle Great Hall. There for the first time she saw her implacable enemies, Burleigh and Walsingham, and a jury of thirty-six peers, Privy Councillors and judges.

She was tried without a counsel for her own defence; the evidence was read to her and she was refused access to the copies of her letters to Babington and his to her. She answered with dignity and humour, defended herself with passionate sincerity, and insisted that she had never plotted against Elizabeth's life. She lied in some matters because she was certainly guilty of the major charge; but she told the truth whenever it was possible. She was not consciously false; the circumstances of her indictment were so palpably unjust, the evidence was forged in places, and the men sitting in judgment upon her were so blatantly biassed, that Mary's defence was only an exhibition of magnificent courage—heroic and admirable and doomed to failure. It was a farce in law, but a grim necessity in common fact. She was too dangerous to the Queen of England and to them, and the legality of the proceedings were relatively unimportant. There were men among them who had written secretly to her in the past, protesting their loyalty, but she knew they would condemn her because she had to be condemned. After two days the Commissioners left her, recording a verdict of guilty on all counts. The sentence was deferred. It must be pronounced by Parliament and ratified by Elizabeth's signature on the warrant for her execution. Fotheringay was silent and empty, except for Paulet and his soldiers and her few servants. She occupied herself with needlework and writing what she knew would be her last letters to all those who had neglected to help her and were unable to save her now.

She wrote to the Pope and to the King of France, and to her son, protesting her innocence and forgiving them their lack of diligence, and lastly she wrote to Philip of Spain. She bequeathed him her right to the throne of England and gave her final blessing to his inheritance. When Sir Amyas Paulet came to her some weeks later and told her that Parliament had sentenced her to be beheaded, Mary only smiled and turned away. There was nothing left now but prayer and patience. When the warrant arrived, she would be at peace.

Sir William Davidson was a rather diffident man; as second secretary to the Queen he usually saw her when Walsingham was present, but at this, the most crucial time since the trial of Mary Stuart, Walsingham was ill, and the onus of conducting his business fell on the unhappy Davidson. He was in the Queen's room at Greenwich Palace, and he was fidgeting as he waited in front of her. The document he had brought with him was held behind his back; in his nervousness he creased it and the paper crackled. The Queen was writing, but she looked up at him and frowned. She looked paler than usual and there were deep lines under her eyes which were red and sunken, for she had been sleeping very badly during the past few weeks.

She watched Davidson with hostility; she was irritated by his shifting nervousness, but then her nerves were so taut with anxiety and strain that the slightest noise made her want to scream. He was stupid and he was pedantic and he was holding himself as if he expected her to throw her inkpots at him.

" Have you brought the warrant? " she asked sharply.

" Yes, Madam."

" Then give it to me."

Davidson unfolded the roll of paper and laid it in front of her. She sat looking at it, and he felt sure that she would refuse to sign it once again and send him back to Walsingham. The last time he had come, she had horrified him by suddenly demanding why she had to make a public spectacle of her cousin's death, when some of those who had been loudest in their demands for the extreme penalty could easily dispose of the Scots Queen and save their own mistress from taking the step. He would never forget the moment when she told him to write to Paulet and suggest that he poisoned his prisoner. He had listened to her, frozen with horror and for the first time he was more disgusted by the Queen than afraid of her, and he managed to make a stumbling protest before she turned on him with an oath and told him to do what he was told. He had sent the letter to Paulet, but that unbending man, true to his iron principles to the end, wrote back refusing to sully his conscience by shedding blood without a legal warrant.

Elizabeth was remembering the incident at that moment; she remembered her rage with that pompous Puritan fool, who no doubt considered her a murderess and presumed to judge her motives by his own vulgar conscience. It was a sensible proposal; it was hallowed by custom and attested by the shades of many Kings of England who had been put to death in prison by a successful rival. If they lost the battle, they were hacked to death on the field, like Richard III when he lost his crown to her own grandfather, Henry VII. If they were deposed and imprisoned, they died by stealth, like Henry VI. But no

256

crowned sovereign in the world had ever been dragged to a public scaffold and beheaded like a common criminal, and this was what she was being forced to do to Mary. And for week after week, as she lay without sleep, torturing herself with indecision, the ghost of her mother stood behind the Queen of Scotland. It was better to die in the dark, to be despatched out of life with some semblance of privacy than to quit the world like a felon, exhibited to the vulgar gaze. The world would judge her as she was already judging herself; nothing Mary had done against her would expunge the crime of severing an anointed head and delivering a crowned Queen to the penalty of the common law.

But nobody would relieve her; Paulet made his conscience the excuse, but his fellow Commissioner, Sir Drue Drury, was no fanatic and he would not do it either. He did not trust his Queen. When Mary was dead she might easily disclaim all knowledge of the murder and punish the men who had obeyed her and carried it out. Still she hesitated; she felt as ill and distraught as she did when she had to sign her first warrant for execution by the axe, so many years ago, when the Duke of Norfolk was condemned.

"How is Sir Francis Walsingham?" she asked suddenly.

"A little better, Madam," Davidson murmured. He was watching her hand holding the pen; the ink was slowly gathering, forming a single drop at the end of the nib. Suddenly she shook it. The ink splattered and then she dropped the paper on the floor beside her. He squinted at it, and saw her signature scrawled at the end. He stood, not daring to move or speak; Elizabeth's face was the colour of a corpse; she pressed her hand to her eyes and he took a step forward, thinking she was going to faint. Her voice stopped him; it was harsh and acid with sarcasm:

"Take this to Walsingham; the bad news will come near to killing him!"

Her unsteady, almost hysterical laughter followed him as he fled from the room. When he had gone, Elizabeth signed and sealed the rest of the papers in front of her and placed them in a neat pile on her writing-table. She stood up very slowly; her legs were trembling and her head hammered with pain. It was a cold, drizzling day in late January, and it had taken her over two months to do what she had just done and send her own first cousin to a shameful death. She went to

E 257 R

the window automatically and unfastened it; the cold, damp air touched her face and she closed her eyes.

Strike or be stricken. She had said that to Robert only the night before when he was pleading with her to sign the warrant, telling her that she was fretting herself into her grave for a worthless principle, arguing that once it was done she would be glad, as she had been glad when Norfolk died. She needn't know the details; he would keep all accounts from her if she liked, shelter her, protect her. Her people were united with her, armed to defend her against attack; her Parliament were loyal and loving and determined to rescue her from the danger of assassination. The life of one treacherous woman was nothing compared to the safety of England and the continuance of her reign.

And now it was done. But at least it would be done many miles away in Northamptonshire. When Burleigh had suggested bringing Mary to the Tower and executing her there, Elizabeth had become almost hysterical. The old associations crowded in upon her, the echo of the Tower cannon, heard by her own father when Anne Boleyn was killed, would certainly reach her ears if she were within a hundred miles. And that sound and her half-forgotten terrors as a child, would drive her mad. . . . The Council had begun to despair, thinking she would never sign the paper. But she had, and already in her own mind she was excusing herself, driven by her own emotional torment to deceive herself for the first time in her life. It was signed, but she could still recall it if she liked, even at the last moment. She closed the window and rang for her ladies. To their annoyance, the Queen announced that she, and they, were going for a long walk in the freezing Palace grounds.

Walsingham glanced at the warrant Davidson gave him, and got out of his sick bed. He knew Elizabeth; he well knew the struggle which had been raging between her and all her advisers to obtain that signature, and he was not going to waste a moment. Within an hour the paper had been sent to Burleigh who called all available members of the Council. He and Walsingham and Leicester, the Lords Howard, Hunsdon, Cobham, Knollys and Derby, were shown the Queen's signature, and the Great Seal of England which had been hurriedly fixed to it. Burleigh looked from one to the other and said gravely:

"My Lords, Her Majesty has done her part. Now we must do ours. We cannot risk a change of mind. And we owe it to the Queen to spare her the distress of further details. I propose that we all take the responsibility and send this warrant at once to Sir Amyas Paulet with instructions to execute the Queen of Scots immediately."

Eight voices answered as one:

"Agreed."

As they were leaving the room, Walsingham approached Leicester. "I have taken the precaution of ordering the Tower headsman, Bulle, to leave for Fotheringay," he said.

Leicester looked at him and shook his head. "You think of everything, my friend," he said.

For the first time he understood why Elizabeth would never like her Secretary.

On February 8th, 1587, Mary Stuart, Queen of Scotland, Dowager Queen of France, heiress to the throne of England and Ireland and Wales, walked to the Great Hall at Fotheringay for the last time. She had been told to be ready the night before, and she had spent the last hours of her life in prayer and a calm preparation. All the turbulence, the ambition and egotism of her adult years had faded, leaving her temperate and resigned. She was able to pray, at last, for her friends and even her enemies, and she meant it when she promised forgiveness as she hoped to be forgiven. And with real humility she prayed for herself. For the first time her regrets were for others, for all those who had suffered through her, even indirectly. She prayed for Darnley and struggled to feel pity and understanding for him, though she could truly say he was the cause of all her misfortunes. She had set her feet towards Fotheringay on the day of her marriage all those years ago. She could think of him and of her half-brother, James, and of Bothwell, without a tinge of blame or hatred. She could not forgive her cousin Elizabeth and she compromised by refusing to think of her at all. She divided what was left of her possessions between her ladies and servants; she insisted with gaiety on wearing her finest velvets and her best wig, and painted her sad, tired face as if she were going to a State reception. At the foot of the scaffold she saw one friendly face—the ageing Earl of Shrewsbury, her old friend, responsible for many comforts in the years she had spent in his keeping. There were tears in his eyes as

259

he looked at her; she gave him her hand for a moment and then began to walk slowly up the shallow steps.

Robert sat by the fire, with his arm round the Queen of England's shoulders. The room was shuttered and warm, lit by a few candles and the bright dancing light from the blazing logs. They had dined together and she had eaten more than usual to please him. She was painfully thin and hollow-eyed, without appetite or enthusiasm even for hunting. It seemed to him that she had aged ten years since the death of Mary Stuart. He had expected her to pretend to be angry when she heard that the sentence had been carried out; he was not surprised when she accused him and the Council of sending the warrant behind her back, and protested to the foreign ambassadors, with tears in her eyes, that she never meant it to be executed. He was not even indignant when she vented her rage upon the innocent Davidson and threw him into the Tower. But he was astonished when she ordered a State Funeral for Mary at Peterborough Cathedral, and buried her at the enormous cost of forty thousand pounds. Then he began to believe in her grief; he believed it still more when her health showed visible signs of decline. She wept frequently, even when she was alone. She paced up and down her rooms at night, unable to sleep, and sent her food away untasted. And night after night, he listened to her outpourings of regret and recriminations and excuse, and marvelled at the effect the death of someone she had never seen and who had been her mortal enemy for over twenty years, was having on her constitution and her will. He had always thought her hard; now she tormented herself by demanding accounts of Mary's execution, cursing the Dean of Peterborough, who had disputed with the unhappy woman on the scaffold, denouncing the religion which was the only thing left to comfort her.

"They have no pity, these gentle servants of God," she said bitterly, turning towards him. They had been discussing it yet again. She knew it by heart now, but she was still morbidly unsatisfied.

"She answered him bravely," Leicester said.

"She was braver in her death than most of the dogs surrounding me would be," Elizabeth retorted.

"Then let her rest in your own mind," he urged her. "It had to be done and you know this. She died more royally than she lived; forget her, Madam. You always said to me that only fools dwell on the past—where has that stout heart of yours gone?"

"Sometimes I think it's in her grave at Peterborough," Elizabeth leant against him and sighed. "I have fought and schemed for Queenship and now I feel as if I had killed part of myself. I feel bloody-handed and degraded, and only you, of them all, understand me enough to know why."

"I understand you and I love you," he answered her gently. "Too well to let you pine away for a thing that was inevitable. She had to die, Madam, and you have to live. Now, more than ever, or it will all have been in vain. . . . Don't think of it or speak of it again. I swear to you now that this is the last time I shall discuss it with you."

She looked at him obliquely.

"Those are high words, Robert. I've had enough of other men's dictation in the past few months."

"I don't dictate," he said. "But I want to see you smile and show your spirit. You've reminded me often enough that you were the Queen in the past, and this is not the time to show that you are just a woman."

"It never is the time," Elizabeth said wearily. "It has never been the time in the whole of my life."

"You cannot change yourself," he told her.

Suddenly she smiled at him and touched his face.

"You grow very wise, Robert; what should I do without you now? You are the only one who sees me as I am, who sees the grey hair under the wig, the lines beneath the paint. . . . How is my Lady Leicester? You've seen very little of her lately."

"She's well," he said, hesitating. Elizabeth never mentioned his wife unless she were about to quarrel with him. "I have even forgiven you that," she said. "If she is impatient to see you, she must wait a little longer. I have the first claim."

"You have always had it and you always will."

Elizabeth was staring into the fire; she was sitting more upright, not leaning against him so limply and some of the lassitude had gone out of her expression.

"I will need you more and more, Robert," she said suddenly. "I will need every man in England who is loyal and able before very long. Now I say it for the last time. Mary Stuart is dead. But like the dragon in the fable, when you cut off one head another grows. I have done what Burleigh and all of you wanted, what had to be done if you like. And now we must take the consequences, and the consequences are Philip of Spain and the Armada he has been building. Our spies report that it will be ready in six months!"

## Chapter 13

HUNDREDS of miles from England, Philip II, King of
Spain, sat in his rooms in the Escurial Palace outside Madrid.
For many years Philip's recreation had been the planning of
this tall sombre building, which even included the magnificent
tomb he had designed for himself. It was lofty and cool, and
the views showed him a panorama of the capital city of
Spain and the brightly-coloured fields and orange groves,
scorching in the fierce sun. Philip seldom looked at the view.
Heat and colour did not excite him; he had decorated
his own apartments with sombre tapestries and dark furniture, and he had dressed in black velvet for over forty
years.

As a young man he had been handsome, but the general
impression he created was one of reserve and coldness. His
hair was receding, it had once been as pale as flax, and his pro-
tuberant eyes were a chilly blue. They were heavy eyes, matched
by an ugly prominent lower lip. He was sixty-one but he moved
and spoke like a much older man. His body was frail, and his
habits were monastic. He ate and drank very little, prayed and
attended every priestly office during his long days, and he
worked and worked until everyone surrounding him was
exhausted.

It was difficult to believe that he had ever experienced an
emotion or succumbed to a passion. He seemed strangely lifeless, and his curious pale eyes were dull. He never raised his
voice, never gave an order without wording it as a request, but
he had buried three wives and kept his mistress in a walled-up
room without sunlight or fresh air until she died because she
had been unfaithful to him. The mistress was the key to the
mystery of Philip and his personality. His wives had been
chosen for him: the elderly, plain Queen Mary of England,
whom he had abandoned to die alone, and two French Prin-
cesses for whom he had no enthusiasm; but he had chosen
Anna Eboli to please himself. She was beautiful and full of
fiery spirit; as a girl she had lost an eye duelling with her page.

She was not moral or religious or meek, and she satisfied the immoderate appetites for lust and domination which consumed Philip, burning away beneath his courtesy and reserve like the deep fires of a volcano.

He was cruel with the brutality of the supreme egotist. He had punished Anna with a positive genius for knowing what would most torture that restless, active woman, so passionately fond of life. And then he had forgotten her completely. He supported and encouraged the Inquisition originally formed to rid Spain of the heresies of the Moors and the Jews, and expanded it into a dreaded political weapon. He had largely isolated the Church from the direction of the Pope and, when it suited him, he disregarded Papal interference. He was the most absolute monarch in the Christian world, and the most feared man who had ever ruled over Spain. And for nearly thirty years he had been pursuing his plan to conquer England. He had been patient, because time meant nothing to him; he was apt to regard himself as immortal, even when he went alone to the magnificent empty tomb under the Escurial. He had never forgotten England. He was unaccustomed to being challenged and treated as if he were of no importance. He had preserved his usual cool politeness during the three miserable years he was married to Mary Tudor; his feeling never showed on the surface when the London mobs hooted after him and published coarse lampoons about him in the streets. He listened politely while the English Ministers and the English clergy talked over his head and disregarded his advice, and he accepted the supreme humiliation of having to ask his wife for the least thing he wanted. He had been calm and patient, and escaped back to Spain or the Netherlands as often as he could; but his pride had suffered a permanent scar. His hatred for that alien country and its people had grown into an obsession, and Philip's whole character was moulded like cement; it closed over an idea or a grievance and hardened for ever. His desire for revenge was even strong enough to consider marrying his sister-in-law Elizabeth and trying to dominate through her, but she had rejected him and, in his heart, Philip was relieved. He wanted war with England, not then or in the immediate future but at some date ahead, when he could give the details his full attention. He was prepared to wait, and while he waited he had personalized his simmering grievance and hatred until the whole of England, independent, rude, scornful of Spain and Spain's omnipotent King, was symbolized in Elizabeth Tudor.

He would never admit that she was clever. Throughout the years when her policy, her lies and interference in the Netherlands had kept him from striking at her, Philip chose to regard her success as accidental. He was not in a hurry. He could wait, and he had waited nearly thirty years.

The table in front of him now was covered by maps. A sheaf of papers, statistics of men and ammunition, provisions for the long voyage, and a list of all the ships of war, were by his elbow. He had read through them, making notes and referring to the navigation maps set out in front of him. It was the largest fleet ever assembled in the history of warfare, and it would have sailed a year earlier, soon after the death of the Queen of Scots, except that Drake, one of the notorious pirates employed by Elizabeth, had brought a small force of ships into the harbours of Cadiz and Corunna, and sunk some of the Spanish fleet at their moorings. Philip's revenge was delayed, but he ordered replacements to be built and set the date a year ahead. Now everything was ready. Nothing perturbed him, nothing deflected his single-minded purpose to reduce England to ashes, put its Queen and all her Protestant advisers to death, and claim what remained as his inheritance. The only wise word that Mary Stuart had ever written was when she made her will and bequeathed him her right to the English Crown. He had done his best to bring about her death by encouraging plots on her behalf without giving the support of troops and money they needed to succeed. So long as Mary lived, he had been unable to declare war; he was not going to subdue England only to give it to a Queen who was half French and bound to serve French interests. He was not going to give England to anyone when he had taken it, except perhaps one of his daughters. It would be like the subjugated Indies, part of the Spanish Empire, and once it was properly pacified, fit to form part of the dowry of a Princess of Spain. He had reviewed his Armada of ships and bestowed the command of them upon the Duke of Medina Sidonia. They rode at anchor in the ports of Spain towering like floating castles, their bright pennants streaming in the wind, cannon massed upon the decks. And in the Netherlands a seasoned force of thirty thousand soldiers were waiting to embark.

The King looked up for a moment, clasping hands swollen

with gout; one of his eyes was succumbing to a milky cataract and he found it difficult to read for more than a short period. He sometimes wondered how age had afflicted Elizabeth. Like a lot of old men he was apt to think of her as she had been when they last met; very slim and upright and not unpleasing to look at, though she was too thin and her features were too angular. He liked women to be rounded and small, with bright black eyes and smooth, voluptuous hair. He could not quite imagine Elizabeth as an old woman. In his heart he still saw himself as young.

He rang a little silver handbell and his secretary came out of an alcove; there was always someone on duty all through the day and night. The King sometimes got up from his bed and dictated a letter. He had no Ministers capable of taking even a minor decision. He loved and cherished his power and refused to delegate anything to anyone else.

"Write an order to the Commanders of the Armada," he said. The secretary sat down at a second small table and waited.

"Tell them," the precise voice went on, "that the King has studied the charts of the tides and approves the route suggested. He commends their enterprise to Almighty God, and orders them to sail for England on the nineteenth day of May. When you have finished, I will sign the letter. Send it at once to the Duke of Medina Sidonia."

He read through the letter carefully, and then wrote his own form of signature at the end of it. Three words: *I, the King.* Then he left the quiet room and walked slowly down to his private Chapel where he knelt in the dim oratory and prayed that God would bless the venture and grant him the victory. It was not a prayer of supplication, for Philip had long since identified his own will with the designs of Providence. He was the King, and God had never failed him.

Elizabeth was alone in her Privy Chamber at Greenwich. It was seven o'clock in the evening and the July sunlight was still streaming through the windows. The room was cool and very quiet; the Queen stood without moving; the black brocade dress hung loosely on her for she had grown very thin; her cheeks were hollowed, and her heavy-lidded eyes were ringed with sleeplessness and anxiety. They had brought her the news that morning: the first ships of the Armada had been sighted off the Devon coast. Up and down the shores of South-west

England, the warning beacons blazed. She had imagined the men standing guard beside them, scanning the misty coastline, and then the first shout, the pointing hand, the moment when the watchers gathered, shielding their eyes, and stood there on the cliffs, looking at the distant sails moving like clouds upon the horizon. The Armada was in sight, and now the beacons were fired and the tocsins were ringing, and in all the towns and villages a drummer sounded the call to arms. After twenty-eight years Philip of Spain was returning to England and nothing stood between him and victory but the will of her people to resist and a small fleet of fast, heavily-gunned ships. A force of thirty thousand men were gathered at Windsor, under the command of her own cousin, Lord Hunsdon, to defend her from capture, and sixteen thousand men waited at Tilbury, barring the way to London. She had almost laughed aloud when the Council proposed this disposition of her forces; she could see Burleigh, greyer and more bent than ever, his face contorted with anxiety, insisting that the person of the Queen was more important than the possession of the Capital. Without her there was no point, no reason for resistance and bloodshed. If Philip captured her, England would fall with her. He had been unable to hide his reproach as he looked at her. She was only a woman, without husband or children, and the freedom of her country and the lives of every man and woman who had served her, were dependent upon her alone. And while the numbers of her soldiers were impressive, the quality was pitiful. They were raw and untrained, poorly fed and indifferently armed, conscripted in desperate haste from a population which had not waged a serious war for nearly thirty years. There was not one military Commander who could compete with Alva, and the veteran Spanish troops were the most highly disciplined and experienced soldiers in the world; they would run through her army like a knife through butter. Elizabeth knew this; she knew that if Alva once landed on English ground, she would be dead and Philip would be in London before two years were over. She had temporized and delayed to the last moment, refusing to let them squander her money in a futile attempt to make a fighting force out of an army of amateurs, insisting that the fleet be maintained as cheaply as possible until the sea captains themselves demanded how they were to fight with leaking ships and men existing on half-pay. She had not listened. She had cursed at them all and sworn to fight the battle in her own way, refusing to bankrupt her throne and mortgage her country to an extent where victory would be achieved at the cost of economic ruin. She knew, and so did they, that Philip must be defeated at sea or not at all, and she argued that a few coats of paint and bribing the seamen with full pay would not affect the outcome. She spoke and acted like a miser, and she could not explain to those men who were all so desperately afraid for their own safety, and for hers, that whatever happened to her and to them, her instinct was to save what she could for her people.

She was the Queen, and now at last, with Mary dead, they looked to her, and loved her; she had so often spoken of them tenderly as her children when she wanted to thwart their desire for an heir of her body; now the addresses of loyalty and affection which came to Greenwich with every courier, brought the tears to her eyes and an ache of anxiety for them to her heart. Whatever happened she would not beggar them to save herself. She had spent her life making her country strong and rich and prosperous, and England was repaying her with men and money and promises to die to the last man in her defence. She gave Leicester the command of the men defending London. He and Hunsdon could be trusted never to surrender. Now at last the waiting was over, the arguments, the indecisions, the doubts—they belonged to the past. She was over fifty and she had been Queen for nearly thirty years. Before the month was out, she would either be dead or she would be safe on her throne until she died in her bed. And now all fear had left her. She felt cold and calm and strangely exhilarated. She had been waiting for Philip for years, not the few short weeks since the Armada left Spain, and she had always known he could not be kept at bay for ever. From the moment of Mary Stuart's death, war was inevitable. Now it had come and in the greatest crisis of her life, Elizabeth was in command of herself and her own situation.

Her brain was clear, her emotions were under control. The war was not a religious crusade, as Spain was trying to make out; it was not the onslaught of the powers of the Inquisition, with which her parsons were terrifying their congregations up and down the country. It was what it had always been, a contest for power between her and Philip, and that was how she was going to fight it, without crosses and banners and priests, but with cannon. God was at the right hand of the victor. That was Elizabeth's belief, and it was the belief of the commanders of her fleet, many of whom were pirates by profession and all the more skilful for that. When she first heard the news that the Armada had been sighted off the coast of Devon, she had retired into her oratory and prayed for a few moments. She had asked God to give her the victory, without arguing or promising, and allowed herself to hope that He was interested in the outcome and prepared to intervene. Then she sent for Leicester and Burleigh and Lord Howard of Effingham, who was her cousin on her mother's side and the Admiral in command of all her ships.

They were announced within a few minutes, and Burleigh hobbled in on his stick, followed by Leicester looking every day of his age, his fine figure running to flesh, and the grey hairs showing in his beard. The tall dark sailor, Howard of Effingham, came last. They bowed and kissed her hand, and Leicester helped her into a chair and stood beside it.

Elizabeth spoke first to the Admiral:

" What is the latest news of the Spanish fleet? "

" They are sailing slowly towards Plymouth, Madam. They're heavy ships and well loaded; they can't make much speed and the wind has dropped. That was my last report."

" And our own ships? "

The Admiral frowned. He wished the Queen would leave the conduct of the war to her captains; he also wished that she did not know so much about sea tactics. The fleet was in Plymouth harbour, and the last he had heard from a messenger who had ridden through the night, was a disturbing account of near chaos when the Armada was first sighted. If the Spanish Commander sailed into Plymouth and engaged in a close attack, his superior armaments would blow the small English fleet out of the water. The order to draw anchor and scatter into the open sea had come as a surprise, and many of the heavier ships had fouled each other's lines and drifted into a dangerous bottleneck near the harbour mouth. He did not yet know whether they had got out, or whether the Duke of Medina Sidonia had seen his opportunity and altered course to engage them.

" Well? " Elizabeth spoke sharply. " Where are they? "

" In Plymouth harbour, Madam."

" If they're caught there, they'll be blown to pieces and we will have nothing to stop the Spaniards from embarking Alva's troops and landing them at Dover! What the devil are the captains doing? Are they asleep down there—tell Drake and Hawkins that if Medina Sidonia catches them sitting like a flock of geese in Plymouth, they'd better sink with their own ships, for I'll hang them at Plymouth dock!"

"They are all men of experience, Madam," Burleigh interrupted. "You can leave your defence in their hands; from our reports on the Spanish Commander it's unlikely he will alter course and disobey his instructions. He has been told to go to the Channel and anchor near Dunkirk to take on the invasion troops. He's not a seaman, and I feel sure he will do as he's been told. We have little to fear."

"I've always found it dangerous to rely too much upon your enemy's stupidity to save you from your own mistakes," Elizabeth snapped at him, and then she glared at Lord Howard of Effingham. She felt the slight pressure of Leicester's hand upon her shoulder, trying to calm her, and angrily pulled her arm away.

"I am anxious, gentlemen, and not just for myself. Lord Howard, you and your captains are responsible for the safety of the whole country, for the lives of thousands of my people, apart from my own. It is a heavy burden, but it is a feather compared to the load I bear. My life is nothing—I'd lay it down tomorrow if it would save England from becoming a part of the Empire of Spain. If I wore breeches instead of a skirt, my questions would seem perfectly natural. Send word to Plymouth, my Lord; tell the fleet that England and the Queen depend upon them."

"I will do better, Madam. I'll deliver the message myself. If the Armada sails round the coast and goes into the Channel we will follow them. My plan is to engage them continuously; with that load and the tonnage of the ships themselves, we should be able to outmanoeuvre them and beat them in a running sea fight. This is agreed between all the captains, and I swear to God, Madam, I'll bring you the victory or I won't come back myself."

He bent over her thin hand and kissed it. He was a rough man, without sentiment or scruples, powerful enough to profess himself a Roman Catholic and loyal enough to enjoy the Queen's confidence in spite of it. He had spent most of his life at sea, and he was irritated with her interference; at the same time he admired her grasp of a situation which they both knew to be in favour of the enemy. She was extraordinarily courageous; there were no womanly tears and flutterings for her own safety and she looked so frail and drawn that his heart was touched and his weatherbeaten face turned red. She was the Queen and she never let him or anyone else forget it for a moment, but she was also his kin, and he was more personally attached to her than he would admit.

When he had left she turned to Burleigh.

" What is the mood in the City of London? "

The Minister smiled.

" Confident and loyal, and ready to fight. Offers of money have been coming in from every Guild and Livery, and the citizens are arming. The Churches have been full since early this morning. When I came here there were couriers from the midlands and the east, all telling the same tale. If Alva lands here, which God forbid, every man able to hold a sword will come out into the streets to fight for you."

It was amazing to Burleigh that, after so many years and so many upheavals, the Queen was more popular than she had ever been. He had underestimated the power of her hold upon the common people of the country; for now the clever speeches and the exhausting, costly progresses through towns and villages were showing their true value. They knew her by sight, and the many personal contacts she had made were rallying them to her when fear of Spain and a disinclination to part with their money and expose themselves to risk might have seriously weakened her authority. It was true to say that there was no peace party; there was not one dissentient group prepared to throw the Queen to her enemies and make a separate treaty with Philip, and he thanked God over and over again that Mary Stuart was not alive to rally those few Catholics still at liberty. And they were few indeed, with the exception of Howard of Effingham who was the Queen's man first and a Catholic afterwards, every notable Catholic or suspected Catholic had been arrested days ago.

" Let it be known that I share their confidence," she said. " There must be no panic anywhere. You must help me draft a proclamation and have it circulated throughout the country. We'll do that later this evening. I shall show myself at the first opportunity and I shall also visit my troops. If they are going to die for me, they should know what I look like. And know that I'm not skulking in some inland fortress while I send them out to shed their blood."

" I will come back in two hours, if that pleases you, Madam." Burleigh took her hand and after he had kissed it, bending with some difficulty, the Queen gave it an affectionate squeeze.

" You've got a grey beard and a gouty foot, but you're as brave as any man I know," she said. " Be of good heart, my friend, Philip won't feed you to the flames, nor poor Robert, either."

She looked up at Leicester and nudged him.

" I know how my navy and my cities are faring; now I want to hear about the army. Come back in two hours, Burleigh."

When she was alone with Robert, she sighed and leant back against the chair as if she were exhausted.

" Come and sit beside me."

He went to the other side of the room and poured out a glass of wine and gave it to her. In the last two years they had both been ill, and she allowed him to bully her about her food and lack of sleep, and agreed to leave the dancing and music she loved when he insisted that she was tired, but he had never been able to curtail the hours she spent on governing, or to take a single State paper, however unimportant, out of her hands. When he was ill, he was subjected to every remedy Elizabeth could think of, supervised like a child and surrounded by fussing doctors who had been made answerable for his recovery to the Queen herself. They cosseted and cared for each other and reacted with terror to the slightest threat of illness. It was unthinkable that she should die, because he would not know how to exist without her, and the idea of death and Robert reduced Elizabeth to hysteria with worry. They sat together like an ageing man and wife, their hands entwined, symbolizing the bondage of two lonely people who had nothing but each other. It had been true of Elizabeth for several years, and it was true of Robert, too. His wife, gay, voluptuous, tender Lettice Essex for whom he had risked so much, was still gay and still voluptuous, and she had slowly tired of a husband whose duties kept him at Court and whose energies were vitiated by the demands made upon him by the Queen. She had always been jealous and she had been in love with him for a remarkable length of time in view of her character, but eventually she discovered that she was no longer irritated and anxious when Robert was away, and no longer excited and eager when they were together. She was still young and handsome, with an undiminished appetite for the pleasures of life. Robert was too tired and too obsessed with the Queen to give them to her, and she was now the mistress of Sir Charles Blount.

At that moment his personal disillusionment was very far from Leicester's mind. He had been working day and night, snatching a few hours of sleep and eating where he worked, in a desperate attempt to arm and organize the army gathered at Tilbury. He understood the problems of provisioning and transport and he had gained some military experience in a short-lived expedition to the Netherlands some years before, but he knew that an engagement with Alva's troops would be tantamount to suicide. Since they had heard that the Armada had left Spain, he had felt as if he were living through a nightmare; it was all the more unreal because Elizabeth had been foretelling it almost since her accession and he had begun to think it would never be an actuality.

The Spanish galleons were enormous; English spies had compared them to floating fortresses; he knew very little about seamanship but something about gunnery and he could not imagine how they could possibly be sunk. He did not know the quality of his own untrained troops, and he thought of Alva and the Spanish halberdiers and pikemen, and the strength of the Spanish artillery, and he could see nothing ahead of them all but defeat.

"Don't be so anxious," Elizabeth said quietly. "I don't want to hear about the army. I know that you've done your best with what you have, Robert."

"They have too few arms and no experience, but they don't lack courage. None of them will desert you whatever the odds."

"I know that." She looked at him suddenly. "I also know that you are losing hope. You see all the odds against us, and none in our favour."

"I haven't your faith in a gang of pirates and a few ships. I'd sooner we had a strong army and matched the Spaniards here in the field."

"Many things can win or lose a battle, and the English are better seamen than soldiers. They'll fight all the harder for knowing that Philip will have every man of them hanged if they lose; he hasn't forgotten Cadiz, or the treasure ships we took from him."

"It will go hard with all of us if he wins," Leicester said slowly.

"It will indeed. He will put me to death, and you and Burleigh and most of the Council. But he is not going to win, Robert." She stood up suddenly. "I did not kill the Queen of Scots and execute so many of my own subjects just to give England to Philip at the end of it all. He is not going to win, and his ships will never anchor in an English port. That is what I believe and what I command you to believe with me. I shall go down to Tilbury and address your troops; I shall show them that I am not afraid of Philip. And by God, I'm not any longer! "

"You think God will give us the victory? " he asked. He had begun to take an interest in religion; it quieted his mind.

"I think we will take it for ourselves," the Queen answered.

"If we win, it will be because of you," he said.

"Not quite, Robert. But if I faltered now, we could certainly lose. And I am not going to falter, and nor is anyone else.—Go and find Burleigh and tell him that I shall go by barge to Whitehall this evening. I shall want you with me, and a proper escort, my musicians and torch bearers. I will write my proclamation there. But first the people of London are going to see me and they are going to see that nothing has changed. I am not afraid and I have not left them. Go now."

At nine that evening the Queen's barge sailed up the Thames, and the crowds lining the river banks and rowing their boats close to the procession saw the Queen sitting in the poop under a crimson canopy, torches blazing beside her, dressed in bright yellow and shining with jewels, with her musicians playing and a brilliant escort of ladies and gentlemen surrounding her. She smiled and waved vigorously, and wiped away tears at the warmth of the cheers. The Earl of Leicester was behind her chair, accompanied by his young stepson, Robert Devereux, the Earl of Essex, who had come to Court under his patronage. It was the same brilliant pageant which Elizabeth presented for her people every time she made a journey, however short, and the approaches to the river banks were packed with an excited crowd. With an invasion fleet sailing within sight of the English coast, her appearance seemed of special significance to them at that moment. The Queen was still in London, she was not panicking or moving to the Tower or further inland for safety, she was painted and jewelled as brightly as usual and she seemed as confident and good-humoured as if they had just won a signal victory. The rumour circulated that the battle had already taken place and the whole Armada had gone to the bottom of the sea.

When she landed at Whitehall Elizabeth went straight to her apartments, stripped off her cumbersome clothes, changed into a loose robe, and sat down with Burleigh to draft her proclamation and a speech she would make to the army at Tilbury. By midnight she received a message from the west coast that the Armada had ignored the English fleet in Plymouth harbour and was sailing round the south coast up the English Channel.

The two fleets had been engaged in a running fight for seven days. Howard of Effingham and his captains, Drake and Hawkins, brought their ships up behind the Armada after leaving Plymouth and the first encounter damaged several of the heavier galleons, reducing their speed. The English were so superbly manoeuvred that they suffered no loss, and when they attacked again and again the following days, they never engaged closely enough to run the risk of being grappled and boarded. Their gunnery was deadly; it had to be because the harassed commanders were already short of shot, but the Armada's pace was slackening and there were more stragglers, partly crippled and drifting helplessly on the tide. This was not war as the Spanish Commanders understood it; the enemy harried the main fleet and picked off the casualties but refused to sail round and face them in a major battle in spite of their superior speed. They were small ships, slightly built with tapering lines and concentrated armament; they chased in and out of the massive galleons, driven by oar and sail, like a pack of terriers.

Admiral Recalde was second in command to the Duke of Medina Sidonia, and he was an experienced seaman who had already begged his Commander to attack the English fleet in Plymouth harbour. His advice was ignored; when he signalled to the Duke on the second day that they should stand to and attack the Isle of Wight and force the enemy to engage at close quarters, his request was again refused. The Duke had received his orders from the King and those orders were to sail to Dunkirk and embark Alva's army of sixteen thousand veterans. He had been entrusted with a fleet of one hundred and thirty-one ships, and a force of seventeen thousand troops. These were to be joined with Alva's forces and landed on the English coast. He respected the Admiral's judgment, but he did not share his anxiety over their present rate of loss. And he did not even consider disobeying his instructions from King Philip.

On the evening of the 27th of July, 1588, the Armada anchored between Calais and Gravelines. It was noted that the pursuing enemy had been reduced; a number of Howard's ships had been forced to return to port for ammunition. As Medina Sidonia pointed out, when his captains came to the flagship *Santa Maria* to dine with him that night, they were now ready to take on Alva's soldiers and return to England.

The next day the crews were busy repairing holes and damaged rigging and burying their dead. There was no time to rest until the fleet was properly seaworthy. In the rare interval the officers relaxed. They had been at sea since May 19th, and they had been fighting for a week without much satisfaction. The night of the 28th was very dark and a strong wind came up, ruffling the banners and rocking the heavy ships in a deep swell.

The first of the English fire-ships sailed into the middle of them at two in the morning. There were eight such ships, and they were blazing from stem to stern with pitch and faggots, and the rising wind drove them along the water, shedding sparks and flame and smoke as if they were toys upon a pond. The stretch of sea became an inferno lit by the glare of the burning wrecks and of those galleons which had caught fire from them. The rest of the Spanish fleet were struggling to cut their cables and drift out to safety. Lines were fouled; there were collisions and explosions as the ammunition in the burning ships went up; the sea was full of charred wreckage and dead bodies and men swimming, screaming for help. Some of the rammed ships began to list so violently that the thousands of troops trapped in them went to the bottom of the sea without even reaching the decks. From the flagship, Medina Sidonia ordered the rest of the fleet to hoist anchor and pull out into the open sea; he had just seen Admiral Recalde's galleon blow up like a monstrous firework after being covered by a shower of flaming timber from a fallen mast. There was no time to save survivors; the fire-ships had sunk by then, but everywhere he looked his own ships were burning. He had been a distinguished soldier and a devoted servant of his King. But

Philip had not told him how to provide for this, and as the *Santa Maria* moved through the smoke and the wreckage, he knew that the English fleet was waiting for him outside the radius of the fires.

The dawn was breaking and Howard of Effingham's ships were now joined by another force under the command of Lord Henry Seymour; the units who had returned for ammunition had made contact again, and as he watched the outline of the Armada sailing out against that frightful background, the English Admiral gave the order to attack. He attacked in the same manner as before, at a safe distance from the heavier ships with their large boarding parties and massive guns. He manoeuvred his light ships at speed among the crippled galleons wallowing in the increasingly high seas, and he sunk them easily. The Spanish ships were separated and disorganized, many of them had damaged gear as a result of the panicked dispersal and were unable to bring about after a broadside. The English cannon smashed through wood and plating into the holds packed with soldiers, and one of the toughest of the English captains blenched at the sight of a Spanish galleon slowly heeling over, while blood poured from her decks like water. The Armada was dying like some great wounded animal in the waters of the English Channel; there was a strong south-west wind blowing up, and the few ships that were left were driven before it. By the end of the day there was no more firing; there was a strange silence. The English fleet stood off and then turned for home; its ammunition was exhausted and there was no more in reserve in the English arsenals. What was left of their enemy was driven up into the North Sea by a wind which was growing into a storm. Alva's army was still intact in the Netherlands but it would never cross to England now. Two thirds of the Armada of Spain were sunk round the English coastline and in the English Channel. The reefs and rocks of Scotland and Ireland later claimed most of those that were left.

The streets of the City of London were packed with a dense crowd of cheering, shouting, waving people, pressed back behind wooden barriers which were draped with brightly coloured cloths. Silks and velvets and tapestries were strung overhead between the buildings, and there were triumphal arches and tableaux depicting the defeat of the Armada. Even the roads were strewn with herbs and flowers. The August sun was shining and Elizabeth thanked God for a light breeze. She was sitting in an open litter hung with cloth of gold and drawn by four pure white horses, and she was the centre of a long, brilliant procession which was returning from St. Paul's in the City after a service of thanksgiving for the defeat of the Armada. The service had lasted for three hours, and her progress from Whitehall Palace had taken nearly as long as it moved slowly through the narrow streets, between crowds of people shrieking with enthusiasm and joy. There had never been a spectacle like this one within living memory; she could hear the cheers within the Cathedral, competing with the choirs and the music and the Archbishop of Canterbury's sermon which the Queen thought went on far too long. She had already been tired when she entered the Church; she wore a heavy gold crown, covered with diamonds and emeralds, and her scarlet train had to be carried by four pages. The dress she wore was white, sewn all over with pearls and diamonds, with more emeralds blazing round her neck and her wrists; she carried the sceptre in one hand and the orb in the other, and she had been glad to lay them aside during the service. Her head and arms were aching again as she rode back through the City, but she was still smiling and turning from side to side to acknowledge the tumultuous reception of her people. It was thirty years since her accession, thirty years since she had made her first triumphant appearance on her way to the Tower as Queen of England, and she felt as she listened to the crowds and the salvos of cannon and the pealing of every church bell in London, that her life had completed its full circle. They had defeated Spain. Of the ships sent against her, a handful had returned to port, and of the full complement of troops and seamen who had set out from Spain to conquer England, less than ten thousand were disembarked in their own country, starving and wounded and ravaged with disease. She had ordered a medal to be struck, commemorating the victory with the simple inscription in Latin: " *God Blew and they were Scattered* ".

She could feel the warmth, the admiration and love of the rough, smelly Londoners enveloping her; there were faces wet with tears among them, young faces and old faces, and the same expression of fondness was on them all. For their sake she had dressed in her magnificent, stifling robes and carried the orb and sceptre, refusing to ease her own burden and put them down, refusing to travel by barge for part of the journey and spare herself the slow, jolting ride through the uneven streets. She wanted them to see her and enjoy every moment of the spectacle, she wanted to re-live the scenes of her accession and her Coronation and remind them that she had fulfilled all their hopes in her when she had come out among them as a young woman at the beginning of her reign. In spite of her tiredness, in spite of the heat and the ache in her neck muscles from the heavy crown, Elizabeth sat as erect as if she were twenty-five again, and the smile never left her face.

It was the moment of her supreme triumph, the moment of vindication for anything she had ever done that was bloody and deceitful and ruthless in order to preserve her power. She was alone in her state and magnificence; no husband rode beside her, no child followed her chariot and was cheered as the heir to her throne. She was surrounded by men who had supported her, fought for her, and governed with her, but it was her victory and her triumph, and like all moments of ultimate success, it was already tainted with sadness. She was happy, and yet her heart was sinking a little, because she knew that she was taking part in the end of a long and incredible era in the history of her country and the course of her own life. Full circle. The phrase chased in and out of her thoughts. Her country was safe and so was she, but after the peak comes the decline. For the first time since she had heard of the defeat of the Armada, since reviewing her troops at Tilbury and making what everyone considered to be the most masterly speech of her reign, the Queen felt drained, as if all her energy and much of her spirit had been dissipated in that desperate time of anxiety and struggle. But they had won and whatever happened, she would leave the country she had ruled in a position of strength and power and wealth which it had never known.

The dynasty would die with her; she was the last of the Tudors, and she did not regret it. She had given England more than any of them and she would leave England when the time came with a sense of achievement which was close to vainglory. One day, the son of her dead enemy Mary Stuart would inherit all this. As she looked round at her Capital, she almost smiled at the irony of the circumstances which made James I of Scotland the future King of England. She had been told that he bore no resemblance to his beautiful mother; he was short and badly made, with an over-large tongue which made his speech a gabble, and a marked preference for handsome young men. He was sly and treacherous, but there was nothing she could do but live as long as possible and delay his inheritance. She dismissed the thought from her mind; it irritated her and reminded her of her own mortality.

It was becoming inconceivable to her that she would really die; even her mirrors were distorted to hide the ravages of time and worry and show her an image of herself which was false. She was tired and she was more often bad tempered than not; trifles annoyed her and her temper flamed at the guilty and the innocent without distinction. She was omnipotent and indispensable and she saw no reason to check her own tyranny; she was entitled to it. She was entitled to be flattered and humoured and glorified, because this day's rejoicing was due to her. She had staved off Spain for thirty years and then beaten Spain when the war came.

If the young men rising in her service and the simpering women who had taken the place of her old friends did not appreciate that and show a proper sense of gratitude and awe, then she taught them to be afraid of her instead. She did not mind fear from the majority because she still had the love she needed to support her. She had only to glance to the right and see Robert riding slowly beside her and catch his eye and smile at him, and she felt that she had seized the best of everything and relinquished nothing of importance. She was alone in her triumph and she wanted that loneliness, but he would be with her that evening in her Palace while the crowds got drunk and danced outside in the streets. And for every evening, as far ahead as she could see.

The hangings were drawn and she had ordered a fire to be lit in her rooms in spite of the warm August weather. It was nearly a week since the Thanksgiving Service, and Leicester seemed to be suffering still from fatigue and from the obstinate low fever he had caught while he was at Tilbury. The Queen had recovered after a few days rest and sleep, but she spent her evenings quietly with him, dining and sometimes playing cards or sitting talking about the past. She looked across at him and saw him watching her; his eyes were dull and tired and he had eaten very little.

"What are you thinking, Robert?"

"I was thinking of the first time I saw you at Hatfield."

Elizabeth smiled. "We were both young then; who could have imagined us now, sitting together like this, with half a lifetime behind us. . . . We didn't marry after all, but we haven't fared too badly."

"You were right to refuse me. I was never worthy of you; I was a poor husband to both my wives."

"You made a poor choice—twice," Elizabeth retorted. "And the second was the worst. Where is she now?"

"At Wanstead," he answered. He could talk about Lettice with indifference now; he was no longer hurt by her infidelity. He felt too ill to care. And Elizabeth, with her jealousy and her acid tongue, had never taunted him with the failure of his marriage or even mentioned it until she knew he could discuss it with composure.

He had been very grateful to her and very touched by her forbearance.

"I hear news of her from my stepson," he said. "She's in the best of health and spirits and I imagine she is too busy entertaining Sir Charles Blount to concern herself with me."

"Forget her. I'm surprised she's produced such a fine specimen as Robert Essex, he must owe it all to his father! I've liked what I've seen of him, quite apart from his kinship to you."

"He's clever and he's ambitious," Leicester said. "But he has a loyal heart. He's never borne me any malice and I've done what I could to advance him. He should be useful to you, Madam. In a year or two you might find a place for him."

"I might," Elizabeth said gently. "I will, if it pleases you." She had aready noticed Robert's stepson, and she had been favourably impressed. There was no harm in liking a handsome face and a pleasing manner, and the young Earl of Essex was one of the handsomest men she had seen in years. Better looking than Robert in his prime, she thought suddenly, with his mother's dark red hair and his father's bold, confident smile.

And by contrast with her memory of someone in the first splendour of health and virility she noticed how drawn and sick Leicester looked and how he sat so close to the heat of the fire. She left her chair and to his surprise she knelt beside him.

"I don't think you're well," she said quickly. "I'm going to make you see my own physician. And you'll take what he prescribes if I have to feed it you myself!"

He held on to her hand; his own were very cold. He looked into her face and saw the anxiety and the tenderness in it, and he yielded to a sudden impulse and leant his head against her shoulder.

"Madam," he said slowly, "I tell you that I feel tired and feverish and sick to death. Whatever is wrong with me, it won't cure in this air. I saw my own doctor for the second time today, and he says I ought to leave you for a while."

He felt the Queen stiffen, and he added hastily, dreading a refusal, "A very little while; just long enough to go to Buxton; they say the waters there have marvellous properties. If I go, I shall come back to you restored instead of moping around like a sick dog until you become tired of the sight of me."

"That danger passed a good ten years ago. I can't spare you, Robert, you know that?"

"Then we won't mention it again. I'll probably do well enough without taking the waters." Her need came first; he felt too low and weary to argue for himself.

"I can't spare you," she continued, "but you are going just the same. You are going to Buxton, and my only condition is that you should write to me every day, as I shall write to you. I want you to be well, my Robert, my poor beloved Robert, because I am so selfish and I could not do without you." She turned his face towards her, and for a moment they looked at each other, then he felt her kiss him gently on the cheek.

"Thirty years after, now that I'm an old and creaking woman, I can say it to you, if it is not too late: I love you, Robert, and I need you. I know now that I always did."

Elizabeth Throckmorton was standing in the shadows at the back of the room. She had been waiting for nearly ten minutes, her eyes fixed on the back of the Queen who had been sitting in front of her dressing mirror, staring into the looking glass without speaking or moving.

The lady-in-waiting held three of the Queen's dresses over her arm which was aching with their weight, but she had not dared to speak. There were other women in the room and they were waiting silently: the wig-maker, the two ladies who helped the Queen into her corselette, another lady with several pairs of shoes, and the personal servant who mixed the cosmetics she used on her face.

It had always taken two or three hours to dress the Queen; in the last few weeks since she had emerged from her rooms and appeared in public, it was an interminable ordeal for everyone who waited on her. She would look at the clothes and throw them on the floor one by one if they didn't satisfy her; she had smacked Elizabeth Throckmorton across the face for suggesting that the metal corset was too tight, and while the tire-woman fitted her with different wigs, she watched herself in the glass and made a bitter grimace. Nothing pleased her; nothing even interested or aroused her unless it was to convulse her with temper. Her women lived in terror and spoke in whispers; when she was not raging at them and filling the rooms with obscenities, she was weeping and reading the letters she kept in a casket by the side of her bed.

The Earl of Leicester had been dead for two months; he had set out for Buxton and died on the journey, and when Elizabeth heard the news she fainted outright. She had gone to her bed and remained there with her doors locked, refusing to come out or to see anyone, until the Chief Minister, Lord Burleigh, took the responsibility for having her door broken down and went in to see her. There were no witnesses to that scene; no one knew what he said or how he persuaded her to return to her duties and master her grief. If he had failed, it was quite possible that the Queen would have fretted herself to death.

As she sat before the glass she looked as thin and bloodless as if she were dead; only her eyes were bright and alive, alive with torment and despair.

"What the devil are you doing? What are you staring at?" Mistress Throckmorton jumped and hurried over to her.

"Your dresses, Madam. Will you look at them and make a choice?" Slowly the Queen turned round.

"Red," she said, "and gold, and green. . . . Are you mocking me, Mistress, that you bring me such colours?" The younger woman shrank and passed the dresses to her friend, Margaret Knollys.

"I beg your pardon, Madam. I shall fetch some more for you."

"Fetch what you please and be damned," the Queen's voice

snapped at her. "Fetch something in mourning colours, for I am in mourning. Where's that fool with the wigs?"

There were three heads of hair, curled and scented and made from fine silk in different shades of red, from auburn to pale gold.

Her own white hair was short and drawn back. She looked at the effect of the darkest first and then flung it aside. Nothing looked right; nothing disguised the pallor of her face and the savage hollows under her eyes; even the cleverly distorted glass showed her that she was old and ravaged and mocked her with fleeting reflections of younger faces as they bent over her.

And there was no one to look at her with an admiration she could believe in any longer; she was surrounded by young eyes, by men and women who went on their knees to the dreaded Queen of England and felt no stirring of emotion towards Elizabeth Tudor. It did not matter what she wore, for Robert would not see her tonight. Robert would not stand by her chair and make her laugh and escort her back to her rooms, and sit with her for an hour or so before she went to bed.

He was dead. He had died out of her sight on the road to Buxton, and she had nothing left to comfort her but his letters; the last of all was written only two days before the end. The shaky writing was blotted by her tears. He had died without her; cruelly died, unfairly died, leaving her to this lonely, empty existence of pitiless State, having her own way for twenty-four hours of every day, governing and conferring with Burleigh, who was so enfeebled in body that he could hardly walk, looking at the ageing faces of men who had once been young when she was young, and the young faces of men who had never known her as anything but tyrannical and old.

Now, with the years making their steady conquest of her, she was in mortal need of human comfort, of the warmth of human love. And now she was truly alone.

Every evening she dined in state with her stewards and her cup bearer, sitting on a dais under a velvet canopy. She came to the table preceded by trumpeters and picked at her food, attended by four ladies who served her and dined off her leavings. She lived in unrelieved magnificence and when she retired to her apartments, she either sat alone or was driven out among her courtiers to sit and listen while someone else played and sang, and to watch while others danced. Burleigh should have let her die, instead of forcing her out into the world and her responsibilities. He could not supply her lack, for by the evening he was nodding in her presence, worn out with his endless work during the day, a tired old man with only enough energy left for his duties, and a wife and a home of his own to go to when those duties were over.

She had grieved and wept for Robert, but now she was beginning to envy him.

She stood up and, leaning on Lady Knollys, held her breath while the corset was pulled in round her waist, and then stepped into a dress of black and silver. She chose the pale red wig, and wound a long rope of pearls round her neck, before her ladies fastened a wide ruff of beautifully worked lace under her chin. The reflection stared back at her moodily; pale and angular and sad.

"Your Majesty looks beautiful," Lady Knollys said. Elizabeth glared at her.

"Don't lie to me."

Knollys was the most docile of her ladies, possibly because she was the kinswoman of Leicester's widow. And now that he was dead, the Queen had shown Lettice no pity; she had remarried with such indecent haste that even her own cynical friends were shocked. She was now Lady Blount, but she was paying every penny owed by her late husband to the Crown, and when that debt was settled she would never be rich or even comfortable again.

"I'm not lying, Madam, I assure you. I heard Lord Essex say the same thing only yesterday when he saw your Majesty in the Long Gallery."

Elizabeth snapped her fingers irritably for her white plumed fan.

"What does that boy know about beauty—he's young enough to be my son!"

She turned again to the mirror; from a distance her reflection was deceptive. She had always been short-sighted and now the woman standing there, very slim and upright in the glittering sombre dress might have shed twenty years. After a moment Lady Knollys coughed. She had been told what to say by her relatives; Essex himself had rehearsed her for days, but she had not found the courage to repeat all she had been taught. He was mad with ambition and mad with impatience to step into the place Leicester had occupied for thirty years. No one could convince him that the Queen was not a lonely, feeble woman so desperate for the illusion of youth and love that she would submit to the unthinkable degradation of accepting it from him. It was hopeless, but at least she had promised to try.

"Madam . . . he is in the ante-room now; hoping to see you."

Elizabeth did not answer; she opened the fan and closed it again. Her first impulse was to laugh with contempt and send the simpering woman out to him with a caustic dismissal.

Essex was waiting to see her. Essex, at twenty-two and in the prime of his splendid manhood, handsome and virile and horribly young. . . . It was ridiculous. It was not only ridiculous, it was an insult. For a moment she was angry, and then suddenly she hesitated. Except for Ministers and petitioners, that ante-room had been empty for two months; as empty as her life and her leisure. If he came they could talk for a few minutes, talk about Robert, talk about anything before the loneliness enclosed her and left her at the mercy of her own thoughts. The temptation came to her, and for yet another moment she resisted. But it was such a small weakness, such a harmless indulgence to see Robert's stepson and exchange a few words.

Lady Knollys was watching her and afterwards she swore that she saw the Queen shrug.

Elizabeth turned back and sat down in her chair.

"Go outside, and tell the Earl of Essex that he may come in."